ICENI

ICENI

Helen K Barker

Published by
Bladud Books

A Beginning…

Was it possible for so much to hurt all at once? Annis moved her shoulders, seeking to lift her head from the forest floor, her long hair catching in last year's withered leaves. Her muscles ached where she had pushed and resisted. Her skin was sore where it had been bruised and torn and held by rough hands. Everything was pain.

Gradually she came to, returning fully from Haven. Her attackers were nowhere to be seen now, leaving nothing behind as they passed through her life save for bitter memories and a stickiness between her legs.

Wait. No, the clamminess was too much for just that. And there it was – she sighed with relief – the grudging cramp. Early and uncomfortable, but welcome with its message that she was not, and could not become, with child this moon.

But where was Cathbad? Where was her husband? He'd been here when they'd, when they'd… Unthinkable. Had he been killed then?

She forced her eyes to focus despite the swimming sensation. He was nowhere near, but neither was his body. So why weren't his strong, comforting arms around her now to make it all safe again?

She listened. There was a trampling amidst the close-pressed trees, confused shouts, and orders in a military tongue. Then a resonant voice rising above the chaos. Her husband's pitch, deep and rhythmic: Closing the Paths. But why was he tidying up his Workings now when she needed him more?

Suddenly she understood. He was trapping them within the forest. That would teach them. Her tormenters would never get out; they'd be doomed to wander aimlessly until Artio allowed them to die. But he didn't need to do it, not now. She could pick her attackers off at her leisure, appearing like a raven whenever and wherever she chose, to swoop vengeful at their eyes. In fact, she'd take the first right now; she was in the mood for retaliation.

She felt within for the Goddess, seeking to tap the Divine power. Surprisingly, there was nothing inside but emptiness. What? Had everyone deserted her then? She felt again. Nothing. But she couldn't be left alone, not now, not like this!

Where was the Goddess? Where had She gone? Annis panicked. Unable to reason clearly she picked up the strongest scent of the Goddess within the forests themselves and threw herself into the cool verdancy before the Paths could shimmer and shut her out forever.

Forget the pain, ignore it, she told herself firmly as she tore further into the waist-height ferns, beseeching the Divine to return. No amount of agony could ever compare to the mental anguish of losing the Goddess' presence, not once it had been known so intimately. The physical hurt would all be worth it, if only she could get Her back.

Then Annis heard her own name being called, as if from a far off place; she paused to see her husband beckoning her back. Cathbad looked worried. So, he'd considered her plight at last then? No, she wouldn't return, not until she had the Goddess again. And not to this ineffectual man who obviously thought more of retribution than of his wife.

She turned away from him. Neither, then, was there any more need to collude with the Goddess for the sake of her husband and marriage. She'd always known instinctively she'd birthed twins and not just one son, but she'd kept up the happy pretence for years for the sake of harmony. How had Cathbad ever thought he could hide the truth from their mother? Now she was finally free to admit it all and grieve for her lost child without her sorrow spoiling whatever he was trying to keep unsullied.

Then she started to run again, deep into the shadows and dark places of these sacred Groves …

Chapter 1

Imbolc

It was a good day for change. Boudicca could feel the earth responding to the stronger surge of life pulsing up to warm its roots and excite its creatures to song. The icy freshness chilled things to their essence, leaving them naked and stark and without pretension, almost as if nature could be seen with a true eye. As she watched the day unfold, she counted two pairs of magpies sprint to the shelter of the nearest fringe of trees. She greeted each of them in turn and smiled for the fresh pairing which heralded the turn of the seasons.

Today was Bride's Day, a portal day, when the land lay prone beneath the equal grip of spring and winter. She felt it as less a battle of the seasons and more an easing between old adversaries. Welcoming in the dawn, she felt the lust of her Goddess enticing the young God and imagined the scent of Their sexual heat. He was bringing energy to Her, energy and determination, and together Their mating frenzy would clear away the old and the tired and usher in growth and fertility. Despite her regret at having no partner with whom to emulate her Goddess, Boudicca Blessed Their coupling – any change would be welcome.

She hadn't slept too well throughout the winter, not yet accustomed to sleeping alone, and had woken this morning in the small, quiet predawn of utter isolation. She had felt the stirrings of a great day from the moment she wrapped a woollen blanket around herself and crept out into the fields, where she watched the dawn throw its rose tinge across the horizon. Instinctively, she knew that vast repercussions were carried in its wake.

These slices of privacy had become like a gift in this bustling life where there was precious chance for contemplation and everyone seemed to depend upon her. A few moments when the world moved at a slow enough pace for her not to have to struggle to keep up, and when she no longer felt different or set apart, for there was no one to compare herself to. These insights came with the grief as a mixed blessing, as unbidden as the memories.

In an instant she was back at the start of winter, to Samhain, when she was last with her husband. Her unfocused starring had stilled her mind to invoke a reminiscence as clear as a vision. Her powers of recall were strong enough to feel the lick of flames upon her wet cheeks and the smell of sickness through the wood smoke. Tears welled gently to mist her sight, reproducing the image etched indelibly upon her mind. She tensed, reliving being torn between staying put and going to him. She had stayed put, in the end, tucked away in the darkest spot of the hut, where only the brightest flames illumined her torc and no one could get at her. Stayed put, with an arm around each daughter, making them stay put too. Three shiny mahogany heads with angry, mad eyes that must have seemed like feral creatures to the doctors and diplomats who enclosed the dying man on the pallet by the hearth.

Despite the crackling of the dry timber and the murmurings of the professionals which accompanied death, she was sure he was whimpering her name, 'Boudicca, Boudicca'. He was coughing blood and fighting for each breath, yet still he called her to him. She was rigid with fear and anger, unable to push through these quacks and sycophants with their formal, defined roles. They had tried to take everything from her and her husband and now they robbed them of their last opportunity for intimacy. She was the only character in this bizarre play with no part, no lines, and so very frightened that if she went to him she would lose her composure, would break down and would keep him here, trapped in limbo, between worlds.

So he had died without her, giving one last shuddering sigh like peace itself and surrounded by the faces of strangers. She had berated herself for it ever since. She had approached the bed at last when only the healers' assistants remained to tidy the body. She had crept stealthily as if afraid to wake him and melted into his eyes, which were already glazing over.

There was no rest. He looked in shock. She had looked up to where he had been staring, to see what he might have seen as his last sight. She was half expecting to see some shining spirit, especially on this day, their New Year when the gates between the worlds were at their thinnest. But there was nothing, just the roof struts. His lips had curled back to bare his teeth in a tight grimace. She made herself bend to kiss him, brushing her lips to his, because she knew that was what she was meant to do. This last picture of him, she realised, would be carved in her heart for eternity, to corrupt any future moment of pleasure which she might have the audacity to enjoy.

Death, she decided, was cruellest in its simulation of life. He had looked so much as he had the instant before, yet with just one vital essence missing. Now here, now gone. And this, showing her tenderness to him too late, with only the slaves to note her compassion, was all she had been granted. Excluded from the pomp and ceremony of death to pick up the rags of their life together from the leavings of others. She couldn't remember how long she had stood transfixed, keeping vigil by her dead husband. Only that, after a period which had seemed both like moments and eons, her daughters had come back and with strong, insistent, supporting arms had led her outside where the wailing had started and the tears had never stopped.

'Mother? Here again? You should go back. Don't you know bears have been sighted in the woods recently and the wolves are still south this early in the year?'

She looked at her daughter as if seeing through her. Being mauled didn't seem so bad when your insides were in such turmoil. 'I have my spear.' She tapped the weapon at her side. Then held her hand out to interrupt her daughter's further remonstration. 'I could hunt wolf and even bear single handed before I reached your summers. I haven't forgotten yet. There's very little I forget, Grania mine, and I don't think I'll be troubled by the wild creatures when I sit so softly and think on your father.'

Grania put her head in her hands in frustration. 'Father was a good king. Prasutagus will be remembered by the children's children's children of both Iceni and Romani for the peace he brought our peoples in difficult circumstances. Now we need a Queen, remember? We need you as you were before you took him as consort and shared your rule. Don't tell me you've forgotten that, or the fact that if the Romani catch you with your spear, there'll be trouble for all of us.

'Oh yes, mother-mine,' Grania continued. 'Our "guests" have been especially busy today, despite the earliness. Something's going on, they're anticipating something and have tightened up their act. Everyone seems very tense. Come to think of it, out here you can sense a keen sort of "motion", like nervous energy.'

'So, you haven't managed to shut your Gift out completely then?' Boudicca teased Grania, enjoying seeing her daughter squirm just a little. 'No, don't sulk, it's your birthright and you'll come to treasure it one day, but I don't want to argue with you. Just help me up and we'll say no more, the dew has seized some of my aching joints.' Grania reached down, bracing her legs and extending a supporting arm.

Boudicca flicked her hand up, catching her daughter not by the hand but by the elbow. Rolling back she pulled Grania over her head and used the momentum to spring into a fighting crouch. There was no need – Grania was doubled with laughter and surprise and quite incapable of retaliating.

'Don't tell me I can't even trust my own mother!'

'Don't tell me you've studied so much war you've forgotten the basics! Just wanted to remind you that I haven't forgotten anything. Everything is crystal clear, by Mother, occasionally it would be a mercy if it wasn't. Perhaps it'll fade in due course, but I've delayed too long already and I betray our tribe for ever thinking I did not. So today, daughter-mine, I move on, despite the binds which bid me still. Today is the dawning of a new spring and a fresh start and a day of many changes. I feel it too, perhaps more acutely because I want to feel it, but these Romani with their ordered psyches confuse the land for reading, and I can't Scry what today brings. I feel it will change us all irrevocably, though, in its passing.

'Now I may still need my dawn forays to exorcise these moods which plague me, but I'm still capable of placing a Ward for wild creatures around me and a Glamour upon a stick to make it a spear. Can you imagine the Romani's evidence melting before their very eyes? Now, perhaps one of the most welcome changes would be for you to stop underestimating your mother? After all, I'm not so old; I was only a summer or two older than you are now when I birthed you.'

The two women embraced, their differences accepted, and started back down the slight slope towards the timbered enclosure they called home. They crossed newly tilled fields, each neat square of land forced to expose its rich black tilth furrow by furrow. Plough teams were already harnessed and working the fields nearest the forest edge, freshly cleared to provide work – and grain later – for the many refugees who had fled for royal sanctuary. It was fertile land; by mid-summer it would be a rippling mass of spelt, broad wheat and bere barley. For once Boudicca couldn't bring to mind the image of the maturing yellow wealth, despite it being such a familiar scene. Perhaps the particular field she was concentrating upon would experience severe storm damage and not come to fruition. She paused, shifting her gaze to another patch of earth, but there was a block here, too, where she could sense only sporadic stumps of stubble. This troubled her.

'What've you seen?' Grania had picked up her concern.

'Nothing,' she lied. She felt like telling her daughter to see for herself, but she didn't want to communicate her anxiety by snapping. It was probably an anomaly anyway. A rain damaged field, a careless fire, they could afford to have no yield from a few fields, after all it had to be sold through the Romani at the prices they fixed and it would be satisfying to see the very land cheat the Romani of their expected profits. It would also be unwise to conclude that all the crops would be ruined just from two Sensings. There was even a chance she'd been picking up rhythms from previous years, or previous places from the new workers, although she'd never known the harvests fail in all her long marriage. She made a note to Scry the land thoroughly in tomorrow's pre-dawn excursion.

There were too many distractions to use her faculty fairly at present, so she withdrew her senses to the narrower view of everyday vision and gave Grania a disappointed smile in the hope of making her feel guilty about neglecting her talent. Grania reddened. She had the technique all right, but she'd always been too caught up in the material world to rely on them. They were a bonus or a refuge for Grania, never an essential part of her everyday life.

Grania was the practical one. The huntress, the charioteer, the wrestler, the maker, the leader. The one who saw the world in a straight line, with her ambition at the end and the next goal always pushing her onwards. Like the sun's rays, inexorable and constant, yet occasionally unbearable. As different as she could be from her twin, Maeve, who dwelt in the dark places of the spirit so naturally that she had taken almost another day to follow her stronger, kicking, twin sister out into the world at birth. Boudicca's issue were like the two sides of a coin, as if someone had taken her own qualities of wisdom and insight and separated them from her physique and pride. Yet the two girls were close and able to learn what they each lacked from each other.

'So, tell me then, what exactly have our "guests", the Romani, been up to today?'

'It's going to take me longer than this brief walking distance home to tell you everything.'

Boudicca sighed. 'I may regret asking, but try me.'

'Well, they pushed over Deirdre's cooking cauldron whilst they were returning an amphorae of wine "to its rightful owners", and spilt the pottage. The slaves I set to clearing it up and giving it to the pigs discovered that one of the piglets was missing from the sty and replaced only by hobnail boot prints ...'

'Try me on the things of slightly more importance.'

'When the gates were opened this morning there were another five refugees seeking asylum. They're kinsfolk from the hamlet at Camboritum. Were from there anyway, and were also most put out at having to walk here. Their horses, livestock and people were taken and their crops trampled, so all that remains are the Lady, her two husbands and their children.'

'The Romani's "appropriation" is so close?'

'Indeed, mother mine, the Romani here sneered when they saw them and jeered that it served them right for not paying their debts and taxes and that they'd make a good lesson for us. I've put the Lady and her children in the main hut where they await an audience with you. I've had to put her menfolk to work for they were fidgeting with agitation. The Romani have put the price of grain up twice since sun up and have searched the forge for weapons again.'

'That's the third occasion this quarter! When are they going to notice that forge never makes anything? A good lesson in not only using your eyes to see.'

Grania ignored her mother's dig, 'Well, while they're busy hassling the smith, they're not hassling elsewhere. Oh, and Naoise had his torc taken by a Romani who thought it would make a pretty bauble, so I've set Teirnon to make new torcs for him and the kinsfolk from Camboritum. And last, but who am I to say, least? Maeve had a dream last night that she had a hundred lovers, but Maeve being Maeve, didn't delight in it and found it all rather disturbing. She wants to see you.'

Boudicca gave Grania another reddening look. 'I'll deal with the Lady from Camboritum first.' The two women had already passed through the massive timber gates of the palisade and were now holding up their thick skirts and picking their way through the midden and mud paths running between the smaller dwelling huts.

Boudicca swept open the heavy cloth which served to keep out most of the draught and strode into the gloom of the huge main round hut. It took a while for her eyes to accustom themselves to the dark; she used the precious moments to hold herself regally, making her presence known. Shreds of grey light penetrated through the wattle and daub and through tiny bald patches in the thatch. The Lady had been provided with hay, furs and blankets and several small oil lamps which gave off a smoky faint light. Although her two toddlers rolled around in the hay with wooden swords, oblivious to Boudicca, the Lady had approached immediately and was kneeling with her palms upon Boudicca's stomach and her head down.

'Get up, Sister-mine,' Boudicca gently ordered the Lady, then quickly asked, 'Did you get the Goddess' trade tokens out?' The Lady nodded. 'Good. Fetch them. We must be quick in hiding them.'

The Lady beckoned her over to a pile of rags and soiled cloths, bundled and tied to look like rapidly gathered possessions. She used the pin of her brooch to unpick the knots and pulled back the coverings to reveal a pile of dull gold bars which gleamed with ancient swirls and etchings.

'You've done well,' Boudicca approved, nodding to the Lady as she checked over what had been revealed.

'The hardest part was carrying them so they appeared to be light, madam.'

'Rub them with earth and help me insert them in the thatch. The Keeper will be here this evening to take them on.' Boudicca groaned as she stood. The Lady steadied her; Boudicca smiled weakly and quickly started to secrete the muddied gold in the thatch. 'It's only my menses. The cramps will pass by the end of the day, it's only just the dark of the moon and I wasn't expecting them so soon. I wonder what has set them off this early? They've been a trouble all my life, I thought that would pass with the birth of my daughters but they've become even more of a burden since Prasutagus died and seem to be quite random. Do you have some moss with which I might gather the flow?'

Having climbed upon the sleeping platform, which ran around the inner circumference of the hut, to conceal the gold, Boudicca settled down upon the furs and gestured for the Lady to join her. A mewling toddler crept upon her lap and dangled over her knee. Boudicca stroked the child's head.

'I always regretted never having any more,' Boudicca sighed. 'I would've liked to have had at least one son to remind me of our love.' The Lady nodded in quiet sympathy. Boudicca relaxed, trying to ease the Lady into informality where she could feel able to talk without first being spoken to. 'So, tell me what happened.'

The Lady sat very still, then started rocking gently. 'They came in the dead of night, with torches and swords and greed in their eyes. They read some document to us which they claimed had my father's mark upon it, agreeing to a loan. But they spoke fast, in their legal Latin, and when we didn't respond because we were half bleary with sleep, they started to destroy us. They had dogs and chains and they rounded up anyone who could still walk and set collars around their necks in long lines of servitude. They killed the old and the infirm and a babe at her mother's breast. They defecated upon the Goddess' shrine and urinated in Her well, trampled our corn, broke our pots, gorged themselves upon our food, stole our torcs. Then they claimed the land was theirs, the very earth, which I don't understand.

'The strangest thing is, I still don't know why. My father accepted the 'Grantus' their Claudius-god made and we invested it back in the land as they instructed us. That was way back, before I became a woman, this sum is much greater and we'd never borrow. That's the only link, but how can there be a connection?' She spoke in rote as if she was talking about something that had happened a long while ago to someone else. Then she was quiet, still rocking.

Boudicca reached out a gentle hand to her. 'I can only promise you sanctuary here, not safety. You know that, don't you? We're experiencing almost as much extortion ourselves; I've even started to wonder if we weren't better off when we warred with the Catuvellauni deep south of the forest. At least we understood the rules of combat then. I'm sorry to be so pessimistic. You may stay here as long as you like, as long as you are able. Set your husbands to building you a hut, be welcome back to your family no matter how distant your blood tie and ...'

'Mother?' A gush of wind set the lamps wavering and a shaft of light transfixed them. 'Come now, very quickly, please.'

Boudicca knew that tone. She patted the Lady reassuringly and followed her daughter. Grania pointed out of the enclosure, past the stockades and pens, across the fields. There in the dim morning light she could just make out a mass of movement, many people, with here and there the glint of armour and the faint trill of war trumpets.

'Romani. A war host approaches. What of the Romani camped here?'

'They've tidied themselves up and armoured themselves. Equipment has been washed and polished. Swords and daggers sharpened. The white robed ones have been writing feverously. Are they the same Romani, then?'

'They're always the same Romani. Despite their different skins, their different names and tongues. That's why they fight us. It's un healthy for a tribe to be so big, they have to travel a long way to find someone to raid.'

As Boudicca watched, the regular tramp of marching men increased. 'They come for their inheritance. I readied it several turns of the moon ago and left it in the temple.'

Boudicca turned and strode away purposefully, Grania jogging to keep up. They approached the only rectangular building in the enclosure. At the door stood a willowy young woman dressed in blue, with a woad moon painted over her face. She wore a wistful expression and an unfocused stare in the vague direction of the approaching army. A young warrior stood by her offering a string of beads with a puppy's adoration. She was ignoring him, but not spitefully.

'Hag Herself! The moon struck and the love struck.' Grania spat and stomped off round the corner where she could see the enclosure gates without having to watch those at the temple door.

Boudicca registered her daughter's wrath. Jealousy? Grania was old enough to choose whom to couple with and mature enough not to need to tie a man to her. Boudicca suspected, with a mother's insight, that despite Grania's bravado, there had not been that many couplings. She often forgot how young and inexperienced her two daughters really were. It didn't matter. Right now she needed both of them, so she set about getting rid of what she perceived to be the cause of the trouble as painlessly as she could.

She recognised the young man as Rochad, a warrior noble in foster to their house. He should be used to giving orders, or should at least be learning to do so, so she directed him to join the other warriors. 'Tell them to arm themselves. Lime your hair and paint your bodies by all means – look as ferocious as possible. We don't know what the Romani's intentions are yet and I want to keep some things secret for now. We may be able to pay them off, that's what I intend and there's no need for them to threaten a client kingdom that has so far brought them little trouble in proportion to its wealth. Just stand together and look strong and confident. Gather in everyone from the fields and be vigilant. Remember you're Iceni; you've reason to be proud and brave.'

'Maeve,' she turned to her silent daughter. 'I need the things I set aside from your father now.' Maeve nodded and pulled her gently into the temple and over to an oak chest. 'We need to take it to the gates. I will need your help.'

Maeve nodded but did not move to lift the chest. 'I have dreams, mother-mine, where unspoken things entwine and strangle my secretest places. I still work at their meanings. I still struggle to read these alien minds which have so little emotion.'

Boudicca suspected that Maeve's powers had heightened suddenly at the onset of puberty, as hers once had. She remembered how frightening the increased awareness and visitations had been and chided herself for not being there for her daughter. She really had been too wrapped up in her own black despair for too long. 'Don't force it,' she advised gently. 'Their reason stirs too few feelings to make a Scryable imprint. You'd exhaust yourself in trying. Now, Maeve, I really must have this chest moved to the gates.'

Together they hauled it outside the temple, then Grania took over from Maeve. The two stockier women lifted it easily to the gates of the palisade. Maeve brought furs and arranged them for the three of them to sit and await the Romani. Boudicca opened the chest and brought forth her husband's personal belongings. They were all here.

Between the two of them, Boudicca and Prasutagus had devised a Will which left half of his personal possessions to the Romani. She could remember their counsel together and the plan he had wheezed out with the intention of bribing the god the Romani called 'Emperor', so their kingdom might be left in peace. Peace was costly now, there were so many taxes and tributes which cancelled out the benefits of having leisure to sow and reap and breed. They had both felt certain this gesture would be interpreted as a generous gift from a people who could no longer really afford to make it, both of them being acutely aware of how much the legendary Iceni wealth had dwindled in the two generations since the Romani came. Certainly the Romani scribes had smiled encouragingly and rubbed their hands together when Prasutagus had finally set his mark to the document they had drawn up.

Boudicca hoped that today would bring the return of some of the more sentimental items at last. To show good faith and hospitality she had stowed away all her husband's belongings, allowing the Romani first choice. There were jewels and fabulous gold crowns and buckles, torcs and brooches. She treated them with disdain, arranging them on display easily.

But there was also a delicate silver ring she had ordered made for him, too light to be worth much; a comb carved from bone with teeth missing which had snapped when he had offered to brush Grania's unruly hair when she'd been a fidgeting infant. Hunting gloves. Boots made from soft doeskin still smelling of his warmth. Delicate glass beads he was painstakingly restringing when his final illness had kept him bed-bound but restless. And a tiny whittled horse, like the ones he loved. Tough, spirited, independent and agile creatures, he had lived for his horses and the magnificent herd he was building up. He had owned the figure since his own childhood and had called it 'Mouse', as he had named every grey stallion he had traded for since. Whoever had fashioned the figure had been a true artist, capturing all the grace and wilfulness of their fierce little ponies. Mouse had been danced, accompanied by the King's clopping noises, along the cots of both little daughters, who had cooed with delight and tried to grab at it with podgy hands.

These things she arranged more tenderly, running fingers over edges and jogging memories that hadn't yet found a resting place. Such a sad pile of items, all that remained of someone's life. Somehow it didn't seem enough; it didn't do her husband justice. Only her heart did him justice, these things were just things, and she only hoped she had judged the Romani's greed right and they would go straight for the items of financial rather than sentimental value.

The Romani were very near now. Those camped over winter to keep the Iceni in check, and otherwise torment them, had gone out to meet the newcomers and Boudicca suspected that it was one of the newly arrived riders who carried the highest rank, because there seemed to be a lot of saluting going on and orders being made.

She was kept waiting whilst they talked and pointed and tapped wax tablets. It was impolite. She was Queen and it rattled her to be treated so dismissively. She was uncomfortable too with the cramps in her stomach which were becoming quite insistent now and inducing a dizzy faintness. She'd never been anything like fluent with their Latin and it was particularly difficult to comprehend over such a distance. Watching them, she noticed that their greedy eyes looked not just at the gold displayed before her but at everything and everyone. The man of rank looked like a bulbous old toad. He kept licking his lips as if he was catching flies and sat squat upon his over-laden horse. She didn't want to have to deal with someone as unsavoury as him.

On an instinct she called over the young noble she had ordered to gather her people together. He had done well; although missing weapons, the Iceni were in full majestic battle array and looked fit enough to go raiding the cattle of the very Gods. 'Rochad, there could very well be trouble,' she spoke under her breath. 'Be ready to loose the horses and run on my signal. Don't try and fight, there are far too many of them. It doesn't matter what they do, nor to whom; we just mustn't antagonise them. Understand?'

He nodded tersely and stepped back. She watched her instruction being passed amongst the lines of warriors. Then a fanfare of trumpets blared and the Toad approached, walking his horse at a steady pace. He was flanked on both sides by soldiers. His scribes followed immediately behind him, holding parchment and tablets. Underneath the curved rectangular shields of the soldiers she could make out their immaculate armour. It was always identical. Boudicca concluded that they were only frightening when they were together; alone or in small bunches they were puny. Not like the Iceni, Boudicca felt proudly; they revelled in their individuality, battle was an occasion for personal glory when one warrior could take out twenty of these soft babies. Bullies, then, that they had to stay together for protection. Only their faces were different, peering out beneath their helmets, although they all wore the same stern expression and exuded avarice. Here and there she spotted the odd familiar person who had plagued her with petty, and not so petty, annoyances over the last few lunar cycles. Their usual javelins had been discarded, she noticed, but their swords were worn readily to hand.

Boudicca rose to greet the Toad, extending her hand in welcome. He urged his horse just past her and commenced his address: 'Peoples of Icenia, hear me. I, Catus Decianus, Procurator of the Province of Britannia, by order of your Emperor Nero, God of Rome, Lord of the Oceans, King of the Earth, and by the Will of your late and most recently acknowledged ruler, Prasutagus, hereby take possession of these lands and property.'

Desperate to control her anger, Boudicca ignored the snub, and concentrated on deciphering his words. She thought she had the gist and took a deep breath to answer his obvious misunderstanding. She managed a meaningless mumble before she was overrun by legionaries. Catus Decianus had already given his order and half his men were stationed to overpower the defenceless warriors, tying them up or stunning them with callous blows to the head. The rest of the Romani were already pushing open huts and ransacking for loot. Boudicca looked down. In the stampede, Mouse had been snapped in two by a clumsy sandal, although someone had taken care to bag the jewellery. She wondered whether it might have been, perhaps, the same person.

Boudicca turned and, bringing all her leadership qualities to bear, caught the harness of Catus' mare. 'I, Queen Boudicca of the Iceni, demand an explanation of this outrageous behaviour.' She was a tall woman. To avoid her eyes yet to still look ahead, Catus had to look up. Boudicca pulled the harness down; she unsettled his seating.

'We do not acknowledge any 'queen'. If you are the widow of Prasutagus you will know he left half his possessions to your Emperor Nero. It was a wise choice. Nero has graciously decided to accept the gift and in his wisdom has decreed that it is ridiculous to tear up cloaks, divide pairs of boots, you know, wheat ears will not grow without the stalks, my dear. So, magnanimously and with his usual excessive generosity, he has decided to adopt all property and possessions into his protective fold that, in keeping it whole, it might not be rendered valueless.'

'That's not what the Will meant. I've put out his possessions, please choose your half. Take all of them.' She tried not to plead but, unused to being in such a position of powerlessness, she felt unnerved by the situation. 'What you're taking from me now is not mine to surrender,' she reasoned. 'What of my Ladies and Chiefs? They hold their land independent of me.' She spoke slowly; she had to translate as she thought.

'All of it. I wouldn't bother to resist, you're nothing against the might of Rome.'

'Nooo ...'

Boudicca did not have a chance to answer him before Grania called out in anguish. Her daughter was screeching and pointing outside the palisade to the corral. The noble fosterling Grania seemed so fond of had been struck down with a sword through his stomach, his body twitching in agony. The ponies were charging off to the forests, a few legionaries stumbling piteously behind trying to catch them. Then, as Boudicca watched the gap widen between ponies and men, at the edge of her vision she saw Grania move quickly and then Catus was unsaddled and nursing a smarting punch to his jaw. Maeve too had edged closer to him and was about to stick the pin of her brooch into his eye.

Boudicca leapt to pull back Maeve. It must have seemed to the Romani that she was about to join in the attack on the Procurator who was screaming, 'Get these Furies from Tartarus off me!' An instant later she was hauled away from her daughters and pressed face-down on the ground. She heard Catus stumble away from her, demanding: 'Treat them as the spoils they are. Their women have such slack morals they'll probably enjoy it – if they're not used to it!'

Then her skirts were pulled roughly over her head and, as she realised what was happening, she started screaming in utter outrage that they should consider such a thing. She flailed her limbs, and bit anything her mouth found, like a rabid wild cat. Then there was a huge, sudden weight on her back which winded her, as three men sat on her to stop her struggling. She tried to catch her breath but her skirts and the soldiers' weight was suffocating. She coughed for air, and then she felt her legs being pulled wide apart and a man sit on each to hold them still too. She moved her toes, hoping to scratch one of them with her nails. Rough hands pulled her buttocks apart and the wadding of moss was torn away, exposing her fully to their hot sight. She felt a flow of thick menstrual blood trickle down her thigh, and sobbed in shame to be seen like this. She tensed, waiting for the first harsh penetration.

The pain, when it came, was not what she'd expected. It was the pain of a kick, hard and mercifully external. The momentum jarred her forward, even under the pressing weight. It was accompanied by grunts of disgust and moans of disappointment and more pain, but now she felt the sharp edge of a strap and knew it must be a sandaled foot. Then she felt spots of wet upon her back as they spat, and more pain as they punched her. Then nothing as she heard an excited fumbling and words of encouragement, whilst the weight shifted from her back to her arms, enabling her to take a deep breath of sweet air.

Then the agony began which bit into her shoulders, scalp and spine. Her clothes were no defence against this flogging and she felt them falling apart around her. She sought, in the regular rhythm of this more predictable torture, the potential of rising above the physical hurt and reached inside for the precious numb place which beckoned. She called upon its reserves, refusing to entertain the lure of passing out, only relaxing into the torment enough to surmount it.

Then she felt for her baby girls, reaching out for them, lending them power, seeking to lead them to the same mental Haven. Maeve was already there, bordered up in a safe catatonia, which, with her impressive Skills, allowed no one in, not even her mother. Boudicca felt saddened, she didn't only want to give comfort to her daughter, she felt the need to receive it too.

Grania was nothing but colour. Furious and livid, her spirit gave off sparks of orange flame which seared any spirit that approached. Boudicca knew that helping Grania would lead to more anguish at first, her barriers would need to be dropped for an instant, bringing total realisation of the violation which was being perpetrated upon her. She prayed Grania would forgive her the price.

'Stop it, daughter-mine!' She used the harshest, most authoritative spirit-voice she could muster. It was enough. Like an infant jolted out of mischief, Grania's defences fizzled out. Boudicca's spirit swooped in and held her tight. Grania yelled and screamed and struggled as her rage cleared and she registered reality, then pulled in her will ready to start up her psychic attack again. 'No, Grania, don't look. Come with me. Come into the comfort of your mother. I'll keep you safe. Relax into me. Come!'

Grania's spirit energy burnt Boudicca as her defences switched back on against the indiscriminate enemy she perceived to be everything that was not-Grania. Boudicca feared her own spirit would bear scars for offering her daughter help, then Grania seemed to swoon into her, and she scooped her daughter up and bore her away to a softer place.

'Mama, I hurt.'

'Yes, I know, but you are safe here for a while.'

'They killed Rochad.' Grania's spirit-face screwed up in rage. 'I loved Rochad, but he loved Maeve more than me.'

Grania's spirit appeared as a sobbing toddler holding its hands between its legs where the pain had been. 'There are many, many people who love you and who will come to love you, little one. Rochad will be waiting in the Summerlands where he'll be free to love you and Maeve equally and you won't mind because you'll be too busy loving other people too.' She cradled the child to her. 'Sleep if you like. I'll wake you when it's safe to go back.' Grania was already nodding against her breast. Boudicca squeezed her tight.

Boudicca could watch her village from here and as she did her anger grew despite the passiveness this Haven placed upon her. She forced herself to watch the continued rape of her daughters, wanting to remember every detail so she could be sure to exact a high enough revenge price when the opportunity arose. It could not be too entertaining for the soldiers, she noted in her detached way; both girls had passed out and the legionaries pumped only at body shells as unresisting as rag dolls. Every soldier behaved differently in his turn. Some who jeered the loudest were the most reluctant to perform, having to be persuaded by their comrades. Some displayed their parts proudly to their fellows before using the girls. Others hid themselves, lifting their armour at the last moment before entry. One knelt, playing with his flaccidity, then vomited. They dragged Maeve away from that mess before they continued. Some urinated, some defecated, those with the iciest, narrow eyes took their turn over and over again, jostling the less enthusiastic out of the way and once pulling off a much older man who seemed to be straining unproductively forever.

Possibly the youngest legionary, still festooned with acne, was dragged away from pillaging the main hut and led forward, giggling nervously, as white as a sheet. They threw him onto Grania, offering advice and suggestions. He climaxed within thrusts and collapsed onto her breasts with a wide-eyed expression of wonder and disgust. He reached up to gently touch her hair before being yanked off and kicked back to work whilst the next took over.

The Toad was nowhere to be seen. Having extracted the choicest baubles for his own keeping, he had obviously crawled home to gloat under a slimy stone. He had taken his scribes and clerics with him, all, no doubt, feeling somewhat conceited and financially improved.

Despite being sickened, Boudicca wanted to remember their faces and acts in every detail. The memories would be fuel to kindle her hatred; none of this would ever be allowed to be forgotten. Her body shell had been left lifeless and wounded, a mass of bloodied strips where the whips and belts had left their mark. She was unattended and neglected, those who remained of her people lay huddled and hidden, they played dead or had fled to the forests.

In these shortened days, dusk fell rapidly with its freezing mantle, and the Romani eventually tired of their frivolity. Laughing and singing they burdened themselves with their hoard of stolen prizes and trophies, set notional fires to several stores and huts and left. As darkness enveloped the village in its own peace, destruction and desertion was all the Romani left in their wake.

'We return now, daughter. It will hurt, but they're gone and I'll still be with you.' Boudicca woke the Grania-spirit with her soothing words. Maeve's defences were impenetrable, Boudicca would come for her later. For the moment it was important that no one mistook them for being dead. She held her daughter firmly by the hand and guided her back to her body-home.

It took a long while for Boudicca to come back to full consciousness. Despite the will of her spirit, her body still protested at being made to experience the full agony of the mistreatment it had undergone. She lay in an exhausted semi-faint for what seemed like an eternity. As she revived, she realised she was not alone. She turned her head, scraping her cheek along the gravel earth, to see her companion.

He was cloaked and hooded in black, and sat cross-legged, patiently waiting for her to reawaken. She recognised sensitivity in his lips, a short trim beard, and kind cornflower eyes that sang of summer. He smiled encouragement to her.

'What day is it?' She stammered, her mind still disorganised.

'It's a good day for revenge,' he answered.

Chapter 2

Crescent Moon

Reality passed in and out of Boudicca's swimming vision. Someone carried her to the main hut with a sturdy, secure touch. The same person laid her in a quiet place and covered her with blankets. Then she was left alone to rest and listen to the subdued, frightened whispers of those who had survived to gather together.

Everything hurt. Whoever had lain her down had placed her on her side so that the weals on her back had a chance to heal. She wanted to stretch, move, sit up, but her body objected so much that she stayed put and lay glaring at those who could move, like an angry child shut out from a feast. She desperately wanted news of her daughters. The forced patience and stillness provided a vacuum in which her imagination ran riot.

Eventually someone came to her; it was the man she had awakened to earlier. He carried a small pot of porridge and a spoon. She watched him approach, noticing his careful grace and slender, strong hands. The porridge pot, she decided, looked very snug in those hands.

'Are you feeling a little better?'

She nodded. 'A bit groggy. I'll be fine in the morning.'

'Something tells me you won't be going off for one of your "forays" tomorrow, though,' he teased.

'How do you know about that?'

He gave her an 'I know more than I'm letting on' look and laughed. Then he held her by the shoulders, keeping her down quite firmly, before admitting: 'Grania told me.'

Boudicca bolted upright. Restrained by his grip her body jolted only a fraction but the pain was enough to make her wince aloud.

'I'll answer all your questions and whilst I do so, I'll feed you.' Boudicca nodded in reluctant assent. 'First question,' he demanded.

'My daughters?'

He spooned a tiny amount of porridge into her mouth. It was difficult and undignified to eat on your side. She chewed and swallowed awkwardly. He offered her more porridge. She accepted.

'Grania is up and about and very full of self-righteous anger. She has used her energy to organise those who are left into what you see around you. Your people are fed and warm, some are being healed, the rest have done their own looting and brought anything of value or, more importantly, of use, here. Most are refusing to think beyond tonight. They will need you tomorrow; I hope you'll be up to it.

'But tonight they have Grania. She will do, for an emergency. She's bossy enough to motivate your people out of despair but not diplomatic enough to avoid putting backs up given long enough. Apart from anything else, she glares at anything remotely male as if to blame us all for her violation.'

Boudicca pushed away the next spoonful to be offered. 'Is she all right, though?'

'Yes. Now eat whilst I talk. She doesn't seem too upset for the moment, just angry. You should watch her over the next few days. When it all starts to register for her, she'll need someone to hold her. That's when her temper won't be enough to pull her through.'

Boudicca pushed away the next offering of porridge too. 'No need,' he insisted, tapping her lips with the spoon. 'Maeve is back. She was more of a worry – I found her amongst the dead.' Boudicca stopped and glared at him. 'Trust me, she's all right. I sensed she was only Absent as I did a quick check of all the bodies. I brought her in, arranged for her to be washed, cleaned up and dressed in some fresh robes. It was better to do that whilst she was still in Haven, otherwise she might have struggled. Then I went to bring her back. Your daughter certainly has some Skill; it needs honing, but the rawness of power is remarkable. It took patience and cunning even for me to prise apart those barriers without being injured myself.

'Now, compared to Grania, Maeve is different altogether. She's become very reserved. She hasn't said a word, just gazes at nothing as if she sees things in the insubstantial air and curls of smoke plumes. If necessary, I can arrange for her to be accepted by the Sisters – I know it's a long way from her home, but it may be the only healing deep enough to reach her. Anyway, I'm talking about worse possible outcomes, which we'll only need to consider if there is no change in, say, a turn of the moon.

'Everyone is keeping their, somewhat discreet, distance from us partly because I instructed them to do so, and partly because they feel a great disappointment in not having protected their Queen from the assault which befell her. There is a weariness in the people here that has cut their spirits and blackened their hearts. Tomorrow you must encourage them to look you in the eye again; offering them forgiveness will relieve some of their guilt, even though the two of us know that it is not them who should be seeking forgiveness, but the Romani.'

Boudicca nodded as she thought his words over. 'You must be the Keeper,' she exclaimed.

He smiled a 'wondered how long it would take you to deduce that' smile. 'Lovernios the Keeper, madam. I don't want the gold yet, you can show me at very first light,' he calmed her. 'Yes, madam, I know you still have it, I can sense the layers of Wards placed around it as the hoard was added to over the last quarter: a most uneven emanation. Now, whilst you dream, think on what has passed today. Don't tidy it away but seek to live through it and rediscover the fierce strength you'll need. It's not only *your* people who desire a Queen.'

Boudicca's eyes had shut whilst she'd been listening to the rhythmic lilt of his voice. As her mind wandered in its pre-sleep meanderings, she realised he was right, it was tempting to push the more disturbing memories away to be dealt with in a later, safer place. Then she found that moving through the horrors, rather than around them, meant addressing their spectres in the mind's equivalent of the brightness of day, giving her a semblance of control, rather than allowing them the power of night's sneakiness.

Still incredulous that what had happened had happened, she slept with the ravages of the day as her uncomfortable bed partner and the memories of the screams of her daughters tormenting her rest. When the dreams came they stirred from a deep well of a place. She felt arms rise from within to soothe and ease her people, to gather the homeless and the cold to her and hold them to the shelter of her breast. Then, as she held them in the strength of her arms, she felt her heart smoulder, kindling a giant rage which demanded justice. Then the rage caught alight, bursting into quick flames, until her whole body flared as if it were made of a massive wicker frame, burning herself and all those who had reached for her.

She awoke later than usual, lost to the lure of this most vivid dream, with no desire to disappear by herself. Today's desire was for constant company as if she feared to be alone. Lovernios was with her as she woke. He brought more porridge and helped her stiff, sore body to sit whilst she ate.

'As soon as you're ready, I'll gather the gold.'

Boudicca nodded between gulps of porridge. She took several quick swallows and then stood up, gasping as she did so. Together they moved to the very back of the hut. There they climbed a rickety ladder and, lit only by the dim light of a clay lamp, they started to pull out the twists of muddied gold bars, spun so thinly as to be mistakable for thatch. Lovernios packed them away into a sack, which he tied and hid away in the folds of his black robes. 'Did you know this was the only hut not to be looted or set to the torch? You set powerful Wards, madam, which distracted the Romani from our real treasure. Well done. You've taken your proportion of the Goddess' trade?' Boudicca nodded. 'Good. The Iceni have really earned it on this occasion; your people deserve this wealth. Now, we must talk.'

They moved away, gathered up a couple of blankets each and went outside to the brisk air. In the clear truthfulness of daylight, Boudicca couldn't avoid the destruction surrounding her. Still she said nothing, not knowing where to begin.

'What are you going to do?' Lovernios whispered the question.

'I'm going to devour them.' Boudicca raised her head to meet his eyes quite calmly and regally. The merciless vengeance in her reply shocked her. She almost felt shame at the quite unbidden idea, but once expressed she realised how much it was meant and how proper it felt.

'I can help you to do that.'

'I know. Do so.' It was a stated request. No pleading. Boudicca made it plain she would exact her price with or without his help but that any advice and influence he offered would be appreciated.

'Fine. Gather everyone you can find and meet me at your forge in the forest. I'll be there within a turn of the moon, after I have deposited the Goddess' trade with the Boatman on the coast. Welcome anyone: those who can walk, those who can't. Bring horses, livestock, weaponry, armour, stores, all you can carry. Send out for those who live elsewhere in other hamlets in the furthest reaches of Iceni land. Gather them all to you.' Boudicca whitened in remembrance of her dream. 'Keep their anger and their memories alive, encourage their hatred of the Romani like a spark which you coax into flame.'

Lovernios led her gently by the arm back towards the doorway of the main hut. He nudged her forward, pushing her in front of himself. 'They need a Queen,' he whispered. 'Address them, arouse and agitate them!'

Boudicca took a very deep breath. She waited for a little silence to fall, then she filled the void. 'We move out,' her voice rang out, clear as a rainbow's promise. 'We take everything and we go by nightfall. I need runners to send for all Iceni kin beyond the forests. Who will go? It's vital that you're gifted in Finding if you offer.' She counted out the volunteers. 'Meet us at the great forge in the forest, no more than a lunar cycle hence. We move with the stealth of deer; let no Romani discover our refuge. There in the womb of the woods we will plan our devouring and imagine the sweetness of their blood!'

From the dimness of the hut rose a ragged cheer which increased in volume as her words were absorbed. 'You're providing them with the decisive action which offers hope, madam,' Lovernios was whispering again. 'I did doubt whether you were up to it, which way your grief would push you.' Then he danced away from her swinging punch. 'Prove me completely wrong, madam – bring me so many Iceni that we can't all meet at the forge!'

Boudicca glared at his retreating figure as he hopped and skipped away from her. He was goading her, she knew, with laughter. He ran east, into the sun – she had to shield her eyes to watch him leave. There, with a nimbus of light around him and his naughty laugh, she could almost mistake him for the Trickster himself.

She let him go and turned back to address her people. She clapped sharply to draw their attention. 'I suggest we pack immediately. Take only that which you can carry. Remember, there are many things you'll be able to reclaim from the Romani very soon.' She knelt and started to gather some newly milled flour, discarding the quern stones as too heavy, after all she expected precious little chance for milling in the coming days. All around her others started to make decisions about what could be taken and what would be left and what was the best way to pack. The children, the old and the sick, were organised into the few places available in wagons. There were no chariot places available without horses to pull them. The wagons and chariots alike would have to have human teams.

She looked around for her daughters. Grania had thrown herself into the packing, snatching sacks off men folk and shoving them out of the way. Most people gave her the wide berth she was so obviously claiming as her most pressing need. There was only one place where there was no motion: by the fire where Maeve sat as vacantly as the simple-minded. Boudicca worried for her. Was there no way of reaching her? She thought of the healing the Sisters in Hibernicus would offer and, as abruptly, pushed the thought out of her mind as unacceptable. Maeve needed her kin, her home, her mother. Boudicca desperately prayed for enough inner strength to be capable of providing what her daughter would require.

Then she went to her. Gently she approached and sat beside her. Across the fire, the Lady of Camboritum was baking griddle bread from a batch of mix. The little flat cakes were at their best fresh and warm but would keep for a day, maybe two, at a push. Boudicca motioned that she would take over.

She wrapped the handle in the cloths of her skirts and moved the hot griddle to her side of the fire, hanging it from the ornate fire-dogs, and measured out a ladle of the thick batter. It sizzled immediately and she watched it gradually brown, deftly flipping it over to cook the other side. Then she added it to the stack already begun. This action of ladle, watch, flip, watch, stack, ladle and so on, was such a familiar routine it was like a meditation. Such an ordinary chore, but Boudicca derived great comfort from it. The world may change, kin might die, rulers may change, but griddle bread stayed the same. She could cook good bread quite absentmindedly, and it gave her an excuse to sit and talk to Maeve without feeling lazy.

'Do you remember when Mama cooked you griddle bread when

you were little, daughter-mine? You would always want to cook a special cake to yourself and it always ended up with a tiny piece burnt when you didn't manage to flip it quick enough. Do you recall how you always used to claim that you liked the black burnt bit best because you liked the crunch? But you always used to pull the most disgusted face when you had to eat it.

'You had pride even then, Maeve, and you loved the unusual, the distinct. Where is that pride now? Is it that which keeps you hidden from us? There's no shame for you in what happened. No one here holds any blame for you.' She touched Maeve's cheek with a soft finger. 'It won't get any better until you come out.

'There, now in talking I've caught the edge of this cake. You'd better be the one to have it since you're the only one who likes it a little burnt and I dare say it'll be the last opportunity for warm bread for a while.' Boudicca transferred the warm griddle bread to Maeve's hands, closing her fingers around it. Maeve did not move. The bread cooled as she held it. Boudicca looked away in anguish, tears crawling down her face.

She turned back to supervising the packing. She hated what she was doing to Maeve by neglecting her, if indeed Maeve was aware of any neglect, but Boudicca knew that from now on her people had to come before even her own daughters. There was not much to pack. Only the most essential, portable possessions had been chosen and furtive meals made of any perishable foods. Gradually, the folk sitting patiently outside, with belongings heaped around them, started to outnumber those who were still busy. Boudicca set Grania to hurrying the rest along, then went to Maeve and pulled her to her feet. Fortunately, Maeve responded to the order inherent in her mother's touch and shuffled along as she was led. Even though her body moved with the grace of a priestess, its precision disguised by a casual air, her face still kept its stony, detached expression.

Boudicca supported Maeve until they were out of the hut and past those who were waiting. She went back to poke out some unburnt kindling from the hearth fire and tucked it away in a bag. Two slaves doused the smouldering hearth-stones by emptying the contents of an enormous iron cauldron over it, enveloping themselves in hissing steam. Then they threaded an iron bar through the cauldron handles so it could be lifted and carried. The next Iceni fire would be lit from the old kindling; the next Iceni meal would be eaten together from the kin-cauldron. These things were the last to leave, and would be the first to be set down. As was proper.

'We move out,' Boudicca called to her people. 'Follow me and stay close. Finding is involved and those of you who do not have the Skill will need to rely on those who do.' Boudicca strode purposefully to

23

the head of the column which had formed naturally, slowing her pace when she reached Maeve and guiding her by the arm. It was like leading a blind woman, except that Maeve's feet missed turf clods and lumps of flint, rendering her as sure footed as one of their brave little ponies.

As they climbed the slight rise, out of the enclosure, stumbling towards the forest, Boudicca glanced back at the rag-tag army straggling out behind. The warriors amongst them held themselves tall despite their limed hair, the spikes of which had bent and drooped. Were sad huddles like this all that was left of the once proud, wealthy Iceni? Boudicca swallowed. There had been a period, within her memory, when they had wanted for nothing, when gold had flowed and they had been the envy of all the other tribes of Britannia. Then they had held off all attempts at conquest or raid, dissuading their enemies by the fame of their champions and the defence offered by the forest and fen flanking their lands. She hated the Romani for reducing them to this, especially following the courtesy and hospitality they had taken and crushed. She swore, with every stamp of her foot, that she would win back Iceni notoriety. Every Romani would regret the day they chose to trick and deceive and steal. They would pay with blood and fire. There was an evil brooding inside her which had started to demand its feed.

The forest started abruptly, running along the ridge of the hill. Birch saplings hemmed in the denser oak which turned the forest to night. She paused to allow everyone to catch up. 'Join hands or tie your skirts to each other, I don't want to lose any of you who accompany me,' she called. 'Leave the wagons and chariots and those who really can't walk the short distance. They'll be brought in very soon as my first priority.' Those who could came forward to follow Boudicca's instructions. As it was, there was only a handful who stayed behind. They crouched together for warmth, confident in Boudicca's promise.

As Boudicca advised, those who could walk formed a windy line which moved forward to snake between the trees and seemed to hiss with the disturbance of leaf mould. Quickly Boudicca placed a Ward to Artio against harm over them. Away in the distance, her sharp ears picked up the lumbering of a bear and knew that the forest Goddess was with them in Her natural form. When she judged the whole line to be within the boundary of the forest, she started to Find. Such workings took effort and concentration and it was one of the few techniques she had not fully mastered. She needed stillness, lack of pressure, no stress. She kept walking. In the chain behind she heard someone trip over a tree root. Someone else coughed. She had to Find quickly, they couldn't tramp around a forest forever, and there were the invalids outside who were depending on her to get them in. Being a Queen didn't provide too many occasions for Finding true Paths; how she wished she had practised more! Perhaps, she reprimanded herself, that would have been a less wasteful pursuit than her morning forays.

Still nothing happened. No footpath opened to show a clear way through the woodland. Boudicca was beginning to feel nervous, realising how vulnerable they all were. Was she really the right person to lead? Was there really no one else? She tried to push such thoughts from her, knowing they compounded the anxiety which clouded the mind and prevented attainment of the necessary clarity. Then, suddenly, she was no longer leading but being led as Maeve pushed off confidently to the left. And then she saw the Path revealed ahead. It was so obvious in hindsight, the click of the mind which enabled the Otherworld to shift into place. Branches lifted, tree roots sank into the earth, tendrils and creepers twisted apart.

She looked at Maeve in wonder, then back at the Path. Maeve still gazed with blank eyes and had relinquished the lead back to her mother. No-one else would have known that Maeve had done the Finding, instead of Boudicca. Boudicca regained control quickly and led them forward, down into a shallow valley where the sound of rushing water encouraged them to hurry to meet it. Maeve had seemed to take control for only a moment, no one else had appeared to notice, but Boudicca could not be certain exactly what had happened. Whatever, she, or they, had Found, and were now safe. That was all. 'Is everyone present?' she asked those who followed. 'You can stop holding on to each other now, we have Found!'

Sounds of relief filtered back to her and the pace lightened. At the river they came to a sturdy bridge, barred by a blacksmith who stood, arms crossed, guarding the way. He wore leather aprons and his hammer tucked into his belt. On the other bank stood his forge with an ever-glowing fire, and stables full of ponies which appeared very familiar to Boudicca. She approached without hesitation and greeted him. 'Sucellus, I am Boudicca of the Iceni. We've met before, I trust you remember – although the years have been kinder to you than to me. You see before you all that remain of the royal enclosure of the Iceni tribe. We beg your aid.'

'Madam,' the smith grinned suddenly with welcome. 'I am hardly likely to forget the face of my Lamer, am I? Once and always bound to serve the Iceni, how can I refuse now?' He limped forward to bow before her, favouring his right leg.

'The years may have been kind to your face but your temper is as sour as ever,' she reached down to raise him up and clasped his hand. 'It was a fair fight and well you know it. I've got one or two scars to show for it myself.'

He grinned, 'Wouldn't be a proper iron-smelter if I were free to wander, would I, madam? You stay here as long as you like, and ask of me what you will. I guessed something was up by the arrival of your ponies yesterday. Been busy shoeing them all. Might I ask, though, just a small favour?' He was rubbing his hands together. 'Perhaps a bit of gold to work? I haven't had any for quite a while. Not for myself, you understand. For the Goddess.' His hand swept around, indicating the river.

Boudicca nodded, as if indulging a child. 'I think we might be able to find you a little.'

Sucellus' face lit up and he started to shake all over in excitement. 'Madam, I'll go and get the old and infirm you left outside. I should be able to find a path wide enough to get the wagons in. You all make yourselves comfortable and I'll take a few of the horses to help with the pulling.'

Boudicca looked at him in astonishment, wide eyed and mouth agape. Sucellus winked and limped off past her people, whistling to some ponies to follow. Boudicca waited for three or four horses to tear themselves away from their hay and trot over the bridge after the blacksmith. Then she led the way over the bridge and straight to the forge fires where her people dropped their burdens and started to warm themselves.

Sucellus was back with the wagons and chariots and their contents almost straightaway. He saw to the comfort of the ponies first, making sure they had a quick rub down and water and ensuring their places at the hay bales hadn't been usurped by their fellows. Then he called Boudicca to him. 'You'll be here for a while, I can see that, and there'll be more to follow. Set them to building shelters. Take only the birch, not the oak. You'll find a bit of food in my hut; kindle your new fire from mine and yours blended together. Grania'll be the best for that job. Then you and Maeve come with me.'

Boudicca did as he bid. Her exhausted people knew they had to work a little more before they could rest the night. If they did not, the lack of shelter might deplete their numbers further by morning. She checked that the work Sucellus had set was progressing, then collected Maeve from the place where she'd left her. They joined Sucellus on a wooden platform which jutted out slightly over the river.

He invited them to sit. Maeve did so without needing to be nudged by her mother. Boudicca was beginning to feel increasingly out of her depth. She sat regally, keeping her back as straight as possible, reminding the others of her status. She was the tallest there. She was trying not to relax, even though she hadn't felt so free for whole seasons. There might be thirty odd people who directly depended on her and looked solely to her for hope, but she was no longer weighted by the demands of running a community or with the diplomacy necessary to appease an occupying enemy. And this was one of the few places in Britannia, unless you went a long, long way north, where they were truly rid of the Romani.

She wasn't going to let herself relax, though. Queens didn't relax.

'Thank you, Sucellus, for all you have done.' Sucellus bowed his head. 'I don't expect we'll stay very long. The Keeper said he'd be back within a turn of the moon; hopefully all the other Iceni will have joined us by then. As soon as we've gathered, we'll move on. Although there is one amongst us who would gladly stay. Teirnon has been working a simulated forge for us. He has some skill, manufacturing cooking utensils, basic repairs ...' Sucellus pulled a face. Boudicca felt the need to quickly explain: 'We needed a forge which was free of all signs of weaponry to fool the Romani. Anyway, he has the way with metal, and he'd make a good apprentice.

'I don't know how many of us there'll be, how many will meet here in total. There have been many, many refugees in the past few turns of the moon. I don't recall how many hamlets still remain, but I'll ensure we don't trouble you unnecessarily.'

Sucellus smiled enigmatically.

'You won't be able to see the trees.'

Boudicca looked round at Maeve. She was staring into the water as if nothing had happened.

'What did you say?'

Maeve continued staring as before. Boudicca started to joggle her, trying to get her attention. Sucellus put his arm out to stop her. He solemnly shook his head, indicating that that would do no good. Then he pointed into the waters which Maeve watched so intently.

Here, by the platform, the waters ran slower. There was a natural depression in the riverbed which had been worn smoother and deeper by the waters that swirled into it and spun so mildly, rendering them almost still. Boudicca watched the clear ripples eddy into the whirlpool before darkening almost to black. She looked deeper, leaning forward to smell the energising air that was being created here, then her sight shifted and she saw bright, sparkling gold, down, down, in the deepest depths. Then she fell herself, seeming to pass beneath the waters that closed over her head, dropping to the treasures.

She blinked and it was gone.

'What did you see?' Sucellus asked.

'Nothing. Only the gold.'

'Then you must make a sacrifice.'

Boudicca looked at him, questioning. His face gave her no guidance. The most precious thing she owned was her torc. Sucellus himself had fashioned it from pure gold twisted into knots and designs so intricate they could only have been produced by one truly Goddess inspired. Her own mother had presented it to her on the day she had abdicated and Boudicca had ascended to Queen. She remembered having to put it on over her childhood torc, before taking the old one off, ensuring that since birth she had always worn the divine mark around her neck. The gold had been collected from three quotas due from receiving and releasing the Goddess' trade – it represented a sizeable proportion of gold due to the Iceni in a year and a great deal of wealth.

Without it she was nothing. Unrecognisable as Queen, or even royal kin, nor even as Iceni. The neck-band was such an intrinsic symbol of her identity that she might even be nameless without it.

But without the Goddess, without her first love, she was also nothing. As Priestess first and Queen second she should never forget that all she understood was held cupped in the balance of the Goddess. She was weary too, it wouldn't hurt to relinquish it all to the Mother. So she reached to her throat and pulled the torc away, casting it softly into the waters that caressed it away.

She instantly felt naked without it and suddenly realised the enormity of what she had done. Hag herself! She might want to lie down and remain in the Haven of the Mother, but there were others who still needed her. She might desire nothingness, but a Queen had no right to impose nothingness upon those who were truly loyal to her.

Then she glimpsed a shimmer further downstream and she jumped up and ran after the fleeting object. 'It's been rejected!' She sobbed and looked to Sucellus and Maeve for support, but they remained as passive as ever. It only took a few swift paces to catch up with the shining torc, then she splashed into the shallow river and pounced upon it as if she were fishing for salmon. She tore it from the waters and defiantly pushed it back on. If the Goddess didn't want it, she certainly still did! Then as the rounded ends touched her skin she realised that the torc was heavier and she brought it back to her view. Still standing in the stream, oblivious to the icy lapping against her calves, she turned the torc over and over: this could have been made by no human hand. Not even Sucellus had the skill to create something as cunningly beautiful and delicate as this.

The torc with which the Goddess had Gifted her, came straight from the Otherworld, spun from Faery gold with secrets which could only be perfected by tiny hands and minute fingers. Boudicca replaced it around her neck. Mouthing a personal apology to the Goddess, she silently repeated her pledge to serve Her as Priestess and Queen. She felt her confidence soar. she would be proud to wear this emblem, there would be nothing she couldn't do whilst she bore its benediction.

Turning to stride from the waters she heard, from the forge, calls of welcome and surprise. There were familiar voices sounding relieved. Sucellus had turned and was already heading back over the short distance with his loping run, which was the best he could manage. Maeve was still staring into the waters – Hag alone knew what she could see, if anything. Perhaps she was simply entranced by the glistening play of light upon the surface water like a child would be. Whatever, it was evident she would need Boudicca to guide her back to the forge.

No one, then, had seen her being Gifted. It was a private moment, one that she had no need to share. Those that needed to know, or who knew her well, would notice the torc; the others would only notice her changed demeanour. She followed at an elegant pace; the heaviness of the torc had affected her bearing and she had to move with an air about her now.

Helping Maeve, Boudicca made her way back to the forge. In the short while they'd been gone, many rough shelters had been constructed which would serve as adequate temporary accommodation, and as the building continued, those too frail or tired to help claimed shelters for their own and crawled inside to rest. A couple of the messengers who had been sent out to other Iceni villages had returned, bringing Iceni kin with them. And that, it seemed, had been the reason for the welcoming calls. Apparently, it wasn't just those from the royal enclave who had been prepared to abandon their former lands; all those in Iceni territory seemed content to leave their homes and gather with their kin, no matter how distant. It was as if they were all aware that the encroaching Romani occupation meant it was only a matter of waiting before they too lost everything. The prospect of change, the chance at some sort of hope, anything was better than just waiting for the inevitable worst.

The following days and lunar quarters passed slowly for Boudicca. The moon waxed to full and then started to wane again. Grania still vented her anger on inanimate objects, seeming to find more energy than all the others put together for coppicing and tree felling. Boudicca had tried to hug her once, but had been pushed aside with an: 'I am fine, mother-mine.' Maeve remained, on the whole, still, but she would take herself off on three or four occasions a day to wash herself in the river. She had also taken to watching Sucellus work. The smith never pressed her for conversation, he just went about his business as if her frightened little eyes were upon someone else. However, Boudicca had noticed how he would angle himself, as he produced fine weaponry, so that he didn't obscure Maeve's view.

Sucellus had pledged himself to arming all the warriors amongst the Iceni, and he was producing a steady stream of iron tipped spears, daggers and honed swords. It seemed he had been building up quite an arsenal before they had arrived, predicting that it would be needed soon. He revealed his cache of weapons which had been brought to him bit by bit in the last decade for safekeeping. In his care, since the Romani's edict against keeping weapons, the Iceni had avoided the confiscation which had blighted other tribes. Each object had been kept oiled and wrapped, and lay perfectly preserved, ready for use after a quick resharpening. He even directed the smallest children to the riverbank to collect sling-stones.

The refugees continued to tumble in, filling the makeshift shelters and stables, and finding warmth amongst the steam of the ponies when needing quick, immediate heat. Grania's team of woods-folk had to travel further each day for available birch, not least to satisfy the fire which consumed vast quantities of fuel. The Goddess kindly provided wood pigeon and hedgehog, boar and deer upon which they could feast. There were also the few root vegetables and mushrooms which could be foraged by those who knew where to look, as well as the grain, sheep and cattle brought in by the refugees.

There were very few disputes or quarrels to settle; the tribe for once were pulling together and making a real effort to curb their naturally fractious characters. There was the odd raised voice, slap, or over zealous punch, but by Iceni standards that was exceptionally placid behaviour. By the end of the first lunar quarter, their original numbers had quadrupled; by the third, Sucellus' large clearing was very cramped. It was no longer simply Gelfine here; the basic royal family had expanded to include cousins and aunts, great-nephews and grandparents: Derbfine. Distant kin met distant kin, often after having been separated for generations; ancestral memories were shared and new allegiances formed. Sucellus returned heirlooms to their owners on recognition; he seemed to sense to whom each weapon should belong, claiming that swords sang to him when their rightful owner arrived. Champions took up their grandparents' swords and wielded them once more, marvelling at the balance and weight of such treasures. The Iceni tribe was almost complete, truly Tuath again.

Everyone, Boudicca realised, was coping fine without her. She felt slightly superfluous. She busied herself organising and participating in battle training for those who were sorely out of practice, but still she couldn't shrug off the mood of agitation which hung over her. Unusually she also felt lusty, as if the rising sap in the greenery around provoked her to rutting fever too. She wondered if Lovernios had been delayed on his way to the Boatman at the coast. Even in Iceni territory there were bandits, beholden to no tribe, who would rob a Druid if they found one. She couldn't Sense him at all, he had Cloaked himself too well. She wondered why she was surprised. Perhaps it was just that he seemed so young, maybe a year or two younger than her.

He could only just be out of Druidic training, yet he was so very gifted. The feelings reminded her of her long yearning after Prasutagus died, and she recognised the desire to push onwards that was indicative of her reaction to stress, her desperate need to do something.

The new torc hung heavy on her neck too. It pulled her deep into nightmarish dreams, full of blood and pain and flapping ravens which clawed at her eyes. There were waking visions, too, hinting at sudden movement just at the corner of her eyes. And there was a brooding badness right inside her, scrabbling for a foothold to reach for release. The tension was permanent, leaving her to feel continually on edge, as if she was about to birth some horror.

On the last day of the third lunar quarter to pass, at sunset, when the low sun flickered through the bare branches as if through a cracked glass, Lovernios came and her mood lifted. Just when she was beginning to despair that she might have to make some excuse to Sucellus and thank him dearly for his hospitality, and move her people on to roam forever like so many lepers, Lovernios sneaked up behind her to tap her playfully upon the shoulder. She knew someone was there well before she tucked and turned because they lacked the stealth of the hunter, even letting their tall shadow fall in betrayal. 'You're too fast for me!' Lovernios chuckled. Boudicca gave him her best patronising smile.

She looked past him to the trees. There was the tiniest unnatural movement, so slight she almost missed it, but it definitely wasn't one of her spirits hovering just out of sight. Lovernios had brought a warrior with him, a skilled warrior. He followed her gaze. 'I've brought someone with me. They would join with you – Addedomarus of the Trinovantes.'

Boudicca stooped, picked up the spear she had been practising with, and turned and threw it in one smooth movement. The spear quivered righteously from the bark of the oak in which it was now embedded. 'How dare you!' she screeched at Lovernios, all the tensions of the previous days exploding at once. 'You drag me here. You make me wait. Without telling me what is happening. Without giving me or my people any hope except that which I have conjured for them.' They had an audience, Iceni were running towards them. Addedomarus had been dragged out from behind the oak and was surrounded, a ring of spear-heads pointed at his chest. 'Then you bring, you dare to bring, a,' she spat, 'a Trinovante, from beyond the forest, to our midst. I know you Druids go where you please, sacrosanct to all tribes, but now you've gone too far with your priestly immunity. I'm surprised you didn't think to bring one of the Catuvellauni with you too, then we could have killed ourselves here, with only the trees to witness our warfare; finishing ourselves off without ever needing to trouble the Romani again!'

'Boudicca, Queen,' Addedomarus addressed her humbly yet without abasing himself. 'Our tribe has a deep desire for revenge too. We would be stronger together.'

'The Iceni don't need to borrow your strength. You might need help, but we don't. We solve our own problems. Our independence is our pride.' She narrowed her eyes. 'Your troubles don't even begin to approach the magnitude of ours.'

Lovernios grabbed her wrists; he was strong. She hissed and struggled like a cat, then remembered who he was and quietened. Lovernios spoke firmly to her, holding her eyes and forcing her to look back at him. 'Let us talk, let us discuss. Then you may decide whether the Iceni will allow the Trinovantes to fight. But first give him a chance to explain; you may be surprised at what has been going on in Britannia beyond the cosseting barriers of forest and fen.'

Chapter 3

Last Quarter

Boudicca snarled at him. She was livid. It was as if some wild beast had taken over. Lovernios stepped back, wary of her. Then, as she swept back her hair before recommencing her attack, Lovernios reached for her throat, touched her torc, nodded and mumbled: 'So it is you. Be still, Andraste, we're not ready for you yet.'

She shook her head as the tension lifted like mist. 'Go back to practising,' she snapped at the warriors around her. They dispersed and returned to throwing spears to each other, still keeping a watchful eye out for their Queen. 'It's warm at the forge and there's food for tired travellers,' she conceded. 'I'll listen. But I expect a comprehensive explanation,' she indicated her throat. 'Of everything.' She held her arm out to Addedomarus; he grabbed it, gripping her roughly in nervous greeting.

Once at the forge, she ordered food to be served to Lovernios and Addedomarus. Addedomarus raised several suspicious glances from the Iceni people who deliberately kept away from him. Eventually one slave was kicked forward, volunteered into serving him. The slave slopped stew clumsily over Addedomarus who lifted his hand to strike the slave then stilled the blow, looking at the culprit as if in recognition. He looked questioningly at Boudicca.

'The price paid for poaching waterfowl in Iceni marshland, Addedomarus. I daresay if I encroached upon your hospitality, I too would find familiar faces.'

Addedomarus was silent. Lovernios ate his stew unobtrusively, watching the two leaders spar with body-language. Grudgingly, Addedomarus picked up his bowl and ate his meal. He dribbled juices down his long moustaches and wiped his mouth with the back of his hand. He discarded his bowl and started to speak. Lovernios halted him. 'Call your leaders, Boudicca. Call Sucellus and your daughters too. Addedomarus doesn't need to repeat his story more than is necessary.' Boudicca clapped a slave over and gave the instructions. It was almost dark; the forge fires were built up for warmth whilst the slave carried out Boudicca's orders.

Soon they were joined by those Lovernios had requested. The Ladies, Chiefs and champions made their obeisances and sat at a discreet distance where they could still hear. Grania turned up, puffing and sweating, complaining at being pulled away from her work. She nodded curtly to Lovernios and sneered at Addedomarus; Boudicca noted how some of her daughter's anger had subsided at last. Sucellus led Maeve; they bore a dish of clear water which they set before them. Boudicca hoped it wasn't for Maeve to wash in, not now, but Lovernios seemed especially pleased at the sight of it.

Lovernios stilled them with a traditional Druid gesture. He started to speak with an even more refined and noble timbre than he used for everyday speech. He was Bard trained, Boudicca noticed, and she settled down to allow him to lull her with his mesmerising arguments. 'The Romani,' he started, 'As we all know too well, are not grouped as tribes, like us Celtoi. Instead they are like one immense people, a conglomerate of states and nations who act, not as individuals, but as a whole. They treat us as one, they aim not to subjugate Iceni, but all Celtoi. They are a strange conquering type for whom it is not enough simply to raid and then allow the enemy to recover so that he survives to be raided again. And it is all of us who have lost to their hunger.

'All Celtoi have suffered from the Romani, and it seems that we have done so forever. First, on the continent, your ancestors fled from them to settle here. Now that the Romani have traced their flight, you suffer in turn. The Druids too have suffered.' He held his hand for silence. Night had dropped and the shelters had gradually filled, they were alert with Iceni ears which strained to hear Lovernios, and Iceni mouths which responded to his oratory with exclamations and gasps. It had been a long while since the Iceni had been entertained by a Bard. 'Yes, even the Druids have felt the grip of the Romani and the Goddess has lost wealth. All things are of the Goddess and She permeates our life. What are we without Her?

'Iceni wealth comes from the Goddess: you have good lands, rich soil, healthy livestock. You are the last link in the trade from Hibernicus too, and as such are due the largest proportion of Her trade of all the tribes on the route. This income is the envy of other tribes.' At these words Iceni faces turned to Addedomarus in hatred and Lovernios rapidly spoke on, seeking to recapture their attention. 'But it's your position in Britannia which grants it to you, and it's not open to others for the taking. Without this gold, without all the other links in the chain, you are nothing.' Iceni faces turned back to Lovernios. 'Just another agricultural settlement without luxury or comfort or the means to make gold sacrifice – indeed, without the gold you would be forced to return to blood sacrifice. But likewise, without you the Goddess' trade would collapse.

'The Romani want the Goddess' gold. It was the legend of Britannia's gold which lured them here in the days of your ancestors. It's fabled how our earth runs rich with seams of precious metal. It does, but not as rich as the earth of Hibernicus from whence the gold comes. The Romani have long realised this, they've little imagination but great powers of logic and reason, and they are now seeking to destroy the Druids. Even while I talk they campaign in the mountains to the west, maiming and killing the Silures, Ordovices and Deceangli, working their way north to Insula Mona and our College there. There are no warriors on the island, only teachers, lawgivers, historians and poets. Most have already fled back to Hibernicus, there will be scant defence now that the mountain tribes-people only offer guerrilla resistance.'

Horror and shock registered around Lovernios' listeners now. The Druidic College at Insula Mona was so famous as to be almost legendary. Several Iceni mothers currently had offspring studying there, their children specially picked for showing intuitive promise. Boudicca herself had passed a few years of her youth in the harmony of its learned repose. She could recall the winds breezing in from the endless seas and the acres of crops rippling in noon heat, as effortlessly as if she had only just returned. The idea of the Romani trampling the holy island to dust, disturbing the lazy scent of honeysuckle and the lessons sang over and over in rote, seemed a desecration as great as the crime perpetrated against her daughters.

'It'll be a sacrifice worth making, if the Iceni do as I say.' Boudicca took especial notice of what Lovernios was saying now. That the Iceni could be connected in any way with the potential loss of Insula Mona, shone a fresh light upon the importance with which Lovernios, and the Druidic Council, perceived the plight of the Iceni. She started to realise the possibility of viewing her situation with a broader perspective, one which would also offer some justification for the presence of Addedomarus.

'The mountain tribes' harassment and the imminent destruction of Insula Mona has led the bulk of the Romani military force away from your lands. If we act soon, you could enact your revenge with relatively little resistance. There'll still be war, but the Romani have left themselves weak and undefended. You have your best chance of victory now.

'To do this, you must think like the Romani think – not as Iceni, but as Celtoi as a whole. It's not enough to be rid of them from Iceni territory, we need to be rid of them from the whole of Britannia. You need join and communicate with other tribes. You need to learn as much as you can about the Romani deployment of legions, where their weaknesses are, what they fear. To do this you need the help of a tribe who have lived alongside the Romani – the Trinovantes are one such tribe,' Lovernios gestured towards Addedomarus. 'To communicate and plan, to translate amongst tribes, and most importantly to bind the tribes, you need the Druids. We are the only universal symbol that every Celtoi tribe recognises.

'Great Queen, the Iceni are the most feared warriors of Britannia, but you can't do this alone. Even Cuchulainn himself would find it difficult to defeat a legion if he did not have his trusted champions with him. United, however, is a different matter – united, Cuchulainn could crush a century or two as he rolled over in his sleep.' Lovernios raised a laugh from those who knew the story of the Hound of Culann. 'You may lose some pride in having to share the victory, but at least this way there'll be a victory to share. It's the Iceni who will lead this rebellion, it's the name of the Iceni that will be sung for generations to come and be remembered with every mention of the word 'freedom'.

'I have the authority of most of the Druidic Council and their full support in this suggestion. The Goddess' Blessing has been sought and granted. The Trinovantes have been near to revolt for years, their tempers are like a cauldron which has been allowed to simmer for too long. I invite Addedomarus to speak next.' Lovernios gestured for quiet while he explained. 'When he tells you the injustices his tribe have suffered at the hands of the Romani, you'll realise that being conquered is very different from being a client kingdom. He'll also tell you the Romani's weaknesses. He has watched them for a long while – watching is all he and his tribe have been able to do.'

Lovernios gestured to Addedomarus. As Bard he had the right to decide in which order the speakers would make their address. Boudicca didn't mind waiting; there was a lot of information to take in. Although her fury hadn't abated at the outrages perpetrated upon her daughters, herself and her people, nevertheless she was starting to feel she had been at least slightly cocooned from the realities of life under the Romani. Especially, she reflected, during the last winter when she had refused to deal with much else except her grief at the death of her husband. She was beginning to realise how selfish she had been, how self-absorbed and short-sighted.

'I am Addedomarus.' Their guest cleared his throat. He was not a natural leader, Boudicca could see that. He was too nervous, although he concealed it well with a show of bravado. 'Some of my words are not your words, but I hope we can manage without a translator. I, my people, the Trinovantes, offer ourselves to the Iceni in fighting the Romani. We would be rid of them from the shores of Britannia forever.

'They set up their Colonia at Camulodunum. Their 'best' city. They choose Trinovantes' land because it is good land, because their fighting men like Trinovantes' land. It is good route to their king emperor

Nero far across the seas. We live alongside old soldiers. They pensioned off, but still act like soldiers, with swagger, with women. They are given land instead of a payment when they retire, and their fellows, who still serve as soldiers, help them in this. They know it is what they will get for their pension too. But they cross at not having money, so they take that off Trinovantes. They take more land, and our gold and then us. They make us slaves and force us to work. My people live in bad places, like small huts for dogs, chained together where the sunlight will not go.

'Then those of royal kin, with gold, we pay for new temple. Temple to their other king god Claudius who brought elephants when I was child. This not like Trinovantes' temple, full of peace in woods and green places. This temple vast. Big enough for several hundred people to live in at once, and room for horses too. Made of stone, with steps so it will not flood in rain, and very high so you have to lean right back to be able to see the roof. There are pictures all around it which do not wash off when they get wet. Not needed for a temple to be that big. Cost too much. Also we are made to be priests and pay for the festivals they say we must perform.

'They also build theatre, senate-house, roads and forum. They make census and tax us too high. They take our weapons so no fighting allowed. We must buy our grain from them at the cost they say.' The Iceni around him nodded their heads in empathy. 'What they did to Iceni very, very bad, but not good what do to Trinovantes. I think our own fault. We so pleased to have them stop Catuvellauni fight us, we thank Romani, but we not that thankful. We would fight now, fight or be swallowed, we have no choice. Iceni have no choice, if you go back you be like Trinovantes.

'Romani frightened of Druid. Very scared of what Britannia people can do with their minds, they not like Otherworld. But they not frightened of Celtoi, they build no ramparts, no palisade, all Colonia open.'

There was silence after Addedomarus had spoken. Boudicca had found listening to the faltering speech difficult and was still trying to unravel all the strands. She had heard of the Temple of Claudius at Camulodunum from the Romani diplomats who had been stationed near the place she had called home up until a few moons ago. She knew it was meant to be magnificent and finely wrought by master craftsmen. She'd also heard that it was a symbol of everything the Romani were bringing to Britannia – culture, health, education, wealth, peace… extortion, mass slavery, poverty, degradation and oppression. She was trying very hard to imagine what the Colonia must look like; it was very hard to conceive of buildings that were so impractically large. Such buildings, she reflected, would take an age to heat and would never feel cosy to live in.

'Maeve will show us.' Sucellus spoke up.

'Of course she may, if she so wishes,' Lovernios smiled at Maeve benignly, encouraging her to come forward. Maeve lifted the shallow basin, careful not to spill any water. She set it down at Lovernios' feet and sat opposite him. 'I had hoped that good would come of ill and this violation might be your making, Sister.'

Maeve passed her left hand over the water, once, twice, thrice. There, by the flickering embers of the forge fires, she Scryed into the still surface waters, willing the images to arise. As the last tiniest ripple cleared, Boudicca gasped aloud. Around her there were mumbles and sighs of astonishment as the others also saw what was happening. Boudicca had expected her daughter to Scry for herself and narrate what she saw in a sing-song distant voice as visionaries before her had done. But there was no need. Maeve had Scryed so strongly that the scenes were reflected from the bowl for all to see.

There, right before them, were the immense buildings of Camulodunum, the confiscated gold, the toiling Trinovantes. The Colonia was built for giants, not for people, it was a place of wonderment, a miracle of structure. Boudicca was amazed at what she saw, but furious too, that they were capable of such fine edifices yet still coveted the rude huts of the Iceni.

Maeve couldn't hold the image for long but it was enough to supplement Addedomarus's description.

'Now, will you host as I requested?' Lovernios' question shook her out of her reverie. For a moment Boudicca had been lost to her inner self. Then Maeve spoke, giving Boudicca longer to form a reply.

'Watch! There is more.' The images commenced again, rolling over the waters. They saw a triumphant war host sweep over the land, rising from the east, leaving destruction in its wake. They saw warriors with spiked hair and woad tattoos dance naked into battle, pirouetting upon chariots and somersaulting into the fray. Fearless of death they fought, tearing the enemy apart, and children with evil faces despatched the fallen with sharp little daggers. Every face wore the same gloating, vengeful expression which stirred familiar memories in every Iceni sat around. It was the likeness of their war Goddess: Andraste. She rose behind the hoard, spurring them on to total victory. She charged ahead of them in the form of a hare, leading them on to fresh slaughter.

The visions faded, leaving the Iceni awestruck. Boudicca caught them a little longer, straining to see before they dwindled completely. She saw the Goddess hot in Her battle lust turn upon everything and everyone, indiscriminate in Her desire for flesh. She saw the leaping little hare change direction. Then she saw water again and felt the stirring within as if some sort of birthing was taking place. On this occasion a bubble burst free and something other than herself used her mouth to announce: 'We fight. How soon?'

Lovernios studied her. 'Not yet.' He looked worried. 'Push Her back down, madam.' Boudicca felt a flutter like trapped wings and then the sensations were gone. She felt wrapped in a cold sweat. Lovernios gave her an 'are you all right?' smile. She nodded to reassure him.

Grania had leapt up. 'If we're invoking Andraste, then we should ready the Groves.' She licked her lips.

'There's no need to return to the Old Ways,' it was Sucellus. 'I've been busy fashioning sacrifices from the gold you've loaned me, there's plenty to appease the Goddess. She always receives any given here most graciously. There's no greater sacrifice.'

'Andraste will demand blood. If that's the form the Goddess chooses, then be prepared to give it. I know the sort of death She'll demand.' Grania had worked herself up into quite a frenzy. There was no response, everyone sat stunned by her outburst. She sat, and let out the faintest sob, then she turned and ran crying from the camp, into the trees. Lovernios looked after her in pity. Boudicca rose to follow her.

'Madam,' Lovernios called softly. 'Give her comfort. Her healing is beginning. Then return. I know it's late but I must talk with you, alone.'

Boudicca ran to keep up with her daughter, leaping over the indistinct bodies which slept near the fire and the sharp knolls of coppiced birch. Somehow she kept her footing, bounding after the wailing left by Grania as a trail. Almost as soon as she left the orange glow of the forge fires she was engulfed by the full force of night but still she blundered onwards after the weeping that seemed to rend the very forest in two. She cursed Grania under her breath for her daughter's lack of control and for being forced into a darkness she had no wish to explore. She objected to being pulled down unwillingly into the depths of Grania's animal despair. Boudicca also knew that only she would be accepted by Grania now and that if she deserted her daughter, she would never have the chance to reach her again, her daughter would be lost for ever and she would regret her inaction for the rest of her life.

The awkward sobbing still seemed a long way off but it had stopped moving away. Boudicca was led deeper into the woods. This seemed to be no Finding; tree branches didn't swing up and out of her path, instead they snared her cloak and scratched her face. For a while she still felt the burning heat of the fires upon her cheeks but before long the black air laid icy fingers upon her. She started to call out, screaming Grania's name over and over until she was hoarse and breathless. Then finally a little way ahead a weak voice acknowledged: 'Here I am, mama. I'm frightened.'

Boudicca stumbled forward. 'Keep talking to me, daughter-mine, mama can't see a thing.'

'Over here, mama.'

Boudicca stepped to the right.

'Mama here.'

Boudicca swung back to the left.

'Mama, mama, where are you?'

The call was from behind. Boudicca froze. There were tricking, trapping old things in the forest who needed to be approached with courtesy and caution, if at all. There were many, many manifestations of the Goddess and the spirits which she didn't understand, but which she had definitely heard of and which needed to be paid respect. In an instant she felt truly unprotected, at the mercy of the instincts of this primeval forest. Silently she reprimanded herself for not placing Wards upon her person. Caught up in her panic and concern for Grania, she'd hurtled into potential danger without thought for the consequences.

Quickly she Warded herself, imagining light radiating from her ethereal body as if she had grown armour. Immediately she felt safer, many little threats evaporating, warned off by her power. Then she called for True-sight, asking for clarity of vision. Gradually the darkness lifted, just a fraction, in what seemed like one circle of her sight. There, as if a hole had been cut out of a sack that covered her, the moon, waning to a crescent, slunk out from behind dense cloud to offer gradual illumination and she could see she had wandered into the wide mouth of a cave.

As Grania called once more, her fresh awareness brought understanding of how Grania's voice had reverberated off the rock to produce the disorientating effect fed by Boudicca's fear and confusion. Lit by the moon's bright shining, she went to her daughter and knelt, holding her tightly to reassure her through her racking convulsions of utter despair.

'Mama, mama, I'm frightened. I'm so angry, I want to kill and maim and rend and tear and torture and hurt. I want to destroy everything.' Grania scratched at her face and pulled at Boudicca's robe. 'I hate so much. I don't understand these new feelings inside of me, they seem to career away without my control. What should I do with them? Express them and let them ride where they will, or deny them? Oh mama-mama, I'm so confused, it doesn't feel like it's me at all any more. I'm not a nasty person, I feel so small and young. I try to be good but all the while I feel men's eyes upon me knowing what was done to me and I hear voices filling me with anger and I don't understand, oh mama-mama help me, please …'

Grania was rambling. Boudicca flew inside her head for a fleeting instant to identify the symptoms she observed. Grania's mind was governed by chaos, too distorted and twisted for Boudicca to want to spend more than a fleeting moment within it. Had Grania concentrated upon learning the Craft, she might have known herself better and understood the mazes and patterns that her psyche was spinning in order to enable each emotion to have a turn at expressing itself. Then she might have been able to unravel and mend the strands herself. But this was not the place for recriminations.

Grania needed love and support and an opportunity to heal. Sadly, Boudicca reflected, that seemed increasingly unlikely now. She'd given Grania those opportunities, or at least thought she had. The anger and bitter temper Grania had demonstrated after her ordeal so far was now proving to be only the surface of a seemingly bottomless cavern. Normally Boudicca would have encouraged her to eject all the rage, now she wasn't too sure whether they were dealing with a finite quantity. For the sake of her daughter, and perhaps for those around, she had to be careful not to misinterpret what was going on for Grania internally.

She held her daughter tight and rocked her. She prayed within whilst doing so. Then she heard the calm voice, low in her mind, and recognised the Divine: 'Let her loosen the reins. There is no other option, even though she travels the borders betwixt life and death. She exudes part of My nature that will not be denied, and there is no other suitable receptacle.'

Boudicca smoothed her daughter's hair and tried to comfort her with gentle words of reassurance. She felt false in the attempt as if she betrayed her child, encouraging hope when she suspected there might be none to be found. Already, well within the space of a lunar cycle, a wedge had been driven between herself and her daughters. Where once they'd been so close, they now seemed isolated each from the other. There was a thin line between being the Goddess' chosen ones and being the pawns in some celestial game where only the Goddess and Her Druids knew the rules. She doubted the prudence of the course that seemed to be being plotted for herself and her daughters, let alone for the tribe. What wild unknowns would be unwittingly released, what dark paths might they be forced to tread? She almost wished she had never birthed her twins, if it was only to bring them into such peril.

No, she banished such thoughts. She was Queen and Priestess, nothing could be hidden from her. If there were concealment she would reveal it, if corruption she would cleanse it. The Goddess didn't work by manipulation and falsehoods but with clarity and cooperation. There'd be no reason to use anything other than honesty in requiring Boudicca to participate in whatever plans had been concocted, she was bound to the Goddess and virtually obliged to do as She asked. Whatever, she had faith too, and now she simply had to trust there was some larger scheme, of which she was aware of only the tiniest part. She was dependent on the expectation that all would be revealed when it was right.

Grania had calmed a little. Instead of the racking sobs that shook her whole body, she sniffled and whimpered quietly. 'Mama, mama, you do love me, don't you.'

'Oh, yes, Grania mine. Of course I love you. What made you think I might not?'

'I thought you loved Maeve more than me. You're with her so often and now she seems so Gifted in the way you wanted me to be.'

'Grania, Grania, daughter mine.' Boudicca was embarrassed, she'd never meant to give Maeve more attention, it was just that her need had seemed more desperate. 'We all thought you were coping so well. It's only now we have a chance to be alone that you're starting to tell me that wasn't the case. Maeve has seemed so much weaker than you, but you've been strong and without you I couldn't have coped in the last few days. Your strength and energy has been truly indispensable. I am very proud of you.

'See, Grania mine, you have gifts in areas where Maeve is very lacking. Even the talents you do see Maeve perform are not honed and trained. They're raw, which can be a very dangerous thing. She doesn't consider the outcome of showing her Gifts, she just does them. Perhaps she's no longer able to exercise such consideration. Perhaps there's very little of Maeve still there and most of her spirit has been subsumed by the prophecy of the Goddess. What if she were to show someone their future, and if that same someone were to see themselves meet a cowardly end? Think what it would do to that person, how it might destroy them inside, how it might provoke them into enacting the same events that led to the ignoble acts. No, daughter mine, half the skill in using the Gifts which Maeve has is knowing when it is appropriate to use them and when it is wiser to leave them be. In many ways, it is more Blessed to be bereft of the Gifts than to use them unknowingly.'

Grania clutched at Boudicca tightly. 'Thank you, mama. But there is still a pulling inside of me. Do I vent what is within or continue to fight?'

Boudicca paused, torn between her own doubts and the Goddess-guidance. 'You must let it go, Grania mine. I'll share the consequences with you and hold you when I'm able, but I don't recognise the like of which you are releasing.'

Grania slumped against her. 'I've done so and I feel light inside and rather empty. It's soothing to no longer be fighting against your own self. I feel ready to go back now.'

Go back. How? Boudicca hadn't noted the route she had taken. She doubted very much whether Grania had either. She'd rather hoped that Grania might be so exhausted she'd need to sleep until daylight.

Boudicca stood, walked silently out of the cave and looked around. She listened too. She could hear nothing, no campfire chatter, nor could she see the rosy glow of warming embers that must be far off between the trees. She smelled for the scent of wood-smoke upon the breeze. Nothing. She wondered whether Grania had coppiced this far and how well she might have become acquainted with the forest, but there was plenty of birch still around at this point and she had no wish to alarm Grania with the possibility that they might be lost.

She could, she reminded herself, Find her way back, but her earlier experiences at trying to Find the forge had lowered her confidence and she doubted her ability not to lose them both even further. She also knew that the best way to counter those feelings was to tackle her dread head-on and attempt another Finding immediately.

'It's this way, Grania. Would you like me to support you?'

'No mama. But I'll hold your hand so we don't lose each other.'

Together they moved out into the night, as stealthy as foxes, seeing by the minimal light of the moon, Her two horns glowing with white light to cast ethereal shadows over the blue landscape. Boudicca set a slow pace, concerned not to let herself wander even further should she fail to Find. She concentrated on the clarity she desired. Then remembered not to concentrate, but to relax. Then her mind fidgeted, alerting her to the forest dangers and producing predators to match the creeping sounds around. She slowed her breathing which had speeded to panic and started Finding again. She searched for the necessary mental clearness, tried too hard and blanked her mind again. She felt for the path she wanted, pictured it, held it, then lost it.

Ahead she heard a different sound, a slow, patient lumbering. She reinforced her Wards, placing them around Grania too. The lumbering paused, then approached more cautiously. 'Mama,' Boudicca turned to looked at her daughter. 'It's a bear, mama. Can you stop it from coming too close? I don't fancy wrestling a bear in the dark – there won't be enough people to watch and inform the Bard of my struggles so I can be immortalised in song. Without that, who'll believe my boasting?'

Boudicca didn't know why she had turned to look at Grania. She should have realised there wouldn't be enough light to see her face. Perhaps it had been habit, perhaps politeness, perhaps an instinctual action to better her hearing of Grania's words. Whatever, she was instantly relieved she had done so. There, behind, quite a way off, back through the clawing trees, moved a thin, yellowing light. She squinted to see at such a distance and nudged Grania. 'Is it a torch?'

'No, mama, the flame is the wrong shape to be a torch.'

Boudicca thought of the stories of will-o-the-wisps and corpse lights she'd been told about as a child. She hoped Grania hadn't thought of them too. She pulled her daughter down into a crouch. They couldn't go forward and they couldn't go back. Boudicca increased the Wards around them and imagined themselves both cloaked in invisibility. They would wait out the twin threats.

The distant light bobbed towards them, weaving its way through the trees but still taking an almost direct line towards them. Whatever it was seemed to know they were there. The clumsy lumbering, too, increased to include a snuffling panting and the crack of snapping bracken. Then, so near, a sniffing as if to define their hiding place, and finally silence.

Boudicca and Grania stayed motionless, holding each other tightly for reassurance. Warriors both, they stilled their fluttering hearts to ease their rising panic and shallowed their breathing. Their presence was barely perceptible. All that moved was their eyes, and those they had shielded with hair to prevent the light from reflecting off them and betraying their presence.

They could see enough though to watch Maeve approach, hands cupped around a soft wavering light, as if she held a burning sea coal, but much, much brighter. She brought illumination with her as if bearing a gift. A couple of paces from Boudicca and Grania's hiding place Maeve paused and turned, revealing a prone bear. Massive in bulk with a long coat and intelligent beady eyes, the bear lay upon the ground as if waiting in supplication. It sat up on Maeve's approach, holding eye contact, and then dropped to its prone position again. Then it turned to look directly at Boudicca and Grania, sat up, nodded its head twice as if directly at them, then dropped back to the floor again. Maeve stood as if she were only there to provide the light, holding her hands up to provide optimum visibility. Then the bear pulled itself to its feet, shaking its weight, and lumbered off past them, each step chorused by the tearing of tendrils and the crunch of dry leaves. Maeve held the witch-light higher and it brightened, showing the bear shovel off to the cave.

Maeve turned serenely and walked back the way she'd come. She took the light with her and the trees opened before her and the paths cleared. 'We must keep up, she's Finding. We should be back soon,' Boudicca hissed, hauling Grania up and pulling her along as they scrambled after Maeve.

As they dusted themselves off, running along to catch up, Boudicca felt like a naughty child who'd been caught by an overly-wise parent and was being punished by being ignored. A crime so heinous could not be acknowledged, let alone mentioned, and for some reason she felt guilty. Then she thought back to what she'd done and realised there was no manifest fault, it was simply that Maeve's behaviour was so superior it was triggering such responses without her realising why. Maeve's poor, confused behaviour was probably not intended that way at all, but Boudicca's automatic response afforded her insight into why Grania had reacted so extremely. Now Boudicca grabbed Grania's hand and laughed, trotting after the elusive Maeve with childish conspiracy.

'I wish I had wrestled that bear,' Grania said with pride. 'It looked docile enough to take on single-handedly, especially for someone of my strength. There may have been no one to see, but we could have dragged the carcass, or at least the skins, home between the two of us. Think of the stories they'd have told of me then! And I could wear the furs into battle – how fearsome I would be – and I would make the Romani quake when they saw me come hollowing at them in battle-lust.'

'Grania mine, I do declare you're getting some of your visionary powers back. A little more practice and you'll be as Gifted at imagining what you desire as Bride Herself.'

'There's never any harm in dreaming,' Grania joked.

That comment halted Boudicca's jovial mood, reminding her of the black visions which had haunted her sleep in recent days. 'Now that,' she conceded, not wishing to upset Grania, 'depends upon what you dream.'

Boudicca caught up with Maeve just as they arrived back at the clearing by the forge. The distance hadn't been far, and had certainly been nowhere near the length of the outward journey they'd made. Apart from anything else, they approached the Iceni camp from a different direction to the one they'd left, and from that Boudicca gleaned a little more of the complexities and nuances of Finding. She stopped Maeve with a gentle touch and turned her around. Maeve still wore the same vacant expression.

'Maeve, daughter mine, do you understand what went on back there, with the bear?' Boudicca asked.

Maeve nodded, and went to turn and continue. 'I want to go and wash now,' she pleaded.

Boudicca held her more firmly. 'How did you learn to do that thing with your hands? That light thing?' Maeve shrugged and opened her hands for her mother to inspect them. There was nothing there. No burns, no scarring, not even any reddening of the skin. Nothing to indicate that anything peculiar had happened.

Boudicca paused, exasperated. 'I've got to see Lovernios,' she stated to both young women. 'I suggest you both get some sleep. Perhaps you could keep each other warm?' She left Maeve and Grania looking at each other, both undecided about what to do, fearing rejection yet so painfully needing each other. They approached from two different worlds, Boudicca knew, but it would take knowledge of both realms to survive in the days to come.

Lovernios awaited her at the forge fires. He stood in welcome, his eyes widening at her arrival and an unnecessarily warm smile playing on his lips. 'You were gone a long while. I was quite concerned.'

'Why?'

'Because,' he paused, thinking, 'Because without you, I... things can't proceed. You're the linchpin of our plans. Without you, lives, homes, gold and land will have been sacrificed without reason. There are a lot of things, and many people, who depend on you.'

'So, I've little choice in helping you. What're your plans?'

'Immediately?' Lovernios asked, Boudicca nodded. 'There are still more outlying Iceni to the north and east, right on the coast at Branodunum and Gariannum. We'll call those in. They live on the outskirts of the forests so I'll arrange for them to be brought here by Finding, that should bring them in very quickly.'

'Arrange? What do you mean?'

'There are more Druids who'd join with us. They camp alone in the forests at present, roaming the countryside in isolation, on the Goddess' errands, safe from all but the Romani. They could be Called in an instant. They are mages and translators. You heard what Addedomarus said about the Romani – they're superstitious and scared of what we can do with our minds. We know how it's possible to live, using the best of both worlds, how a fuller awareness can take away fear. They don't have that awareness. They live entirely in the material world and are very easy to frighten. We could do a lot of damage to the Romani without even leaving the forest. Half the battle is already won with the Romani massed at Insula Mona, another quarter could be won with 'omens and portents'. Maeve would accomplish that very easily with her Skills.

'Also there are Trinovantes who live amongst the Romani. They could help too; they'll certainly keep us informed. And they're ready to rise against their enemy. Together your host would outnumber the Romani at Camulodunum by ten to every one. They're old soldiers, your victory would be as easy as squeezing the neck of a goose at Yule, when you hunger for food to comfort the winter snows. That'd be a sore blow against the Romani – it's their model city, their showpiece, and it would hurt their pride to lose that. Other Celtoi would flock to you then. The host would number whole tribes, and you could choose your next target at leisure. The easiest pickings perhaps, or the most challenging combat? The odd defended fort? Their mewling little harbour at Londinium? Whole legions in their battle plumage? You could even see if you could identify those who perpetrated the outrages upon you, hunt for familiar faces. Then there's the Catuvellauni nobles swanning around at Verulamium in their summer clothing, enjoying their leisure and their Romani bribes. Yes, you'd like to destroy some of the Catuvellauni, wouldn't you? There are many, many others who share your hatred. Together you'd be unstoppable.'

Boudicca was tempted. She didn't want to let Lovernios know that and give him the advantage. 'I don't like you using Maeve like this. She should be able to choose.'

'She does know what she's doing, madam, be assured of that. She communicates constantly, if only you'd listen. Of all of us, you have the most difficult task, straddling both worlds and keeping them in equilibrium within. At least for everyone else it doesn't matter if they become unbalanced in this way. I do appreciate how difficult it must be to pay equal attention to both ways of knowing, but you must try, otherwise Andraste …' He paused. 'Andraste won't Manifest as She should.'

Boudicca stared at him in disbelief. 'That's what's happening, then, isn't it? Isn't it?' she demanded. 'You're using me to invoke Andraste, using my body, my mind, as a vehicle for Her to Manifest in the world. That's why I have these rages and fits of confusion.'

Lovernios calmed her with a simple gesture. 'We're not using you, madam – not the Druids, not I. Andraste chose you. It just took us a while to recognise who She'd chosen. Personally, I was only certain after I saw your torc.'

'So, if She wasn't me, and I wasn't Her, you wouldn't be helping the Iceni now in their revenge against the Romani? We'd just be cast off like all the other Celtoi tribes who've suffered?'

'I don't wish to get involved in 'what ifs', madam. First of all, Andraste only chose you because you were receptive to her. Your anger, your desire to destroy, to 'devour', you said yourself must have been so strong that you opened floodgates in your spirit which might have been held shut by others. You have tremendous powers for one who walks the paths of reality, but it's not to be unexpected – you are Queen and Priestess and Druid trained, it's a volatile combination. Whatever, you opened those depths and you called upon that dark inner strength. Now you'll need Guides, like me, to control what you've unleashed.'

Boudicca slumped in awareness and resignation at what must be. 'At least,' she comforted herself, 'it's not my daught …' She sat up in horror and realisation. 'She's within Maeve and Grania, too, isn't She?'

Lovernios nodded. 'They offered suitable 'hospitality' too. They can be helped to channel the Divine also.'

'If they accept help.' She finished Lovernios' sentence for him. She was thinking of Grania. He nodded again. 'Who are you?'

'I am Lovernios the Keeper. Recently graduated Bard of Insula Mona. Respected, shall we say, within the Druidic Council. Prince of Hibernica and Chosen, too, in my own way. I'm here as Guide and perhaps …' he leaned over to give her a wet kiss which lingered upon her lips. 'Lover, too?'

Chapter 4

Waning Moon

Boudicca took Lovernios to her bed that night. They left the forge fires and huddled close in mutual warmth upon a mattress of dried leaves which scrunched as they turned together. Then they slept, wrapped snug in each other's cloaks.

The whole experience was very strange for her. She had started to wake early again and thus had a while to think it all through before Lovernios stirred. Certainly the Iceni, like the Celtoi as a whole, had a very relaxed attitude to sex. No one would judge her or refer to the incident, there was no shame or obligation incurred, and there'd been many other similar muffled noises around the camp last night. She knew how relaxed and good she should feel, how perfectly free of recriminations, but still she couldn't shake a feeling almost of guilt. That set her remembering what she'd heard of the Romani matrons whose bodies were assets like those of brood mares, to be kept chaste and precious, and she felt sick at the thought that such people could heap so many responsibilities onto such a natural act.

No, she couldn't hide from the fact that this was her first coupling since her husband had died. She thought she was ready to resume that part of her life but it had moved her like she had secretly known it would, if only she'd been more honest with herself. Old vulnerabilities had been opened up, reminding her of the possibility of being cared for and the pain of losing that affection. This was why, until now, she had avoided such contact with the men she knew, guessing they wouldn't be strong enough to hold her through the emotional tide which might erupt if she opened herself to their giving. The wounds were painful and this felt like someone was picking at the scabs.

Lovernios, though, held her constantly through the night, waking at her every movement, all concern at her well-being. She came to, finding strength in his arms which promised protection, and she relaxed into his warm and perfect body curled up around her. There was something about him drawing her to him, something alluring in his eyes which triggered memories of sadness, something impossible to resist. Something which suggested to her that he would be a worthy recipient of her love and that she would be a fool to reject his.

He was nuzzling her hair, rubbing the bristles of his trim beard against the back of her head, and stroking her body. She rolled over onto her back and kissed him, then they dressed quickly.

'Shall we start putting your plans into action today?' she asked.

'They're not my plans, madam. They were devised by the Druidic Council, and I hope you'll come to see them as our plans.' His eyes were all concern.

'What do we do first?' The intimacy of the night was over; she had to make that plain. If there were peoples other than the Iceni about to join them, then she couldn't afford to be seen as a lovesick little girl

Lovernios drew himself up to his full height. She liked the fact that he was taller than her, few men were. He was thinking. 'Give out orders to intensify their training, they don't have much longer to work off their fat and flab, we'll have hosted by new moon. Then bring Addedomarus and come with me.'

Boudicca did as he suggested, leaving Grania in charge of the battle training and Sucellus hotting up supplies of weaponry. Then she woke Addedomarus and they followed Lovernios' long strides, rustling through the forest floor. They walked until they could no longer hear the camp activities. There were very many peoples gathered now, and the raucous noises drowned out all other forest sounds until they'd travelled far enough for the trees to gradually muffle out the various calls, shouts and excited screams. Still they walked, and then the paths eased as if the Faery folk had been out sweeping their way clean with miniature brooms. Boudicca realised that Lovernios had been Finding, but he had done it so subtly that the changes which clarified their route had been almost imperceptible.

They were at the cave which Grania had stumbled into the night before. In the morning light, Boudicca could see how the tunnel had been formed by regularly placed sarsen stones fronting a low hillock. It would be just high enough inside for her to stand upright.

Lovernios was about to enter. 'No!' Boudicca warned. 'It's a bear's cave.'

'How do you know?' he asked accusingly. 'This is a holy place, how come you know anything about it?' He stepped towards her.

'Bears sleep in caves. This would be ideal. There're droppings here too,' she kicked a lump of black wood over, hoping he believed her and didn't come over to check. 'Don't you know anything about staying alive in a forest?'

Lovernios hesitated. 'I'll do my Workings outside,' he announced and beckoned them over to sit with him. Boudicca and Addedomarus joined him as deferentially as if they were his apprentices.

The Druid lit a fire, carefully choosing young green wood which would give off a heady smoke. He sprinkled some dried herbs on it to deepen the scent, arranging the fire so the skein of smoke drifted straight upwards without dispersing, trickling out of the makeshift hearth as if it were the long silky tail of a wildcat.

'What are we waiting for?' asked Addedomarus.

'For the Druids to arrive,' intoned Lovernios. 'Then you'll return with them to your people and then you'll bring your whole tribe to us here. Some you'll leave behind to ensure the Romani don't realise something is afoot, but they'll have important tasks to do and not long in which to do them.'

'Well met, Brother Lovernios,' came a greeting as a hooded figure stepped from behind an oak. 'I was expecting your bidding.'

'Well met, Usnach. Please be seated and wait with us.' Usnach nodded to Boudicca and Addedomarus in greeting. He sat silently. Others joined them, making greeting as they stepped into the small clearing and sat around the fire. Most, but by no means all, were men, cloaked and hooded in black or white, of varying ages but all with the same gentle concern and wisdom showing in their eyes, the same tenderness Boudicca saw in Lovernios. Before long the new arrivals numbered enough to form a circle around the fire with but one gap. They were still silent.

Lovernios looked around at the faces gathered there. 'Where's Cathbad? Everyone I summoned is here except for him.'

'He was delayed at Vernemetum after the Imbolc rituals. He was so concerned at the Romani threat to Insula Mona that he pleaded with everyone with any Gift to set Wards around every sacred site, in the hope the Romani will pass them by.'

A smile played upon Lovernios' lips. 'How very like him,' he commented. 'If only wars could be won without sacrifice. Never mind for now. You know why you've been summoned, you've all heard the Council's decisions: we're to Work to open the old routes into the forest. All routes are to drive straight to Sucellus' forge. First, I want all Trinovantes to have access here, then open the forests to all tribes. Let it be known that the Celtoi are hosting to drive out the Romani; Camulodunum is to be our first target. Let any who would fight come to us with ease; connect the woods of Britannia so even the remotest tribe might Find us with speed. Let the trees read the hearts of individuals so any true Celtoi may Find their way to us.'

'Not the Catuvellauni.' Boudicca was shocked by Lovernios' speech.

Lovernios was indignant at her interruption. He made it very clear in his terse response that she'd spoken out of turn.

'Madam, every Celtoi who seeks to join us will have their heart read by the forest. That means any Catuvellauni or Romani, any sycophantic Regni even, will be doomed to wander for ever in this tangle of thorns. Artio will provide no water, no berries or roots, no comfort of any kind. They'll be picked off one by one by Her sacred creatures, tormented by the sight of fruit hanging well out of reach and tortured by the trickling sound of sweet water that they can never find. Do you forget, madam, how Hidden we are, how our presence is assured here only so long as Artio and Her forest tolerate us, how we stay at Her whim? Her bountiful Gifts are easy to take for granted, but that is when they start to dwindle.'

Boudicca fumed at his words. She hung her head to contain her anger. She would talk to him in private. Yesterday, she thought, that would never have occurred to her. How quickly everything was changing.

Lovernios continued to address the Druids. 'We also want to ensure the Romani get a sense of our Powers. Make them aware they're not only dealing with mortal enemies but also that the entire land rises up to eject them from our shores. Ideally we want every Romani at Camulodunum to spend the last of his days looking over his shoulder, aware of a constant but unspecified threat.'

Lovernios gestured for Addedomarus to speak. 'I can arrange for things of greatness to fall, our women can sing stories of destruction, our people can start to look confident and free again.'

'That will supplement what we can do. Do the Romani have any monument which has especial meaning for them?'

'There is a statue they call "Victory"', Addedomarus confirmed, 'It is of a woman. My Gerbfine paid for it.'

'Good. It sounds particularly symbolic. Can you arrange for it to be toppled, say two nights from now?' Lovernios chuckled. 'Perhaps face down as if fleeing from the woods?'

Addedomarus nodded.

'No.' Boudicca interjected. 'Isn't there something else of equal significance?' Even at the risk of incurring further wrath, Boudicca felt obliged to disagree. She continued rapidly before Lovernios could object. 'Andraste is Victory, Victory is Andraste. Whether She is worshipped by Romani or Iceni, the two are the same, only the name changes. You'd be desecrating Her. There must be something else.'

'Is there?'

'No.' Addedomarus shook his head vigorously. 'Nothing of quite the same meaning for Romani. We Trinovantes never think of it as Andraste; we have no Victory Goddess, until now.' He shrugged, holding his hands out as if he could do nothing for them.

'We'll make sure Andraste is appeased.'

'Apologising before angering Her won't right your wrong.' Boudicca was aware she was being very protective of her Goddess. She felt extremely defensive, as if shielded an unborn child.

'We have to, madam. Now,' Lovernios addressed one of the other Druids. 'I want the Faery invoked. Request that they shriek and wail by night for their lamented lands in the west. Let them do it in whatever place the Romani meet to govern.'

'There is a place they call "senate-house"', Addedomarus explained to the Druid.

'Is there anywhere where sound will carry well? As it does in a cave?'

'Yes, there is a great open theatre, with step after giant step of stone; each step is many, many seats. Our children often call to each other there and play with their voices.'

'How would it sound if a wolf was in there, calling to the full moon? Might it sound as if a whole pack of ghouls and ghosts screamed for the entrapment of their spirits?'

'It maybe make their blood cold.'

Lovernios turned to another Druid. 'Ask Artio to tame us two wolves for a night of Her choosing. Let them be very vocal wolves!

'These are all things which look like sabotage.' He turned back to face the group as a whole. 'We need something more, something which a superstitious mind will nurture and work at, incorporating all these little inconveniences. We need a Glamour which will appear as an unmistakable message of doom.' Lovernios was thinking hard. 'Madam, with your leave, Maeve could weave a river of blood and a vision of what will come to be.'

'Would it harm her?'

'No, it wouldn't harm anyone. It would just look frightening. If she can conjure up those images we all saw of Camulodunum in the basin last night, then she can produce such images upon any water.' Lovernios was thinking aloud, partly to himself. 'If that water is still enough then the Scrying can be seen by any number of observers. The Colonia is built by an estuary; she should be able to Scry such images onto it when the waters are fairly still. Any ripples disrupting the images should only heighten the effect of tumbling, unstable buildings.'

Some of the Druids mumbled at the skills he was attributing to Maeve. One or two looked almost in awe. Lovernios held up his hand to gesture for silence.

'We'll be able to work out between us when the waters are due to be still from our observations of the moon's phases, and when a red sunset is likely to clothe the Glamour in a tide of blood. We can work cloaked in invisibility upon the shores. Maeve might be exhausted by the Working, but she won't be in any danger.' Lovernios chuckled in delight at his ideas. 'We will, of course, need some of the Trinovantes to "spot" this dreadful sight and bring the Romani to the lapping shores to share in the terror. Do you think you'll be able to do that, Addedomarus? Feel free to include as much hysteria as you deem fitting.'

All around Lovernios, heads nodded. His creativity had set many of the others to imagining what could be produced, how terrified and demoralised the Romani could be made to be.

'It will, of course, need to be followed up very quickly with the sort of total destruction which has so far only been hinted at by our omens. These prophecies must only be seen as preliminaries. Our attack must be perfectly executed and a total surprise. All Celtoi who host upon Camulodunum must be gathered here within days. The descent of the horde must come at the peak of their paranoia, or else our efforts will be wasted. It's essential,' Lovernios stared directly at Addedomarus, 'That we are kept thoroughly informed of what's happening in the Colonia.'

'Of course. Each Trinovantes who comes to join you here will bear news, every refugee will find some small way in which to add to the fear of the Romani before they leave their home. Have no doubt, this has been a long while in the waiting.'

'Then we open the old routes,' Lovernios announced to the other Druids as if he had been finally convinced he was right to continue with his scheming. 'When they're open, Addedomarus, you will re-turn to your peoples and instruct them in our plans, then direct them here in their dribs and drabs. They will be welcome.' His look told Boudicca not to argue.

Lovernios stood and gestured the Druids to follow him. He led them a little way from the barrow entrance, then they seemed to take up established positions and gestured together, pulling sickles from their robes with which they made cutting motions in the air. They danced an old, old dance, moving in and out of each other's paths, curving around, seeming to reach the central position and at the last moment sweeping back. They stepped familiar steps, each footfall marking its traditional place. Their robes moved with them so they appeared as strutting ravens, or folded together to look like one vast magpie.

As the ancient dance slowed to a halt, Boudicca noticed a quite tangible change in the feel of the forest. It was as if nature's chaos had become slightly more ordered. Then the Druids dispersed, as mysteriously as they'd arrived, each walking away into the dense trees, disappearing one by one, the forest swinging over to seal their passing.

Lovernios returned to join Boudicca and Addedomarus at the fire. 'Now we've opened the routes to Sucellus' forge. Any who'd join us will be able to come directly to us as easily as reaching out to any tree. Addedomarus, I'll direct you back to your peoples so you can start to effect those things we'd planned.' Addedomarus nodded. 'You've only a few days before we host. Send anyone, anything even, that is not in-dispensable directly here. Come and Find me at the forge if you need additional help, and keep us informed. I know it's been difficult for you to talk in a tongue foreign to yourself and I appreciate that you were making the concession so that the Iceni could understand you better, but at our next meeting it should be in more formal circumstances and I'll be pleased to act as the translator your rank deserves.'

They clasped hands, exchanging a few words of farewell in Addedomarus's own language. Then Lovernios pointed out a path leading between two oaks and the Trinovantes' King set out for it, his form dispersing in turn leaving Lovernios and Boudicca alone.

'Do you realise, madam, that you're the only person who doesn't pay me the respect due to my position?'

'That begs two questions then, doesn't it? What exactly is your rank and why do you put up with me?'

Lovernios chuckled again. He put his hands on his hips and gave her an admiring look. 'I find your attitude so refreshing, I wouldn't want to risk losing it by telling you.' Then he cupped her face in his hands and gently kissed her. 'I take it that's allowed now no one else is around?' She smiled softly. 'Did you actually see the bear when you were last here?'

'Yes, but it didn't do any …' She shut her eyes. He knew.

'I knew something had happened when you went to get Grania because of the way Maeve slipped off. I also knew that both you and Grania were in too much of a state to worry about where you were going, and with the strength of both of your Gifted birthrights blundering around Artio's forest it was almost inevitable that some sort of Finding was going to take place without either of you realising it. What you see here is a layer deeper than Sucellus' forge. Fortunately both you and Grania have similar levels of ability and you ended up in the same place. Your 'skill' at Finding is somewhat notorious even as far as Insula Mona, so I doubt if you'd have been able to get back without being rescued.' He dodged out of the way of her punch. 'There was something of the Divine glowing in your faces when you returned, and a certain placidity in your spirit, so I assumed you'd met Artio Herself.'

'You had no intention of going in the cave at all when we first got here, did you? Of course not,' she accused. 'No one's going to be able to achieve that snaking effect with wood smoke and get it to curl out of a cave too. It was all a ruse to get information out of me, wasn't it?' She stamped up and down wondering how she could have got to be so stupid. 'If it wasn't for the fact I seem to have very little choice in anything I do these days, I wouldn't trust you at all. Now, since what must be must be, why don't you make it all a little easier on my heart and start being more honest? Stop playing games. Just ask. What do they say about me on Insula Mona, anyway?'

He stroked her hair. 'You're very beautiful when you're angry. I like your eyes, they're as constant as the sea on a rough day: merciless and turbulent. But the waves can't help themselves, they just are.' He paused. 'Actually, what they say is a sort of compliment: that you don't like to lose control and always seem to need to influence whatever direction you take. That's why you have such difficulty Finding, because it's the only Sensing to require so much relinquishing. Your qualities are rather more vital for a Priestess who is also a Queen, particularly since there are so many natural Finders scattered around. You can always grab one of them to do your bidding, wouldn't you agree?'

'For someone who has to walk both paths and be an expert in each, yes, it is very difficult to let go.' She agreed with him. 'It would be ideal, perhaps, if I could relinquish just enough. So I could walk ever nearer the Goddess yet without straying further from the material path.'

'Well now, that so happens to be why we're here.'

'Let me guess. There's something else you have to tell me?'

Lovernios shuffled his feet like a naughty boy. 'You still have to contact Andraste. It's necessary. You'll understand afterwards. There's still some rawness in you, some healing to be effected. We, these plans, can't progress until you and Her are one. I've brought you here to this place of contemplation. You wear Her torc, the sign that you're Bound to Her, ready to relinquish everything for Her. Until now you've not really meant that; to go on, to succeed, that must change.

'I'll await you here until you're ready to return. I'll be here to rescue you if you call out, too. You must go into the tomb,' he gestured to the cave mouth. 'The tomb of your ancestors, to meet with Her on equal terms.' He gestured to her not to interrupt. 'Artio won't harm you. Yes, She sleeps within, but She'll bow to Andraste, at least for now.'

Boudicca didn't move. 'What if I refuse? How many more things are you going to spring on me like this? What if I fail?'

'You can refuse. Then we can go back to being slaves and pets of the Romani, and we'll lose everything we've ever known or ever held precious. Or else we host with an unbalanced, unrealistic and uninformed Queen at our lead. You won't fail, not if you learn what you must learn. You must feel the pulling within. It fairly shrieks at me, madam, whenever I look in your eyes. There's a need in your spirit for repose and rounding; without it you'll never move on from the things you've seen and suffered.'

'What if I don't want to move on? What if I still want to remember the outrages perpetrated upon my daughters, my people, and the very earth that sustains us? What if I want to continue mourning my husband so I'm not free to love you? Yes, that's what you want, isn't it? I'll be easier to manipulate if I follow you around with puppy eyes.' She wavered. 'I don't want to forget Prasutagus. I still love him. At least he was always honest with me.'

'If you do as I say, you'll understand I have never lied to you and have never sought to mislead you. You won't appreciate what I'm saying until you're able to see things from my perspective. To do that you must make one last, final, leap of faith, madam, and be alone with Andraste. I wouldn't try and replace Prasutagus in your heart, Boudicca. I had hoped there might be room for the two of us.'

'Yet again,' she caught back a sob that nearly escaped her throat, 'It doesn't seem like I have very much choice.' Then Boudicca swirled around, sending her cloak flying out as she marched into the cave. Lovernios reached out to stroke her arm as she left, but she pulled away from his touch and ducked between the sarsen stones without so much as a backward glance. She hoped very much that he was gazing after her longingly – somehow she managed to resist peeping to check.

Within the long barrow there was just enough room to stand for perhaps three people abreast. She waited for her eyes to adjust to the gloom. She could hear heavy breathing from way back in the pitch-blackness and deduced it came from the bear, sleeping during the day. She must ensure, above all else, that she didn't disturb it; she didn't have Grania's confidence for wrestling.

The visibility was virtually nil, a thin shaft of tentative daylight from the entrance serving only to illuminate the area immediately around the portal. She wondered how both she and Grania had ever managed to stumble into the cave the night before. Even with the night as black as death and the magnification and distortion the fear of dark casts upon things, she found it difficult to accept it was the same place. She ascribed it all to the magic of the place: it was a sacred site, its nature would change with the day and year and the receptivity of the visitor. She wondered again what it was she was meant to do and just what was meant to happen here.

Adjusting a little more to the available light, she could just make out, as various shades of grey, several side caverns inside the tomb, separated off by low walls of stones, piled flat, each upon the other. Inside each cavern was impenetrable black. She edged a step forward, further back, away from the only available light, towards the thick breathing, but so quiet as to ensure the sleeper wouldn't be woken. She slipped her other foot forward, convincing herself she was meant to separate from the things she clung to. Right now, the only thing offering any comfort was the light from the entrance, so she kept on moving, consciously shunning her security and the man who awaited her outside. She had to challenge her structures, the things she relied upon, face all her fears.

Nothing was happening. All that was going on was that she was terrifying herself out of her wits and walking into a bear's den to receive a mauling. And that only if she was very lucky and was going to get off lightly. Perhaps the bear had eaten recently. Perhaps it just sounded like a bear snoring. Perhaps it was really the sleeping of the royal ancestor who slept here. No. That was worse. Don't think thoughts like that. This was a place of death. There would be many, many remains here of, perhaps, hundreds of people. People of her bloodline. Spirits who knew her. Who watched her. It smelt of death here, musty and damp. It was cold. Was it getting colder? Had the dead awakened?

Boudicca backed herself against a wall and slid down until she was sitting on the wet earthen floor. She reminded herself that the jagged edges biting into her buttocks were jutting flints and very unlikely to be bones. She drew her knees up to her chest and sat, rigid with panic, glaring into the ebony which was all she could see, defying the murkiness to send forth its test. Waiting was worse. Keeping alert, looking all around, convinced of movement where there was none. Her eyes were tiring, darting all around at the imaginary threats she was certain were waiting for her just to drop her guard for a moment. Yes, a split instant would be all they would need for her to lower her vigilance and then she would be at their mercy. So, just as long as she kept up her watching, watching, they would not attack and she would be safe. Eventually Lovernios would come for her and she would be safely outside again and they could laugh about the phantoms she was sure she had seen.

Then, in the stillness, she remembered her husband and his last illness. She remembered the love they had shared over the years, their joys, their tears, their arguments. The way his eyes crinkled when he laughed, his kindness, his touch. How those glinting eyes had turned to pain, then to agony as the illness had eaten into him bit by tiny bit, eroding him from inside, gnawing at his body and his spirit and taking him from her a little more each day. His brave smile as his failing body heaped indignities upon him, and a little squeeze of her hand to tell her he still loved her and appreciated her presence.

Was it any wonder, then, that other more worldly concerns had been pushed aside to care for themselves? That her most fierce priority had been the welfare of Prasutagus? That occasionally she had snapped at others or made rash, unconsidered decisions? No, she wasn't about to criticise or punish herself for some of the unfitting ways she'd behaved when she was under so much pressure. No. People could understand or judge her forever; she had done what was best for her husband and had survived herself.

Death had taken hold very quickly when it had finally come. Quick and sudden, although the preceding days had seemed drawn out and stretched, she remembered. In hindsight it had all been over so fast. He had pushed away the healers, wanting release, not realising they sought to soothe, not to extend, his sentence. She had comforted him in those moments, like with a frightened child, promising that treatments wouldn't hurt and poultices wouldn't sting. Some had. Some had seared and racked his thin, weakened body and she'd caught the accusation of betrayal in his eyes, deducing he could no longer trust even her in a world where everything seemed set to destroy him.

Back then and in the days following she could only flash in return a shamed glance full of apologies at the way of things and whisper, 'Sorry'.

The funeral had been worse in many ways. On the one occasion when she needed him there beside her, even if just to be, he was gone. There was so much to organise, so much to endure, his mere presence would have been a comfort. Many things had been taken out of her hands by formalities and traditions, but her role had never been explained. Perhaps the part of the widow, the chief mourner, was only felt so acutely by her because of her sensitivities. Perhaps what she had felt was unexplainable and no one could have forewarned her.

They came for her when the body had been readied and the pyre stacked. She'd been left with her daughters, alone and undisturbed. She felt like an embarrassment to the tribe, as if her associations with the deceased rendered her so close to death that she had partly crossed the border out of life herself. Had she belonged with the living or the dead that day? She'd felt set apart by her people, familiar faces would not meet her eye; she was other, the focus of their grief. For one day she was not Boudicca, she was Prasutagus' widow, her personal identity swamped in her tribe's sorrow.

The weight of her people's grief had hung heavily upon her as she walked behind the wicker chariot upon which her husband's remains lay. It jerked slowly forward to the cemetery of the Iceni. It was a burdensome responsibility where the pressure of so many strong emotions seemed to suffocate her. She felt the collective feelings from those attending the funeral like a blanket. Somehow she coped. Somehow she got through the experience. Somewhere deep within provided some inner strength to draw on to see the day to its close. But it was an alien strength, it hadn't felt at all like a part of her. She had felt as if she'd been in a trance all day, drugged by a pervading numbness that was surviving not living, lending an aura of unreality to the whole proceedings.

Images invoked themselves unwillingly. Of taking a shaky place amongst the women folk who shrieked and howled to eject their grief, whilst on the opposite side of the pyre stood the men, bedecked as warriors and sounding war trumpets. A cacophony of noise to disguise any unqueenly sobs. Someone lit the pyre and cheery flames licked over and round the body as if tasting and scenting its meal before devouring it completely. It was as if the glowing fire delighted in the sacrifice it had been given. How Boudicca hated those flames then, how she resented their amber warmth which stole her husband before her very eyes. She watched the pyre with pure hatred until it burnt out, seeing abstract shapes of torment in the flames which she took a savage delight in, using the images of cruelty as an unexpected outlet for her anger. Then the ashes were raked in and placed in an urn which was buried amongst the urns of their forebears. The earth was marked with a wooden stick-man who took his place bravely amongst the other male and female markers which pitted the burial field.

And during the whole ceremony no one touched her or spoke to her, too embarrassed she might break, or too frightened of her asso-ciations with the dead. Whilst everyone else had seemed to have someone to comfort them, she was different, she was utterly alone. Yet, despite this almost avoidance, her presence had been intrinsic to the whole ceremony; without her, there would have been no focus for Iceni grief. She had been their figurehead for the day. Despite her own very real bereavement needs, her tribe had placed the onus upon her to lead them through their grief: to put the needs of the whole before the needs of the individual. And now, although others might be able to leave that place, part of her would be remaining there forever.

Here in the cave, the whole episode seemed so distant; it was like remembering someone else's memories.

The front of her tunic was wet. She'd been crying. Had she woken the bear? She listened carefully. Nothing, then the sound of rhythmic, gentle breathing. She sighed with relief, then wondered if Lovernios really was waiting for her outside. What good would he be against a gigantic bear? He was no warrior, that was certain; his lean body was definitely toned although it lacked the muscular definition and scar patterns of a seasoned fighter. Could he work his magic quickly enough to fend off an attack by a raging bear? She still didn't trust him totally, she realised; she was coming to depend upon him, but she still lacked the essential trust.

She couldn't explain the strange attraction she felt for him. He looked nothing like her late husband; he was of a longer, less stocky, build with a beard instead of drooping moustaches, but he smiled with his eyes as Prasutagus had. His smell was unfamiliar but safe and musky; she had liked his body smell, wafting from his strangely un-blemished skin. It was a good, man's scent. Certainly, he didn't possess the usual looks which would normally draw a second glance from her, but there was a fascination with him that she could not deny, some sort of binding she could no longer resist.

How much, then, of her distrust was linked to these strenuous ef-forts to stop herself falling in love with him? For that, she realised now, was what she had been striving to do. What of her husband, her late husband? What of his memory? Would she be betraying him? Lovernios had already reassured her he didn't seek to replace Prasutagus. Did she have enough love within herself to love them both? Since when had love been finite? If her intimate relationship with the Goddess had taught her anything, it had been that there need never be any constraints upon the quality or quantity of love.

And how much of her distrust centred upon his strange and incommunicable wisdom, with his secret plans to be hinted at just enough to keep her in line? She realised that in many ways he was right. No matter how much she might resist change, she did have to move on and somehow she would have to find the strength to do so. She understood now that she and the Iceni, even the other Celtoi, had been fools in their dealings with the Romani. Even she had been seduced by the promise of luxuries like sweet wine and pretty trinkets, cosseted by the lure of comfortable town living, civic amenities and soporific pleasures such as under-floor heating. They had paid with metals and dogs, hides and grain, even slaves. How many nameless faces had she personally sent, chained and whipped into vast, creaking ships never to see the shores of Britannia again? No hope for those captives that a raiding party might bring them home. And what had she got in return? Some amber beads, glassware and some empty amphorae, the wine long guzzled in an orgy of waste, to boast to the other Celtoi of Iceni riches.

She'd been tricked. The Romani had demonstrated their consumable commodities and encouraged the Celtoi to procure them. The Romani had funded Celtoi bragging, interpreting it as greed and not tribal pride in displays of wealth. They'd bought all the Celtoi offered for barter, and then they'd taken even more, more that was not on offer. But these Romani were conquerors, not traders, and their promises were nothing against the price of freedom.

Had Lovernios seen this? Would she have listened to him back then if he had tried to explain? She doubted if she would have done; she was too headstrong, she needed to have worked these things out for herself. In his wisdom, with his broader view, he must have understood all these things and known how useless it would have been for him to try and explain. But now it seemed to her as if Lovernios was asking her to do the same as she had had to do at Prasutagus' funeral: to put the whole before the individual, to preserve and kindle the atrocities performed upon herself and her daughters – not to let the memories heal, but to use them to rouse the Celtoi of Britannia into a frenzy of nationalistic fervour against the Romani. There was reason aplenty for revolt, piled up like so much dry wood; all it needed was one spark to set it alight.

She was intended as the tinder. A sacrifice in a way, but a sacrifice of identity not of life. That other price would come from the warriors she'd lead, some of them, inevitably, to their deaths. If she did as Lovernios asked, if she provided the figurehead to his scheme, she would be seen by many thousands not as Boudicca the woman, but as Boudicca the Queen, Priestess, and Destroyer.

'And as Boudicca the Incarnation of Andraste.'

Boudicca sat up, alert. She had started to drift away into the realms of her thoughts and imagination, where she was unaware of the present material world. She could no longer hear the bear's breathing, but she had distinctly heard the voice which had spoken to her from within, the voice that she now recognised as belonging to the Goddess.

'Is that what is required?' She asked tentatively.

'At last, little one, you acknowledge Me. Just a slight shifting over should do.'

Boudicca felt a strange sensation in her skull, like the tension before a thunderstorm or before a headache, then her thoughts seemed to converge into one place, into one side of her head, and then suddenly it was as if she was sharing her psyche with another. Concepts seemed crowded at first as her mind filled with wobbling images, then her thoughts settled like ripples in a well after pebbles have been dropped into it. Clarity returned, but with a sense of compactness as if mentally things were still a squeeze. Clarity yet with the benefit of a perception beyond her own.

She sensed the shared aspect of herself make itself aware of its surroundings, the cave, the forest, the wider land. She shuddered. 'We would be rid of these Romani, they have no feeling for this land. They have no feeling at all. Everything falls before their order.' Then she desired to leave the barrow and see Lovernios. Her need of Lovernios was strong.

Almost tripping over the rough floor, she stumbled outside into the warming spring air. The world had depth to it now. Boudicca saw significance where before there had been none; the emphasis of importance had shifted in nature. Lovernios was ruffling the neck of the great bear, lying prostrate before him.

'Lovernios!' She called. 'What have I done? What have I unleashed?'

He looked up. The bear turned and dropped in supplication to her.

'Beloved.' Boudicca felt her arms open to sweep Lovernios to her. 'At last we are together again. How long has it been?' Then as Lovernios cradled her to him and kissed her forehead, the pressure waned and the Goddess left her once more.

Chapter 5

Insula Mona

The Goddess' influence diminished, leaving Boudicca without the sense of personal invasion but still with the benefit of divine sagacity. Lovernios, she noticed, was holding her as if he would never let her go, tight, like some fragile, precious thing. As if he had lost her once too often before.

'You're back,' he sighed in relief. Boudicca looked at him in surprise and recognition on some deeper level. 'You were gone a long while,' he explained, rapidly covering himself. 'Nearly three days, you must be exhausted.'

Boudicca nodded. She was tired, and hungry, and started looking covetously over to the wood pigeon Lovernios had plucked and slowly roasted over his fire.

'It's for you. Help yourself.'

Unable to control herself, she grabbed the skewered bird, lifted it to her mouth and gnawed off chunks of flesh, chewing voraciously as if she had never eaten before. The pigeon was consumed in moments, leaving Boudicca with grease around her still full mouth and a wariness akin to any scavenging animal. Lovernios set a leather flask of water beside her. She drained the flask then turned and faced him, crouching down upon her haunches as if anticipating an attack.

Lovernios nodded to himself as if trying to sort his thoughts out before he committed them to words. 'Your eating habits always were quite despicable.' He looked at her sternly. 'You're not a raven, nor a wolverine. You're a Queen. A little more dignity is called for, madam. You really will have to learn to control Her.'

He sat cross-legged in the teaching position, across the fire from her. The huge bear shuffled to its feet and docilely lumbered over to fall with a lollop by his knees, positioned so Lovernios could absent-mindedly tickle its ears with the minimum of exertion whilst he talked.

'Madam, you know, as well as I, who Andraste is: The Mother in Her Darkest aspect – the slayer, the destroyer, the keeper of secrets. You know the carnage She brings and the price She demands. But She promises victory and triumph and it has been a long while since the Iceni, or any of the Celtoi, have seen Her Manifest. You know we need Her presence for what's to unfold and you've seen She was willing to be a part of it. Look how readily She has come to you, how easily She sits upon your psyche.

'But Her nature is such that Her desires are often relentless in their pursuit. That is part of Her appeal for those who worship Her. It's the appeal a woman has when she displays impetuosity and flightiness, pushing a man's desire to its limits as he realises her untamed mystery. Often it's a frivolity, occasionally an unrelenting driving force. In its purest form, it is never controlled by logic or reason. But, Manifest in you, She can be tempered, persuaded to wait, cautioned even. She's wild and uncontainable but you're strong willed enough to master Her by insisting She works through you, rather than you through Her.'

Boudicca shifted position, making herself more comfortable and assuming a less defensive stance.

'She's quiet now, but when She erupts again, let Her know She stays as a guest, not by right. All things Divine are of the One and acknowledge Celtoi freewill. Our peoples are loved for our fierce pride and enjoyment of all life can offer, without choice our exuberance would not provoke such delight in the One.'

Lovernios softened his voice. 'There's a part of me that loves you as much for Her presence as for yourself. That part of me has learned to be tempered, for it's Her consort, and I've lived with the God within for many years. So I, too, know the things which you're now experiencing, and I know them well.' Boudicca gasped. 'Together we've awaited Her return and I've had to teach the God patience or be torn in two by the pain of His desire. Those years have been long and we've come to such integration I can no more imagine life without His presence than He can bear to contemplate the loss of purpose without me.'

Lovernios reached out to touch her hand. 'I can teach you the path to integration, for it is smooth and easy once it's been discovered. Once more it's the Finding of the route wherein the difficulty lies, once Found it can never be lost.'

Boudicca watched him, wide-eyed in wonderment. 'Show me,' she whispered urgently. 'I can't continue so fragmented, never knowing when I'll know what my left hand might do, and when I will not.'

Softly he taught her: 'See your mind. See the barriers which distinguish you from Her.' Boudicca closed her eyes to concentrate. 'See them as fences, as lines, as impassable defences. See them clearly, they divide you from each other, they keep you distinct so you squabble over your resources rather than share. The road doesn't lie along those boundaries. I myself have travelled for days in my mind following the line of those defences to see if they ever ended or weakened. I've travelled in both directions, there's no change either way. I've climbed and I've tunnelled. The way through the defences is to invite the Divine to dissolve the boundaries.'

64

Boudicca blanched and pulled away from him, staring in disbelief. He stroked her hand. 'I know,' he reassured her. 'I understand how frightening it must be. But only She has the power to destroy the lines which keep you apart. They were put there, I know, for good reason, to preserve your sanity and identity, but they're a false security. Without them She'll have no need to erupt and smother you, it'll be like it is now, in the lull between Visitations. Yet you'll have constant access to the Divine, continual communication, and She'll have no need to use force to make Herself known. Hence, through a gentle coexistence, you'll maintain control without either of you needing to compromise.

'Trust me,' he whispered. 'With the benefit of hindsight, it is the better way.'

'Trust you. Again?'

'When have I ever been wrong?'

Boudicca closed her eyes and called upon the Goddess to dissolve the barriers, adding the proviso that the invitation to share her mind was as a guest. Her own voice sounded weak and wavering in her head, like a thin child's speech echoing around the halls of her mind as it uttered the invocation. It was a leap of faith for her, so she asked, as an afterthought, for the Goddess to be gentle.

The sturdy boundaries shimmered and undulated. They thinned to insubstantial wisps and dissipated like a spider's web in a summer's downpour. Boudicca expected some sort of onslaught from across the line where her defences had been. There was none, just a wash of warmth and gratitude. She wondered whether this was intended to lure her into a false sense of security.

'Don't you trust anyone, girl?' A giggling question, quite sardonic in tone, then: 'I'm not surprised; you've had a rough ride of it recently. Still, it's not for Me to cosset you – I'm here to put it all right.'

It was a surprisingly comforting voice now. One which no longer needed to overexert itself to get what it wanted or to demand attention. It seemed more relaxed, more willing to consult her and work in harmonious partnership.

She looked at Lovernios in quiet thankfulness for finally providing the means to still the persistent voice inside her. She saw him in a fresh light, through the Goddess' eyes, which softened his features and let her see his character emerge through his looks. He was not Prasutagus, he was different from that, but Prasutagus hadn't been the only attractive man she'd ever met. She realised how very handsome Lovernios was. He chuckled as she appraised him a little longer than was possible for her to be able to get away with and still pretend she'd not been assessing him. Then he offered her his profile, sweeping back his long dark hair and holding his head up proudly.

Then it was her turn to laugh at his pretence at vanity. She reached up and pulled his head back down towards her and kissed him quite intensely. There was a raging passion within her now, like a torrent, driving her towards loving him. It might have been the Goddess at work; perhaps there were no longer two separate people here at all, just two Divine Beings. She didn't care. She had mourned too long. It was all right to live now, not just to survive.

'Tell me everything that's happened since I've been gone,' she demanded excitedly.

'Everything? Well now,' Lovernios had an evil twinkle in his eye. 'Sucellus broke a hammer this morning. Goewin's child fell in the river yesterday and has caught cold. Fionn failed to …'

He was stopped by a blow from Boudicca which knocked him off balance. He nursed his arm with exaggerated tenderness. 'Grania used to do that to me. You know what I meant, Lovernios.'

'First let me reassure you I never once left this clearing during your meditation in the barrow. I didn't desert you, rather the Druids brought me news as they went about their business and I feel I've been kept well informed. I'm telling you this because the trust between us is still a fragile thing and although I'd antagonise you for fun, I'd never seek to have you question my loyalty again.

'Now, let me tell you about how things have gone at Camulodunum to begin with. All of the tricks and terrors we devised to haunt the Romani veterans have worked a treat. They're scared out of their wits. The Romani are a superstitious lot, their faith in their pantheon of deities is so weak that curses, fear and state ceremony are all they really have left of their religion. That, madam, is why I have no fear of destroying their Victory statue. Symbols have power only by their associations in peoples minds. For the Romani, their Victory statue has no connection with Andraste. For some of our peoples it will, but together we can reframe their mental meanings and no offence will be caused to the Goddess.'

Boudicca nodded, still not entirely convinced by his logic, but there seemed to be no objection from Andraste Herself, so she let it pass.

'Maeve's been an essential asset in all of this, without her the other things we've done wouldn't have made such an impact upon the Romani.' Boudicca sat up at the mention of her daughter. 'For two nights now, some of the Sisters have led her to the shores of the estuary. They travel fast by using the Finding routes opened within the forest, and the shores lap against wooded land so they emerge from the forests in an ideal place to perform their Workings. The waters are calm enough for the images which Maeve projects upon their surface to be identified as the pillars and columns of Camulodunum. They work from just before dawn so that, as the sun rises, the images are quite strong and well defined. The dawn is red, as we calculated it would be, so the images appear as if tinged in blood. Fortunately, the moon has just passed its last quarter and its waning to new has produced a powerful ebb tide. During the stillness, before sunrise, we heaped earth and shaped logs so, as the tide retreats, it appears to a casual eye that bodies of men and women are revealed.'

Boudicca widened her eyes, revealing how impressed she was.

'Of course, on close inspection, they're shown to be no such thing, but the fisher folk who creep down at dawn are Trinovantes; their screaming and panic brings the Romani running to come see and also prevents the Romani from too near a look. The images fade soon after dawn as Maeve is brought back to camp quite exhausted …'

Boudicca frowned at that last comment. 'She's fine? As you promised?'

'She sleeps a lot, but I don't sense any distress. Of course, as her mother you may pick up nuances in her that I've missed. You've the last word in this matter, but we plan only one more day's Work, and she doesn't seem to be at all coerced by our scheming.

'Anyway, on the second day, that is this morning, more Romani came to see the awful marvel which confirms their greatest fears. When the images faded, the Romani townsfolk departed and returned to their Colonia but the Trinovantes continued to stir up their fear. They gossip constantly about the dreadful images, so hopefully tomorrow morning the whole town should be there to see what we make! The Romani are so rigid with fear now that they've no will left to build defences. When suggestions were made, apparently for a moat and rampart, our Trinovantes conspirators persuaded them it was totally unnecessary by using fine words and exemplary behaviour.'

Boudicca smiled as she imagined the panic of the Romani.

Lovernios continued with his narrative. 'With this amount of panic and fear, any other remotely unusual event is interpreted as a portent of impending doom. There are, of course, the things we've arranged. Artio has sent wolves to howl in the theatre.' He ruffled the bear's neck a bit more vigorously. 'And very vocal they are too! I don't think I could sleep through their singing. Stealthy too, prowling around the stepped seats so as not to be caught, then calling to the waning moon when any investigator has departed. The Faery have possessed the senate house and are weeping for their lost lands: all in return for the bowls of milk which we reminded the Trinovantes to leave out in thanks for their assistance.

'Then there are the things we've not arranged, the things of the Romani's imagination. They see a bird fly to the left – it's a bad omen. They see some pebbles fallen in an unusual way – it's an omen. A sandal strap breaks, a pot cracks, a loaf burns – all these things are omens and render them too scared even to go about their daily business. There're Romani spies everywhere, but even they're not exempt from the fever of superstition overwhelming these people. They may have their suspicions fuelled by their fears but they can find no evidence for the level of insurrection which is about to unfold. We're cloaked too well by the forests, and the Trinovantes are on their most 'civilised' behaviour; no fault can be found.'

'When should we horde? It would be better if it were soon.' Boudicca licked her lips in anticipation.

'Has it really been so long since you've tasted blood, Andraste? Did the water sacrifices of gold and precious things never quench you? It'll be soon. You'll choose the right moment. You'll know when.'

Lovernios sat back and shrugged. 'There's little else I can tell you. The majority of Trinovantes have drifted away from the Colonia now. Key personnel remain and conceal the absence of their extended families. Sucellus' forge clearing is very packed, you will be surprised by the difference.'

'There were a lot of people there before we came here,' Boudicca stated.

'There are many, many more now. Britannia is one now – Celtoi, not individual tribes. We're horde. It's not only the Iceni and Trinovantes tribes from whom the warriors come, but from far afield too, wherever there is Romani oppression. There are some from the Dobunni in the Vale of the White Horse, the Atrebates to the south, and from the north some Coritani and a few from the Corieltavi. All are trusted warriors who've learned of our gathering from the Druids and have Found through forests near to them.' He held his hand up. 'There're none from the Catuvellauni, nor from the Regni in the far south, whose King, Cogidubnus, as you well know, is a Romani sympathiser and paid too well by them to want to drive them out. More surprisingly, none have come from the Dumnonii, nor the Durotiges, both tribes from far to the west.

'You'll understand, when you hear the number of different tongues that assail you, why none of this would've been possible without the Druids. At the very least, madam, you'll need us as translators.'

'I'm starting to realise, Lovernios, how very much we, I, do need you.'

'Not soon enough, madam. At least the two of us can return to Sucellus' forge as a united front.'

'What about my other daughter, Lovernios? What about Grania?'

'Oh yes, Grania.' Lovernios paused. 'Grania's much better, but I'll let you find out how for yourself.'

Boudicca gave him a puzzled look. He reached out to take her hand.

'Shall we go? I should warn you that you've changed in your absence. It didn't disturb me because I was expecting it, but it may unsettle your people. Let's just say it's more obvious that the Goddess' hand is upon you. You shouldn't have any problems with authority anyway.'

'I never did!'

Lovernios conceded the point. 'You might have done with peoples other than the Iceni. Your torc, Andraste's torc, has its very own luminescence now, almost dazzling. Leastways it lights your face with a subtle glow. I just thought I ought to warn you.'

'Thank you.' She touched the torc at her throat. It felt warm, but she'd known it would. 'Let's go.'

Lovernios turned to the bear. 'Thank you Artio, we'll meet again soon.' Then he took Boudicca's hand and stepped into the trees. 'Just to show you how easy it is now, I'll let you do the Finding.'

Boudicca cleared her mind and pictured where she wished to be. She took several random steps forward, leaving herself open to the whims of wherever the forest might wish her to be taken. Instantly the paths appeared and she gasped at the ease with which she had gained the Skill. She squeezed Lovernios' hand in excitement. 'I've done it!' she squealed.

'Well done, but don't get too carried away. I hate to ruin your moment of pleasure but you won't Find so easily when the Druids have shut the old paths again. If our successes are as I hope, you should be able to take advantage of our Workings for a full turn of the moon yet, so you can have a chance to appreciate what it really means to master the technique.'

Boudicca was about to hurl abuse at him when she realised that beneath his serious, somewhat condescending expression, he was desperately trying to hide his laughter at her reaction. She'd bitten at his sarcasm again; was she so obviously quick to anger? She was, she decided, but it must be part of her appeal, for Lovernios' eyes were shining with an appreciative love.

She tossed her mahogany hair back with mock contempt and strode off towards the forge. Lovernios let his suppressed laughter betray him as he jogged to keep up.

'What on…?' She exclaimed.

'Told you she was feeling better, madam.'

'Where did she get that old thing from?'

'Sucellus found it.'

'But we haven't made them pay that fine for almost a whole generation.'

'Shows how lazy and flabby you Iceni have become then, madam.'

Boudicca ignored him, she was getting used to his jibes as a means of expressing affection which indicated the new informality existing between them. She'd have to think of a few retorts to do with Druids and gently insert them into conversation as revenge. But not for the moment, now she wanted to watch what Grania was up to.

Her daughter was calling up warriors from the huge crowd surrounding her. She stood upon the wooden bridge where Sucellus had first greeted the Iceni, and was using a leather belt to measure the girth of each warrior she called to her. Most of the warriors passed the test and the belt fitted easily upon their firm frames, but every so often one would fail and the belt wouldn't be able to be done up despite the exaggerated pulling and heaving of Grania and the sucking in of midriff by the man in question. Then would start the hilarious taunts and jeers of Grania and the crowd and the loud laughter and clapping as Grania sarcastically asked how fond the warrior was of beer and mead, whether he preferred twirling a spindle to throwing a spear, grinding grain to handling a sword?

There were plenty of retorts about relaxed muscle and putting on weight over the winter, about how they'd been such a notable warrior they'd always been awarded the champion's cut of meat in feasts and must have had one too many such prizes. But Grania never relented and always demanded her punishment: a piece of gold for the river upon which they stood.

Bracelets and rings, armbands and filigree belt buckles all were submitted as a fine for having grown too obese, as the old laws had once decreed. Some of the objects were ritually broken by their owners before being delivered unto the water. And many an eye followed the airborne curve of a precious thing as it was cast away to plummet into the fast little stream before it swirled into the deeper whirlpool. Many a mouth formed a longing 'aah' at its plop on hitting the water and sinking into the river depths forever. Many a warrior left the bridge feigning deep disappointment and resignation, dragging their feet and pulling sad, sad faces, but then it was the turn of the next man and the cheerfulness returned to the crowd whilst the returning one submitted to back slapping and commiseration from his fellows.

Boudicca and Lovernios were soon laughing with the others. She stopped Lovernios from joining the crowd, keeping them both back to the vantage point that was the slight rise around the clearing, and shielded by patchy tree cover. Boudicca was, as Lovernios had warned, astounded by the numbers of people who had come to her cause. The clearing was extremely packed; she would have to push through hundreds of people to get to her daughter, even if she skirted around the fringes.

'I don't want to ruin it by announcing my presence yet,' she explained. 'Especially wearing this,' she gestured to her torc.

'Sucellus sent word he'd found the belt yesterday. We thought it would make a good 'treatment' for Grania. I didn't think it would be quite so comical, though.'

'She loves the attention, doesn't she? That's the warrior in her, she'll be a great champion, held in awe by Celtoi peoples for her prowess in combat.'

'Look at her! She's really disappointed when they fit into the belt. She's even trying to tickle that one to make him relax his stomach.' Lovernios shook his head sadly. 'A generation ago, no one would have failed this test.'

'I failed it once. But I was expecting my twins then; perhaps four, five moons into my pregnancy.'

Lovernios looked at her with admiration. 'I think that's excusable.'

'I made sure I passed at the next testing, a year later, and the next. Then the tests sort of petered out. Why isn't Grania testing any of the women?'

'No idea. Sucellus told her it was for all of those who intended to fight. Has she seen this before?'

'When she was very young. But I know she can remember it – she kept a cord with her play weapons when she was a little girl. She used to make me measure her waist before she'd start to play. She took herself quite seriously, even in those days. She should know to test the women too. Let's watch a little longer and see if she moves on to them.'

'See, there.' Lovernios pointed. 'The woman with the plaits has stepped forward to be measured and Grania has pulled out the man behind her instead. It's all good humoured at the moment. It is the sort of mistake that could happen in any crowd; I'm not too sure if it's intentional.'

'I don't share your lack of concern, Lovernios. She's enjoying this a little too much, you know. In fact, if I know Grania, I'd say she was actually enjoying humiliating the men folk.'

'A mother's intuition?'

'Look at her eyes.'

Lovernios looked more carefully. On inspection, Grania's expression was grasping as she relieved warrior after warrior of gold and hurled the items over the swirling stream. As she measured their bulk, she would survey them as if they were so much midden to be treated contemptuously.

'Fortunately for Grania, the crowd are in the mood for this ribaldry, but it doesn't take much for a crowd this size to become a mob. Come on, with me, let's see if we can prevent a diplomatic incident!' Boudicca pulled Lovernios after her, bellowing as she charged down the hillock. Those in the crowd who turned to see who was making the noise moved rapidly aside, hauling their companions with them.

Boudicca registered the look of awe upon some of the faces as they recognised first her, then noticed the torc's effects.

'Make way for your Queen!' She called as she pushed, attracting Grania's attention.

'Mother mine, you're back. Well met!' Boudicca clasped Grania's offered hand as she finally pulled herself up onto the bridge. The crowd had closed around her, leaving Lovernios to push his way more gradually through the throng of heaving bodies; Boudicca couldn't afford to worry about him for the moment. The warrior whom Grania had been dealing with edged himself back amongst his comrades in the hope Grania would forget he'd failed the test but not yet paid the fine, and considered himself granted an informal reprieve in which to rapidly lose some weight.

Pulling Grania to her in an unusually flamboyant demonstration of affection, Boudicca took the opportunity of such close quarters to hiss: 'Pick a woman. Any one will do. Quick. Test a woman.'

Grania pulled back and smiled a tense grin; she spoke through locked teeth. 'Only the men have let themselves go slack. Only the men need punishing.' Only Boudicca heard her. Only Grania saw the look her mother gave her.

Still smiling stiffly, Grania gestured to the corpulent woman with plaits to climb the bridge for testing. Boudicca nodded to her, still watching her daughter warily. The woman seemed oblivious to the undercurrents of tension between mother and daughter, Queen and subject. To whistles of appreciation she lifted her tunic to reveal magnificent breasts covered in looping tattoos and a plump stomach scarred with stretch marks from multiple pregnancies. She held herself tall, flexing muscles as her male counterparts had done, flaunting her physique and playing to the crowd. The woman was justifiably proud of her body, Boudicca could see she would make a formidable enemy once she loosened her long plaits and let her hair trail streaming behind her as she charged into the fray of battle. Many would fall in terror before her without so much as a blow.

But would she pass the belt test? Together, Boudicca and Grania measured her. The belt didn't quite fit. Grania was just about to tighten it for a moment's discomfort to let the woman pass so she could dismiss her into the crowd, when Boudicca stopped her by yelling, 'You must have a well trained husband, Lady. One who doesn't need to be kept in line. It seems we've let ourselves go a little, doesn't it?'

The Lady blushed. Behind her in the crowd, a man, presumably her husband, suffered some taunting. Then the crowds erupted into laughter and the lady chortled, paid up her fine, replaced her tunic and returned to her man. He looked her up and down appraisingly and slapped her buttocks. Her husband's comrades were also giving her lecherous looks. She reddened again, but with pride now, and returned their admiring gazes. Boudicca realised, with heightened insight, that the display had been perhaps one tiny part in a grander scheme to acquire an additional husband before long.

'Now a man,' hissed Boudicca. Grania pointed one out and he came up. 'And another two women straight after.'

Grania glared at her mother, but did as she said. The testing continuing until the crowd had started to dwindle away and Lovernios could join them again.

'What do you think you were doing?' Grania was furious. 'I was enjoying that.'

'The question is, what do you think you were doing, daughter mine?'

'I was measuring the men's girth before they went into battle. They're meant to keep themselves fit and firm, but they've let themselves go. How will they be able to protect their tribe when they're so ineffectual?'

Boudicca paused. There was more at issue here than Grania's need to debase men folk.

'Firstly, daughter mine, you were doing very well. It was very entertaining to watch and the people enjoyed your show very much. The Goddess, I'm sure, is appreciative of all the tribute. However – and you will just have to take my word for this based on years more experience of rulership than you – it was only a matter of course before the womenfolk noticed they weren't being chosen.'

Boudicca saw the look of disbelief on Grania's face so she tried to explain in more detail: 'This isn't a normal bunch of people. This is a displaced horde of people who are quick to anger. Tempers are running high and the tribes gathered here are tense, like a hidden animal about to bolt. It would take very, very little for them to turn on you – many of them are not Iceni and have no reason to pay you homage – and from where I was watching I could see you were playing with fire. If they'd mobbed you, neither I nor any of the Druids would've been able to save you – they'd have been out of control, and so would our plans. We're aware of that potential, and we're keeping it in reserve for when we can release their fury against the Romani scum.'

'And, daughter mine.' Boudicca gentled her voice. 'These aren't the men you should be punishing. Save your anger for the Romani, find the ones who hurt you and vent your revenge on them. The horde will be glad of your fierce anger in the days to come, and believe me, soon you'll have all the blood price you could ever dream of.'

Grania was starting to look convinced. Boudicca continued to talk. 'It's not the fault of the Iceni men that they didn't come to your aid when you were hurt. They weren't impassive because they were weak or lazy, but because they knew that if they saved their strength they could exact revenge. An Iceni death here, an Iceni death there, means little to the Romani and is as easy to acquire as a single swing of a sword, but together we'll massacre them – togetherness is our strength. Don't blame your kinsmen, we need them. Don't alienate the womenfolk, we need them too, for they're as noble in battle as any man.'

Then Grania turned to storm away as if in a sulk. Boudicca pulled her back and held her. 'There's no shame in what you did, Grania mine. No one knows except you and me and Lovernios here. To the people gathered here you've gone up in their respect and they'll look upon you in battle now as a great leader. You should be proud; you created an afternoon's diversion for a restless people which provided them with more of a group mind. It was good work. You're truly a daughter of mine.

'Wait just a few more days and I'll lead you to all the blood you could ever want and more. You may drink it, bathe in it; I'll give it all to you.'

Grania returned her mother's embrace but still did not talk. Boudicca noticed that her daughter was biting her lip as if to hold back tears. Boudicca didn't push her. Grania, she knew, would want to keep her pride. 'Come, let's go to Sucellus,' Boudicca offered. 'I'd like to see my other daughter too.'

'I'll continue with the shelter building. No mother mine.' Grania pulled away from the hand that sought to hold her. 'I already know the wondrous things Maeve's been doing. There are more people every moment who need shelter for tonight. I'm of better use out in the woods, although we are near short of birch.'

'It's very much appreciated, just as long as you understand that. It's work of at least equal importance to that which your sister does.'

Grania shrugged her shoulders. 'I think it's doing some good,' she affirmed in a smaller voice, and turned and walked away without once looking back.

Maeve was by the forge fires, still watching Sucellus work miracles with metal. It was obvious from the dampness of her hair that she'd washed recently, but the heat from the forge was drying her quickly. More horses had been brought in, and sturdy goats and sheep wandered around the clearing bleating and nibbling hay. Battle chariots had been arranged around the forge and wagons were piled high with a few basic supplies.

'Sucellus, you have been busy.' Boudicca looked in awe at what he'd produced in her absence. Despite the thousands of Celtoi who had massed to her call, everyone who desired to fight would be armed with at least one weapon. A few were fine heirlooms, wrought with decoration, but the majority were purely utilitarian. Sucellus had produced bosses for the many shields he'd made too. Each finished shield would be long enough to cover virtually all of a warrior's torso. He'd set the more artistic amongst the Iceni to painting the shields with bright designs and the rough oblongs were laid out in rows, drying in the thin spring sunlight.

Sucellus looked up from his work and smiled briefly to acknowledge her, but he didn't stop what he was doing. 'My apologies, madam, but we've just got this iron ore hot enough. Poor old Teirnon has spent most of the morning working away at those bellows – it'd be a waste to stop now and ruin all his hard effort.' Then, with a glance at the somewhat surly Teirnon, 'I don't think he would be too appreciative, either.'

'I didn't realise this was what being a smith was all about,' Teirnon muttered.

'Then there's the traditional laming,' Sucellus gloated. 'But if you keep that mood up, you might find that there's nothing ceremonial about any limp you end up with!'

'You're the most dreadful tease, Sucellus, and quite a bully too. Teirnon, I can see you're doing a wonderful job, you look quite exhausted. The Iceni appreciate your labour.'

The apprentice flushed. In his sulk he'd obviously forgotten his Queen was present but, like anyone used to motivating people, Boudicca had achieved the equivalent of three days' holiday in her few words of praise. Sucellus winked at her. Boudicca knew he didn't have the resources to let Teirnon pause, and the words wouldn't have meant the same coming from him, but he'd relied upon Boudicca's charity and given her the opening lines to provide the young man with renewed impetus.

Maeve seemed to have just woken and Boudicca's heart sank at the sight of the dark circles under her eyes and her thin cheeks. 'Have you been eating, daughter mine?'

'It disturbs my concentration, mama.'

'You must eat, Maeve. Lovernios, will you find some broth for my daughter, please? Someone should have a camp fire going and a bowl to spare.'

'I was right, mama, you can barely see the trees. Look.'

Maeve pointed and Boudicca scanned the clearing herself. There were so many people now it was difficult to see the forest foliage between their bodies. They wouldn't be able to stay here for much longer. Not only was the tension, the need to do something, anything, becoming quitetangible, but the woods would simply not be able to sustain them. They'd need to horde soon, even if only to raid.

Lovernios had returned with two bowls of broth. 'Your daughter isn't the only one who needs to eat, madam.'

Maeve picked at her soup, taking tiny sips even though the meal was barely warm, staring at her food more than eating it. The bowl was full of a thin stew, flavoured with early wild herbs, but most of the lumps of barley, parsnip and mutton had sunk to the bottom of the bowl. Suddenly, Maeve gave a little cry and demanded that Lovernios bring her a basin of clear water. As he did so, Boudicca noticed how the still surface of the watery broth had been just enough for Maeve to manifest images upon it. Poor child, she thought, what must her waking life be like now that every surface offered the potential for Scrying, bidden or not?

When the basin was set between them, Boudicca leaned forward as eagerly as her daughter, straining to see the images Maeve was bringing forth. The picture was faint and less distinct than before and, as she came to recognise the scenes, she realised why – the images came from far over the other side of Britannia, from her beloved fields of Insula Mona. Then they homed in on the shores of the island, at the very closest point of its connection with mainland Britannia. There, arranged along the shoreline, stood thousands of Celtoi warriors. Dotted amongst them were Druids, some recognisably familiar teachers from her college days, raising their arms to the sky, shouting prayers and curses, and Sisters dressed in their traditional black with dishevelled hair, running around brandishing torches and screaming and shouting at who or what strange threat?

'Can you show us what's on the shores of Britannia? What are they so scared of?'

'There's no need; watch.'

Lovernios' breathing was fast and deep now; he was panicking. 'The Romani are attacking Insula Mona then. I never thought they'd dare.' Then he went very quiet as they watched the flat-bottomed boats, crammed full of shining soldiers, edge nearer to the banks of Insula Mona. Romani horses, too, swam in their hundreds towards the Celtoi, each one's rider swimming alongside. It was only a short distance to the island, but the boats moved fractionally nearer and nearer as if they would take forever. As Boudicca watched she realised that very few of the Celtoi warriors awaiting the Romani attack were armed. They were bolstered purely with their religious faith. In a sickening moment she realised that any killing on the shores of Insula Mona would be simple butchery.

Frenzied and hysterical, the Celtoi's behaviour was clearly causing alarm to some of the younger Romani who were obviously expecting less savage adversaries who might show more restraint and propriety. The ideal enemy was not one who laid down and died or who submitted to the might of Rome quite voluntarily, but one who embraced Romani ways to the extent that they would give all they had to the

State; even delaying the sacrifice of their lives to match Rome's choosing if Rome ever deemed it necessary.

Boudicca's eyes darted over the Romani faces to see if she could recognise any of those responsible for her daughters' degradation. She could not. Most of the faces were battle hardened and impassive, seemingly immune to the emotions of battle. This was a job for them, not a part of life. A task to be completed, an order to be followed, with total absolution from any of the personal responsibility of their actions. These were not thinking, caring individuals, these were killing things, stealing lives for some grander plan they neither knew of nor felt for. It was only the hardness in the eyes, engendered by such attitudes, which Boudicca recognised in those faces.

Then the first was ashore. With a helmet as reflective as the brightest mirror and plumed like the proudest horse, the Romani splashed through the shallows, stabbing with his short sword and calling to his fellows. The first few legionaries were cut down, sending wriggles of blood into the lapping waves, then the onslaught began and the trumpets blared and the Romani ordered themselves into a solid wedge and charged. Brave Celtoi warriors fell tumbling around the wall of shields, turning the sea red, with here and there a tattooed limb poking out of the waters and a limed head crying in agony.

Useless against such unaffected coldness, the Brothers and Sisters of the Druidic Council had backed away, realising their magic and curses were no threat to the Romani. Death's encroachment was delayed solely by the warriors who fell to give the teachers, priests and poets some opportunity to flee. The Romani hacked on, efficient in the ruthless murder they dealt out to any caught in the lick of their swords, and oblivious to the dark Spells and Workings hanging over them now like a shroud.

Together both black and white robed Druids scuttled for the trees and the shelters of the Groves. Those who dawdled, those who were lame or old, those ritually blinded to enhance their clear sight, were picked off as they stumbled, and were left prone, with awful wounds upon their bodies, where they fell. A white haired child pulled at an older man, urging him to hurry. The older man jogged along, responding to the urgent tugging as best he could, then tripped, turning for a fleeting instant to see the horror of the Romani close behind. Reaching within his black robes, he pulled out a golden sickle which glinted for the tiniest instant before the boy grasped it and darted for the trees. Boy and man shared a last yearning glance of mutual understanding before the Groves enveloped the boy and the Romani trampled the old man.

The killing was finished quickly. Boudicca saw the Romani send troops into the Groves to seek any stragglers, while the cavalry circled the beachhead to capture any who'd escaped. She saw the foot soldiers emerge, incredulous, from the Groves, and knew that once between the stout oak trees they'd have found no sign of human passing. She saw the Romani's puzzlement turn to frustration. Then she saw the Romani bring axes and stoke fires and destroy the sacred Groves of Insula Mona out of sheer rage that anything so simple should dare to trick them and cause such vexation. Then the vision faded and her emotions returned from the calm repose they had melted into whilst she Scryed.

Now there was no return. This was the only consequence of Romani rule and there was no going back to their former existence in which they were all subservient to Rome and some god Emperor who cared not for his people. There was no longer any alternative but to horde, and their first target was one to bring union between Iceni and Trinovantes: Camulodunum.

She looked up with a new resolve, only to gaze deep into the troubled expression of a white haired child who held out a golden sickle to her. 'This is Andraste's own knife. He said you're its owner now.'

Boudicca took the cruel blade. It fit snug in her hand, worn in the same places her calloused fingers would eventually wear it down had the sickle been presented new and she about to wield it for a generation's passing and more. This was not being thrown in the stream; this marked a new style of sacrifice.

'I've just understood what he'd been trying to teach me. All his lessons make sense now. May I be alone to think on it, Teacher?' It was the child, still talking in his high piping voice, but to Lovernios now.

Lovernios nodded. 'There's only this evening and this night. I hope that's enough for all of you.' Boudicca looked past the child and realised Lovernios was addressing a whole crowd of Brothers and Sisters, all ragged and bloodied, and recognisable as the same Druids she'd seen moments before running on the beach at Insula Mona. On reaching the trees they'd Found and the Pathways had brought them here, in silence, to stand before her and await her presence.

'It has to be enough.' She announced, raising her voice so everyone in the whole clearing paused their tasks to hear her words. Everyone that is except Grania who could be heard a little way off complaining loudly about how there was no more beech to be had anywhere and that the first oak would have to be chopped down if any more wood was needed for shelter. Then even Grania was silent, as someone must have nudged her to be quiet.

Boudicca winked at Sucellus, who'd limped over to join her. 'We can't have that, can we?' she whispered in an aside.

'No, Madam, it's right for you to leave now,' he whispered back.

'It has to be enough, my people, for there's only tonight left. Tomorrow we horde!'

Chapter 6

Camulodunum

The horde that hurtled out of the forests which divided Iceni territory from the Trinovantes', enveloped Camulodunum like a low black cloud during a sudden April shower. It swept over the levelled defences, left from the earlier use of the land as a fort, and scattered the few Romani farmers who were still toiling to ready the fields for sowing. Swarming into the tight ordered streets, it fanned out to destroy anything, or anyone, with the misfortune to come within its grasp.

Naked warriors danced upon the trestle tables lining the open shop entrances, kicking the various wares to the ground. Shop keepers were kept alive long enough to point out the amphorae holding wine, as opposed to those storing pungent olive oil or sharp fish sauce, then the sounds of their dying would be drowned out by the cracking of pottery and the guzzling of the contents. Children in a street school had been ordered to fold up their wax tablets and stylos neatly and were still doing so when a champion decapitated their Greek tutor's head and held the grisly trophy up for them to see. Like so many lambs the children turned as one to look their own death in the eyes. Women were executed whilst at their baking or sewing; the old, weak and infirm were wounded or lamed and left to scream out their agonised death throes, increasing the cacophony of noise.

Everywhere was chaos, with the horde herding anyone who could still run – away from them, ahead, anywhere, just away from the terrors snapping at their heels. At the head of the host, amongst the very first out-runners, Boudicca rode her chariot, deftly steering her horses around spilt sacks of flour and piles of abandoned laundry. The harbinger of disorder herself, she drove her horses onwards through the cobbled roads, controlling the reins with one hand whilst spearing the exposed backs of civilians with the other. She rode with her bright tartan cloak flapping behind her like the wings of a massive raven and she shrieked as she seemed to fly at her fleeting enemy, urging her army to retribution. Her face was of one possessed, absorbed in the moment, yet glazed as if she'd not yet registered the horrific carnage littering the town.

Life, it was apparent to Boudicca, had continued much as usual in Camulodunum. Despite being induced into a state of agitation and foreboding which had rendered the townsfolk of the Colonia somewhat nervous and jumpy, it was obvious, by the number of faces she saw die struck with a look of abject surprise, that the horde had come as if from nowhere. Certainly there were a few more troops than her intelligence had led her to believe, but even they were scattering before her champions, seeming to aim for some sanctuary which she knew could not exist. Resistance was negligible. Quite simply, she knew, the Romani had heard rumours, some had suspected something was wrong, but the vast majority had found the idea of an insurrection totally inconceivable.

What was even more vital to the painstakingly planned rebellion was that no Romani of importance or power had suspected anything was untoward until the blast of Celtoi war trumpets had sounded at the Colonia's perimeter. The butchery was almost too easy. Boudicca felt confident the news of the attack would come as a revelation to jolt every Romani in the empire out of their complacency.

The chariot swung out wide as she rounded a corner and for a moment she thought she'd driven right through the town and out the other side, for suddenly the shops and terraced houses came to an abrupt end and before her opened a wide area of space. It took an instant for her to realise the town continued on the other side of the square, but as she cast her eyes about she found she had to look up – way, way, high up above – to see the gigantic building of stone which dominated her view and invaded the very sky.

Her horses came to an uncontrolled halt as she was overawed by the sheer scale of the Romani's construction. Around her the other fearless warriors who'd chosen the danger and glory of the advanced troops, faltered, their onslaught also checked by the sight before them. Veterans and semi-armed Romani soldiers used the brief lull to scamper from their hiding places and scurry up the dozen or so steps of the massive building –joining their comrades who'd already survived the rout – to their chosen sanctuary. Transfixed by the monument, Boudicca, and the Iceni around her, let the Romani have their bolthole. Close behind, the Trinovantes rounded the corner and jolted the motionless Iceni back into renewed action. The Trinovantes were not so impressed by the steps and colonnades of the massive structure ahead, they'd become immune to its majesty since being forced to live in the shadow of its oppression. They saw the Romani escape into this hated symbol and their rage at their lost quarry sent them into a renewed passion.

'Destroy the Temple of the Claudius god!' They cursed and ran across the precinct, which soon became a killing ground as javelin after Romani javelin was hurled from the safety of the temple doors. A few Celtoi died, caught unprepared that the Romani might have been perceptive and organised enough to identify the one defendable structure in the whole Colonia and provision it.

It took Boudicca the first few Trinovantian deaths to comprehend the entire situation and appreciate the Romani achievement in erecting this edifice to the conqueror of Britannia. 'Back!' she commanded, ensuring that no other warrior charged into certain suicide. The Temple of Claudius was too soundly built and too defendable to take by storm, but it could at least be sealed off, guaranteeing that no other Romani reached the haven it offered.

Miraculously her troops obeyed. So close to their kill and the symbol of their subjugation, the hot-headed Celtic warriors would not normally have been so easily controlled. But there was an edge of authority in her voice now, trained by the events of the last lunar cycle and tempered by the fire of the Goddess, Andraste, which could not be resisted.

Her warriors edged themselves around the perimeter of the Temple precinct, out of range of any Romani missiles. Gradually their numbers swelled as those champions who tired of looting joined them, thirsty for more blood, aware that the majority of booty would keep. This was an area of relative peace, but around the town the sounds of destruction continued; occasional screams tore the air as concealed citizens were discovered, and fires roared as forges were upturned and hearths kicked. Chickens squawked and dogs whimpered as they too were caught in the massacre. Fabrics could be heard tearing as Celtoi wives argued over ownership of fine clothing, and metal chinked as precious things were bundled up and stolen.

But around the Temple there was only the sound of shuffling restless Celtoi feet and faint coughing from the trapped Romani. Boudicca ordered fires to be built up around the sides of the Temple, out of sight of the doors. She set the Trinovantes to the task as they were the ones who chafed most openly to be upon the Romani. She might have the Goddess' authority but she, especially, knew that a Celtoi warrior in battle frenzy was a volatile force to be handled with respect. There was plenty of scaffolding at the place she indicated; the Temple might appear magnificent now but it was still incomplete. The smoke would blow, she knew, directly through the doors and make the air inside insufferable. Then she called for Lovernios.

When he came, he followed her away from the Temple quietly and seemed sickened by the sight of so many dead, even though they were Romani. He shook his head as he walked, casting his gaze around about, and muttered to himself: 'Even the little ones, even the children, babes.'

'They're the spawn of Romani, not children. They're Romani in the making, in miniature. They're already tainted by the deeds of their parents, look, even by the clothes they wear.' Boudicca kicked a body as she justified what they had done.

'Now, Lovernios, will you please spare a few moments from your misplaced grief to tell me why I have a more organised Romani resistance on my hands than I'd been led to believe was even possible? I thought everything had been so well planned. With the bulk of the Romani force being at Insula Mona with their Chief-governor, leaving little defence against our rebellion, right down to the little details like that hare you sneaked beneath my robes this morning for me to release before the horde. I should've known something would go wrong!'

Lovernios tried to calm her with a gentle caress but she was too agitated to respond. He sighed and led her into one of the little houses lining the street which hadn't yet been reached by the plunderers. Once within he turned and Warded the doorway so no one would disturb them, then he gestured for her to follow him into the atrium which opened to the sky and sit with him in the teaching position.

She watched him wait for her breathing to still a little more, and for her to calm down; in such a state she wouldn't even be open to reason. She knew what he was waiting for and gave in; she didn't want to get into a battle of wills with someone who'd be a formidable enemy if she pushed him too far. Finally, he spoke.

'Last night, as you know, we took Maeve out to the estuary for her final Scrying. You slept during this so you might be refreshed for today. The Scrying was again perfect and the images rendered upon the surface were clear for all who might come and see it. And come they did. This morning the shores and banks were filled with every veteran and townsperson who could hobble their way and stand to watch. Then as the sun rose, casting the water and its images into red relief, we learned from those who were the last to leave the Colonia and join our cause that our Glamours had been too good. Indeed the toppling of their Victory had been the last straw.'

He stopped her exclamation. 'Yes, I know you warned us. Anyway, it became apparent that a few of the townsfolk, not many you understand and certainly no one of status, but enough, had contacted the Procurator, Catus Decianus – I believe you've already had the pleasure of meeting him? – and he hurriedly sent a small force to reassure the Colonia. It seems that a rider slipped out of here without our noticing, then the imperial messenger service would've swung into action, providing fresh men and horses all the way to Londinium and back to Othona with orders to release some of the garrison.'

Boudicca shut her eyes at this thwarting of their plans. 'Madam, it's not that bad. He sent two hundred legionaries, that's all.' Boudicca widened her eyes. 'Two hundred legionaries who're used to protecting

Catus Decianus at his palace in Londinium and his clerical cronies. Men who've arrived here after a long river crossing and a forced march and who're exhausted. Do you realise how weak and feeble those troops are? Do you realise how poorly armed they are? Hag herself, madam, those men – just! – have never needed to protect themselves, or anyone else, since they were first assigned to the Procurator's Office. They haven't seen active service in the last two years! The only reason they were at Othona was to protect Catus' back should he need to retreat at speed from his dealings with you. They've grown fat awaiting their recall, and I suspect that, until extremely recently, they supposed this assignment required broadly similar duties to what they're used to.'

She turned on him. 'They seem to remember enough about shoring themselves up in a highly defendable position. That retreat didn't look like a spur of the moment idea. That Temple looks like it's been readied for a siege with a stock of weaponry. I suppose you'll be telling me they've got supplies with them too?

At least you've got the decency to redden slightly, oh lover mine.'

'Madam, it's still not what it seems. Yes, there's a store of weaponry, mainly javelins as you saw, and yes, there're some supplies, maybe enough water for a day, perhaps two. But it wasn't arranged by the Procurator's guard. No, madam, it was all arranged by the veterans themselves. They are the real professionals here; it's them who hold out against you, with perhaps a handful of the legionaries to aid them. A legionary won't forget twenty years of soldiering in two years of farming; he'll have lived the life for too long. It takes more than a plough team and a nagging wife and squalling babes to make a man go soft.

'I suggest, madam, there is little choice but to wait. I know you don't like it, any more than I or anyone else in your army likes it. But there are some who need the respite even if they might not want it.' Boudicca frowned and crossed her arms as Lovernios explained further.

'Firstly, there are the sick and the young who need to rest. The wagons have only just joined us in the Colonia and that can be a most wearying jolt of a journey. Secondly, under cover of night, those Romani who haven't been discovered yet will attempt to crawl out and flee from you; I think your champions will find good sport in that.' Boudicca smiled a cat grin at the thought. 'Thirdly, there are many, many Celtoi warriors who have heard of our plans but who've been reticent in throwing their lot in with us until they see how things fare. We've a decisive victory to show them now. They know we'll go on to better and greater things. Any true champion will be too proud to be able to resist such glory. The Dumnonii especially, from far, far in the southwest, should join us now. If you stay here a while they'll know where to find you.'

Boudicca nodded to herself while she thought it over. Lovernios continued. 'Then there's your army. They come for plunder and Romani riches. Let them destroy and devour all that's available to them here. Then, when we're ready to march on the next settlement they'll do so greedily, not hankering back to the treasures they left here. You also need to be aware that, although the bulk of the Romani are at Insula Mona, their Governor will know of this soon, if he doesn't already, and he'll send others to defend against you. These he'll probably order from Lindum, north of here in the lands of the Corieltavi, where a large force is kept, so be prepared for them.

'When those considerations have been made, madam, you must choose Andraste's sacrifice, and give your Goddess Her demands for Her own special blood. You'll know who to choose, they'll make themselves apparent, and how to kill them.' Boudicca felt a flutter within herself at Lovernios' suggestion, as if raven's wings flapped in her stomach. 'I suggest a feast tonight, in the Temple precinct, with fire and war songs and the loud boasting of champions. We'll drink Romani wine, eat their food and openly waste what we don't want, knowing there is plenty more. We'll torture them with our enjoyment whilst they hunger, we'll frighten them with talk of the things we Celtoi do to our enemies and we'll rejoice in the tears we'll hear from the Claudius Temple.

'Finally, you must look for the hare who still courses before you and see where his long legs carry him. You can see him still, if you look in the right way and the right places. Today he led you here, as the most fitting place for you to start this terror. Where will he lead you tomorrow?'

'That was a nice touch before we left, Lovernios. Very fitting.'

'He was Artio's idea. She sent him to me. I found him as I wandered off for my morning toileting, caught loosely in some willow boughs which had formed a natural snare. I've never seen anything like it before. He wasn't even kicking, quite placid, so I sang to him and worked his bindings off, checked him over for injuries and set him down to go free. But he just sat and looked at me quite quizzically, thumping his hind legs at me. Then I saw the bear prints passing quite near and three magpies chattered to me from atop an oak, which set me thinking of a girl – which is how I think of you!' Boudicca scowled at that and Lovernios chuckled at her expression, 'And all the connections suddenly clicked and I realised what I had to do with him. You felt yourself how calm he was tucked under your cloak, even with all that shouting and jeering from your Ladies and all the other Chiefs around you. How confidently he ran, in a straight line, in the direction of

Camulodunum. How the old pathways opened wide before him, so your army could follow in one mass and emerge from the forests close to the Colonia so we could fight refreshed and with surprise on our side.

'You must have Seen, as I did, that in the Otherworld the same hare kept running, straight to Camulodunum and then beyond? But where beyond has not yet been decreed. I know only that we've released the dams on a river of blood and now we must ride with the flow until it's run its course and we reach the sea.'

'Do you need me to be able to see the hare, then?'

'I can see it, so can several others of the Brothers and Sisters who are Gifted in this way. Maeve, I know, sees it very clearly. But you're the one who released him; the strongest link is with you. I know you need your Queen's skills now, with all the responsibilities being piled upon your shoulders, but use your Priestess skills too and your Goddess eyes. Don't neglect that half of yourself. Use this lull in the storm, this pause in the terror, to find where we should horde next. Our success, our lives, even our land, depends on you using your latent abilities.'

'You sound just like me when I talk to Grania.'

'I wish it wasn't necessary, madam. Now, we've been gone long enough. Let's return to the Temple precinct and set our mighty army to the things we've decided are necessary. There'll be feasting this evening, just as in the old days of raiding, and there are bards aplenty who'll entertain us through the night. There'll be fires too; we can use them to Scry upon.'

Boudicca nodded; Lovernios' words made sense. Perhaps this unexpected siege could be used to the rebellion's advantage after all. They stood and made to leave the Romani town house. Whilst Lovernios lowered the Wards he'd set at the door, Boudicca found the tiny shrine to the household gods. It was a bronze figurine of some little god with wings on his head and on his ankles, but what really set it apart was the number of erect and bulbous penises sprouting from various parts of its anatomy. She counted six, each portrayed as if having a life of its own like a vine's tendrils, seeking to inject its invasive seed into a suitably pliant receptacle.

A Celtic artist would have been less blatant, would've created a stylised, elegant pattern to hint at the form it invoked. Even now she wasn't able to appreciate such Romani art as a thing of beauty. A lunar cycle ago too, she reflected, she might have at least laughed at the lustiness portrayed so bawdily in the statuette. Now she felt sickened by it, yet strangely excited, too, if she were truly honest with herself.

'What is it?' Lovernios asked.

'Nothing,' she replied, not wanting Lovernios to see, afraid the sight might ruin something between them. Some pain, she realised, she had to bear alone or risk driving a wedge between herself and her lover. Then she spat on the greening statue before striding regally out into the streets, pulling Lovernios close behind. A party of looters emerged from the shop opposite and seemed to notice the existence of the town house as if it had been missed before.

'Has anyone been in there?' they called, checking with each other whether the property was worth their effort or whether some other party might have been in earlier and taken the choicest items.

'No,' Boudicca reassured them. 'It's all as it was when the Romani had it and quite intact.'

Some recognised her and bowed. They looked uncertain.

'You may go in now. We've finished what we were doing.'

The looters gathered up their sacks and started to call to others who were still dawdling in other places. 'Quick, hurry! This place hasn't been touched yet. It's got to be one of the last few left – at last we should be able to get some real treasures.'

'One thing more.' Boudicca stopped them. Yet again her divine authority seemed to halt them in their tracks, provoking reasonableness where there would usually be none. 'Anything you don't take I want destroyed. Totally, completely. Nothing is to be left. You understand?' A few glum faces nodded, quite confused. 'I'm aware it's a strange request but I have my reasons, they're not for you to ponder. Raze it to the ground when you've finished. I want this fire to be hot, I want an inferno, it must give off as much heat as any forge. The flames must be capable of melting metal. Rake through the ashes, ensure there's nothing left but grey dust. Oh, and don't touch the shrine to the household gods. Leave Romani superstition for the fire.

'When you've done this you'll have earned my thanks and you may all present yourselves to me at the feast tonight and take your meat directly from me.'

The looters bowed once more. They were still puzzled, Boudicca knew, but they'd do her bidding no matter how weird it might sound. Meat might be plentiful in Camulodunum tonight, but it was still a vast honour to be granted meat straight from one's Chief. No Celtoi would let such an opportunity be passed up, so before Lovernios and Boudicca had even started to take steps away from the house, the looters had commenced the work she'd set them to do.

'What was all that about, madam?'

'I wouldn't want to ruin anything by telling you.'

'That's usually my excuse.'

'You're learning.'

Lovernios laughed quite heartily out loud. 'Whatever did I do in previous lives to deserve this?'

'You were very, very good, of course. And you must've worked very hard, to benefit others, not yourself.'

'Let that be a lesson to the just man, then.'

Boudicca looked puzzled.

'Plato, Boudicca mine, but I wouldn't want to ruin the beautiful expression on your face by explaining it to you!'

Boudicca scowled. 'Have it your own way then,' she retorted and she laughed, despite herself. Why could she never stay angry with her Druidic lover for long? 'Let's get this situation into some semblance of order then.'

She strode off, back to the Temple precinct. The wide square had filled in her absence, although no one had ventured within firing range of the besieged Romani. The bodies of the Trinovantes who had taken that risk still lay prone upon the Temple steps. Warriors came and went, some left to do some looting and mindless destruction, others put down their booty sacks and came to stand and glare at the hated symbol which still defied them. Some of the more daring rode their chariots tantalisingly close to the Romani's range, running out as graceful as dancers along the central poles which swung between the galloping horses, to hurl insults at the Romani.

The smoke had started to build now and those nearest the fires had to partially cover their faces with their cloaks. The crowd was restless. Women warriors, as well as the men, taunted the Romani with obscene gestures and threats of Celtoi revenge. There were many, many dogs which had been brought, too, and they slavered at their leads, eager to be at their enemy and excited by the sound of the war trumpets. Fortunately, there were still games to be played and fun to be had with the besieged Romani, and as yet no one had led an assault upon the Temple. No one seemed in a hurry to rush the Temple – the Romani were too well defended – it would be better to weaken the enemy first. Certainly there wouldn't be so much glory in that, but then the Celtoi had had to be weakened before the Romani had been able to conquer them, and it seemed fair retaliation. Let the Romani know how it felt to be disadvantaged in a fight. The Temple, too, may have been dedicated to a foreign Claudius god, but it was a holy place and it wasn't proper to war in sacred space, no matter whose honour it was set aside for.

As Boudicca watched, the centre of the crowd heaved and parted as it ejected a huddle of warriors from its midst. There was a struggle as a captive was led forward by those who'd just pushed their way to the front. Several Celtoi women had discovered a young man and they pulled the Romani with them so he was in view of the vast Temple doors. He was still young enough to be someone's son, Boudicca realised, with just a hint of fluffy hair upon his lip, but he managed to hold himself tall. They stripped him and poked him with their spear tips in all his soft places. His resolve crumbled – inside he was still a child, nowhere near an adult really – and he started to blubber. Boudicca laughed. The spears were thrust more forcefully and he started to cry out loud for his mama, begging the women to leave him alone, that he had done nothing wrong, and how his father would save him.

'Quintus!' A voice boomed from the temple. For an instant the Celtoi cowered, thinking it was the voice of the Claudius god come from the sky. Then they realised it only heralded an echoing heroic charge by an old sweat who came hammering down the Temple steps despite his colleagues' attempts to hold him back. Their attention diverted for an instant, the boy ducked under his tormentors' arms and ran for his life across the square to the safety of his father and the sanctuary beyond.

They never even reached each other. Despite a hail of Romani javelins to cover the veteran's sally, a chariot whipped out from the Celtoi ranks and rode between father and son. Deftly the warrior standing on the wicker frame cast a spear with each hand, in different directions, neatly into the chest of each Romani, leaving their bodies stuck through. They died at the same moment. The driver hadn't even slowed the horses to allow the manoeuvre, but kept the chariot at the same furious pace until it had travelled the length of the precinct. Then the chariot turned tightly, and to a riotous cheer from the Celtoi ranks, made a victorious pass back to where it had appeared from.

Lovernios tapped Boudicca's shoulder to divert her attention back to her purpose. She realised she'd been shouting in triumph as raucously as everyone else at this marvellous display of the charioteer's skill. The chariots were usually ridden upon uneven grass; these cobbled streets were a veritable treat. Lovernios nudged her again; he'd obviously been giving their situation a lot of thought.

'Madam, we need the force to be divided into three, a third to rest immediately. We need to keep a constant vigil over these besieged veterans – they're professionals, remember? They'll realise soon how hopeless their position is and will probably start some sort of diversion so they can bolt. We must be wary of that, so we need a third of our force to be constantly on guard here. Those that rest now can be set to take over the next shift here. We need another third to continue searching for those who've secreted themselves around the Colonia and who might still try to escape and those who might have been sent to bring relief to the town. When the Celtoi who choose to remain here tire of their current entertainments, I suggest we set some of them to arranging the feast to end all feasts, as we promised. They should be warned to be continually wary though. Lets see if we can't tempt those Romani out.'

Boudicca contemplated his ideas for a while. 'We not only need to split the army into three, but to do so evenly. There's no good in setting old women and little boys to watch the temple. Also, we need to do so diplomatically. If we're Celtoi now, as you claim we are, and not Iceni plus other lesser tribes from around Britannia, then we need each tribe to be represented in each third.'

Lovernios grabbed her arm and squeezed, hard. She pulled away. 'Don't be so antagonistic, madam. You only need the wrong tribesperson to hear choice remarks like 'lesser' and you will be Iceni. Yes, Iceni alone, and it'll be you the Celtoi will turn on instead of the Romani. Have a care, madam.'

Boudicca looked around her. 'No one heard,' she hissed.

Lovernios gave her a very serious stare.

'I need...' she corrected herself. 'Request, the aid of your Druids as translators to aid my Chiefs in ensuring each part of our force is evenly balanced.'

'Call your Chiefs to you, I'll request your translators.'

Boudicca sent a runner for two selected leaders, Addedomarus from the Trinovantes and whoever the Coritani would choose. Grania was also sent for as second in command. Addedomarus arrived along with a huge woman from the Coritani who was almost as broad as she was tall, but her frame was built of muscle not fat, and her strength bulged out of the gaps in her makeshift armour. She introduced herself by uttering 'Fand' and punching her chest, and once again Boudicca realised how very reliant the whole operation was upon the goodwill of the Druids. These armies before her would never have been able to even communicate without Lovernios' assistance; the rebellion would have been nothing more than a half-baked shambles without him.

The translators arrived, taciturn and learned. Two wise women, ill-equipped for more social discourse, their white robes emphasising the paleness of their skin gained from years spent in recluse. They nodded sagely at everything Lovernios said to them in their own private Druidic tongue, of which Boudicca knew only a smattering. He explained to Boudicca what had been agreed whilst one translator communicated the information to Addedomarus, and the other conversed with Fand. Discussion followed. Boudicca felt uneasy; this was out of her control. How could she be certain they were saying the right things? Even an incorrect inflection might stir up animosity. She watched and listened to the conversations, desperately trying to discern how things were proceeding from universal body movements and nuances of language.

Finally Addedomarus clasped her hand, smiled and said, 'Good plan, we watch, you rest.'

The translator explained the exchange to Fand. She in turn nodded and grinned, grasping Boudicca in a suffocating bear hug to confirm her agreement. Then she gabbled something at the translator, who muttered, 'Queen Fand says she is pleased to be still looting, and will find some especial trinket for Andraste.'

'Does she mean some gold or a sacrifice?'

The translator communicated the question back to Fand who laughed and slapped Boudicca playfully. 'She says you understand her in the way that only a woman would and she is honoured to answer to your orders.'

'Well, I'd never have suspected such a character to be so enigmatic,' Boudicca muttered under her breath as soon as they were all dismissed.

Lovernios gave her a warning stare, then sniggered at her observation. 'Just go careful who hears you, madam, that's all.'

'What is it you're so very scared of, Lovernios mine?'

'This is all new territory for me, too, madam. We've received Blessings from the Goddess beyond anything I'd ever dreamed of in formulating this enterprise, but still there's a part of me which questions how long free spirit of the Celtoi will respond to your authority, indeed to any authority?'

'The horde is like my horses, Cloud and Mouse,' she mused. 'Battle-trained and hardened, it seeks the thick of conflict but stalls at the slightest hint of reticence. Our horses are fiercely independent, any sense of control stems from an illusion which conceals a cooperation between partners.'

Having thought this through, Boudicca was able to answer Lovernios more fully. 'We must let the hoard have free rein, only making steering adjustments, if we're not to lose its wild momentum. We won't really be commanding, we'll be suggesting. It's the divine authority of Andraste which results in a suggestion being responded to as a command. It's only if the Goddess influence wanes that we shall appear to lose any control, and She shall continue to wax as long as there's blood to be let.'

Lovernios gave her his odd little bow and seemed to be reassured by her words. She felt strangely tired and, taking his arm, withdrew. She left Grania to ensure that enough warriors took the opportunity to snatch some sleep so they might be alert to guard the Temple through the night's feasting, although Grania was as reluctant as anyone to be drawn away from the trapped Romani. It took argument before Grania conceded there would be more chance of a Romani to kill during the night when they were most likely to attempt to escape. Boudicca imagined Grania twitching and flinching in her sleep between shifts, like a cat dreaming of mice.

Already, edible spoils were being piled in preparation for the evening's celebrations and wood was collected for bonfires. Eagerness paced the temple precinct in anticipation of the grand feasting and laughter that would ring out tonight, although for now the Temple was as silent as a tomb, as if the Romani within already considered themselves dead. Gradually the Colonia was being razed out of total hatred for what it had symbolised; buildings were levelled and commodities destroyed. Soon there would be nothing but dust.

Maeve had travelled with the wagons. They'd been drawn up to block the main exit from the Temple precinct and contained all the non-combatants of the horde. They represented only a small proportion of Boudicca's army because even the barely active had taken up arms in the hope that an easy kill would ensure that their names would be sung in memory. No one had wanted to miss this opportunity for glory.

The oxen had been left harnessed and brooding and, on first sight of the wagons, Boudicca felt that the beasts summarised the mood of all the passengers. There was little activity, as if the excitement of this raid hadn't yet filtered through to those who'd been left out. Boudicca felt bad about insisting on Maeve being transported in this way, but it was easier to keep track of where she was when she was packed in with children and those too sickly to fight. Fortunately, Sucellus had largely taken over Maeve's welfare while they camped at the forge and had chosen to accompany the horde when it left, travelling in the wagon since he was too lame to run. He sat patiently with Maeve, gripping her hand and accepting her strange, far away look.

Festooned around the wagons were the trophies of war: heads of slain enemies hung by their hair from the wickerwork above the wheels, their severed necks dripping blood and globs of brain which trickled over the cobbles. Lovernios blanched a little when he saw them and shook his head in disbelief as one little boy leaned precariously over the rails of his wagon to prise open a mouth stuck in its death grin and work out the blackened tongue. The children around him giggled and squealed as he prodded the head further, trying to alter the expression or push in the eyes.

Boudicca ruffled his hair. 'Sorry, little man, you can join your mama soon when she comes to bring you to the feast.' There was a chorus of aahs and oohs from the wagon and lots of wide eyes looked to Boudicca. 'There'll be stories and songs too, but only for those who wait here for their parents to come for them.' Some of the children still looked in need of reassurance. Boudicca guessed their question. 'There are very few Celtoi dead, your mamas will come for you. The Romani didn't want to fight at all, they just ran away.' There were cheers and claps from the children, and from those in the other wagons. 'If you stay here, your parents will know where to come for you and then they won't be distracted from their fighting by worrying about your welfare.'

Celtoi children were boisterous but obedient in general. They were also equipped with lively imaginations and could keep themselves amused for long periods quite happily. It was a characteristic which tarnished only fractionally with age. Boudicca felt quite calm about leaving them to the peripheral vision of those warriors just inside the Temple precinct. More and more people would soon be enjoined to rest, and they'd come here first to seek out their dependents.

Maeve, though, she wanted to gather to her. 'Daughter mine, please come to me.'

'Is there water to wash?' Maeve pleaded.

'No, Maeve, but there are fires prepared and we can warm ourselves next to them. We should stay together, for a while at least. We can rest. I would talk with you too.' Boudicca gestured to Sucellus and he led Maeve through the muddle of those squeezed into the wagon and helped her down to the ground.

The four of them made their way back into the Temple precinct to where the fires had been prepared and meat had been set to roasting. The noise of jeering warriors was still deafening as Druids moved amongst the crowd inciting them to further fury by reminding them of their ancestral glories and past outrages of the Romani. A place had been prepared for Boudicca by the largest fire. Blankets and swathes of rich cloths had been earmarked from plundered homes for Boudicca and her Chiefs to rest upon, wine had been set apart along with some of the choicer cheese and bread which hadn't suffered too much trampling.

The seating allowed maximum warmth without burning and a clear view of the Temple. There was enough smoke to make Boudicca's eye smart, but she ignored the discomfort, aware that the veterans would be barely able to breathe soon. She scanned the precinct and noted how the crowd had already started to gather around the Nobles to whom individuals owed allegiance.

'Lovernios?' she whispered. He bent to hear her quiet voice. 'Can you ensure your Druids do all they can to keep the horde as Celtoi and not revert to tribes?'

'It's inevitable, madam, that they'll collect around their own people.' He thought for a moment. 'However, for every quarrel they can remember between them, there can be found another memory of alliance. Every Celtoi here can name at least one ancestor who quarrelled with an ancestor of every other Celtoi, but they forget their unions quickly, too. The Druids have memorised the ancestry of every Celtoi family back to the days of the Faery. We can use that knowledge to remind them of the inappropriateness of their rivalry.'

'Keep their anger directed at the Romani then. Must we provide continuous diversions to prevent them turning in upon themselves?'

'Madam, you still have to realise that every advantage can equally be a disadvantage, it depends upon how it's viewed.'

Boudicca took a deep breath. It seemed that every attempt she made to reach out to Lovernios for reassurance was answered with detached rhetoric, yet on other occasions he'd offer total emotional support quite unbidden. She felt pulled between relying upon him and being independent, the balance shifting continually.

'I'm going to rest now,' she announced. 'I want to be woken if I'm needed, for the slightest reason, you understand?' Lovernios nodded. Boudicca pulled Maeve to her and covered her with blankets, as she had when her daughter had been much younger, clasping Maeve protectively, her motion effectively shutting Lovernios out from the comfort she offered her own.

She heard Lovernios give a few orders and felt Maeve relax her stiff unyielding posture, and then, despite the excited noises and all the tension, she slept a light, disturbed sleep where she was running, always running, to keep up with… who knew what?

Chapter 7

Visions & Revelations

When Boudicca awoke, the afternoon had vanished and the sky was grey against black where the many camp-fires and smouldering remains of once fine homes had emitted billows of smoke. The same fires now served as sources of light to illuminate the smoke which was refusing to dissipate in the still air. The ravaged Colonia would be easily seen from afar, she realised, perhaps as little more than a hint of orange in the east, like a particularly fiery dawn, but it would be an obvious warning to all Romani who saw it of what had come to pass. Then a scent of succulent roast mutton and beef filled her nostrils and she started to salivate, realising how hungry she was. The same still air wafted the sounds of a harp gently picking out the refrain of the legend of Bronwen accompanied by a more raucous drunken chorus.

The Romani wine had flowed freely during her rest. As she shook the remaining drowsiness from her limbs, a gold flagon was handed to her and she gulped the fruity liquor to the dregs, thrusting the cup forward for a refill. From the sounds of the carousing around the Temple precinct, she knew she had some catching up to do, and from the earlier triumph over the Colonia, some celebrating to enjoy. As the wine took effect, sending a warm glow over her face and neck, she called for the Bard to play something lively from the Tain Bo Chuailgne and she laughed at the opening chords and retelling of the argument between Queen Medb and her husband Ailill over who owned the more possessions. As the song closed she noticed the harpist moving nearer and nearer to her. She peered under the hood of his robes to see if it was any Druid she might know and gasped to discover it was Lovernios. He passed the harp to another Bard before he sat beside her. The next harpist lacked the same understanding of the music and his interpretation of the wooing of Emer was flat in comparison to anything Lovernios might weave.

Boudicca looked at Lovernios in astonishment. 'Well, madam,' he explained. 'You're so constantly full of surprises yourself I just thought I'd demonstrate a few of my own skills.'

'How did you know it was one of my favourites?'

'A song of a marital row? Let's say it was an educated guess.'

'I'm impressed – more with the playing than the intuition.'

'Thank you.' He nodded, quietly accepting her praise. Boudicca had noted before how that sort of acknowledgement was often the way of the true artist who would disdain flowery acclaim in preference to more genuine appreciation. She suspected Lovernios derived all the justification he needed from the expressions of wonder being conjured all around whilst he played.

'Is this an appropriate point for me to hand out the champion's portion of meat?'

'There've been a few fights between some of your more boastful warriors, but in order to avoid tribal rivalries the Druids advise you should award prizes to warriors from several tribes rather than just one champion.'

'And those who completed the destruction of the house for me.'

'That'll have to be done separately, madam, if you're not to provoke favouritism.'

'Has there been any progress with the Romani?'

'No one's emerged from the Temple, but we know they're still there because there's coughing and sobbing and a baby cries intermittently. Any approach is still greeted with a storm of spears so they must be well equipped, with those at least. We ride just within their range now, hoping to entice all their spears to us so they might be left with nothing. Your warriors find it good sport to taunt them and fly in the face of such danger. However, I'd advise against a massed attack for now; too many Celtoi deaths so early in our campaign could prove disastrous for morale.

'There's no mention of surrender, madam, and I suspect they're holding out in the hope of being relieved soon. There's no other reason for them to want to survive in such a desperate situation. Surely they're terrified by now and short of supplies?'

'Do you think that even the Romani would've tried for a brave death in battle rather than this slow death, if those were the only two options they were aware of?' Boudicca asked.

'I do,' replied Lovernios. 'I've been concerned for a while now that help may be on its way from Lindum, and the reports from my Druids confirm my doubts. It'd make sense for the Romani to have also sent a rider to Suetonius Paulinus if they were sending one to Catus Decianus, as we know they did.'

'Who?'

'Suetonius Paulinus is the Governor you saw launch the attack upon Insula Mona – it's common knowledge that he is at Insula Mona and the distance from here to there is at least thrice and thrice again what it is from here to Londinium, so it's quite probable that rider's were sent to Londinium and to Insula Mona, as well as directly to Lindum.

'Nevertheless, we have to remember these Romani are creatures of rules and regulations. It's doubtful that Cerealis Petillius, the chief of legion nine in Lindum, will attack us without his Governor's command. However, this forewarning means he is likely to be gathering his legion together from all the little forts and scattered camps in which they're billeted, ready to respond at the slightest notice. The command could arrive at any moment and he'd then be in a position to answer it immediately; realistically we should expect them here within a couple of days.'

Boudicca shut her eyes in exasperation. 'So what do we do?' she asked.

'Well then, if we take a select force out to meet him at Durovigutum, which is where he'll leave Ermine Street for the Via Devana to Duroliponte, we should be able to ambush his force from the advantage of the thick forests which sweep around that area. He won't expect us to be quite so organised. Just as long as the Romani continue to underestimate us, we'll continue to have the element of surprise.'

'Then we could ride back in triumph,' Boudicca butted in excitedly. 'Bearing their heads as trophies, and the sight will quake these Romani here if they're still holed up in their Temple. Then their resolve will fail and we'll be totally victorious!'

'I suggest, madam, we're very strict about this. We'll need to take a large force of our noblest champions only, our most elite warriors. This will be a very different battle from today's easy slaughter. This will be a defeat of Rome's finest, hardened professionals. As I said, this early in our campaign we can't afford any mistakes – we must ensure we win. So far our objectives have been simple and our targets meek, but we're committed now and we can't go back to being the friends of the Romani. We must go on, and to do that we must kill. This town, this Colonia, is only a tiny part of all who must die if we're to drive the Romani from our shores forever. I expect that over the next few days we'll be joined by many more Celtoi who wish to cast their lots in with us and be counted amongst those who expelled this most insidious enemy from our land. I'm relying upon their coming for our numbers to swell, for although we're horde, we're still not enough.'

'Perhaps a direct victory against a mighty Romani legion will show they're not invincible, as once we thought? We'll force some Celtoi into joining us to prove where their true hearts lie and that they're not Romani supporters.'

'Exactly madam. So I insist we take no camp followers at all when we go against this legion nine. No children, no audience, the minimum of Druids as translators, although we should be able to ensure everyone knows what their roles are before we leave.'

'We'll need at least one Bard, to remember the deeds of valour and sing them over to the tribes.'

'Madam, I most humbly offer my services.'

Boudicca clapped her hand to her mouth. 'Apologies, Lovernios mine.'

Lovernios feigned exaggerated surprise. 'You'll have to lead them, madam.'

'But I'm needed here. And I want to be alone with Maeve for a while.'

'There's no way we'll be able to achieve such tight control without your, and Andraste's, authority. This is one occasion when we'll have to have battle plans as strict as the Romani's.'

'As restrictive, you mean.'

'Just for once we might have to play them at their own game. Use the best of both worlds, if you like.'

'So no individual challenges between champions of tribes before the hard graft of war?'

'They'd cut down our best quicker than we could blink, as they've replied to such challenges before. Have any Romani emerged from their Temple to answer the many challenges set to them today? It would've been a chance for them to win some glory whether they're rescued or whether they die. No, it's not their way, it places too much emphasis upon the individual, whereas the Romani live for the collective. We'd lose the flower of our tribes if we fought in our traditional way.'

'So, we can't insist they fight in our way, but they can force us to fight in theirs.'

'That's another disadvantage which we can turn to an advantage. They still expect us to fight in our own distinctive way. They're a people prone to prejudice, and already we've been stereotyped along with all the other peoples they call 'barbarian'. Displays of pride, like these before the temple, reinforce those beliefs. They've come to assume we'll always start our battles by casting our very best troops against their short swords and impenetrable shields. They, on the other hand, keep back their most seasoned soldiers until the third rank, which is why their lines rarely crumble – their foremost troops have nowhere to turn to.

'In the same way, madam, that we've come together as Celtoi, and not as individual tribes, it heralds many other changes in our warring. We could so easily be invincible just by learning a little from our foes. There's no need to abandon everything we Celtoi hold dear.'

'So, we can still use the forests to Find the right place to lay in waiting for this legion nine and transport our warriors so they fight fresh and unwearied?'

'Artio will lead us to the ideal place to destroy any Romani, if we trust Her to do so. But that's another reason why we should only take those who'll be of real use in battle: if too many warriors pass through the old routes into the forests at once, then all the pathways will have to stay open for a long while, not just the ones we wish to use. That was fine whilst the Romani didn't know about our gathering, but now they know we're horde, it could be used against us.'

'I thought only those who sympathised with our cause would be granted the ability to Find? I was under the impression that that was how we'll so far managed to avoid any Romani, or even any Catuvellauni or Regni sycophantic scum, from stumbling into our schemes.'

'This would be a slightly different Working, madam. The previous Working had a, well, the nearest way I can describe it is a screen. That's fine and sustainable when people are passing through it in ones and twos and small family units, but not when they're in their thousands.'

'Thousands? Lovernios, exactly how large a part of my force do you want detached for this ambush?'

He thought aloud. 'Let's see. According to the Druids' reports, you should expect your ranks to swell to half as many again within the next few days, and we predict the horde to eventually be thrice the size it is now. But we can't take anyone who's newly arrived. And about a third are non-combatants. So, madam, if you count everyone here, we should take half the total force you have at present. And that half should consist of the very cream of the horde.'

'That won't leave anyone to guard the Temple, unless you Druids are planning to take up arms. We might as well just let the Romani escape now.'

'Yes, it will,' he spoke slowly. 'First, as I explained, there'll be more Celtoi joining us very soon. If half your force here were suddenly to drop dead, they'd be replaced within two, maybe three, days. Secondly, well, have you ever met a Romani matron?'

'Once or twice.' Boudicca shrugged, uncertain at what point Lovernios was trying to make.

'And what did you think, madam?'

'What is there to think? The ones I met didn't utter a squeak during the whole encounter. They barely moved. I suspect their make-up was so thick and their hair so ornamental and their clothes so elaborate they couldn't.'

'So they didn't frighten you then? Didn't chill your bones to the very marrow?'

'Only in as much as seeing what I myself might have become had I continued to embrace this stinking Romani so-called civilisation.'

'I see. And what emotional effect, madam, do you hope to procure in your enemy when you come charging upon them with your bright cloak flying and your red hair streaming behind and your spears brandished in your strong arms?'

'I hope to turn their stomachs to liquid that they might mess themselves, change their hearts to stone that they might know the meaning of defeat, and chill their bones to the very marrow in comprehending total and utter terror.' Boudicca hesitated, realising what she'd just said.

'And having seen you in action myself, I'm very sure that's exactly the effect you do produce. But, for the Romani, it's not very feminine behaviour.'

'Well, I can't imagine one of their matrons acting like that, either.'

'They still find it hard to believe how any woman could act like that.'

'I think they'll get used to it. I'm not the only one. You may have noticed.'

'Indeed. But the point is, madam, they're not used to it yet, and therein lies our advantage.'

'So, what you're trying to say, in your usual round-about way, is that the higher the proportion of male to female warriors in our horde, the more intimidating they find our force.'

'Exactly.'

'But that's ridiculous. Everyone knows women make better warriors than men – look at Scathach who trained the great Cuchulainn, or even Aoife whom Scathach sent him to defeat. Even our Goddesses are more ferocious than our Gods – Andraste, of course, and the Morrigan. I could go on.'

'Certainly, I too would expect the Romani to have learned from their own history and have remembered Cleopatra, or even from Greek history, which they are so fond of, with Artemisia.' Boudicca looked puzzled. 'They were women who once commanded great armies, with some success, against mighty empires,' Lovernios explained, then thought for a moment. 'Perhaps they were bad examples to choose.'

'Didn't they win?'

Lovernios hesitated and covered himself quickly. 'They didn't throw themselves into the thick of battle with quite the same enthusiasm as you, madam. They were more like military commanders than warriors, whereas you embody both traits.' Boudicca didn't push the point but felt certain Lovernios wasn't telling her the full truth.

'Essentially then, what you're suggesting is that if we take a higher proportion of women warriors, say most of the Ladies and chiefs' wives, to ambush this legion nine, leaving a majority of male warriors to guard the Temple, it won't appear to the Romani trapped here that much of the siege has been lifted.'

'That's right, madam. We use their preconceptions against them. And the beauty of it is that the ambush will attack so fast the soldiers of legion nine won't have a chance to register that they're beset by a force which is mainly female. So we'll be using our resources in the best way: effectively doubling our numbers.'

Boudicca nodded, thinking through the ideas Lovernios was leading her to formulate. 'I like it, Lovernios. It serves the Romani right for being so narrow-minded. As long as the Goddess' hare leads me in this direction I'll follow and I'll wreak destruction where it pulls me. If She wills it, I'll lead your detachment out tomorrow evening to ambush and destroy any forces that might march to attack us. How can we fear defeat when the womenfolk take up arms? We'll return with our gory trophies of war and parade before this Temple of Claudius. The Romani we've trapped in there will die with all their prejudices turned upside down and the Celtoi women will never be underestimated by the Romani men again. You'll see.

'But for now…' Boudicca was mindful of the present and the feeling of anticipation around them. 'Please bring those who've won the right to the champion's portion to me and ensure the celebrations continue all through the night with music and song and story-telling. Then I must talk to Maeve, if she'll listen. Together we'll Scry the flames for the hare, and perhaps that way, at least, we can recover some of our former intimacy. I still worry so about her. Grania seems to be fine, especially now the blood letting has begun, but with Maeve there's so very little change. She's calmed down considerably since Sucellus took over her welfare but there's no sign her trauma has started to heal. Lovernios, I desperately want to reach her.'

'You can, but keep trying, madam. I commend you for your efforts when you've so many other demands upon you. I'll bring to you those champions whom you request. Put on a show for your peoples – that's what they want to see – then be alone with your daughter.'

'Before you go, my lover, share my bed tonight?'

Lovernios squeezed her hand and smiled his promise, then he left to find those who were to be presented with the finest cuts of roasted meat, carved by their war Queen herself.

While she waited, Boudicca arranged herself regally upon the cloths that had been arranged for her comfort, plumping up a few cushions to give herself more support. She still carried the golden knife that had been presented before she left Artio's woods, and wondered whether she should use it to cut the meat. She pushed it away back into the folds of her robes again, not realising until then that it had just worked its way into her hands. It itched to be used. Perhaps

Fand would bring her something to provide the opportunity.

When the champions came they arrived drunk and sweaty. Boudicca wasn't in the slightest bit surprised to see Grania amongst the men and women who'd been picked for their display of prowess at arms. They held their heads high, as well they deserved, and there were whoops and calls of praise as they played to their audience.

A steaming pig was lifted off the fire where it had been roasting and, still dripping with fatty juices, it was laid before Boudicca. Taking up a sword from each warrior in turn, she cut thick, generous hunks from the haunches of the animal, stuck the meat with the point of the sword and passed it back to the owner. She paused in her carving only once when Grania passed her a bloodied sword. Boudicca handed it back to her daughter, saying, 'Grania mine, you know better than to not clean a sword after a kill, please wipe it.'

Grania did so, for once without any retort. The blood was fresh and left smears upon her daughter's trousers. Boudicca felt herself staring at the stains for longer than was proper before she tore her gaze away and continued cutting meat. Then every champion held their prize aloft for a moment before bowing to their Queen and gnawing at the meat they'd won as their right. It was a great honour. Boudicca felt like an immense mother, dishing out food to her many, many children; but this was more than mere food, this represented a deeper type of sustenance and Boudicca felt the tug upon her spirit as she re-enacted a ceremony which had been performed by her people for many generations.

The carcass had offered up the choicest cuts, but still plenty of meat remained. Behind the warriors, at a discreet distance, hovered the looters who'd promised to destroy the Romani house with its hateful little effigy. Boudicca beckoned them forward. 'Have you done what I asked?' They all nodded their nervous heads, aware of her royalty more so now than when they'd met before. 'Then you've done well and are worthy to be served by your Queen now for having served her faithfully before. Here's your meat, eat and drink all you will with me tonight.'

Suddenly there was a tremendous roar of applause from the crowd who'd heard her words, a cheering beyond even that heard for the champions. It was a rallying cry to unify spirits and lift hearts, and Boudicca felt euphoria at being at the centre of such accolade. She swam with the sound, letting it lift her with its heady praise until she felt quite light-headed.

Then, with her Goddess insight, she understood how in praising these looters, she'd done more for Celtoi oneness than anything Lovernios had devised. These were the little people, the smallholders and petty crafts-folk, those who were very rarely noticed by the nobility, let alone acknowledged as individuals in their own right with their own feelings and daily worries. But they were the mainstay of the land, the backbone of the horde. Rich only in numbers, lacking decent weaponry or armour, perhaps hoping to acquire some from still warm Romani corpses as the destruction progressed, nevertheless these tribes-folk had left everything they'd known to answer a cause they could barely understand.

Boudicca's heart went out to them as she was swept upwards by their support. Then she felt something like ravens' wings rise majestically from her sides and wrap all the massed people before her in a protective fold of her own manufacture and she realised she was conferring the Goddess' Blessing upon all who'd come to Her. For all who gathered and for all who were still travelling to gather, this rebellion had just been transformed into a crusade with deeper meaning than simply the expulsion of the Romani. The feeling of mission from everyone in the Temple precinct rolled over Boudicca like a wave of almost tangible emotion which visibly rocked her. Her reaction was extreme, she knew, because of her heightened Goddess awareness, although she could tell that even the most insensitive person there couldn't have failed to notice the distinctive difference in atmosphere either.

Maeve had felt it strongly, too. Boudicca was certain of this by the rapture she saw engraved upon her daughter's face as soon as she regained something more akin to normal consciousness and could focus once more. Boudicca decided not to disturb her, but Maeve's expression of such serenity gave her the idea that her daughter might be more approachable in this state. She transferred her energy within until she could see her spirit-body shine around her. She was definitely showing more red in the ethereal since the last opportunity she'd had to do this Work, whereas Maeve appeared as a pure blue-white light. She tried to approach but her daughter's energy was almost searing with its intensity, she was repulsed with every attempt she made to draw near.

Even with Andraste's presence, Boudicca couldn't make contact with her daughter. She sat in her Other form and waited patiently for a while, in the hope of learning something about her daughter's new existence. The light within Maeve-spirit flashed and dazzled with its effervescence, like a clear crystal being turned over and over in bright sunlight. Boudicca could have watched the wondrous patterns forever, she could easily lose track of how long she waited. Then the flickering stars cleared a little, forming features as wise as Maeve's which smiled a benign benediction upon Boudicca. She understood then why she'd been unable to approach and why Maeve rarely responded to any contact on the material plane.

She watched the beautiful lights for longer than she'd originally intended and let herself be subsumed into their swirling eddies, aware it formed some sort of communication with Maeve. Although not unwelcome, this contact was still not the sort she desired. Then she was aware of movement, of the lights coalescing into some form with life of its own, some creature running helter-skelter away from her at a vicious pace. The bright animal jelled into floppy ears and long, muscular legs propelling it inexorably onwards, onwards but always away.

Boudicca felt herself struggling to catch up with the fleeing hare but always it was just out of reach, never pausing, never tiring, just continually moving and leading her on. She cast a quick look behind. Her robes flowed out around her for what seemed like forever, casting a curtain of night all about, populated with the huddled masses of her horde, their camp hearths shining like so many stars in the firmament. She dare not look too long, she might lose sight of the hare, and she whipped her neck back round to scan for it. It was just disappearing over the horizon. Boudicca put on a mighty effort, drawing physical strength from reserves she'd never thought to use, and pelted after the hurtling creature. She topped the crest of a shining hillock and looked down upon the desolation stretching before her.

The little hare hopped between the burnt houses and dead bodies, all horribly disfigured and mutilated, it leapt over cracked pottery and spilt grain, it sped over ruined fields, then darted into dense woods. Boudicca didn't have the same energy, but she jogged after, jumping over the destruction littering her path. Soon she became immune to the pain all around, failing to flinch even at the sight of familiar Celtoi faces lying slain before her. She ducked to pass beneath the trees only to emerge almost immediately upon a clearing filled with a strange strong scent. She caught sight of the hare at the edge of her vision, rushing past the oaks across the clearing and she bolted after him. As the long grasses stuck to her skirts and brambles tugged at her clothing she pulled herself free, breathing deeply of the perfumed smell of woman permeating the area.

Then she was released and moving forward again into a tangle of black branches which snagged and blinded her like so many clawed fingers reaching for her eyes. Here there was confusion and fear and a deep musky smell of masculinity and dominance dissipating into a feminine smell of blood and tears. Bewildered, she pushed through the forest, listening now for the gentle thud of hare paws running over dried leaves and young shoots, until she was out again into open countryside. Just ahead was the little hare, too close. She hurled herself upon it, hoping to catch it for good, but it struggled free at the last instant, wriggling more than necessary in its escape. Prone upon the earth she looked down at what she'd almost caught to see hare after hare loosen itself from her grasp and go tearing across the ploughed fields, hither and thither in all directions. As she watched, the entire horizon filled with hares, all bounding away from her and running onwards and onwards, never tiring, never stopping, bobbing up and down in their crazy flight until she could see nothing but hares.

Mesmerised, she let them dance in front of her vision, unable to break her gaze away from their erratic movement. Then the hares metamorphosed into ravens and crows of darkest ebony gorging themselves upon human flesh. They swooped and flew, calling greedily to one another and squabbling between themselves, pulling bloody globules of food off their quarries and flying with the morsels into the face of the yellow sun, which beat inexorably down upon the whole scene and bathed everything as if it had been cast into a sickly furnace. Then suddenly all the creatures coalesced into bouncing flames of myriad colours enthralling in their intensity.

'Madam, madam, I think you should move back from the fire now, madam!'

Someone was tugging at her body, her brow was sweating quite feverishly and she felt dizzy.

'Boudicca, Boudicca,' more urgent now. 'You drank too much too quickly. Come, move back from the fire, the timber has caught alight now and the heat is quite stifling here. I don't know how you could have stood it so long.'

Delirious with the temperature and the things she'd seen, Boudicca allowed herself to be hauled back to a more comfortable distance.

'I wish you'd warn me when you're going to go into Goddess trance, madam. If we hadn't pulled you back then, I doubt very much whether you'd have been able to return and tell us what you'd seen, and all your effort would have been wasted. And I know you've seen something, I can tell by the renewed glow in your face, and it's not just the redness from the fire. Here, drink this water. Slowly, madam.'

The cooler air washed over her body, turning her sweat to rivulets which soaked her clothing. The water trickled down her parched throat, seeming to separate the walls of her gullet which felt as if they'd been stuck together. She sagged where she was lying and they brought damp cloths to place upon her skin and cool her down even more.

'Lovernios, Lovernios?'

'Yes, madam, I'm here. I never left you; I've been beside you all the while. It was I who realised you were overheating where you were and got you back here.'

'Lovernios?' Her voice was weak. 'Lovernios-mine, you are like an old mother hen.'

'She's going to be all right! Everyone! She's going to be all right!'

'Of course I'm going to be all right. I'm fine. Just Goddess inspired. In fact, everything's going to be all right.'

'Just as soon as you've had some sleep, madam.'

'I sleep too much. I slept plenty this afternoon.'

'You should take as much sleep as you need, and right now you need plenty more than anyone else. Doze. I'll be beside you all night, I promise.'

'Lovernios mine? Lovernios, I ...'

'I know. I know. Sleep, madam, tell me everything in the morning. Believe me, it'll all keep.'

Boudicca's vision and Lovernios' favourable interpretation of the symbols she had Seen did not wait until the morning. Boudicca had taken to waking just before dawn again and it was then that they talked and made love quietly. They held each other tight under the rich Romani blankets which smelled of herbs, and they watched the dawn light steal over the heavens. Secret, muttered conversations could be just heard around them, too, and Boudicca guessed they were not the only ones to discover the day's start was when a little privacy could be found by a people already crushed together and lacking personal space.

'So, Lovernios mine, it seems we're on the right course, and your scheming fits nicely with the Goddess' own plans for us. Somewhat comforting that we're doing what we've been ordained to do, fulfilling our destinies if you like.'

'Mm.' He mused upon her words. 'I'm relieved, truth be told. One gets fleeting inspiration from the Divine and it's impossible to corroborate the experience unless someone else receives similar insight. Thank you, madam, for confirming my own visions.'

Boudicca felt a digging in her ribs, which reminded her of an issue she'd forgotten. 'Did Fand find a suitable sacrifice for Andraste?'

'What? Oh yes, yes,' he sighed. 'She found a very suitable offering. I'll let you find out for yourself. You might need a strong stomach, mind, but I think Andraste'll make sure you're up to it.'

'That's intriguing. On both counts. I'll leave Fand 'til the morning; I've learned patience since meeting you.'

'That is a blatant lie, madam. You've just become good at feigning patience in the hope of spoiling my fun!'

'I'll treat your remark with the disdain it deserves. Tell me, you keep referring to Andraste and me as separate, but I thought we weren't any more?'

'That's a mystery, madam, and one which I've tried to explain to myself so I might frame the words for your elucidation. But I can't. It's as if there are two of you, which are also only one. I see the changes in your face myself; occasionally you are you, and occasionally you are

Her, and occasionally the difference between you is indeterminable. As for the young God, he comes to me as a constant companion, but I think that is part of the aspect of the Divine you've invoked. Cathbad might be able to clarify my words, but the task is beyond me.'

'You've mentioned him before. Isn't he at Vernemetum?'

Lovernios stiffened. 'From what I've been told, yes, he's there. For what good it'll do him. Us, even.'

Boudicca said nothing, forcing Lovernios to fill the silence by continuing to talk. 'He's trying desperately to set invisibility Wards upon each individual shrine and Grove in the hope the Romani might pass them by. Such Workings allow people, places, even things, to go unnoticed or overlooked. Anybody under the influence of the Wards seems to have their attention diverted. It's a simple Spell to invoke, whereby the energy can be maintained and held over several centres; many centres for the skilled practitioner. He, and those who've stayed with him, claim some success with this tactic. They say that where the Goddess allows Romani to chance upon our holy places, a profound yet gentle change is effected. Even the Romani's hardened spirits are apparently touched by the seasons of our worship at these sites, they feel the sacredness of the spaces we have set apart and make their own consecrations there in turn.

'Cathbad claims this veneration is the evolution of our ways necessary for them to survive. He insists all things must adapt if they're to last perpetually, that these are not the first nor the last changes to occur in the religion this land chooses for its own.

'So, he won't be joining our cause. He'd prefer for us Druids to drift and slink away into the forests, to play a more spiritual role in the ways of this land and relinquish material power.' He shrugged. 'To the Romani, I presume. He argues that the wealth we've acquired with our gold routes is at odds with the true spiritual life and such temporal power should be relinquished. I don't know where he expects so many of us to go. Artio's forests can only sustain so many wandering hermits. The north is wild beyond the Brigantes' land, even for the Goddess' own, whilst Hibernicus is already harbouring many of our number who've fled from the Romani advances in Gaul. Perhaps he'd have us disappear deep into the impenetrable layers of the Otherworld, which overlap each other in the woods and forests? Then we might spend eternity peering in awe at the earthly world we've left through the knotty bark of oaks and the upturned faces of flowers.'

Lovernios shook his head in disbelief. 'I don't agree with him, as you've no doubt worked out for yourself. I've always felt the stirrings of the Divine within a person's heart is something not just for the spirit but an urgent message to be manifested within the material realm. Else of what value are these tuggings? The material and the spiritual are indivisible, and both can lend wisdom to the other.' Lovernios had raised his voice, his eloquence becoming more forceful as if he was repeating well-rehearsed arguments. 'We Druids cannot leave the Celtoi to the destruction of the Romani, we've been your shepherds for too long. And anyway, he seems to conveniently forget the Romani pledge to exterminate all Druids.'

Boudicca gripped Lovernios' hand to try to tell him she would never let the Romani exterminate him. Lovernios smiled at her attempt to comfort him and continued. 'Fortunately the majority of the Council side with me, else things would never have progressed even this far.' Lovernios' voice quietened, as if something had saddened him.

'Hush, Lovernios mine. It's only me you're talking to in our sweet pillow talk. There's no need to address the horde and awaken them.'

'Sorry, madam, was I becoming too passionate?'

'I've not seen the like in you before. You're usually more contained. I feel I may have opened a wound. One which you assumed had healed until you had need to let a healer examine it.'

'You may be right. Perhaps I did get a bit carried away. It's only... No, there's no point even wishing for such things.'

'What?'

'Just that I hate this division. It'd be better if we could all be united in this.'

'Does he outrank you then?'

'No. We Druids don't understand rank and authority in quite the same way as you do. There's not exactly the same need. You must have noticed that when you trained with us?'

'There was a distinctive difference, but since there was no need for orders to be given and received during my stay I hadn't been able to reach any such conclusion, only to make observations.'

'You surprise me, madam. Again.'

'You're avoiding the issue. Why is Cathbad's support so very important to you?'

Lovernios hesitated and closed his eyes as if trying to decide whether or not to tell her. 'I shouldn't really let it be. It's just that he's my father.'

Chapter 8

Legion Nine

They heard them well before they saw them. A steady tramp-tramp, precise in its rhythm, echoing along the straight, exacting roads which had been one of the very first marks the Romani had etched upon the land. Britannia had been scarred ever since by the lines of cobbles appearing like swollen veins upon the skin of the earth.

The sound of marching got nearer. Boudicca felt certain that this legion nine was almost upon them, and she tensed, ready to bolt from the trees.

'They're still a long way off yet, madam. Relax, you're affecting those around you.'

Boudicca tried to release some of the tension in her shoulders, but she was like a coiled spring and it was hard for her. Even as she slackened her hold upon her spears, she noticed those nearest her doing the same, filtering the slight lifting of tension through to all who were massed in waiting with her.

They had slept the night in the forests, watched over as ever by Artio, huddled in stolen blankets and cloths with dried leaves piled up for additional warmth. There were no fires to betray their presence and they'd slept a light, warrior's sleep which woke them instantly to any unnatural sound. They'd left Camulodunum with no provisions, still gorged from the orgy of plenty, and had easily found fresh springs from which to drink and splash the travelling dust from their faces. Then they'd waited, as perfectly quiet as could be managed from such a huge force, until the Romani they expected passed the carefully laid trap.

The wait had passed agonisingly slowly for Boudicca, who seemed as anxious for blood and death as Grania. She tried to pass the moments by reliving the sacrifice Fand had brought her the morning before. It was only the memories of life-taking which seemed to slacken her thirst. Unknown to Boudicca, Trinovantes looters had discovered a bronze statue of the Romani Claudius god, he who had brought elephants to Britannia and he to whom the Temple at Camulodunum was dedicated. More familiar with the Colonia than any of the other tribes, the Trinovantes had known where to look for the best trophies, having grown in slow hatred of such symbols and having long earmarked them for future retribution.

The plunderers had been unable to move the whole life-sized figure, heavily cast as it was with precious metal and sunk with Romani cement into its plinth, and had instead hacked off the exquisite head with its bejewelled eyes which twinkled when it was moved. Then they set the hollow head over the next live Romani they found cowering in some dingy cellar: a pregnant woman terrified out of her wits, and brought the whole offering to Fand who escorted it ceremonially to Boudicca.

Boudicca had woken in Lovernios' arms to the sight of a naked, obviously fertile, female figure with a golden head shining in the weak rays of the early morning sun. At first she thought it was a Visitation of the Goddess, or a vivid dream which still endured. Then she heard the fight for breath as the woman suffocated inside the improvised mask and saw the trembling limbs as the captive floundered blind before her.

A closer look and she saw the sight for what it was. A distraught mother-to-be with a grotesque crown, the edges of the Claudius head sharp where it had been cut from its torso and now digging into the very human neck which drizzled blood. Fand stood by, roughly holding up her captive who was so heavy with child as to be almost unable to stand. Fand's expression said it all. Cruel and calculating, she was flushed with her assured success at bringing an especial token for Andraste's pleasure. It was not quite a gold sacrifice, but the effect was magnificent, and, according to the almost purring within, extremely pleasing to Andraste as a blood offering.

The woman's belly was round and taut and vibrated slightly with the new life it promised. New Romani life to trample the Celtoi as easily as it would suckle milk and fill a napkin. Normally, Boudicca would Bless such a sight, placing her hands upon the womb in veneration of the Goddess' gift of life, but now she felt no such benediction. Now she felt pure rage and destruction and she let the powerful emotions erupt through her body and burst from her hands.

There was a cheer from the massed horde and a triumphant celebration of the destruction Boudicca had just wrought. She looked down at her handiwork. The woman had fainted, her life pumping away fast to puddle at Boudicca's feet. The little golden sickle had self-assuredly worked its way into Boudicca's hand and she'd split the woman's stomach, pulling forth the grey not-quite-formed child pulsing within and now held it aloft, still attached by its cord, to more rapturous approval.

Then they cut off the woman's head, still bearing the thick bronze statue head, and hoisted the whole trophy upon a long pole. They draped the umbilical cord around the pole too, letting it wrap itself around the shaft like a bizarre parody of the tree poles they'd erect to dance around, with streamers of cloth, to welcome in summer. Then they paraded the whole gruesome creation around the precinct. When the riotous noise finally subsided, a long while later, Boudicca heard retching from the Temple and she knew her actions had had many profound effects, not least upon the cosy contentedness she felt exuding from deep inside her own self.

Now they waited for more Romani to kill and Boudicca still wore the blood which had spattered from the Romani matron's almost-babe as a battle-paint. The next Romani to die would give better sport, she hoped, before perishing in a complete Celtoi victory, ensured by the sacrifice.

Whilst she'd been thus absorbed in providing some diversion to distract her eager mind, the even tramp of Romani marching boots had increased in volume. The anticipated Romani were here at last, and the numerous Celtoi lurking within the shadows to either side of the road were clearly agitated to be at them and released from this somewhat ignoble camouflage. Most unsettled of all was Boudicca. Despite her contrived mental re-enactments, she fretted at her concealment like a wildcat trapped in a hunter's cage as soon as she realised her prey had come into range. Even her customary pacing was denied her, lest she rustle undergrowth and expose the ambush.

'Why are we still waiting? They're here!' She urged Lovernios to give the order she'd agreed to wait for.

'No, madam. We can just see the first of them now, you see?' He pointed to the lead horses of the column. 'After the cavalry, or equites, the infantry marches in blocks of men.' Lovernios was very calm, as if he was telling a story to a demanding child. 'Each block they call a cohort. And if you watch, each block is led by a tribune. Then, every subdivision of each cohort is a century, led by a centurion.' He indicated each rank with a sharp dart of his pointed finger as he spoke. 'Those were the ones I told your people to slaughter first; without commanders these Romani are nothing. I have to count those blocks of men before we attack, then we'll know our odds. Any calculation can only be approximate because at the very back of the column will come the auxiliaries, and their numbers could vary considerably. Most of those will be from Hispana, a hot, black land far to the south, from whence this legion takes its name. They're neither as well trained nor as well armed as the legionaries, who are purer Romani.'

Boudicca tapped her foot restlessly. 'We can't wait much longer. They'll be gone if we sit and count them.'

'No they won't. You know as well as I that your force is strung out along these forests for as easily as far as this strutting column stretches. I can deduce so much by the sound these men make as they march. No, madam, our success is imperative, as I've explained to you over and over. If they've brought all their legion our fight is hardened, but if they haven't, then we have a certain victory before us and your peoples will fight all the better for such a boost to their confidence.'

'My peoples don't need their confidence to be boosted.'

'Whatever, it would be best if the Romani were well and truly in our trap before we attack them, else they'll simply retreat and reform in quite an orderly way, and then they'll have regained some of their advantage and the outcome will be more in the balance.'

Lovernios was counting quietly. 'Now, there's at least three.'

Boudicca watched the bobbing plumed heads stride past her hiding place. They were like so many displaying birds, as if they sought to imitate the colourful courtship displays of nature whilst being its very antithesis. 'What's that one?' She asked.

'Which one?'

'At the front. Those there. What are they?'

'The one at the very front, madam, is the legatus, the chief of these men, Petilius Cerialis himself. With him is the praefectus castrorum who takes over command from the legatus if it's ever necessary.' Lovernios went back to his counting.

'Four.'

Every soldier's face was stony and emotionless, every legionary unnaturally similar, as if a mother had birthed each one, one after the other like identical, multiple births. Boudicca shivered at this sinister enemy, acting in unison, fighting as a whole.

'What about them?' She pointed.

'That's the aquila and the imago. I told you about them, remember?'

'The soldiers will lose heart if those fall?'

'That's right. The eagle is the standard of the whole legion.'

'Do they take heads then, like the Celtoi do? I didn't know that.'

'Why do you think...? Oh, the imago,' Lovernios chuckled. 'No, the imago is a portrait of the emperor. They carry a little statue of his head as a further standard. Five.'

'Are they gold? Why are they dressed in wolf skins? There, and look, there!'

'Yes and yes, I'm sure Andraste will think it a suitable sacrifice, and they are dressed in wolf skins because they are the signifers. Each century has its own standard too. Six. There are six cohorts, madam; if you're taking heads today there should be enough for one between every three warriors. And that's an omen in itself.' He grinned widely before raising his trained voice. 'Go!'

Boudicca took an instant to realise he'd given his order, then she screamed in battle rage, setting her fierce chant reverberating off the tree trunks and Iceni shields which surrounded her. Her cries were the signal to set the war trumpets blaring and the host clamoured out of the trees after her, releasing their war dogs ahead of the Celtoi charge.

It was the only warning the Romani got. The roads had been cleared either side for twenty paces. It took the horde moments to cover that distance, bursting out of foliage which was capable of hiding many more of their number. The advantage of surprise was with the Celtoi for meer moments. These legionaries were alert for all dangers although obviously not expecting such a well-planned attack. Shock registered on their faces before they were hastily ordered into battle formation, unable to react fast enough to throw their javelins, but still quickly enough to form a firm defence with their raised shields. The foremost warriors were already upon the outlying legionaries and casualties were falling equally on both sides.

Still the Celtoi tumbled out of the forests, champion after champion leaping into the fray to be dashed against an impenetrable shield wall or to hold back and assess the weakest spots before attacking with renewed vigour. The noise was ferocious. With their limed hair sticking up in abandon and their faces and bodies painted in woad whirls, the largely female force couldn't be identified as such in this close hand-to-hand fighting. The warriors screamed at the Romani and slung spears and sling-shot at them. The Romani were taunted and yelled at; remarks were made about their sexuality which were reinforced with obscene gestures. The legionaries could have made no distinction between the behaviour they associated with Celtoi males and with the behaviour now being demonstrated by Celtoi women.

The Romani were frightened. That much was obvious. It showed in their nervousness which was smoothed by their professionalism and training. They hadn't been quick enough to throw their javelins – the deadly weapons which usually caused such chaos amongst the primary Celtoi ranks, decimating the most prestigious champions in any charge. For once, though, these pila hampered the Romani rather than their foe. The long spears were discarded, kicked out between hobnailed boots, so their shields might be drawn up into the formidable turtle formation from which only vicious swords would extend. Surprise, however, had meant the legionaries were more scattered than they would perhaps have chosen for their optimum defence. Each century was divided, each defensive unit was small. At first, individual legionaries who had been just too slow to jump into order were picked off one by one by the attacking Celtoi, perhaps still with the distracting pictures of their sweethearts in their dying minds. Then a sort of stalemate was established for a short while, during which the classical Romani manoeuvre was adopted and the Celtoi milled around, unsure of where or how to attack first.

Then the cavalry rallied and started to harry the outlying Celtoi troops, galloping in close and dispatching Celtoi warrior after warrior before darting off to turn and attack once more in a fresh place. Vastly outnumbering the Romani, the Celtoi charged as one, oblivious to the massive losses they bore. Equites were unhorsed as they drove in for the kill, only for fleet footed champions to leap from their path and onto their saddles. The horsemen were dead before they hit the cool of the road. Celtoi horses had been left at Camulodunum for fear that an inopportune whinny might disclose their hidden location, but now the warriors had horses again with which to meet the Romani cavalry in more equal combat.

Boudicca led the assault upon the grouped Romani as turtle unit after turtle unit fell, inefficient against the sheer weight of the Celtoi charge. The tide of battle turned, leaving those Romani who still stood in the minority against those who'd fallen. Only isolated squares of men remained, waiting stoically for the last charge they could withstand. The cavalry, Petilius amongst them, had assessed the situation as useless and turned their horses to flee as fast and as far as they could. Back to Suetonius and Insula Mona, Boudicca guessed. She let them go, they could warn any Romani still to come of the true terror being unleashed in the east of Britannia.

'Andraste, Andraste!' Her warriors yelled as they challenged and destroyed the last bunches of Romani. The legionaries died together – even Boudicca had to give them credit for their bravery on this point – their firm discipline not even wavering at the very end, despite their desperate, doomed situation. She'd caught a Romani horse, which pranced very prettily between her thighs until she accustomed it to her will. She used her new height advantage to salute those who were the last to die and her vantage point to assess the deaths which had occurred.

There were very, very many Celtoi numbered amongst the dead. Those who'd survived were gathering heads as trophies of war: there were enough now for maybe two heads each, probably more. She watched a moment longer, calculating quickly. At least two heads each. She must have lost over half the force she'd taken to fight this legion nine, and this hadn't even been a full legion they had attacked. Boudicca realised the truth in Lovernios' words, when he'd warned them before they left Camulodunum how this battle would be. How they'd laughed that they wished for better sport from those they challenged! Would they laugh when they returned? Perhaps. They'd exalt in their victory, certainly, but they wouldn't be able to laugh so loudly as before. There wouldn't be enough of them to match the volume for one thing.

Then there were the babes waiting behind at Camulodunum. Weeping would be heard from other places than just the Temple of Claudius and the barracks at Durobrivae tonight – the nearest fort for the Romani cavalry to retreat to and the halfway point between Camulodunum and the legion nine's headquarters at Lindum. Ultimately, Boudicca was responsible for Celtoi as well as Romani grief, but she tried to push any thoughts of that nature from her mind. The battle was won but their work was by no means finished. There were still more sacrifices to be made before the end.

'All those of you with horses, listen to me!' she called. 'Take your horses, leave your glories of war – there'll be plenty more to be won – and chase the Romani home to their pathetic defences like whipped puppies. Take the war trumpets and make plenty of noise so they fear our whole host still harries them all the way north, stay well behind so they're not able to count your scant numbers. Then return to Camulodunum and share in our victory – we'll save you Romani heads from those we take from the Temple.'

Lovernios joined her and she jumped from the fine horse she'd procured, giving the harness to Grania who plainly itched to be up and after the retreating cavalry. 'Remember my words, Grania mine; you're not to catch up with them and challenge them. I want you to return to me. Do you understand?'

'Certainly, mama,' Grania licked her lips in anticipation. 'But some might fall if they ride too recklessly or if their horses are driven too hard.'

'Yes, you may consider them yours in such circumstances,' Boudicca chuckled. 'But no outright attacks and no heroism. We've lost too many warriors today to risk losing more.'

Grania was off, as fleet as the wind, riding to catch up with the mounted Celtoi. 'Some might indeed fall if they ride too recklessly or if their horses are driven too hard,' Lovernios observed with a slight scowl.

'Not that one. She's my daughter, after all. She rides extremely well and will consider the horse hers now and will treat it kindly. She knows horses and she knows her own limits. She also knows my rulings. She'll be back.'

'After us, though, madam. She'll be back after us because we should be returning right now without any further delay. Those upon horseback can return as soon as they're free to do so. There's no point in us waiting for them, they'll probably be at least another lunar quarter.'

'Not yet. I want some heads to take back myself.' She withdrew her golden sickle from the belt where she'd tucked it for safekeeping and picked her way through the bodies showering the road. There were a lot of Celtoi dead. She was surprised herself at the number. Only a comparatively small number of warriors were left to mull over the spoils which were theirs for the taking. The battle had been close. Closer than she really chose to contemplate. And over so very quickly too. She desperately hoped Lovernios was right and more Celtoi would rush to join them and rejuvenate the horde just as soon as news of this double victory reached them.

There were too many familiar faces for her not to be personally moved by this visitation of death. Individuals she'd known and loved were too readily found amongst those bodies she limply flopped over to gaze at. It seemed to her she'd seen plenty of corpses now and that she should by rights be growing immune to the horror of staring eyes and stiffening bodies. But still she couldn't accustom herself to the rising nausea at the sight of fresh wounds and missing limbs.

Then she came upon the first of the Romani dead, clustered together, some still in their last wrestle with their slayer or those they had slain, locked in some final embrace like eternal lovers. Further on were heaps of dead legionaries, piled upon each other where they'd fallen. Boudicca stealthily approached them. She knew what she was looking for. She'd listened attentively to Lovernios' lessons.

She peered down at the bodies and through the spaces their tumbled corpses had made. Eerily, these men had been alive such a short while ago. She glanced back to Lovernios. He hadn't partaken in the combat; he wasn't trained, she knew, but she still felt he was less of her partner, not quite an equal, for it. During the whole episode, he'd held back, like a particularly craggy tree, robes folded in over himself like a bat's wings, motionless at the very edge of the forest. Ready, she secretly suspected, to vanish back into the foliage the instant he came under any personal threat. His distinctive non-involvement gave her further insight into just why his body had managed to remain so unusually free of scars and blemishes.

Now she saw him survey the dead and feel for any life pulses he might register in the bodies strewn before him. Any Romani he found still struggling for life he knifed, cleanly, in the throat. An expert butcher's cut to extinguish life immediately. With the Celtoi he examined them more carefully for their potential in responding to healing, but still the majority he finished in the same merciful way. Those Celtoi he did decide were likely to recover, he made comfortable as best he could with a sip from some flask he carried and arranged for them to be separated from the dead, ready to be brought back to Camulodunum to start their convalescence.

Boudicca left him to it. He had enough authority of his own to pull warriors from their messy trophy gathering in order to help him if need be. Most of those whom he selected for the return journey were suffering from concussion or broken arms, they should be capable of walking with some support from their comrades just as soon as Boudicca was ready to leave, although she doubted whether they'd be fighting again for a while.

She'd been tugging at Romani bodies in order to free the specific thing she was after whilst keeping one eye on Lovernios and, more awkwardly, one hand upon her sickle. Suddenly a bent piece of armour gave way to her relentless pulling and the treasure was within reach. Stuffing her arm into the midst of the bodies of legionaries, she felt around blind for the gold she wanted until her fingers closed upon the precious object. She could feel its sacredness even as she released it from its last guardian. The eagle. Exquisitely cast in cunning detail and painstakingly polished, the bird sat in her hands, wings open as if it sought to envelop all the world within the fold of its feathers. It looked so insubstantial now that she actually had a hold of it, but still she could feel its power, imbued as it was with the hopes and aspirations of so many men.

This object was a stunning replica of the real birds she'd only ever seen in the mountains on her journey to Insula Mona, soaring through the crisp air, oblivious to the people far beneath that must have appeared like mere specks upon the ground. She'd recognised the intrinsic aloofness of the eagle even then, had been dwarfed by its majesty even when she was younger and had less understanding of the concept of rank. The beautiful regality could make even a princess feel insignificant; was this why the Romani had chosen it for their totem?

Boudicca didn't care. It was hers now and soon she hoped there'd be another three for her to display with it, once she'd destroyed each of the other legions in Britannia. She tucked it securely into the folds of her clothing. There was something else she wanted before she left, the sickle wouldn't let her forget to take that.

She cast a cursory look over the bodies. The imago, she'd seen, had been taken by the equites. It didn't bother her. She found the Nero god to be similar in appearance to the Claudius god in the way the Romani depicted him: rather an ugly man with a balding head and a huge hooked nose. Not a pleasant image to want to keep as a trinket, and if she didn't find it attractive then it wouldn't make a suitable sacrifice for Andraste either, no matter how much gold it was made of. No, Andraste would be pleased with the eagle, what she wanted now was something for herself, and Lovernios had given her just the education she required to find the most prestigious trophy.

All of the legionaries had been equipped with fine shiny armour, all their heads protected with wonderful helmets, for what good it had done them. But the ones Lovernios had called 'centurion', they had the most magnificent helmets of all, and Boudicca wanted one for herself. Those helmets had shone like mirrors at midday, but across the top of them, arranged transversely, were a crest of proud white feathers. Any head which Boudicca bore back to Camulodunum to show off to the rest of her horde, would be wearing one of those helmets. And she remembered slaying a centurion just around… here. Greedily, she sliced off the head, using her weight to press through the bone, and hefted the prize under her arm. The helmet was held on firmly by a chinstrap, so she turned the head upside down so the blood dripped into it.

Then she looked for one of the wolf-skins worn by the signifiers that she'd coveted. Heads could only be taken by those who had made the kill, but clothing and armour and any other spoils of war were there for anybody. She found the skin and hung it round her neck; she knew she looked fierce in it. Then she thought about some armour for herself, perhaps some greaves or a chest plate. Romani javelins were there aplenty, but she discarded the lot in disgust. Their long untempered shanks were designed to bend upon impact, their disposable nature making a mockery of Lugnasah spear-throwing games devised by a more opportunistic people.

She continued to search greedily, like a child at her first travelling fair tempted by so many foreign traders with an abundance of exotic wares. Suddenly and capriciously the wolf-skin was dropped and all thoughts of armour abandoned. Such things were fine and glorious but would only hamper her in battle and she enjoyed the freedom of light-footedness where she might dance death's dance hand-in-hand with the Life-Taker Herself.

She came back to Lovernios now, grinning like a child who'd eaten too many autumn fruits and proud of the things she'd acquired. She showed them to him, hoping perhaps for some sort of approval. He just nodded at her and continued with his healing, either not willing or not able to give her the recognition she desired. She looked down at the things she'd taken. Suddenly they seemed so very insignificant. Valuable as they were amongst the Celtoi, nevertheless she'd have gladly traded them all just then for a moment of Lovernios' attention. Immediately they'd been rendered as nothing.

'Have you found many of our people alive?' she asked, determined for him to take some notice of her.

'Not enough,' he replied sullenly.

'One death would be too many.'

'Remorse, madam, after such a great victory?'

'Remorse, Lovernios, even for some of the Romani. They were so young.'

Lovernios busied himself with the broken wrist he was setting in a simple splint. A sharp pull and a quick binding with some torn cloth and the bone was set ready for mending. Then he came to her, gathering her in his arms. 'We can't afford to be like this. Neither of us. We can spare no regret at the things we've done, wallow in no second thoughts, else the leadership of our people crumbles in indecision and doubt. Such is the price we both pay, to put those who come to us before even ourselves. We must harden ourselves against the realities of this rebellion, even at the cost of our own compassion, or for us, our own humanity.

'The Romani are anathema to us, an alien race who seek to utterly destroy; the only language they understand is that of our swords. They'd treat us no better than this, and have indeed treated us far worse, as well you know. As for the Celtoi who sacrifice their lives for us, they are now in the Summerlands, with our ancestors, basking beside eternal meadows and presiding over their abundant herds. Didn't you see how they embraced their deaths and fought for you so willingly? Death in its stark aftermath is always disturbing, but in its actuality the spirits gladly return to their true homes as soon as the illusions of this world drop away.'

He finished his speech with a pause. 'I don't Sense any more Celtoi are still alive. Have your warriors collected all the heads they want?'

'It appears so. They're limited to taking the heads of those they actually killed.'

'Really? So, that explains why such an avaricious bunch of collectors have left this battlefield relatively tidy!'

'It's a sort of loose code of honour between warriors.'

'I see.' And so did Boudicca. Lovernios' words had illustrated the wide gulf that occasionally existed between the two of them: the secular and the profane. Her training meant she understood some of his world by her own experience, but his understanding of hers came from a detached observation which was so much less involved.

'Do you think,' he continued, 'that some of them will be able to carry some of their comrades back to Camulodunum and still be able to hold on to their prizes?'

'We hook the heads onto our belts. See!' Boudicca showed him by looping the chinstrap of her centurion's helmet onto her belt. 'Unfortunately it means the feathers will get crumpled, but I'll straighten them out for display. Usually we attach them by knotting their hair, but it's more difficult with the Romani because they keep their hair cropped short.'

'Well.' Lovernios swallowed awkwardly. 'Can you call over some help for these wounded? Some of them can walk – although gingerly because of the bumps to their skulls – and will just need support. A couple will need to be carried because of leg wounds, but they'll live once they regain consciousness.'

What remained of this select detachment of Boudicca's force were now growing bored with picking over the remains of the battle and responded quickly to Boudicca's command to help the wounded and follow Lovernios back through his Found paths. The forest would take them directly back to the wooded area nearest to Camulodunum, but as Lovernios had advised, the Workings were open now and would soon be less of a secret.

Boudicca was the last to leave, waiting in the hope of hearing the return of horses, perhaps bearing her daughter Grania back to her. As she stood patiently, alone amongst the dead, she felt like the Morrigan herself, the female destroyer resplendent over the things she'd wrought. She felt the power diffuse through her body, like a tingling of the Divine, that was transferring her spirit, no matter how unwillingly, from the maternal to the destructive. She was slipping into a change of being utterly profound and over which she had less and less control. Then, almost as if at her silent command, her thought was answered and the ravens swooped in, the Goddess' birds and the first scavengers of war. They settled like a cloud of dust, seemingly birthed from every tree around with their screeches and greedy cries of 'never more, never more'.

They were wrong, Boudicca knew then with her elevated insight. She'd be providing them with many more feeds in the moon cycle to come. The next would come that afternoon as soon as she returned to the Colonia. Then the Temple of the Romani's Claudius god would fall and all within would become evening sustenance. Would these birds know to roost near Camulodunum tonight?

She turned from the ensuing feast, which reminded her too well of the massed Celtoi looting and destroying the Colonia, leaving the bones of foe and enemy to be picked clean. The ravens were indiscriminate in their taste. Still with these images clear and fresh in her mind, she returned to Camulodunum, the paths clearing before her to bring her out within a short walking distance. When she emerged from the woods nearest the town she joined the remains of the detachment that had been awaiting her. Lovernios had halted them, assuming she would be only moments behind and wanting her to lead them back in victory. It wouldn't do for her to be absent from such a parade. Such a low profile might result in the horde concluding she'd lost her life during the ambush and they couldn't yet afford such demoralisation.

She took her place in the lead and they strode quickly back into the streets of Camulodunum with its flattened buildings and burnt shells of houses. They could not run for fear of jolting the wounded unnecessarily, but their steady pace meant the warning of their approach was carried quickly back to the mass of Celtoi in the Temple precinct.

Before they had even reached the open square, they were greeted by a welcoming cheer virtually worshipping them back amongst their kin. Boudicca was astounded by the number of people waiting to acknowledge their victory with the full honours due to such military prowess. It was as Lovernios had promised it would be. Their numbers had been replaced in their absence; many more Celtoi thronged the precinct than there had been even before she had left with her sizeable detachment. She could identify from the chequered patterns on their clothing that some were from far, far outlying tribes occupying lands she could only ever imagine as swathed permanently in mist. The horde was larger now than anything she'd ever dreamed possible; it was hard to comprehend so many peoples had come ultimately at her beckoning.

Still more were coming to join her force. Even as she'd walked down the broken roads of the Colonia, groups of tribes-folk had questioned where they might find Boudicca's rebellion and the returning warriors had directed them towards the Temple, keeping themselves anonymous for a while longer. Now, nearer the Temple, she noticed huddled groups of pale and weary men and women with dreadful sores upon their necks and weals upon their backs and she deduced that slaves, ensnared by the Romani for their tile factories and mines, had been released and won to their cause. The only thing bothering Boudicca, as her eyes swept over the mass before her, was how much the overall proportion of warriors had lessened. Though their numbers defied the imagination with whole tribes rising against the Romani, they now seemed to be carrying many more non-combatants and those who were totally untrained in warfare.

No matter. Battles could be won and lost with psychological tactics. This amount of people would be certain to terrify every Romani in Britannia even if the legions were to stand all together. Such a horde might be unwieldy but they could overwhelm the Romani now simply by their appearance.

To tumultuous acclaim from the crowds parting before them, Boudicca and the remains of her detachment made their way to the open area before the Temple. Once there she addressed the crowd, which quietened, straining to catch her words. She told them of their victory, of the annihilation of the Romani's legion nine and of Grania's mission to ensure the remnants of Petilius' men whimpered all their way home. She spun her story out for her peoples, entertaining them the way Lovernios might. She told them of the way the Romani looked and the way they marched. Of their fine shining armour and their skill with weapons. She built up the picture of how formidable a foe they'd faced so her audience might guess by inference how much greater were the Celtoi.

She lowered her voice, the crowd becoming even more attentive, to tell them how they'd waited patiently in ambush, desperate for the sight of their prey. The Goddess, she assured them, had chosen the right place for them to attack, the best moment to run from Her forests and had assured them of victory, sending Her ravens in readiness for the meal which would certainly be provided. Then she lifted the head she'd loosened from her belt, holding it high above her head, her arm straining with the weight.

'This,' she screeched, 'is your foe. These are the ones you should be most afeared of. But these are the ones who stand back in conflict, letting their more junior, less hardened soldiers fight before them. Even the centurions quake before Celtoi battle lust; even their chiefs are cowards. We've destroyed the might of Rome. Their most beautiful town, their most celebrated troops. With such ease! We're unstoppable!'

Her words had been especially chosen to both rouse the Celtoi and also intimidate the Romani still trapped in the Temple. The shouts and cheers for her wove a sound so complex it was as if it could be worn like a blanket; the noise was so great as to thicken the very air.

Boudicca was very aware of the effect she was creating. It had been staged so very professionally; she had gained the ability from years of experience. Even Lovernios would be pleased with her. She made sure all the Romani heads were displayed by turning with her trophy to show it off to everyone in the Temple square. Even the Romani in the Temple would be able to see what she carried. Every warrior who'd returned with her did the same. The effect could not have been missed, even if her words had been unheard. It must have been glaringly obvious what had happened to legion nine, and any hoped for relief for the veterans, from the evidence of the captured heads and unusual mixture of legionary armour with which her army had festooned themselves in triumph.

Just to make sure the point had been driven home to the beleaguered veterans in the temple, and to ensure they turned now to desperate measures, Boudicca had one more prize to show. She'd prepared the measure of her speech carefully, with one eye upon the cloudy sky. As she neared her final glorious words, the sun emerged from behind unfolding clouds and she thrust her other arm up towards it, as if in salute.

The first rays to shine down fresh upon her caught the glinting thing she held in her open hand. The massed Celtoi saw it and understood its meaning. The golden eagle being lifted in triumph seemed poised to fly from her touch as the sun illuminated it for all to see. The spectacle could have been lost on no one. Here was all that legion nine stood for and represented. Such a thing could never have been taken unless the legion had been totally destroyed and routed. If such a detachment of the main force could effect such success, then there could be no stopping this much larger horde which still increased in size even as they watched.

Boudicca prayed the sunlight would stay for moments longer as she turned sedately, grinning in wild excitement, to ensure the besieged Romani saw the message of their doom. Her grin broadened.

They had.

Chapter 9

Waxing Moon

With both arms held up as if in praise of the sky, blood dripping down her left side from the centurion's head, and a manic grin stretching her cheeks, Boudicca was the first to see the stirring from within the Temple of Claudius. Her speech and actions had created the desired effect and pushed the Romani who cowered there past hope and into a last forlorn action.

They came out like newborn rats. Blinded by the sudden exposure to light and stumbling forward upon weak, unnourished legs. Their faces wore dark circles under their eyes and furrowed brows, their skin tinged with a grey pallor. They swung swords before them, optimistically hoping to find blood for their blades. They appeared in ones and twos, limping forward to engage in combat.

Boudicca let them come. They were no threat. They moved too slowly. She guessed they wouldn't even have the strength to cross the open precinct. Just waiting like this, refusing to grant them the last chance to die bravely in conflict, allowing them to collapse exhausted in front of their victors' impassiveness, was torture sweet.

Despite herself, she had to admire their bravery and resolve. They seemed so few to have defied the Celtoi for so long. There was strength in their purpose now and Boudicca saluted, not the Romani, but the dedication of the eternal warrior she saw portrayed before her. There was no chance of escape or victory here, this was a last request to die with pride. She gave the order for the slaughter to begin.

Silently now, without war cries or shouts, the executions began and the Romani died without sound. As soon as the first fell, more revealed themselves. Even women and children hurled themselves down the Temple steps, summoning courage from some unknown source for a last charge, hoping they might be killed quickly and cleanly. The Romani had deduced that no captives were being taken for ransom or slavery and knew there was no hope of safety anywhere within the east of Britannia now. Weakened by lack of water and food, there was nowhere to run to even if they had been able. No resistance was offered; they simply ran against spearheads and sword edges with a pretence at some form of attack. They offered themselves up as willing sacrifices to a mightier force, acknowledging in their choice of death the real power in the land.

For Boudicca, there could have been no greater compliment.

Together, she and Lovernios watched the destruction of the Temple of the Claudius god. Celtoi scrambled over the walls, some still under construction, and dislodged blocks and stone where they could. White chunks of plaster were worked free of their fittings to be sent crashing to the ground. Decorative mouldings were smashed and disintegrated on impact. This was the Trinovantes' moment. One tribe at least had their hearts' desire.

'Will the Trinovantes still fight, do you think, now they've destroyed what they came for?'

'We'll have to make sure they're grateful to us and will remain loyal. With the eloquence of so many Bards lent to your cause, the persuasion should not be too difficult, madam.'

'And where do we go next?'

'Where did the hare run?'

Boudicca shook her head. 'It wasn't clear. None of it was really decipherable, only about the destruction of the legion. I think there's a lot more lazy blood to be shed yet.'

'What do you mean?'

'I don't think there'll be any major confrontations with the Romani for a while. I think the horde will rest and destroy anything remotely Romani in the area. We can't go anywhere until Grania returns anyway. What do you think the rest of the Romani will do now?'

'It'll take a couple of days for the news of this latest destruction to reach Suetonius Paulinus at Insula Mona, although he's probably already started to march back. He is, no doubt, somewhere on Watling Street by now. Then I expect he'll be extremely surprised by the damage you've done to his legion nine: you probably destroyed the best part of a quarter of the total troops available to him in the whole of Britannia. That will have stung him severely. Then he'll try and delay meeting you in battle for as long as possible. His forces are strung out around the country. He'll collect troops from those forts and barracks he passes on his way to meet us in battle, but he'll have to send for some of the more outlying forces and wait for them to join him. He won't engage us in combat until he's at his fullest strength.'

'So, it's in our interest to host now, as soon as possible, and meet him along Watling Street?'

'I'm not sure, madam. He'll be expecting similar tactics, for that's what he'd probably do himself, but he also thinks we're an unruly mob led only by a woman. I've already told you how the Romani opinion of women is prejudiced by their opinion of their own matrons. That should go some way towards explaining why I suspect he might be hoping this horde will become unmanageable now you've had two complete victories.'

Boudicca rolled her eyes in exasperation as she imagined the stereotyped view that the Romani had of her; she spat in disgust.

Lovernios was talking as he thought his plan through; Boudicca could see him become excited as his ideas fitted into place. 'Anyway, if that is the case, then he'll hold back and offer no resistance until your army approaches his legions for the final battle to decide the outcome of the Romani occupation of our land. Now it makes sense to destroy as much as he allows us during that respite. Let it appear that your army is indeed out of control. We can systematically destroy everything remotely Romani in Britannia, clear whole tracts of land at our relative leisure. If we're unpredictable enough, we could even wash over some of those outlying troops he intends to call to arms. Then we can turn upon and obliterate all the legions quite easily, since they'll be gathered in one place awaiting our swords and the death we deal.'

Boudicca nodded her approval as she started to see what Lovernios was describing.

Lovernios continued. 'Then there'll be no Romani in Britannia and we'll be free of their stifling yoke. It won't be the only occasion on which they've been cast from our shores. Our historians tell us they've tried to subdue Britannia once before. That was way back, in the age of our ancestors, when Cassivellaunus of the Catuvellauni was hounding the Iceni, or so our historians advise us. Even if the legions dare to return for a third attempt they'll have to start their conquest afresh. There'll be nothing Romani left in Britannia once we've finished. We'll annihilate them and ensure they know Celtoi to be the most formidable enemy they've ever faced. We'll teach them their Empire should never have been considered invincible.'

Boudicca liked his suggestion. 'It seems very right, Lovernios mine, I'd like the opportunity to ruin and maim myself. There's an increasing need I have to rend sinew from sinew; the feeling rose in strength as the moon waned to new and I must answer this wanting. More people join us by the moment, our numbers grow considerably by the day, and yesterday I even heard the lilting mountain accents of the Silures and the Demetae. Soon we might well become the uncontrollable chaotic mob the Romani chief assumes.'

'Not with Andraste and the Druids to Bind you.'

'Despite the immense debt I owe you for arranging these things, and the gratitude I have for your invaluable aid, still my warrior's awareness screams that our size means stealth and order are being lost to us. I'd judge, if our forces were to start moving towards Londinium now, the wagons wouldn't start to trundle after until our forerunners had reached Caesaromagus. Our horde would stretch thick along the roads. We move far slower than the Romani soldiers and we're too many now to hide as we move.'

'So, do you think we should attack Londinium next? It makes sense, madam. It's not quite the model Romani Colonia of Camulodunum, more a sprawling network of timber buildings, but it's important for Romani trade and will still be a severe blow to their new province if it falls.'

'I didn't say that.'

'Yes, you did. You said that if we were to horde upon Londinium our force would stretch from Camulodunum to Caesaromagus.'

'I was just using it as an example, I didn't intend for it to be interpreted as an order. I could just have easily illustrated our situation by saying we would cover an area from Camulodunum to Combretovium, but that's in the opposite direction and I presumed we would be advancing into Romani territory, not retreating back into our own.'

'But the point is, madam, you didn't say that. You said Londinium.'

'Don't read so much into my slips, Lovernios mine, else I'll have to watch all the words between us and our affection will lose its spontaneity. I doubt very much if it was an interjection from the Goddess – see, I'm not even in trance.'

'It's not necessary for you to be in trance, you know that. You just need to be receptive. Andraste will come through when you're relaxed, and you were then, busy calculating numbers and distances and remembering the nearest settlements. Quite distracted. At least give me the benefit of the doubt by testing the idea when the next trance falls upon you.'

'I can't see the point. I want to stay here for a while. Consolidate things. It'll all wait. I want to rest.'

'What's made you so listless, madam? This mood's come over you since your return.'

Boudicca lowered her voice. She wasn't ashamed of what she had to tell him, just discreet. 'It's my menses. They're late again, chopping and changing with the phases of the moon so I feel my womb is being tugged around with the forces. It's been well over a full lunar cycle since my last bleeding and I feel pulled between the two strongest tides of the moon, distended and weakened as if both vie for my spirit. Even today's exercise hasn't brought them on and I feel trapped in this state of anticipation, continually on edge as if something important is going to happen. At first I thought I was with child, but I can't be because we first loved well after the middle of my cycle.'

She sighed, dismissing her worries. 'I usually feel lethargic around this point, especially if my bleeding is late.' She continued, guessing some sort of apology was due, 'It's not detrimental to you, it's just the way I am.'

'New moons are for fresh starts, whilst full is for consolidating those beginnings made at new. And you're more sensitive now, too. Perhaps that's why the Goddess' guidance has seeped through.'

Boudicca looked at him in disbelief that he was still persevering with his argument. She felt a wave of anger gather, bottled within, with herself as a cork.

'Anyway, madam. Catus Decianus is at Londinium.'

The wave broke, bearing Boudicca before it at its very crest. 'Catus?' Just a hoarse whisper.

Lovernios nodded, watching her intently. Boudicca couldn't help but betray her emotions. Despite all the training and experiences she had undergone, still her feelings ran too high. 'Catus Decianus. The toad. I would kill him slowly.'

'So, madam, you'll try to Sense whether it is indeed Londinium we should horde upon next?'

'Is it truly possible? Is Catus really within my grasp? I didn't think, I'd ever …'

She smiled a slow predator's smile. 'In just two quarters it'll be Eostar and full moon. There'll be rites, of course? And celebrations. This Colonia should be nothing but dust and ashes by then, even if everyone here shatters just one sun-baked brick. Before we leave, Camulodunum will be as if it'd never existed. Then we'll gather up our people and cleanse the land, sweeping further west and destroying everything Romani that carelessly wanders into our path.'

She looked Lovernios in the eyes with a new determination. 'I'll do your Sensing for you, even now as the summer is nearly upon us and the days wax to equality with the night, I feel the Goddess' hands upon me. But She exhorts me at this moment not to walk in Trance with Her, but to join in the razing of this edifice and to mingle with Her people. Later, perhaps, I'll feel more want to repose in Her presence, but not now. Anyway, I have to stay and await Grania's return before we move on.'

Over the next lunar cycle, Boudicca increasingly left Lovernios watching the various stages of the destruction of the Temple to the Claudius god and went in search of inanimate objects upon which she might vent her rage. She felt, perhaps unreasonably, angry and grumpy, when really she thought she should be pleased everything had gone so well, but she attributed her emotions to her still late menses and dismissed the nagging tension. However, the idea of revenge upon Catus as a real possibility brought her a satisfied gurgle of pleasure which entertained her for days.

Then, on one day near to the full moon, when she was contemplating the things she might do to him, she took a large stick to a wall of one of the few remaining timber-framed houses and really started to work her temper off. The wattle and daub had been plastered with an attractive lozenge pattern. Neat and ordered and very precise patterning. Boudicca took especial delight in her wanton damage, hacking at the plaster as if it was Catus' face.

The wall didn't last long. The house had only been a loose shell and had never been constructed to withstand the worse the climate could chuck at it, let alone a thrashing from a tall and wrathful woman. Boudicca had built up quite a sweat. She felt a little better, but still inclined to destroy something else. All around her similar acts were being carried out, although less enthusiastically and perhaps more methodically, as her orders were adhered to. The hard slog of ensuring nothing was left for the Romani was considerably less fun than the first onslaught upon a civilian population.

Most of the labourers were not the sort of people one would have expected to have taken to such work. By their clothing and simple manner, Boudicca could see they were farmers, used to tending crops and breeding flocks to increase their wealth, nurturers and creators, procuring richness by working in harmony and understanding of the land. Boudicca would have thought such labour might have been against their very core of being, but she'd learned not to underestimate such folk. Here before her eyes was another example of the eternal resourcefulness of the little people who really ran this land, those who had to be able to turn their hands and minds to any task asked of them. Doing so was the only way in which they could ever survive.

She turned up her robes to hide her torc and watched them for a while, not wanting to betray her presence and enjoying the sheer pleasure of not having her status recognised immediately. Somehow she felt more real, another person rather than a mere title, despite the increased vulnerability. There were a lot of bodies around, she noticed. All Romani, dressed in their simple tunics or dresses, and lying where they'd fallen. No one had bothered to tidy them away, no one would. Here and there fingers had been chopped off to remove rings, or occasionally whole hands had been amputated. A few heads were missing, but not many. The spirit resided in the head and the taker would be imbued with the victim's qualities. These Romani were cowards who'd run and not fought – no Celtoi wanted those characteristics. Slightly more disturbing were the pools of dried blood and gaping holes around the groins of some of the male bodies. Boudicca wondered what strange traditions the distant, outlying Celtoi tribes might perpetuate. Then she realised she'd have to accommodate such practices in the name of diplomacy, no matter how distasteful she might find them.

The other scavengers wouldn't come until the Celtoi had left, the slinking creatures under Artio's care would not venture too near the horde – they had been enemies of mankind for too long. The Celtoi would have to move on soon, though. The bodies had hardened more than a quarter ago and were now rotten and stinking. Despite the earliness of the year, there were flies and beetles and other small carrion, lacking the sense to comprehend mankind as enemy and desperate enough just to consider him as competitor.

Boudicca moved on, she'd come to the outskirts of the town and had passed through the west gate to the road which ran south-west for a short distance. A little way ahead, Boudicca could see stone markers and she made her way towards them, curious about what this place might have meant for the Romani. Dotted on either side of the road were blunt stone pillars, rising out of the earth like uneven teeth. Boudicca could see the stones were carved in beautiful detail and she bent to examine them more closely. This was an uneasy quiet place, the air cut only with the call of crows. Feeling within, Boudicca sensed death's presence and she knew this ground to be a place for the dead, the atmosphere imbued with grief and sorrow where so many people had come to mourn. These pillars, then, were the Romani equivalent to the Celtoi stick markers they placed over their own cremation pits.

Such information aided Boudicca's understanding of the images she saw encoded for eternity in the stone. The first picture she recognised as depicting a centurion. She noted his military equipment, which had been exquisitely detailed in stone, and compared it to the soldier whose head she'd taken earlier. This man was grim-faced, his left hand resting upon the pommel of his sword which swung elegantly by his side, whilst in his right hand he carried his vituus, or vine stick, the symbol of his office. There was something arrogant in the way this centurion was shown swaggering around with his vituus, obviously considering himself so very much better than everyone and everything else, even in death. Boudicca was intimately acquainted with such attitudes and her blood boiled at the sight. Suddenly, as if in a fit, she kicked the tombstone, felling it in one fluid attack, rendering it prone before her, split in twain.

Her anger had been aroused again. She cast about for the next picture she might be able to decipher. Those without images were meaningless; she just couldn't understand the patterns of straight lines which told their own story if one only knew their language. She wondered if Lovernios might be able to read them; after all, the Druids had their own Ogham script. Did these marks serve a similar purpose?

The next picture she found froze her in her tracks. This was of a mounted legionary. She peered at the detail so she might be able to learn about him and feed her temper. Around the top of the tombstone were snakes and strange, fanciful animals, some of which fitted the descriptions she'd heard rumoured of the outlandish creatures brought to be slaughtered in the Romani's amphitheatres. The rest resided only in the memories of her deepest nightmares. The snake though, she knew, was an image of death, although the Celtoi would portray the slithery animals as swallowing their own tails and thus symbolise the everlasting cycle of rebirth – a more positive message for soothing the grieving than these creatures being squeezed by the more fearful monsters. This was clearly a Romani officer, but what sort she could not discern. He was mounted upon a fine horse, shown with good, strong bones, which was poised, static, as if waiting for the stonemason to finish his carving before it would move. What was so hurtful to Boudicca about this image, though, was the strange cowering figure under the hooves of the horse. Desperately holding up its long shield in abject humiliation, the Celtoi warrior being subjugated was portrayed as more animal than human. The Romani, meanwhile, held himself so confidently upon his steed, raising his shield in his left hand and carrying a bronze lance in the other which was fastened into a hole in the stone.

Such triumph over her people, shown so insensitively, disgusted Boudicca. She tore out the little lance and snapped it into many pieces before tossing it to the winds. Then she took Andraste's knife – quite calmly, all things considered – and prised off the stone where it had been worked to produce the soldier's face. She twisted the knifepoint in the eye sockets, loosening grains of stone. Bit by gradual bit the dust came away until whole chunks fell off. She used the edge of the sickle to saw at the stone and then the handle to smash at the horse's nose. She was quite absorbed in her task and satisfied, when she stepped back to review what she'd done, with her handiwork. Her blade hadn't blunted at all.

Most of her immediate rage now seemed to have worked its way through her, both by the heavy physical destruction of smashing a town house, down to this more detailed obliteration of a personal memorial. Every tomb here, she reminded herself, would need to be destroyed eventually. Every trace of Romani would have to be washed from these lands. Celtoi and Romani differed in every way, even to their funereal practices, she realised. Worlds apart. She contemplated the sheer waste of resources invested into these monuments; the complete extravagance arranged before her, paid for by Celtoi sweat. Then she recalled what the Celtoi had been reduced to. Simple cremation pits marked by fragile stick-markers which crumbled to dust within years. Reduced from what? Why, from the fine chariot burials the Bards still sang of, where the feasting and games in honour of the dead would last three days and three nights and no one or nothing would go without during the mourning of the recently departed. How she had wanted to send Prasutagus upon his journey to the Isle of Rebirth in such a manner. She had known for a long while which of his chariots she would choose for him and exactly which possessions he would need with him. Circumstances had conspired to prevent her from fulfilling such plans. She swore, in revenge, that no Romani in Britannia would ever be able to aspire to such abiding sepulchres again. The highest honour such corpses could hope for would be a scattering of earth cast over a mass grave.

Horsemen were coming in upon the road to the north. Boudicca had been aware for a while of the irregular stream of people trudging towards Camulodunum. Some brought wagons full of the possessions of perhaps whole settlements, some rode chariots, others led pack donkeys or staggered under the weight of their families' burdens. Quite a few brought ferocious dogs with them, trained for the hunt with wicked jaws. Already Boudicca knew there had been fights between dogs, staged for the owners' delight, and the victors set to feed upon Romani corpses. The Druids had had to impose strict rules about the tethering of such beasts whose growling worried the children. Lovernios had been concerned the dogs might develop a taste for human flesh if it was encouraged, but Boudicca had reassured him of their tight obedience and indispensability upon the field. And anyway, surely Romani flesh would differ in taste from Celtoi?

All these newcomers entered the remains of the town, unaware the strange woman skulking amongst the tombs had been their inspiration. Perhaps, thought Boudicca, it might be for the best if things remained that way. So she let them pass by at a distance and without acknowledgement, merely monitoring them in her peripheral vision.

These horsemen, though, were different; they attracted more attention from her. Celtoi didn't normally ride their horses; they were used for pulling chariots, occasionally wagons, and for breeding. They were one of the many ways in which the Celtoi measured their wealth. Not only were they too valuable to be ridden, but they were also too small. The Romani's horses, on the other hand, were tall and bred to be ridden, and these particular mounts were Romani. Those foot-travellers whom they passed on the road recognised the horses' stock and instinctively hurried to the run offs to let the horses pass. Such habits, thought Boudicca, take longer than two victories to diminish.

The riders, however, were definitely Celtoi. So much was obvious from their cheerful chequered clothing, augmented by the odd item of Romani military issue, and the way they handled their weapons. Not even a Romani spy would have the audacity to walk into this hornets' nest and, anyway, the language they called out in greeting was familiar, without any hint of an accent. Boudicca peered at them, squinting a little so she might be able to determine any familiar faces or hear their voices.

Grania was back! At last! Boudicca gathered up the folds of her clothing and pelted back along the road, through the Colonia gate and along the ruined streets. As she neared the temple area she pulled at her throat to loosen her robes and revealed the Otherworldly glow of her torc. As the first bystanders caught sight of the object, they moved aside to provide passage and nudged their fellows to do the same. Boudicca nodded in gratitude to them, astounded by the instant change Andraste's torc provoked.

Now she was back as Queen and Priestess, as war leader, a quick change from one role to another. She wondered briefly whether she alarmed any of her people by her unquenchable need to be an individual separate from the mass, then reflected that probably the only person to be affected was Lovernios and he wouldn't dare question her. She stumbled upon him more or less where she'd left him earlier. He was sharing a simple meal of stolen bread with Maeve and Sucellus. Grania had still not joined them.

'Grania's back.'

'She hasn't come here yet, madam,' Lovernios mumbled through a mouthful of loaf.

'Where can she have got to then? She was on horseback, she should've been here before me.'

'Some riders did come in. But they just joined whoever their respective Chiefs were and reported to them. I should get the information relayed to me by the Druids before long. No hurry, have something to eat, madam.'

'But what about Grania? I want to see my daughter, hear the information she must've gained. Did no one see where she went?'

'Madam, calm down. We're in no immediate danger. We can wait awhile for Grania's news. Perhaps she's unpacking, or washing, or tending to her horse.' Lovernios shrugged and popped another morsel in his mouth.

'Get someone to send for her.' Boudicca walked up and down a few paces, unaware her fists were clenching and unclenching. 'No. No. I'll do it. I'll go and find her myself. Anyway, aren't you curious about where I've been all this while?'

She stamped off without waiting for an answer.

Disappearing into the crowd, she sought out any of the riders she'd just seen return. She could not understand the language of some of them and, becoming more and more infuriated, she demanded, no, requested nearby Druids to translate for her. They were so careful, every one of them, questioning the warriors precisely, wanting to prepare a translation as exact as possible, before uttering it to Boudicca. She felt like screaming: 'It doesn't matter. I only want the gist, get on with it.' But somehow she contained herself, trying to remember that as far as these translators were concerned, their skill was Goddess-given and she was asking them to provide their version of a holy act. She was also desperately trying to hang on to the idea that these people were still just people, individuals like herself. Her needs might be paramount to her, but they were only a means to an end for those who served her.

Finally she had the information she needed and she pushed through the crowds once more to the place where she'd been told she might find Grania. Traipsing around the streets, kicking orphaned stones, she was alone again. Just any mother looking for her child, although recently, she knew, there'd been many more of the latter forlornly looking for the former.

It did not take her long to reach where she had been told to go. The building was the second largest after the Temple and its precinct, and had a distinctive semi-circular plan discernable even from the ground. Boudicca wasn't really too surprised to learn of Grania's stay there. On hindsight, if she had only applied a little Romani logic to the situation, she might have been able to work out for herself that Grania would have made straight for the Romani's theatre.

There were several entrances. Boudicca chose one; she knew it would not matter which, as they all led to the same place. She crept under the ornamental arch, keeping her footfall as noiseless as possible. Wanting what? To eavesdrop on her daughter, to surprise her, or equally to not frighten her? Boudicca herself didn't know; somehow secrecy just felt appropriate, as if there was an air of it all around.

Edging forward, she peeped out from behind the stone wall which would bring her into the view of anyone in the theatre. She could just make out the tiers of seats rising to surround the elevated stage. Grania was nowhere to be seen. Just as Boudicca was about to stride into the theatre for a better appreciation of the architecture, albeit produced by a Romani architect, she caught a hint of movement behind the stage. Grania was burrowing amidst some rubble, hiding something – a sack perhaps, or a rough bag, Boudicca couldn't tell from this distance. What she could see, quite plainly, were Grania's hands completely covered in blood.

Just as fervidly, Grania scrambled off the stage and scampered out of the theatre, apparently not caring now whether she might be seen or heard. Her fleeing feet sent echoes of sound bouncing off the theatre to herald her departure. Boudicca turned and ran back the way she had come, hoping to cut her daughter off as she headed for the temple precinct. Boudicca had not given her own actions much thought up to now, responding purely to her instincts in trying to ascertain what Grania was up to. Now she did, hoping Grania might never know what she'd seen and would interpret her sudden appearance purely as that of a distraught mother come to greet her long awaited daughter.

Boudicca contrived to weave back through the narrow streets and double-back to bump into Grania, feigning surprise at finding her daughter there when they collided. She hugged Grania, exclaiming at her return, and started to ask her what had happened to the remains of the legion nine. Grania briefly returned the hug and broadly started to describe what had occurred, regaining her composure extremely rapidly.

'We did as you said, mother mine, and followed the remnants of the cavalry back along the Via Devena, hollowing loudly and sounding our war trumpets all the way. They barely looked back the whole while, so fearful were they for their very lives'

'How far did you chase them?'

'Through Durovigutum, pausing only to rout that settlement.'

Boudicca looked shocked.

'Mama, you should be pleased, they were Catuvellauni.'

'There really weren't enough of you to take such a risk, Grania.'

'Most of them scattered as soon as they saw the Romani hurtle towards them. It was the legionaries who did most of the scare mongering for us. The pro-Romani settlers fled before our eyes, all we had to do was stick a few defenceless backs and slit a few awnings as we passed. We didn't even pause to make sure the fires had caught. There was enough smoke to suggest they had, though.'

Boudicca couldn't help grinning at Grania. She was quite proud of her daughter for taking such initiative, even though she worried now about the unnecessary risks she might also have taken.

'Well, I still wish you'd told me you were going to do those things.'

'You wouldn't have let me then, mama.'

Boudicca smiled, Grania was growing up.

'Anyway, we were only taking advantage of the opportunity afforded us – none of us knew the legionaries were going to be so panicky, did we?'

'I don't expect even Lovernios had thought of that,' Boudicca mused, half to herself. 'You followed the Romani further then?'

'Oh yes, all the way to their fortress at Durobrivae. You should have seen them desperately digging their defences and rallying those they'd left behind. Suddenly were all go, standing to attention, issuing contradictory orders, grabbing weapons. They're quite amusing when they have to deal with chaos. I don't think they were very pleased to see how few their pursuers were, though.'

'You let them see you?'

'Oh yes, mama. We turned our horses around and around to show them how well they preferred to be owned by Celtoi. We stood along the skyline, antagonising them and flouting our victory, then we turned and melted into the woods, Finding our way back here within moments.'

134

Boudicca wasn't learning anything she wouldn't have been able to work out for herself. Grania was evasive if anything, and there was that feeling again, of a desire to be secretive and keep things to oneself. Boudicca realised she was starting to pick up Grania's own emotions. Their relationship had always been close, until recently. Now she knew intuitively that Grania was not telling her everything.

'I'm very proud of you; you've done well. We celebrate Eostar tonight. With so many Druids it should be quite a festival. I wish you to join me as Priestess.'

Grania's face dropped, and she made as if she would protest.

'It'd mean a lot to me, Grania, and to our people. All you'd have to do is stand with me. Tomorrow we'll make preparations to leave these ruins, but we're not yet sure which road we'll take or where it'll lead. I hope that will become apparent during our rituals tonight.'

'But mama!' Grania started to protest. Boudicca quietened her by raising her hand.

'Before we go, we must ensure everything is destroyed that can be destroyed; it's taking too long with our current methods. The main problem's these larger buildings,' she gestured around. 'The Temple isn't a worry. The Trinovantes will erase it even if they have to chip away at it for a year. No, it's the forum, the theatre, some of the larger houses.' She watched her daughter carefully for any betrayal of emotion. Nothing. 'Fires will have to be built against them to crack the stone and make it easier to lever the walls down. Tiles will need to be smashed, decorations will need to be defaced. Everything in them will need to be razed.' Still nothing from Grania. 'Will you do it for me? Will you be in charge of such responsible work?'

'Of course, mama.' No protest, no requests. Whatever Grania had hidden, as carefully as if building a nest, she had no concerns about it during the destruction process. Was it something capable of surviving the flames? Something she no longer cared for? 'If you like, I'll start on the theatre straight away.' Or perhaps something she'd arranged for someone else to remove even now whilst she talked to her mother?

Boudicca was confused. Grania's face and words revealed nothing. Only this all-pervading atmosphere of something being kept back. Something secret of Grania's was not being shared with her mama. Boudicca had to let it go, she had no choice. To do otherwise would drive a wedge between the two of them where already there existed a dreadful gulf. She could have Grania watched; she could have the theatre guarded. No, there should be trust between the two of them; it was natural for things to be kept separate between mother and daughter, wasn't it? Wasn't it all part of growing from girl to woman?

She leapt then, a jump of faith in her trust that Grania was not intrinsically bad and her daughter's secret hoard was something of her business and hers alone. 'It'd be appreciated, Grania.' She forced out the words. 'The sooner there's nothing Romani left here, the sooner we can be after more of their blood. Procure the labour you require – you have my authority in this matter.'

The two women clasped hands in farewell and smiled at each other. Then they both turned and walked away. Boudicca forced herself to keep walking, not wanting to look back in case Grania interpreted her action as spying. She'd just about mastered her natural inquisitiveness and concentrated her mind upon the forthcoming Eostar rites, when she heard Grania call out.

Boudicca swung around, not pausing to worry about interfering now, and dashed back to her daughter. Grania hadn't moved from where they'd separated except to double up, clutching her stomach. Boudicca wrapped a protective arm around her back, trying to pull Grania upright as she did so. Boudicca took a lot of her daughter's weight as Grania relaxed into her mother's arms, obviously in agony.

Grania's face had whitened and was twisted in spasms of pain which weakened her body. She called out again, a grunting sigh, as if she hoped to eject the torment along with the sound.

'Mama, mama, help me!' she screamed, and Boudicca heard other Celtoi come running to offer assistance.

'Tell me where the pain is, Grania mine.'

Still doubled over, Grania pushed her hands from her abdomen to reveal the blood starting to seep through her clothing.

'Mother Above! Are you injured?'

'No mama,' voice weak now. 'It's my menses.'

There was quite a crowd forming. Boudicca shooed them back to allow Grania air. 'Do you usually bleed so much? No, let me take your weight.'

Grania groaned again, lower now, as if the pain came from deep within her womb itself. She sagged into her mother's arms. Boudicca wondered in admiration how long Grania had been in so much agony without betraying a hint of it to her.

'No, mama mine, not this bad usually.' Another groan, as if her body was responding to contractions which brought the pain to irregular peaks. 'I'm sorry, mama, I didn't want you to know.' Gasping words now, little more than deep breathing.

'Know what? What?' The crowd edged closer, fencing them in.

'Oh, mama, mama. Don't hate me, please mama. I didn't mean to.'

Boudicca blanched. Had Grania done this to herself in some way? She gripped her daughter tighter, as if to squeeze the information out of her.

Grania started to swoon. Just before passing out, Boudicca heard her fragile whisper: 'I think I'm losing my baby.'

Chapter 10

Eostar

Grania's condition somewhat marred the Eostar rituals that Boudicca and Lovernios presided over. Even with the massive crowd watching her actions from the Temple precinct and those pushing from without for a better view, Boudicca found it difficult to concentrate.

The rite was a familiar one; she'd performed it every year for her Gerbfine, in the royal tribal territories of the Iceni. Those events had been more of a family occasion, attended just by the inhabitants of their enclosure who were almost all immediate kin. But this was far more formal; there were Druids in attendance and many, many thousands of people, all intent on her movements and words. And this year she enacted the ceremonies with Lovernios; last year it had been with a frail Prasutagus.

At first she'd thought she might be getting to be too old to stand as the embodiment of the Goddess in Her Spring Maiden aspect. Such doubts had been her reasoning behind inviting Maeve and Grania to attend with her. But her daughters were together for once and with some of the Sisters who had healing wisdom and knowledge of herbs. It seemed to Boudicca she'd tidied away the two of them, yet again, so they might not disrupt or disturb her things of higher importance, but she also knew she'd been grateful the two girls were eager to take solace in each other at last, and she knew it was guilt making her think such crippling thoughts.

In many ways, though, as the motions and litany came back to her, she was able to take comfort in the familiarity of the ritual and relax as the Goddess within took over much of the role of Priestess. She was content to let the Divine guide her through the rites and Blessings and absolve her of some of the sombre mood hanging over her. From the look in Lovernios' eyes, she could tell the young God had been granted similar freedom with him. The crowd, too, might be oblivious to the transformation of their Priest and Priestess, but the sheer reverence of the huddled masses was testament to their experience of the sublime.

Boudicca held up the eggs she had Blessed. She'd asked the Druids to bring her a variety from every species of bird in Artio's forests and the nests yielded an abundance of coloured and speckled fragility which sang of the summer to come. Her brief inspection showed a hedge-sparrow egg and three from a starling, but there were an abundance of blue-green magpie eggs. She could count seven merely from her cursory glance.

The crowd were waiting to be addressed now. She knew what she had to say, but not yet how she wanted to say it. In desperation, she gave her voice over to Andraste. For a long moment nothing happened, and then she felt the sudden surge as her torc shone and the Goddess came to the fore.

'My loyal peoples, welcome to the equality of days! We are now between the start of spring and the beginning of summer. The seasons cannot be halted in their progress and summer will soon be upon us, for who can stop the yearly cycle from turning? Not I, no, for I am summer's herald.

'The winds rush and whip our clothing and the sun brings heat to shine upon our upturned faces. All around us new life buds and we cannot deny the calling beckoning us, too, to join its celebration. However, before the summer can be birthed, the old ways must disintegrate, for we still bear the vestiges of winter. Thus all the elements of life have been brought into new balance and you have felt the chaos in nature as the wildness courses even through your very beings. And so a new tide of life begins and the day length equals that of night. Nothing in nature is ever constant, the light is gaining and soon future days will exceed future nights.

'As it was in the beginning, so it is now: out of this chaos, fresh ways arise. As it is in nature, so it is in you.

'These eggs show the emergence of light from darkness, of life from non-life, of ideas from inner stillness. Laid in the secret season of early spring, they hatch in the new warmth. These eggs are you – you are these eggs. For it was your plans that were formed after Imbolc in the secret hearts of Artio's forests, and now they have opened to reveal the first steps towards something we only dreamt about in the depths of winter.

'Yes, my peoples, for it is just as if the Celtoi have emerged from their own personal winter of desolation, as well as the winter we know we are leaving behind in the material realm. Is winter not an apt description of the feeling of Romani oppression?

'These eggs are fertility, rich with promise and the potential of life. Let us leave the winter behind, finally, along with what belongs to winter. This is the festival of new balance: as the sun gains strength, we must joyously accept the change and our rebirth in freedom!'

The crowd burst into tumultuous applause, deafening Boudicca with their cheers of wholehearted approval. She felt light-headed with the Goddess' influence and uncertain of exactly what she'd said, only how it had been met with such obvious endorsement. She stepped towards Lovernios, hoping now to complete the ritual. But the Queen in her could not resist turning back for one last look at the people gathered before her. The loyalty she sensed flooding towards her was an emotion she would never want to forget.

They were waving their arms now and the noise was growing in volume. Louder and louder, their arms moving faster and faster. Boudicca felt herself falling and reached out to Lovernios for support. He caught her arm, lending her strength, and gently took the eggs from her and laid them at a safe distance. It wouldn't do for her to fall and crack them. Still the arms waved, swaying back and forth, like ears of ripening corn. No, not like corn, just like ears, long grey ears, twitching and listening, then hurrying away to scamper west into the setting sun.

'The hare,' she uttered, before Andraste descended upon her once more and she pulled herself out of Lovernios' arms and stood to address the crowd.

'The sacred hare is amongst you, amongst every one of you. Can you not feel it running with your heartbeat?' There were so many hares, all bobbing away amongst the crowd. So many, it seemed there were no longer any people in the mass, just hares, all running away in a multitude of different directions, trailing blood as they ran. Boudicca felt sickened by the motion – she could no longer focus.

'Whilst the hare runs separately within each and every one of you, so should you run as individuals. Sweep the land. There are enough of you to divide into small units and still be within calling distance of each other for aid. Destroy anything Romani you find. If they will not join with you, then they are against you and they should be killed. There is no opposition all around the remains of this Colonia, just small farmsteads and fortlets. Ruin them all, put them to the sword and the flame. There will not be much blood – the trail is watery here. Enjoy the sport.'

Then she watched as the hares coalesced into one massive hare with vicious claws and nasty yellow teeth. Then a river appeared and the tide rose and fell. When the ebb tide was at its lowest point, the hare drank from the river, and the blackened waters made it grow even more.

'You have until the new moon to raze the lands in these environs of the glory which once was Camulodunum. The horde will host again outside Londinium and then destroy it. The new moon is for fresh beginnings; it is proper to attack the second Romani settlement then, it will mark the next stage of our rebellion.

'Some of you will want to stay behind to ensure the total eradication of this Colonia. Then you will want to return to your homes and raise your families and crops. How easy it will be for you to slip away whilst the horde is temporarily disbanded. I say to you that the land is not yet ready for this! There will be plenty of summer left for farming, but first the entirety of Britannia must be cleansed of the Romani threat, else you will plough and be forever checking over your shoulder for the tramp tramp of Romani soldiers coming to take your land.

'Those of you whose lands have been already freed of the Romani are not the only tribes to have answered my call. There are other Celtoi tribes here too. Without them we would never have come so far. But their lands are still not free. You owe those tribes loyalty! Every Celtoi here owes their neighbour and their neighbours' neighbour loyalty for what you have done for one another. Such loyalty cannot be repaid until every Romani and every Romani supporter in Britannia is dead.

'Do not return to your homes yet. We still have need of you, and if you would only be patient the Romani will provide you with loot and blood to your hearts' content. There is more, believe me – much, much more – enough to sate even the greediest amongst you.

'The wagons and camp followers will travel to Londinium at their own slower pace. They will follow the Romani road leading southwest and will engulf first the settlements at Canonium and then Caesaromagus. I estimate the former will be reached after two days' journeying and the latter after five. However, it is unlikely we will be ready to leave Camulodunum for at least another three days.

'Move with the wagons, scout out for Romani and then return, or come and go as you will. I ask you one thing, my peoples, and one thing only: meet us on the outskirts of Londinium on the night of the next new moon, bring with you tales of bloodshed and cruelty perpetrated by Celtoi warriors, and be ready to horde upon Londinium!'

Boudicca could not have imagined that the crowd was capable of raising a louder cheer than the previous one, but it did. Andraste, however, had not yet finished, and neither had the Eostar rites. The noise subsided once more. This was the part Boudicca had been dreading, the part she had been unsure about going through with. Now it seemed as if the decision was taken from her.

'The God too is young, yea, and also ardent!' Lovernios joined her, responding to her signal. They clasped hands and held them high above their heads, their hips so close as to rub together. Everyone will know the extent of our relationship now, thought Boudicca, there can be no more pretence. 'It is He who breaks the chains of winter and Our union breathes life into new order.'

They clasped each other then, openly before all the crowds, signifying the sexual union of the Goddess and God. There was a brief lull and then the crowd shouted and cried and cheered louder and more enthusiastically than ever. Everywhere amongst the horde, lover grasped lover and wife grasped husband, everywhere the desire of the Goddess and her Consort was emulated.

Still disoriented from Andraste's influence, Boudicca allowed herself to be led by Lovernios to the bower set up for the two of them. The Druids had strung sheets of rich Romani material over a lean-to structure of branches and poles, garlanding the whole with the earliest flowers, bluebells and trailing cascades of ivy. Sunlight streamed through the thin material, causing shadow-play to ripple around the interior. Delighted with the effect, Boudicca laughed, still saturated with Andraste who cooed and purred with pleasure at Lovernios' touch. The finest Romani delicacies had been set aside for those who would act as incarnations of the deities for this ritual, and arranged with the best that Artio's forest would yield of natural fare. They could want for nothing.

For a single, precious evening, Boudicca had been granted liberation from her cares and worries. Grania was fine and recuperating steadily; there was nothing, the Sisters had reassured her, she could do. The Romani were far away, too far away to affect her. And the people had seen the Goddess herself, whether they actually realised it or not, and were busy celebrating the Eostar rites with their own festivities.

This tent-like structure, then, was like an island in a sea of turmoil, an oasis of bliss, open to Boudicca to accept its offer. Only she could not. Her insides were knotted into a tangle of cares and burdens, and part of her could not stop going over and over the situations she'd bound herself up in. Lovernios sensed her tensions and brought her wine to steady her. She sipped it slowly, not wanting to fall into trance like on the last occasion she had drunk alcohol. He waited patiently for her to finish; she sipped repetitively, still tugged between her wearing concerns and the pleasures available to her for the rest of the night.

Lovernios was a good, kind man, she decided then, looking at him in consideration. He'd been very patient with her when she had thrown so much at him; lesser men would have dissolved back to an easier wife. So, he had perseverance; good, she liked that, he'd need it to love her. This was not going to be an easy relationship even now that they'd publicly announced their union, their promise to each other. No, two people so strong in character, so plainly obstinate, could never share a relaxed love. But Boudicca thought she might reject such a simple relationship if it were offered now, opting in preference for the heat and excitement she got from Lovernios. Nothing, with him, was ever boring; she hoped she was an equal inspiration to him.

And there was certainly an unmistakable desire between them, whose flush she could feel even now as she gazed for a prolonged period upon his handsome face. She had, she realised, been reluctant to commit herself to this man, too scared of being hurt or betrayed in her vulnerability. It was becoming slowly obvious such reluctance was long past, and she'd already fallen deeply in love whilst she'd been clawing at her independence, too busy to notice her true feelings.

She reached up then, to touch his tender expression, drawing him to her in desire, yet in more than that too.

'Lovernios mine?' She hesitated. He kissed her trembling lips. 'I love you, Lovernios mine.'

He smiled softly, and nuzzled her face with his short beard. 'I know you do. I love you too.'

Then she pulled him to her in a tight, desperate hug, trying to describe some of the fierce emotions inside and starting to show him in actions what she could not say in words.

Their lovemaking was like nothing Boudicca had known before; certainly there was a sacredness about their motions, but there was something more too. It was as if something deeper and older than the earth took place within their shelter, something primeval and basic, raising power and energy to accentuate their awareness of each other and the cosmos around. Their restless rhythms stirred parts of themselves previously not awake, whilst their spirits soared around the heavens, their loving seemingly liberating them from their own bodies.

When they dozed fitfully in each other's arms during the late evening, still drifting to the sounds of merrymaking in and around the Temple compound, Boudicca asked Lovernios the one question left burning. 'Do you know, Lovernios, what the main thing is which attracts you to me?'

'Madam,' he chuckled. 'Surely that could be any one of a number of virtues?'

'No, shush, I'm being serious.'

'So am I!' He replied tersely with mock indignation.

'No, what I meant to point out was the look in your eyes of half-remembered pain. It's that which I recognise from the look in my own eyes peering back at me from a bronzed mirror. It's the same look I identified with when I first met you, and instinctively knew, even then, that you'd understand me and the things I've been through. You never talk of your childhood, nor of your past. It's only a few days since you first spoke of your father.'

Quite abruptly, Lovernios pushed himself up onto his elbows and leant over to pour himself a large goblet of wine. He gulped at it, not enquiring whether Boudicca wanted any. He had resumed the barriers between them, she realised, typified by his sudden indifference to her. She felt as if he had hung a veil to divide them one from the other.

'I'm sorry, Lovernios, I didn't mean to pry. You don't have to tell me anything. It's just my hope that you might jog things I've put from my own mind and can no longer remember; I often ponder what horrors I might have blotted out.'

He was still thinking. Wondering what? Whether to tell her, or what bits to tell her, or how to tell her? She waited, certain now there was some awful story to be told.

'There are things which have happened to me and those around me which I haven't been able to bring myself to tell you, madam, for fear you might not be ready to hear them.' He poured more wine. 'I should, by rights, have told you before we were publicly joined, but I was concerned they might be too near to your heart and your own experiences for you to be able to bear the telling.'

Boudicca put her head on one side as she paused to listen more carefully.

'Those are the reasons I've delayed and those are the reasons I give now for still wishing to spare you. It's a pain I've learned to bear alone; I can still do so. Sharing will not release this particular burden.'

'I would there was nothing between us, Lovernios, including whatever horrors you've lived through. Come, lie down in my arms and let me comfort you while you tell me the things I need to understand.'

After more wine he snuggled up to her embrace, laying his head upon her breast as if he were her child. Then he spoke softly, his voice wavering and nervous, as he started to tell her who he was.

'I was born, like your daughters, as one of a multiple birth but, unlike your daughters, not identical. I shared my mother's womb with a brother, and we formed together, sharing her ample sustenance. My mother was from Hibernicus, a princess from an ancient royal family of Insula Sacra, and as magnificent in looks as a Faery Queen from the oldest tales.

'Boudicca mine, I could embellish this tale with all the skills available to a Bard. I could sing of my mother's legendary beauty and compare her to each of our Goddesses in turn, but I'd be detracting from the events and I trust you'll believe me if I just speak simply.' Boudicca stroked his hair in reassurance. 'Forgive my ineloquence, madam, lost in favour of brevity?'

Boudicca nodded that she would.

'My mother was named for the mother Goddess Anu, being called Annis. She was as lovely as the most skilful depiction of any of our Goddesses. Like a graceful willow, she was tall and slim; her hair was as long and straight as yours, and black as glossy jet; her hands were slender and pale, her nails neat where she'd never needed to labour in the fields.

'She was proud, too, as a Celtoi princess of the royal line should be, boastful of her looks and confident of her ability to stir any man's heart. But she was not a callous woman, never using her beauty for destruction, just proud and rightly so. When her father decreed she should wed and choose a fitting husband, she politely refused all the champions and warriors who offered themselves and picked instead a young Bard whose music and sweet words had lightened her days of maidenhood.'

Boudicca raised her eyebrows in surprise; it was unusual for someone of a royal line to marry outside the Celtoi aristocracy.

'It was, of course, a great honour she bestowed upon the Bard, and one which caused consternation in her father's court. But she had her way eventually, for she was wilful even then and her wondrous looks had meant no man could deny her desires for long, even her own father.

'The Bard, of course, was Cathbad, my father, and he was soon recalled to complete his training at Insula Mona. My mother accompanied him, leaving Insula Sacra despite never having done so before. It was when she had left that she started to waken her own not inconsiderable Skills. Imagine, then, the joy for this young couple when they learned they were to become parents, not to one child, but to two. The same joy rushed through the Druidic community like a fire in summer brushwood: such children would be certain to be naturally Gifted, beyond even the usual Skills displayed by Druidic offspring. And when the news reached back to her home lands, it found a doting father glad he would soon be a grandfather and relieved his daughter's choice had been so Blessed.'

Lovernios and Boudicca exchanged smiles at the thought.

'The couple stayed at Insula Mona until the birth. My mother went into a long and protracted labour, as would be expected for two babes. Her womb was distended and swollen, rich with new life, but she lost copious blood and was exhausted from the work the Goddess had ordained for her. First one babe was birthed and screamed at its first intake of breath. Half a day later the second was still not birthed. By now my mother was weakened and feverish, desperate for sleep and torn with pain. The Healers did all they could, with kind words and encouragements, Spells and Workings, and every knot upon the island was ordered to be untied, but to no avail. The second babe was finally birthed stillborn, a bloody mess, with the birth cord wrapped tight around its neck. It would, as I've told you already, have been a son.'

Boudicca hugged Lovernios tighter as he told her what had happened to his would-be brother and his words brought back memories of birthings for her too.

'Finally, my mother slept, with herbal draughts to staunch the blood and cloths to keep her warm and clean. My father wept, for joy at the gift of one perfect son and for grief at the death of a boy taken before he could even be named. My father wept alone, for the Healers had left and even I was too exhausted from my birth journey to do else but sleep. It was then, so I learned, that he decided to spare my mother's sorrow and tell her there had only ever been one babe. The last, he concocted, had been a midwife's error over a particularly difficult afterbirth, easily made when twins are so rare anyway and a son is born so large and healthy. My mother, he knew, had been virtually delirious when the last child was birthed, and she would believe him if the Healers kept to the same story. Why, he decided, should the joy of a new mother be shattered when it could so easily be complete?'

Boudicca shook her head in sadness and disbelief at the foolishness of the man. 'Did your mother fall for that?' she asked.

'Warily at first, and only after the story was corroborated by the midwives. My mother accepted what my father told her, loving me, her baby son, with heartfelt gratitude for the happiness I brought her. My father, though, grieved the loss of his other son more than he'd anticipated, and the grief cut even deeper for the fact he'd consigned himself to endure it without his wife's shared solace. My mother, seemingly oblivious to the fact that her son had once been half of twins, became absorbed in her new babe and the wonder of the creation she'd helped bring into the world, not noticing my father's pain. He withdrew gradually, letting his mental agony guide him into realms of the mind usually only reached by deep meditation.

'As so often happens with survivors of trauma, his exploration of his feelings opened him up to new levels of awareness and the transformation of his psyche was soon noticed by his fellow Druids. Recognition of his Talents meant my father was recommended for Druidic duties at Vernemetum, and our young family was sent there. My earliest memories are of the great Shrines and Groves in the midlands of Britannia as my father travelled to each, officiating over rituals in every one.'

Lovernios shifted position and he changed his tone, interrupting his narrative with an explanation of the background to his story.

'You may be unaware, madam, of the layout of holy places beyond the territorial lands of the Iceni. I know you've used the Druidic roads, from Insula Mona to the easternmost coast of Britannia, and that you would have taken shelter at various shrines along the routes as and when you needed rest, but such a path wouldn't reveal the web of sacred sites stretching across Britannia. Insula Mona is a holy place, certainly, because of its strong links with the sacred isle, but it's the midlands where Druidic power has always been concentrated, and

Vernemetum is the most holy of all these places: a great sanctuary preserved only for the Druids, where the Goddess may be approached directly amongst Her oak trees and Her pools of forgetfulness. The boundaries between the layers of worlds are at their very thinnest here, which is why access is so restricted: anyone not sufficiently trained would become lost, perhaps being returned to this world only after many years have passed.'

'No I didn't know that, but I am slowly learning that I know less than I thought.'

'Well, anyway, my father was assigned to Vernemetum and it was there that I grew up. Those were drowsy days when the gold trade was at its peak, flowing healthily through Britannia to the Continent, enriching all whose hands it passed through and providing ample sacrifice to the Goddess to even sate Her thirst for human life. Even the skill in fashioning beauteous things from the gold was transformed amongst our smiths and metalworkers into a religious act in itself.

'Soon, too soon I remember, I was of an age to be fostered. Even amongst Druids a son may not come into his father's presence from leaving babyhood until he's passed puberty, so, like the sons of warriors, I was sent back to my mother's kin. I remembered then my father's weeping for my leaving being out of proportion to the tears of other fathers or those of the rest of my family. In hindsight, I can understand it was because I was the second son he was losing.'

'And you still suspected nothing?'

'No, nothing! Well, not until later. But I remember how my grandfather received me as if I represented the return of his daughter rather than just a part of her, treating me like a prince and training and protecting me as was due my status. I wanted for nothing. Those days were happy too, although I missed my beautiful mother and the tender songs she'd sing to me before I slept. But I was the son of two Gifted Druids and my own Talents soon became apparent, although I kept them to myself for a few years before I was old enough to realise they were Gifts for the benefit of more than just a naughty boy's tricks.'

'So, you're more like my Grania than you would really care to admit?'

Lovernios laughed before continuing, 'Two other things happened in that year, I recall. The first is related to the flowering of my Skills and concerns my stillborn brother. I'd always been aware of another presence – a male entity linked with me – although, of course, no one had ever mentioned I'd been one of twins. This must've been similar to the intuitive bonding you've seen between your own twin girls. When I played I'd invite this male entity to play too and would chatter to him in the same way other children might talk to an imaginary friend. He

146

was a secret, though; I'd sensed strongly I was meant to tell no one about him.

'My brother was good company for me in Insula Sacra for there were only a few others who shared my Talents and I was still in a strange land. Although my father was unreachable, I felt my mother with me too, but she was fainter. With the help of the tittle-tattle from some slaves about how I'd always been a robust child with a healthy appetite, so much so that twins were revealed as a singlet, I finally made my own deductions. My mother's presence felt distant because she was physically distant. My brother's presence didn't have the same restrictions, because he was not physically manifest. That he was a presence like my mother's, dissimilar only in sex and strength, could mean only one thing: this presence was my brother who had died at birth, and he and I had been twins.'

'How disturbing for you!'

'Not really. You see, there came a point when my mother's presence suddenly vanished and my brother's became very much stronger. I learned then to subsume him within myself and to share my Being in much the same way as you do with the Goddess. It had always been natural to have him with me, a constant source of friendship and wisdom. As the years increased, I noticed the grace and truth in his presence, and I came to understand him as a Manifestation of the Divine: the Young God, Andraste's consort. It's only recently, with the gathering of the Druids for this rebellion, that I've finally been able to confirm my suspicions.'

'But I still don't understand why Cathbad, I mean your father, is now like he is.'

'Well, the other thing to happen in the year I was sent to my grandfather was, I believe, connected with these things, especially since it preceded my experience of the Young God: it was the return of the Romani.'

'How?' Boudicca was extremely puzzled by how these things could be related.

Lovernios explained. 'Although I was safe in Hibernicus, still we heard of the things being done by the Romani. We heard of their gifts and their money and their luxuries. Wondrous travellers' tales filtered through of beautiful goods to trade and warm rooms to sit in, of food and plenty and games – we heard it all. We also knew it wouldn't take the Romani long to covet the Druid gold, and perhaps then for them to come for it even into the depths of the sacred isle itself.'

Boudicca nodded in agreement; the Romani hadn't been able to resist the lure of the Celtoi gold for long.

'They were all friendly and open-armed at first, of course. But we knew about such things – how they would try to lull those they wished

147

to conquer. And we knew, too, of their use of Celtoi sacred sites for their own worship. They took Druid trade routes – paths we've always walked along where our feet have worn away the grass – and covered them with brick and sand to make their hardened roads and stop the earth from breathing. They carved their straight roads through our sacred land, scoring the earth and cutting Britannia's flesh.'

Boudicca winced as she too remembered the changes the Romani had made when they came and how she had felt their infrastructure pierce the earth itself.

'They'd heard of our gold by then, and had been told Vernemetum was the holiest place in the land. So they went there and my father granted them audience. They sat amongst the oak trees and their words were chorused by birdsong. The Romani numbered only a centurion and a few soldiers, and my father brought only my mother to sit with him. Everything was informal, everything polite, there were no threats, everything quite amicable. But no, my father told them, the gold was sacred; it was not for trade, nor for purchase. The Romani couldn't have the gold. Neither would he tell them where it came from nor where it went. Such information, he told the centurion, was the Goddess' own secret. Of course, he offered, if they would only stay a while and listen, the Goddess might Bless them with Her own wisdom and then they would understand for themselves.'

Boudicca could feel tears come to her eyes. The story Lovernios was telling her was so very tragic: she knew how the Romani were going to respond before he told her; she had already seen enough of their nature to know that they would not even try to comprehend such an alien concept.

Lovernios continued, his voice catching as he too, sought to control his emotion. 'My father could tell that the Goddess' presence, emanating from Her most sacred place, was starting to pervade even into the dense armour of these Romani. Certainly the soldiers had shuffled nervously and kept glancing around at every raven call, but gradually they'd calmed. My mother, too, had made them welcome, serving them with fresh water and fruits and nuts from the forests. She was a Celtoi princess first, remember, before ever she'd become Druid, and she knew the hospitality due from one royal family to another. She'd also missed the attention from the brave warriors and champions of her father's court in her younger days. She saw in these Romani, perhaps, an opportunity to relive some of the attention she'd received before she went to live amongst the Druids. So she prepared for the meeting by unbinding her black hair and bedecking her pale skin with the finest gold. She was still rightly proud of a beauty which had refused to fade despite a difficult labour and the years that had passed since.'

Boudicca closed her eyes. She was willing Lovernios to stop, afraid of how his story was unfolding, aware of the fear that was reawakening in herself.

Lovernios spoke more slowly now; it was getting difficult for him to recount his story. 'Like any Celtoi woman she held herself with pride, using her bearing to display her looks. My father, proud to have her as his wife, encouraged this boasting, pointing out to the Romani how soft her features were, how shiny her hair, how white her teeth. The same had been done by countless Celtoi couples before, had it not? Wasn't it natural to boast of the things of which one was proud?'

Boudicca nodded. Yes, in Celtoi society this was acceptable behaviour. In Celtoi society only.

'My father had misjudged the Romani in several ways. They're not open to the sense of the Divine, as we are. The Goddess was all around them, a powerful feminine force, but all the Romani knew about it was their own arousal. Here before them was a man seemingly teasing them by thrusting his woman before them. Didn't he know that Romani soldiers were not allowed to marry?

'All thought of gold seemed to vanish then as the centurion himself was overcome by his desire. Romani men, as you know, madam – and it is for this part of the tale that I've prevented myself from ever mentioning my background before – Romani men don't have the same control over their urges as Celtoi do. We're not starved of physical love because there's no shame in any part of it. For the Romani there is. They did the unthinkable, perpetrated the unspeakable crime upon my mother.'

Boudicca clenched his hand tightly as he confirmed in words what his manner had already betrayed.

'My father was too shocked to respond, not appreciating what was going on and then unable to move because he was pinned to the ground. They all took their turn with Annis – the centurion made sure of it, not wanting, I presume, to be the only one to be tainted with such a crime.'

Boudicca felt sickened by his story, reliving again what she had seen done to her own daughters.

'But they hadn't stopped my father's mouth. Silently he spoke the Spell to release the barriers between worlds, so easy to do in such a place where the boundaries were already veil thin. He felt the shift in consciousness; the Romani did not.

'When the Romani had finished and had straightened out their cloth skirts and smartened their armour, they turned and ran, like the cowards they were, into the trees. My mother lay breathing heavily, battered and confused, and wondering why her husband didn't rush to comfort her, but my father delayed casting a Healing upon her. Listening first for his revenge, he heard the Romani charge into the Grove of oak trees, penetrating deeper into the layers of worlds between worlds until their footfalls and shouts faded to nothing. They were lost, he knew, for eternity, and no benign spirit would ever offer guidance to their wandering.'

Boudicca could not help but smile a little at the thought of such rapid and apt revenge, but then Lovernios reminded her of where his father had been less attentive.

'My father should have cared to my mother first, but he delayed too long. Whilst he paused, savouring his triumph, she'd pulled herself up and instantly understood what had happened. She noticed my father, too absorbed in his own emotions to come to her, and my mother panicked then and dashed into the trees, too quick for my father to close the portals. She was gone, tearing through the trees, running blind through the forests.'

Boudicca was close to tears now with the sheer tragedy of what Lovernios' poor mother had been through. She desperately wanted to hug and comfort Lovernios, but she held back, sensing that he still had more to tell.

'Cathbad followed her for days – even whole turns of the moon – wandering aimlessly, looking for his lost wife. He continued to grieve, whilst he searched, for the death of his stillborn child; although one, me, still remained, separated from him only by distance. He had plenty of opportunities to think on his mistakes and to consider whether his wife's sudden grief might not have panicked her into headlong flight had she been allowed to mourn her stillborn child. Or, indeed, had it been the half-forgotten memories of two babes birthed which had pushed her into madness? He formulated, too, his present Teachings on the Romani, apparently flitting at first from abject hatred to complete indifference. He concluded, as I've told you, that the Romani should not be fought, but pitied and brought to the fullest awareness of Celtoi spirituality as is possible only by sharing our holy places with them. Too many others had tried to defeat them with physical strength and most of them were dead, my father reasoned, whereas he had submitted to the Romani and was alive, having defeated them in his own way.'

Boudicca shook her head. 'He's wrong,' she whispered. 'He must be wrong. Did neither of you ever see Annis again, then?'

'Yes, he saw her again; he still sees her in fact, once or twice a year, always fleetingly through the trees, sipping from a pool of water or scavenging for food. Raven and crow call always precede her appearance, and over the years he's noticed she's transformed into a savage hag with long nails and blue skin. He still returns, year after year, hoping the boundaries will be at their thinnest between our world and hers if he returns during the same season he lost her. He hopes he might transport her back to be his wife once more.'

'Have you ever seen her? What about any one else?'

'Oh, he's certainly not the only one to have seen her. The local folk call her Black Annis. They blame her teeth and nails whenever one of their lambs goes missing and tell stories to frighten their children of her blood soaked cave lined with the skins of babes who stay out playing too late.'

'But it's not true, is it? Just stories to frighten little ones, surely.'

Lovernios shrugged. 'That's what they say.'

'So your father has changed Druidic policy as a result of this, as a result of his 'feelings'?' Boudicca was incredulous.

Lovernios nodded in agreement. 'It was my father who issued the guidance that Celtoi gold should not go to the Romani, though, seeking to preserve at least some of the Druidic power. When I came into my own Skills and realised I wanted to train to be a Druid, I began to feel most strongly that these Romani should be ejected from our lands, forcibly if necessary. The younger members of the community felt the same. It was a while before I came to understand that the same man who argued most forcibly against my ideas was also my father. I managed to unravel this story bit by bit to help me comprehend not just what he believes, but why.'

'Which is?'

'He believes the Goddess will prevail above all. I agree with him. She will, but in what form? Would their religion be identifiable as that of the Celtoi? I believe our worship should continue as it is, as it has been pleasing to the Divine for so many generations. Our ways are sacred, our places holy. We shouldn't risk losing our accumulated wisdom of the ages, because it might never be regained. We can't entrust our faith to the unfeeling and grasping Romani, not when its very essence is being eroded. The Romani have already destroyed the western and the eastern ends of the golden trade route. Without them the sacred web at the centre is like an amputated limb which will wither and die without a life force to pulse through it. We must fight.'

Lovernios sighed, pausing for breath after his outburst. 'But although Cathbad advocates these things as if he were the most learned elder, I always have to remind myself that when he lost contact with my mother, he also lost contact with that part of himself which was Divine. The two Manifestations are inextricably entwined, so when he preaches, no matter how wise his words may sound, I have to ask whether they derive from him or from the One.'

Boudicca was lost in her thoughts for a moment while she assimilated this new information.

'Boudicca, you're so quiet, have I upset you?'

'No, Lovernios mine. I'm just thinking on what you've just told me. I need to sleep now. Can we talk in the morning?'

Lovernios smiled gently and closed his eyes. Soon he was snoring gently; he must've been exhausted, thought Boudicca. Boudicca held him to her, shifting his weight a little so he was more comfortable against her. His words had awakened half-forgotten memories, and her conscious mind was working hard to grasp the tendrils of ideas and thoughts that his story had evoked. She let them drift away, giving in to the sleep which was insisting upon sweeping over her. She dreamed, strangely enough, of Maeve walking in a meadow full of flowers. When she looked down at Maeve's feet she realised the flowers sprang from wherever Maeve stepped.

Chapter 11

Disseminating Moon

Boudicca went to Grania at dawn. Her daughter was still weak from the loss of blood but had started to regain some of her usual colour. Maeve was with her, as silent and non-intrusive as ever, but nevertheless, just to see her two daughters together gladdened Boudicca's heart.

'How are you feeling, Grania mine?' Boudicca asked, settling herself gently on the edge of the makeshift bed. She took Grania's hand and rubbed it between her own, more for something to do than Grania's need for warmth.

'Much better now, mama.'

'You missed the celebrations last night.'

Grania smiled secretly. 'I know. I'm sorry, mama. Did everything go all right without me?'

'Yes.' Boudicca glanced at Maeve so she'd know she was included in the conversation too. 'Everything went fine. Surely you heard the noise?'

Grania nodded. 'I knew you wouldn't need us, mama.'

'I wish I'd shared your confidence! Now, what've the Healers said? How long before you can start to take Romani heads again?'

'I'll be up in a day or two.'

'What did the Healers say?'

'*I* said, I'll be up in a day or two, mama.'

Boudicca didn't push the point. 'Just as long as you're sure you'll be all right. You're likely to feel quite fragile after a miscarriage. It's nothing to be ashamed of.'

Suddenly, Boudicca went quiet as if she was trying to stop herself or had been caught in shock. For a moment she seemed as if she were a vast distance away, then she collapsed with unbidden tears streaming down her face. Great racking sobs poured from her as if they would never end. 'Oh, my little Grania, my little girl. How I wish you'd never had to live through the pain of this.' Gingerly, Boudicca reached out to her daughter, groping for comfort, yet careful not to apply any pressure upon Grania's sore body.

As they held each other, Grania too started to cry, a quiet sobbing to acknowledge the start of her own grief. Then Boudicca felt other arms around her and she twisted her neck to see that Maeve had also come over to offer her support. 'We haven't been together like this for quarters, my daughters. If only it could be in better circumstances.'

The three women clung together, alone, for a while. Boudicca couldn't remember who withdrew first, only that none of them did until the first flood of their tears had dried. They sat, no longer embracing, but still close. Boudicca still sniffled.

'I'm sorry, mama.' Grania broke the silence. 'I didn't want you to know, didn't want you to remember the babe you lost.'

Boudicca gave a brief snort of a laugh. 'Was that when we three were last together?'

Grania nodded, so did Maeve. 'You wouldn't tell father. You didn't want to worry him.'

'He was too weak. I was scared the news might quicken his illness. He wanted a son so much.' Boudicca sat shaking her head, fresh memories returning quickly, loosened by the previous night's conversation. She was surprised at how much she had refused to acknowledge those particular memories; she'd even convinced herself she'd forgotten until this brought it all back. She mopped at her eyes. They were perpetually damp these days and were starting to puff painfully.

'But you still needed someone to grieve with, remember? You chose us, when it should have been the father, your husband.'

'Is that why you're grieving with us now, Grania? Because the father of your child isn't with you?' Boudicca clamped her hands over her mouth. 'I'm sorry, I didn't realise. It wasn't from the…?'

'No, it wasn't. I was already with child when the Romani came to our settlement. This child was nothing to do with them. The father was Rochad. He died without knowing.'

'Why didn't you tell him?'

Grania's eyes narrowed to slits. Then she looked straight through Boudicca to stare at Maeve. Maeve was still impassive, ever serene. Grania dropped her malicious glare. 'Because of Maeve,' she admitted, then stilled Boudicca with a touch to her arm. 'It's all right, mama. We've sorted it through and come to an understanding.'

'You've talked to her? Grania, did Maeve speak to you? Maeve, can you speak?'

Grania stilled her again. 'Not in the way you're thinking, mama. We're twins, it's a different form of communication.'

'Have you always been able to do this?'

Grania nodded her head sullenly.

'All the while? Even when Maeve was in abject shock and responding to nothing or no one?'

Another sullen nod.

'Why didn't you tell me? Why didn't you talk to her?'

'Because I didn't want to, mama, and I didn't want you to make me do it!' Grania snapped back. Boudicca recoiled from her daughter's outburst, sitting back quickly to place some physical space between them.

'Not even with all the help I needed? Could you not have overcome your feelings for me?' Nothing. No response from either daughter. 'What happened between you to separate you like this? Was it something I was supposed to notice, something I missed because I was too wrapped up in mourning for your father?'

'I've told you, mama, we've come to an understanding between us.'

'Oh no you don't. This has gone too far. You're not just any two girls, you know, you're Iceni princesses. How can we keep the tribes united when two of the rebellion's most prominent figures are divided? Out with it.'

Grania sulked, refusing to look at either Boudicca or Maeve.

'Grania mine, I know your moods too well. You're jealous!' Grania inhaled sharply. 'I knew it.' Boudicca sat back triumphantly. 'Come on. Tell me. Then we can have it all sorted out once and for all.'

'There are still some things I need to check with your Lovernios first before I'll go back to how it was.'

'Grania.' Boudicca used her no-nonsense tone. She felt her torc flare with energy. She willed it down again; she didn't want to use Andraste's power in this domestic situation, no matter how exasperated she might be feeling.

'Rochad lost interest in me because of her,' Grania mumbled. 'That is why we've been like this. But she's just told me she wasn't interested in him because she hasn't even started her menses yet.'

Boudicca thought for a moment. She was obviously only going to get one side of this story and that was going to be blatantly biased. She had to be careful how she was going to interpret the things she was about to learn.

'So why should this affect your love for each other?'

'Don't you see? If it weren't for the Romani, she'd still be maiden. Rochad never loved her, not in the same way he loved me.'

'I see.' If only all human love was so simplistic, thought Boudicca. Grania had so much to learn. Such revelations reminded Boudicca how very young the twins really were. 'And what do you need to check with Lovernios?'

'She said,' Grania gestured at Maeve in her accusation, 'that Rochad didn't want to be a warrior but had chosen to train as a Druid. He came to her out of interest, not out of passion. The Keeper, who arrived the night of Rochad's death, was apparently coming not only to take the gold but also to interview Rochad and accept him for training if he was suitable.'

'Isn't it enough just to accept your sister's word she didn't encourage your lover, that she only responded to his spiritual interest? Surely he wasn't worth this carving up of affection between yourself and your own twin?'

Grania fidgeted nervously. 'I was desperate, mama. I thought I was losing him.'

'Occasionally, if you love someone, you have to let them go.'

'Just like you did when you miscarried? Or when father died?'

Grania's words stung. Somehow Boudicca ignored the rebuke and let the words wash over her. She swallowed, shocked at how much Grania had hurt her, and how much she'd obviously hurt Grania in the past for her daughter to lash out so vehemently now. 'I'll go and get Lovernios,' she whispered, and hurried to fetch him.

Lovernios was not far away; gathered with the Healers just outside the temporary shelter, discussing Grania's condition. He looked pale and sombre, as if he'd been deeply affected by the miscarriage. Boudicca too, felt shaky. She thought they must look a fine pair together, wobbly on their feet and with faces as white as spring clouds.

As she approached, he withdrew from the huddle of fellow Druids and joined her. 'Madam, you look like I feel.'

'That bad?' They smiled lover's smiles, not quite able to muster laughter. 'I need you to talk to Grania. She needs some confirmation concerning your first visit to our royal enclosure.'

'What about it, madam?'

'No, I can't tell you. She needs to hear it straight from you, without any hint I may have primed you with the right answers. If she isn't striving to listen even now as we talk, she'll definitely ask me whether I told you what to say when she's finished interrogating you. She's remarkably defensive at the moment; I'll have to be able to answer her with an honest face.'

They clasped hands for companionship and Lovernios pulled Boudicca to him for a quick kiss. 'I have some more information for you, madam. I don't think it's urgent yet, but you do need to know.'

'And I have some for you, too. Let it all wait then,' and they ducked under the loosely strung awning. Their eyesight adjusted to the gloom fast enough for them to catch Grania shifting back to a sitting position, having been straining to the sound of their voices. Her eyes darted to both their faces, trying to discern whether they'd been talking about her.

Lovernios stood before the bed in the customary servant-pose used by Druids to convey their presence was at the Chief's pleasure. The unexpected courtesy was not lost on Grania who visibly relaxed, although not enough to gesture to Lovernios to do the same. It was obvious to Boudicca that Grania did not have enough confidence in this situation to share her power.

'What do you require of me, madam?'

Grania smiled like a contented cat at the use of the formal title, carefully choosing how long she'd take to answer Lovernios. After all, the Druid was there purely at her bidding. Boudicca wondered whether Grania realised how privileged she was. She tried to hide her escaping smile, doubting whether Grania would be able to keep up this patronising pretence so well, especially if she was made aware of just how much rank and influence Lovernios carried. She admired both of them intensely then: Lovernios for his tact in dealing with this temperamental young woman, and Grania for the status she continuously strove for and often got.

Eventually Grania deigned to speak. 'Tell me why you originally came to our royal settlement,' she demanded, as imperiously as she could manage.

'Madam, I came mainly as the appointed Keeper to collect the gold sent by Druidic trade to the Iceni, where it is stored at the royal enclosure. Your mother hid it, by means of a secret Glamour, in the main hut and I duly took it from there onto the coast, where it was passed to the Ferryman for custody.

'Madam, forgive me if I try to teach you what you already know, but your settlement has been a station on the gold's trade route for many generations. Your tribe receives a generous commission for its part in this trade, enabling your peoples to make gold sacrifice rather than blood sacrifice. The visit of a Keeper on each of the four quarter-feasts should be familiar, although it was only my first visit to your settlement myself. It was actually my first assignment as Keeper, entrusted to me as I was in your area. I trust my appointment was not displeasing.'

'You said 'mainly'. Why else did you come?'

'The Druidic Council at Vernemetum had received a message from a young Iceni noble in fosterage to your Gerbfine, requesting training as a Druid. The mere fact that such a plea had been received by us, by our own methods of communication, suggested the young man in question had considerable Talents. We were led to understand he'd been receiving some rudimentary training to hone his Skills whilst under the guise of learning warfare and the way of the warrior.

'It was deemed most practical to interview the young man one to one, with a view to immediately admitting him to our way of life if he was found suitable. Someone fully trained, with a full range of Druidic Skills, was considered to be the most suitable judge of our supplicant. In order to ensure efficient use of resources, it was decided to send someone of at least Keeper rank to complete both tasks at once.'

'Did he tell you his name?'

'He called himself Rochad, or the prince of Gariannum, madam; his family were from the easternmost coast of Iceni territory.'

'What about his teacher? Did he tell you her name? Are you certain it was he who Sent to you, not someone else on his behalf?'

'He didn't mention any names other than his own, madam, and we're as sure as we can be that the message was directly from him. There's an unmistakeable Mark which gets associated with each Sending, it makes each Sender somehow unique. Do you have some reason to believe his teacher was female?'

Grania reddened. Lovernios' quickness and his round-about method of conveying his own considerable status had registered with her. Boudicca could see her daughter was starting to lose her nerve; she sincerely hoped Lovernios would choose to be sensitive to her

'Mama will tell you, won't you, mama?' There it was, a plea for assistance, a hint of feeling out of her depth. 'What happened then?'

'Sadly, madam, when I arrived at your settlement I found it to have been the subject of Romani destruction. I'm sure you would not have me repeat descriptions of what I saw. Those memories are still too raw for all of us here.

'Although I was fortunate in being able to retrieve the gold, thanks to your Queen's proficiency in Warding, I was too late to speak to Rochad. He'd already been killed by the Romani. I gleaned the details from those who saw what had happened, the feelings of the place where he died and the condition of his corpse. He was a brave man who died for his tribe. He may have passed into the Summerlands too soon to have been accepted as a Druid, but there is no doubt in my mind as to his prowess as a true warrior.'

Lovernios stood, still in the servant-pose, awaiting Grania's next request. It never came, only masses of tears and cries where words had been expected. Boudicca rushed to comfort her daughter again. As she swept past Lovernios she hissed, 'Go now, wait outside for me; don't go far.' Lovernios winked slyly before doing as she ordered and left the three women alone.

Only when he'd gone would Grania speak through her tears. There was resentment here, Boudicca knew, but at what? Jealousy for a mother's love transferred, or for a father too soon replaced? Or was it simply the fact of Lovernios' maleness still prejudicing Grania's confused feelings? It would be a long while, she realised, before her daughter would accept Lovernios in the same way the rest of the tribes-folk had. And what of Maeve? What did her other daughter think of Lovernios? There was no animosity emanating from her, certainly, but neither was there any encouragement.

Grania's grief was louder than it really needed to be, but Boudicca let her vent it all. Hopefully those tribes-folk remaining in Camulodunum, and there were still considerable numbers who hadn't yet ridden out to destroy the surrounding settlements and forts, would be too busy with the final dismantling of the Colonia to notice this more human noise.

'He should've been a father. His children would've been wonderful like him, tremendous warriors, and I'd have been Blessed to carry his child.' Grania wailed.

'Hush now, daughter mine,' Boudicca tried to soothe her. 'Think how hard it'd be to fight with your belly all swollen and distended. Why, you wouldn't even be able to get close enough to take all the heads you deserved and then your name wouldn't be sung by the Bards in the lengthy ballads being composed to commemorate our rebellion.'

Boudicca was trying to reassure Grania that all was not lost. But she knew it would feel to her daughter as if it all had been. After all, she could remember the feelings quite keenly herself.

'Why do the Romani matrons have babies so easily? I've seen so many of their bloated stomachs around even the Colonia. It's not fair, mama. Why should those brood cattle be so fertile when even my own body rejects the child I'd already come to love?'

'Grania, Grania, there'll be other men and other babes. All as handsome and all as lovely and all as different as each other. You'll just have to trust your mama on these things, believe me, I promise.' Boudicca was trying not to be too patronising, aware of how Grania would respond. 'I know it seems like the skies have fallen and the seas have risen and the earth has cracked, but first love always feels so painful when it ends. Your circumstances are far, far worse than anything I've known anyone else endure, I know, but you're beautiful, Grania. Rochad won't be the last lover, nor will this be the last baby.'

'But it's still not fair, nor right, and I hate them for it!'

'I know, Grania, I know.'

It wasn't fair. Boudicca knew that as much as any woman. She remembered acutely every twisting ache of losing a baby, when your body yet screamed that the child was still there, and other women seemed to flaunt their fertility. How you'd look in every cradle and at every sucking babe. Or respond to every cry in the night and listen as some other woman answered the call first. Then desperately seeking some form of comfort, how you might fondle the things you'd readied for your unborn child only to finger them empty and unused, not even tainted with the ghost of a gurgle.

'We should make them pay.'

'What? How?'

'We should punish the Romani women for taunting us.'

'What? Who?'

'Us, mama, you and I. We've both lost babes, we both feel identical pain, and yet the Romani women still show off their lazy pregnancies. How dare they! We should make them suffer for their audacity.'

159

Boudicca felt her torc start to glow, and begin to burn. Grania's words had a certain appeal to them. 'And how should we do these things?'

'The Goddess needs sacrifice, you heard Lovernios say so himself. The gold routes have dried up because of the Romani destroying them and the Druids who operate them, so what shall we sacrifice now? There's no choice, is there, mama? If there's no gold then we must feed the Goddess with blood. You know that's so, it's always been so.'

Boudicca listened carefully. In a strange, foreboding way, Grania's words seemed to make a ridiculous sense, as if they'd all been spoken before, over and over down through the ages, like distant echoes.

'You must feel it yourself, mama, growing stronger every day since the rebellion first started: a desperate, urgent need to slay and ravage. It's the Goddess, mama. Even I feel Her, so She must be insistent. There's no more gold to appease Her, therefore, it's proper now to open the Groves and let them flow with blood once more as they did in the days of our ancestors. I say we should pick out blossoming Romani matrons for Andraste's special offerings, just like the one you sacrificed with the gold Claudius head. What do you think?'

'Hmm, it does have a certain appeal, little one.'

The voice shocked Boudicca into alertness. She'd been as if in a trance, thinking carefully over Grania's ideas and how appealing they felt to a secret dark part of herself. An aspect of herself which she preferred to keep hidden but which still kept bubbling up to the surface of her psyche. Now it seemed she'd spoken directly from that dark well of a place, although she couldn't be absolutely certain from whence the voice had originated, only to agree involuntarily with her daughter's gruesome plans. Yet, if she acknowledged all her feelings and was true to herself, she had to admit she really would like to vent her rage in such horrendous ways. In worse ways too, if only she could invent them.

Before her a movement suddenly caught her eye. A shadow dance upon the material of the awning, a twitching hare flicking its ears at her. Boudicca gasped at the clever creation, wondering who was casting it. Instinctively she looked down to Maeve's hands, moving and gliding into set patterns.

'That's amazing Maeve, where did you learn to do it?'

But Maeve just smiled an idiot's grin and continued with the shadow play.

Boudicca shook her head to clear the madness she felt she was sinking into. She turned back to Grania. 'I'll speak with Lovernios. It does seem you'll be all right to be moved soon, after all.' Boudicca stuttered the words, unable to concentrate upon what she was really saying, and rushed out. Both her daughters had disturbed her far more than she liked to admit. Grania for what she was turning into and Maeve for her lack of involvement in anything Boudicca considered important. It wasn't until a long while later that Boudicca started to question how Maeve had managed to create shadow creatures from inside the shelter when the source of light was outside.

Lovernios had done as she'd asked and stayed outside, out of earshot yet within close reach. She rushed to him and clasped him in a tight hug; the public announcement of their relationship allowed at least a few advantages.

'I don't feel much like eating, but I suppose I ought to. Let's find some left over scraps and a place to sit and share our food.'

'Better make it a prominent position then, madam. You're going to need to grant quite a few audiences. Why not make them informal?'

'Has so much really happened in such a short while?'

'This many people generate a lot of news.'

There were no longer any shops or stores left intact, but a more than cursory search could still find the odd amphorae or smoked ham. They pilfered what little they needed and sat on a pile of loose rubble which gave them enough of an advantage to watch the last vestiges of wanton demolition. It was amazing to think that such a model town, admirable despite all it stood for, could be reduced to so little so fast. One of the rules of life, contemplated Boudicca, was that it was easier to destroy than create.

'Did I say the right things to Grania, then?'

'Oh yes, the correct information and the proper way of saying it. I honestly don't know how you managed to stay so diplomatic. I wouldn't have been half as polite.'

'It was easy, madam. I just imagined she was you. It didn't require such a great leap of creativity.'

'I shall take that as a compliment, Lovernios!'

'Up to you!'

'I'm glad to see you've cheered up since this morning, Lovernios. I thought, perhaps, when I first brought you in to see Grania, that you'd had some bad news. You looked dreadfully pale.'

'No, not bad news, just Grania's miscarriage affecting me worse than I thought it would.'

'Me too.'

'I know, madam. But inevitably my brother's death has certain repercussions. A healthy babe can't birth from a womb from which his companion doesn't emerge alive, without also being tainted with death. What Grania's going through has just reminded me of my own insecurities.'

Boudicca took a bite of food and a generous swig of wine, provoking an uneasy silence. 'Tell me to stop if I upset you,' her words broke the awkwardness. 'But have you seen your father at all since you were sent home to your mother's family?'

'No. I don't want to either.'

'Oh.' She paused and made another conversation attempt. 'Do you still feel your mother's presence at all any more? You hinted before there was some form of link between you and her but that it ended suddenly when the Young God came into your life.'

'No, I don't. I did, but not now. The link I have with you, now that Andraste's residing in you, is so very similar to how it was with my mother. Anyway, I don't miss it any more. That's how come I know why Grania's miscarriage is upsetting you so much. Why didn't you tell me yourself?'

'I was trying to change the subject just then.'

'I know, madam.'

'If you know everything, why do we even bother talking?' She spat the words at him and took another bite of food; she couldn't even taste it, her mouth was so dry. 'I'm sorry,' she relented. 'I thought I'd dealt with the loss of my child, but I obviously haven't. Like losing my husband, the wounds are still too fresh and too deep. Your love's like a soothing salve but I'm still not whole yet and I'm sick of crying.'

'The Trinovantes are staying with the rebellion.'

'Now *you're* trying to change the subject.'

'Not really, madam.'

'How so?'

'I thought you'd like the good news before the bad, and from me rather than from Addedomarus.'

'Why…? Oh, that's why.' Addedomarus was approaching, crossing the Temple precinct with a purposeful stride, a troop of champions from the Trinovantes with him. They were laughing and joking, slapping each other's backs in seeming self-congratulation. 'I take it this is the first of the audiences I'm meant to give?'

Lovernios nodded. Addedomarus reached the foot of the rubble and hailed them. Boudicca stood gingerly, some of the larger stones settling beneath her weight, and saluted him in return. The Trinovantes might be a conquered tribe but they had conducted themselves bravely during the sacking of Camulodunum. Even Boudicca would admit that the Iceni would have had a harder fight on their hands if the two tribes had not united.

'Invite him to join us here and share our food,' she ordered Lovernios.

He did so. The Trinovantes' language was close to that of the Iceni – most of the vocabulary was common but the inflections and rhythm were not. Boudicca and Addedomarus could understand each other well enough in a halting manner, and asking Lovernios to translate was meant as a courtesy.

Addedomarus playfully ordered his elite warriors to go back to their plunder, indicating he would talk to Boudicca and her new consort alone. He started to climb the rubble carefully, putting out his arms for exaggerated balance and laughing as he almost lost his footing. He seemed in good spirits, almost as if he were lighter than before, or possibly rather drunk. 'Tell him I'm glad to see he's full of the joys of the season.'

Lovernios did so and Addedomarus grinned a huge face-splitting grin and made the final few bounds to the top of the rubble. Small pebbles trickled down to the ground in his wake. Boudicca grasped his hand in salute, indicating he should sit. She resumed her place only when Addedomarus had also sat down. She passed him some food as if serving him and waited for Lovernios to start translating.

'My peoples,' Lovernios relayed, 'have nearly finished with the Temple and the destruction of the Colonia. As you can see, there's little left of their fine buildings. This sight is what really brings joy to me, not the season. This all means so much, I thought I'd never see it happen. We'd started to assume the Romani would be our masters forever. Soon we Trinovantes will leave the horde to raid all around. We know where some of their villas are and we've some debts still to be settled.'

'Will you see Londinium destroyed, and beyond Londinium, all the legions in Britannia?'

'We will. Your words in the rituals struck a chord with us. Some of us, our lesser tribes-folk, you understand, not our nobles, had planned to return to their homes. Not because they're cowards or fear death, but because the call to this revolt came so quickly they didn't get an opportunity to plant their crops. Unless they get their seed corn sown, there'll be no harvest this year. Lugnasadh will be sparse and we'll starve come winter. This is something which concerns the farmers and peasants more than us, but it should concern us too, even the best venison bores if it's eaten for every meal.'

'I hadn't meant to cause offence by accusation, Addedomarus. It was the Goddess who spoke through me during the Eostar rituals and I'm certain Her words were meant for all who could hear them. There'll be other farmers in every other tribe gathered here who, no doubt, have the same worries. Her words were not intended to single out the Trinovantes, even though this hated Colonia, your primary motive for joining with us, has now been obliterated. Rest assured, We never doubted your loyalty.

'As for the crops,' she continued, reassuring him point by point, 'There're rich stores of grain all around Britannia, without the demanding Romani mouths to feed there'll be plenty for all Celtoi to share. There are our own small granaries, plus, in the clay soil of the south, they store seed in deep pits in the ground and that'll be ours too. The Romani have their own stores and there'll be ships still ready to sail in the harbour at Londinium, perhaps only half loaded. No doubt there'll also be plenty to claim in the client lands of the Regni, south of Londinium, and the Brigantes, north of the Cornovii, not forgetting the Romani sympathisers amongst the Catuvellauni.

'All these sources may only amount to residues, but put them together and all the women in the land won't be able to bake all the bread it'll make. As for Sucellus, we'd better not tell him or else he'll start dreaming of all the multiple ovens he'll design to cope with all the dough!'

Addedomarus laughed. 'These are the same reassurances I've given my own people, Boudicca,' he replied. 'And although they're important and you've repeated my own thoughts, there's another reason why my peoples are staying: our revenge isn't complete yet. We would destroy the Catuvellauni as well as the Romani. They've been our tribal enemies for so many generations, we can no longer remember when it all started. They've been rivals with the Iceni too; I'm sure I won't have to remind you how bitter some of the raiding and fighting was. If it weren't for Trinovantes' lands shielding Iceni lands from Catuvellauni encroachment, it might be you now, Boudicca, asking me to join you in destroying them.

'First they took our land and then they gave it to the Romani, now they live in peace with the Romani, they intermarry and share their lives, mixing Celtoi and Romani culture together in an unnatural blend where the Celtoi elements are subsumed and altered and the Romani elements glorified. If we destroy the Romani without destroying the Catuvellauni, then the Trinovantes will never be free of oppression. My peoples aren't against raiding, we're not unwarlike, we're as fierce as any other tribe and aren't asking for permanent protection. Our tribe's too proud for that! But these Catuvellauni don't merely attack and steal, they stay and they conquer. When the Trinovantes are gone, fallen to be their slaves, our lands trampled and no longer an effective bulwark against invasion, then they'll come for the Iceni.' He nodded. 'Yes, they will, exactly as the Romani did before them.'

'What do you suggest? The Goddess has already directed our path to Londinium; it would be foolhardy not to follow Andraste's guidance.'

'I'm not suggesting any deviation from the inspiration you've channelled from Andraste. Without the Goddess we're nothing. But there's been no guidance beyond Londinium, am I right?'

'Not yet, no.' Boudicca was cautious, turning to Lovernios for his help.

He coughed. 'If I might interrupt?' He spoke rapidly, translating for both leaders. 'It's as if we cross a stream at night. We put a tentative foot out for the next stepping-stone, never certain one will be there, but it always is, just where we need it. The Goddess always provides, but occasionally we must trust and take a step without being absolutely sure She will find us the foothold. If Addedomarus' suggestion doesn't meet with Andraste's approval, we must trust She will show us where our feet have left the path.'

Both leaders thought about Lovernios' teaching and its relevance for their lives. It was an analogy they'd both heard before, but for Boudicca it spoke to her in a new way. 'What would you have us do, Addedomarus?'

'My peoples, the Trinovantes, will raid north, in the days before we gather at Londinium.' He held up a hand to calm her. 'We'll be there for you at new moon, as directed, but in the days between we'll attack the Catuvellauni settlements between here and Londinium and slightly to the north of the route the wagons and camp followers will take. This, we suspect, will scatter any refugees back to their capital city at Verulamium which lies directly west of this Colonia, or northwest of Londinium. If Andraste wills it, when we leave Londinium we'll head towards Verulamium and attack their tribal capital itself.'

'You've put a lot of thought into this, Addedomarus, and I like your ideas. However, we must allow the Goddess an opportunity to add Her endorsement, or otherwise. May I contact you as soon as I've done so? There's nothing here that's personally unacceptable to me, but we'll all feel more confident when we know we're acting out Her will.'

Lovernios nodded his approval to her quite emphatically even as he translated for her. Addedomarus and Boudicca exchanged formal farewells, as did Lovernios, who added, 'If you see Sucellus, would you ask him to join us?'

Then, as soon as Addedomarus had run back to his comrades, he explained to Boudicca: 'Such a plan would put us in an ideal position for meeting the Romani troops as they march down to Londinium from Insula Mona by Watling Street for a final battle. I think Andraste will agree.'

'What was the bad news?'

'Madam?'

'The bad news? You said there was some good news and some bad to tell me. Addedomarus' was good news, at least I presume so, although if you're going to better it I shan't complain.'

Lovernios took a deep breath and gave her a nervous look. 'I received news that Catus Decianus has fled Londinium.'

'Where to?'

'He took ship back to Gaul.'

'How long ago?'

'A few days.'

Boudicca snorted. 'Sorry,' she apologised. 'It's not funny. I just thought "If only we could have kept this quiet and crept up on him", and then I realised how ridiculous that was. We couldn't keep this quiet, we're not a stealthy raiding party, we're a massed horde, and it was obvious he'd bolt as soon as he heard. Even someone as wrapped up in his own greed and selfishness as him would've been able to work out I'd be coming for him. I hope his boat sinks with him on it, shame it's too late for me to even Cast a sea-storm upon him; I so wanted revenge.'

'You can still have it, madam. Don't let being denied his blood spoil your taste for destroying the Romani.'

'Spoil? Oh no, Lovernios mine, it hasn't spoilt it, not by any means. It's made me more determined to ensure that every Romani who dies knows it's at least partly because of Catus' avarice and cruelty. There'll be a lot of Romani throughout their Empire who'll learn he was responsible for awakening the Hag within me. They'll die wondering whether perhaps the deaths I bring might have been more merciful, or less tortuous, if he'd not been one of the contributors to the causes of this uprising. They'll know, I'll make sure of that, and then they'll be certain to punish him for the additional shame he's brought upon the Romani, even if I can't.'

'You've got something in mind, haven't you, madam?'

'Yes, I'll tell you after you've spoken to Sucellus; he's here already.' She waved down to the smith. 'What was it you wanted to speak to him about?'

'Something I was discussing with the Healers, but I didn't want to mention it without you being present. Addedomarus found him quickly.'

'Well met, Sucellus! Shall we come down or will you be able to manage?'

'Well met, Boudicca! I'll be fine, my leg can cope with worse than this gentle slope just so long as you two lovers have saved some wine for when I get up there.'

Boudicca swished the almost empty jug of wine around. 'There's a good glass left,' she called.

After much huffing and panting, Sucellus reached the top of the mound. Immediately he grasped the jug and downed it. 'That's a very poor glass,' he complained. 'What has Iceni hospitality come to?'

Taking mock affront, Boudicca answered him, 'I offered you all I had left, that is true generosity. Had you come as a guest to me at our royal residence I would have provided so much wine that even you would be unable to drink it all.'

'I'll keep you to your promise one day, Boudicca!'

'One day soon then Sucellus! I look forward to receiving your company. It's always cost the Iceni so little, I've heard, what with you never being able to hold your drink!'

Succellus chuckled, then turned on Lovernios. 'What did you want to see me so urgently about then? Hope it's important enough to justify me running across half of Camulodunum!' Sucellus smiled to excuse his cheekiness but his grin froze and dropped when he saw Lovernios' expression. 'Serious is it? 'Bout Maeve I expect.'

'The Healers are worried about her. How's she really faring? You've been with her a lot, she seems to like your company. Have you seen any improvement in her condition?'

'No, none, but she's all right, that one, so long as she gets enough water to wash with. Just healing slowly and more gently than others I could mention.'

'Grania's improving in her own way,' Boudicca responded protectively. 'You can actually see her heal a little more each day. She's doing things, getting on with life, taking her mind off what's happened. And she's started to communicate with Maeve again.' Both men swivelled to look at Boudicca. 'Well, don't look so surprised, I am their mother after all. They're twins, they have this sort of empathetic bond.'

'And?'

'And what? I don't know, you tell me, Lovernios, you're the one with... Sorry. I didn't mean to... but you've probably got more chance of appreciating their ability than me.'

'Has Grania come to any understanding of Maeve's condition?'

'I don't think she's bothered. All she wanted to know was what had happened about Rochad. As far as Grania's concerned, this ability fits in the same category as all the other Skills she refuses to practice. If she can use it for her own secret, personal use then fine, otherwise she doesn't want to know. She's suspicious of anything Other. You won't be able to force her either, so don't try. Forget Grania, she'll be fine. Maeve is the one I'm most worried about, and I say that as a mother and as the one who knows them both best. Haven't the Healers come across anything like this before?'

'There're a few similar cases like shock or a numb sleep which patients never awaken from, but Maeve is so different. She lets us lead her around, she'll eat and even dress herself now, but she's completely withdrawn from any attempts at sustained communication.'

'It's more than that. I don't think there's very much Maeve left there at all. I think she's almost all Maiden now; her Spirit suggests as much.'

Both men nodded. 'Quite a few of the Sensitives amongst us have also found that to be so,' Lovernios agreed.

'What do the Healers want to do?'

'They want to take her to Vernemetum and the Groves there. They say it's the only place in Britannia where she might find solace enough to improve.'

'I'll think about it. I am her mother, I have that right. I'll consider it along with Addedomarus' suggestions and allow Andraste to grant her approval or otherwise. Who knows, perhaps if we follow Addedomarus' ideas we might be able to accompany Maeve ourselves.

'Whilst you're here, Sucellus,' she continued before she could be interrupted. 'I've something to ask you, too. If I ask now it'll avoid any unnecessary 'running around' on your behalf. Have the horde made any gold sacrifices since we left your forge, or have any been made on our behalf?'

'No, Boudicca, your peoples made plentiful sacrifices before they left. In addition I've dropped the odd ring or bangle into the trickle of a stream by the main gate. The Goddess should be sated for a good while.'

'But She isn't, though, is She? She thirsts for more because Her appetite is greater now then you've ever known it to be before. Am I right?'

Haltingly, Sucellus agreed, uncertain of what Boudicca was trying to prove and unwilling to commit himself before he knew what she was driving at.

'I think Grania's right. In fact, I think we should've listened to her earlier. We'll open the Groves again and provide blood sacrifice to Andraste once more. I believe She desires the death of Romani women who are with child and I'll offer them to Her, cut open with this.'

Boudicca fumbled with her belt, reaching into her clothing, with the intention of brandishing Andraste's sickle with a staged flourish to finish her persuasion. She knew it was there, safely tucked amongst folds and ties, and she shifted around and fiddled to dislodge it. She pulled off a layer or two of clothing, checking each garment before discarding it. Then she noticed Sucellus and Lovernios watching her intently, both wearing worried expressions.

She stopped searching and looked away, ashamed and cross. 'It's gone,' she finally admitted in a voice of abject loss.

Chapter 12

Basalmic Moon

The horde that creaked out of the remains of Camulodunum was far more docile than the one that had swept in upon it. Although the numbers had swollen significantly, this mass of people were not warriors in the majority. Instead the travellers comprised the sick and injured, old and infirm, the very young, those women from tribes where only men were unaccustomed to fight, and a variety of other non-combatants such as those in charge of the supplies or those skilled at handling the draught animals.

Neither were the numbers constant. As the wagons rolled along the Romani roads, some Celtoi died of wounds or fever, and a few were even born. However, by far the largest proportion of those gathered together in the name of rebellion were away scouring the surrounding countryside, scouting further afield for news of the legions or combing the forests to protect these camp followers. Thus, a steady stream of warriors rode back in to see their families before turning their chariots around and charging back to their smaller fighting units in search of new Romani or pro-Romani settlements to put to the flame and destroy. And still more Celtoi came to join the rebellion, although Boudicca would never have thought Britannia's soil, despite being rich, would have been able to sustain even those that had already risen to revolt.

Then there were the Druids who came and went as they always had done, as mysterious and elusive as the breeze, bringing news and information and taking fresh messages with them. It was from them Boudicca learnt that the newest Celtoi to join them were from far to the north, where snow still lay upon the ground despite the lateness of season, from the furthest outlying reaches of the territories of the Cornovii and the Parisi. She was astounded at the distances some of those champions, together with their families, had journeyed to join them. She was grateful to them too, taking care to greet them personally or else send individual messages of welcome.

Boudicca sensed Lovernios was troubled at their arrival. When she questioned him she learned of his continuing concern at the apparent lack of support from the Dumnonii and the Durotiges. No members of either of those tribes had yet risen to join them. If distance hadn't been sufficient to dissuade these newest recruits, then the expected warriors from the south west of Britannia must be absent for some other reason. It was contemplating that reason which so obviously occupied Lovernios' thoughts.

Such a convoy moves piteously slowly. Wagon wheels will stick in runnels and potholes, skipping children will fall and graze themselves, imaginary foes might be sighted from between the trees, even the freshly dead need hurried graves. Boudicca had moved beyond frustration, fuelled by the stories she heard of warriors' fun, and was openly pushing the horde to speed up. Her nerves were at breaking point as she suffered the interminable domestic conversations drifting up in snatches from the column she led. She rocked violently backwards and forwards in pent up urgency, even as she steered her chariot grindingly onwards. She drummed her fingers upon the wickerwork sides and banged her hands against the reins.

Sucellus had insisted she swap ponies. Her usual pair, Cloud and Mouse, were tethered to some cripple's wagon or loaned at a price – she rather hoped it was the latter – to some noble who'd better be treating them well. The old creatures she'd been lumbered with instead were good only for dog meat and seemed to respond to orders a full day after they were given. They flicked their ears at her annoyance but responded no faster. Boudicca was too good a horsewoman to resort to whipping or goading them into greater speed; it wasn't their fault they'd obviously been raised purely to draw a death wagon.

In many ways this slow progress was necessary even for Boudicca, and her resignation to it was a result of her bending to her own standards.

Both Maeve and Grania rode with her. The chariot was cramped, but she had the security of knowing both her daughters were definitely with her. Grania was still in pain and very weak, it showed in her strained face – white with the loss of blood - and the way she winced with every jolt. Maeve was still impassive, stirring only when they passed a well which might offer a chance for her to bathe, and it was over her that Boudicca wished to keep especial watch.

Ever since Andraste's golden sickle had been discovered missing, Boudicca had been a knot of different tensions. Her stomach stewed upon itself, seeming to tie her intestines together. She felt sick and full of agitation, desperate to be up and doing something. Lovernios had reassured her, or at least had tried. 'It's not lost,' he'd comforted her. 'It's not the sort of thing that can be lost, it's just found another Keeper for a while. It'll come back, when it wants to. You'll see.' It hadn't worked. In fact, his words had made things worse. Boudicca was obsessed that the blade had been stolen, taken, found, borrowed, by someone, anyone, without asking, without checking with her: the rightful owner. She still felt it upon her, she felt the ache of its absence as piercing as the loss of a loved one, her whole being felt 'lacking' in something. She couldn't help but go over and over in her mind when she'd last seen it, whom she'd seen since and when she might have lost it. But she couldn't think straight and she still didn't like to accuse when everyone looked equally guilty.

'The Divine is like a lightning strike,' Lovernios had patiently tried to teach her in consolation and explanation. 'In a flat field of corn, the lightning will strike and hit the tallest object, whether that is a tree or a bush or even a standing person. For a while, you were the tallest thing in the field, Boudicca, and the Goddess struck you, reaching through you to the earth and the ground beneath your feet. Now, something else has grown up taller than you, yet the lightning storm still rages. Who will the Goddess conduct Herself through now?'

But Lovernios' explanation had only made Boudicca mad with jealousy and she'd cried a child's tears at being separated from something it wanted and wanted now. It had also made her suspect the one person she had until then believed blameless: Maeve. For who else was so obviously emanating the Divine? And what would Maeve want the holy sickle for? Boudicca's over-active mind had gone to task on that question too and provided an answer to chill any mother's heart. Maeve, Boudicca suspected, had found her own way to cope with the atrocities perpetuated upon her poor, virginal body and also serve the Goddess. The tiresome miles from Camulodunum, with only her fertile mind for company, had convinced Boudicca that Maeve meant to kill herself, and to do so soon.

Just as she believed any concerned mother would, Boudicca set herself the task of constantly watching her daughter, keeping alert for any violent movements or suicidal motions. She couldn't share her fears with anyone else for fear she might alert Maeve to her suspicions. For the same reason she couldn't bring herself to question Maeve about the disappearance of the sickle. Any sudden interrogation touching too close to sensitive issues might startle Maeve into action which might then prove to be all too disastrous. Boudicca couldn't risk losing Maeve too, not after all the other losses she'd endured so recently. So she stayed silent, watching, ever watching, growing more and more exhausted with the impossible standards she'd set herself and making herself solely responsible for her daughter's continued existence.

The journey then was not boring by any means, not with all the constant comings and goings, but for Boudicca, stuck leading the camp followers, it was agitating knowing there was more excitement to be had not very far away. All she wanted was to be free to loosen the reins and have the ponies respond, but she was constrained too by her guarding of Maeve.

They passed through settlement after settlement. Some were grand Romani villas with whole wings in the process of construction, some were little more than tiny huts with perhaps a piglet or a bleating goat. All were ruined in one way or another; some trampled in vengeance, others deserted by their inhabitants who had gone to join the rebellion, taking anything of any use with them in their hurry to leave.

They passed through Canonium after three days, and confirmed they were keeping to their loose schedule by meeting up with the bulk of their warriors waiting to check whether they should proceed. The more mobile combatants had scoured ahead of the baggage train as well as sweeping the land all around the proposed route. The tactic ensured their families and supplies were never surprised by a Romani ambush, and the entire force knew more or less where the rest of the horde would be on any given day. Of course, the information wouldn't be precise, but that was virtually impossible given the mobilisation of so many people.

The enthusiasm of these warriors was too much for Grania, who pleaded and begged and whined to be allowed to join them in roaming the countryside for Romani to slay. She didn't let up until Boudicca conceded she was probably much better and able to ride behind in a chariot. Boudicca allowed her to go on the condition that the driver was experienced and trustworthy; and she called him over and made him swear to choose level terrain and not bump her daughter around too much. Grania sulked openly at Boudicca's protectiveness. Better loss of face, Boudicca knew, than loss of blood that wouldn't stop flowing. But the parting embrace Grania volunteered made her motherly concern worthwhile.

On the approach to Caesaromagus, after five day's travelling overall, Grania returned to her mother's chariot, complaining she was exhausted but conceding that it was a good tiredness. Boudicca was pleased to see her back, especially when she noted the absence of Romani heads and concluded Grania had kept herself out of the fray and close combat. There'd be plenty of opportunity for heroics later.

Whilst Boudicca was welcoming back her daughter and enjoying the presence of both her girls, Lovernios disappeared. Not for long – perhaps half a day – but long enough for Boudicca to notice his absence while she supervised the overnight camp arrangements in the minimal shelter afforded by the remains of Caesaromagus. They hadn't spoken much during the journey. Lovernios had been too taken up with furtive whisperings with his Druids, who always approached him secretly first before even acknowledging Boudicca, and Boudicca had been absorbed in monitoring Maeve.

He kept her informed, of course, of the things the Druids had discovered about the Romani, often more detailed than the reports from the scouts, and especially of the legions' progress down Watling Street to Pennocrucium and Letocetum, the road which led directly to Londinium and perhaps to a final confrontation with the Celtoi. They'd rough estimates of the number of legionaries already gathered; it seemed the Romani were outnumbered ten to one by Celtoi. Easy odds, and Boudicca would have relaxed if not for Maeve.

Meanwhile, she knew that Lovernios was still bothered by the non-appearance of the tribes from the distant west of Britannia. He was also concerned by the proximity of the Romani legions to Vernemetum, which harboured his father and perhaps his mother, and its surrounding sacred sites. Was he absent now in order to find answers to those questions?

They'd travelled half of the distance to Londinium from Camulodunum now. In less than another quarter, the warrior elite would be able to surge ahead of this column of camp followers and still be safe in the knowledge their families and baggage would be close behind. When Lovernios finally returned, worn and haggard in the late dusk, she learned how those few days might be crucial.

'Madam, I have news.'

'Where've you been?'

'Into the forests, madam. I have news.'

'I was worried. I missed you. Grania is back.'

'Madam, I have news of great importance.'

'Go on, I'm listening.'

'Suetonius Paulinus has beaten us to Londinium, we were too quick to complacency.'

'He's the Romani Chief, yes? But how can he have got so far? Only the other day we received news his troops were still near the sacred sites by Vernemetum.'

'Only he and his cavalry came as far as Londinium, madam. His main force is indeed still near Vernemetum. We never imagined he'd have the audacity to split his force and ride a small unit right into the jaws of his foe. Such manoeuvres give him a valuable advantage in speed, even over our fleet chariots.'

'So, he's decided to make his stand in Londinium, then? Well, if we hurry we can destroy him and the town before his legionaries join him. Then we can pick them off leaderless at our leisure.'

'No. He hasn't made his stand at Londinium. The town is even more sprawling than Camulodunum, with perhaps less defences, if that is possible. What he's done is almost unbelievable and totally unlike the usual Romani tactics. I wouldn't trust the information when I first heard it, dismissing it as a ruse until I sought out the truth for myself. Then Addedomarus found some Romani refugees creeping around the forests, flushed out by Artio who sent them running into our arms. They corroborated the rumours for us, eventually, with their own eyewitness accounts. I think in hindsight they might have preferred to take their chances with a bear hug and a mauling from Artio herself.'

'Which was why you were away for so long?'

'Yes, I had to be certain before I brought you the news. I didn't want to alarm you unnecessarily.'

'Alarm me? Why?'

'Basically, Suetonius Paulinus rode ahead of his main force with all his cavalry. They could make very good speed without being hampered by their foot soldiers or their supply wagons. They reached Londinium a couple of days ago. According to the refugees, the inhabitants of Londinium have been living in dread since they heard about your sacking of Camulodunum. At first they hoped help might be at hand from the legion nine, which was sent against you, and then that the Governor, which is Suetonius' rank, would come with all the military force available to him in Britannia to be their saviour.

'You have to bear in mind that the inhabitants of Londinium are as different from those of Camulodunum as are the buildings in the two towns. Camulodunum was intended as a model Colonia, laid out identically to the imperial city of Rome itself. Its inhabitants were veteran legionaries plus their families. Londinium, however, is the Romani's trading base within Britannia. It's a loose collection of warehouses and hovels, wharfs by the Tamesis, the remains of a fortress and a few prestigious houses. Those who reside in Londinium are traders, wealth seekers, procurers and acquirers of valuables. They've very little allegiance to anyone except themselves and they acknowledge Rome only in the trade opportunities afforded to them as a result. Perhaps that's why Catus Decianus chose to build his presidential palace there? It'd make sense for such low morals to attract him to the place.'

'So they're different?' Boudicca shrugged. 'They're still Romani, they're still going to die.'

'Well, these citizens of Londinium aren't soldiers like those of Camulodunum. They've studied balance sheets not warfare. Faced with such threats as this rebellion they look not to themselves for their welfare but to the Governor himself. Who will dig the ditches to keep us out, who will provide the swords? Why, the highest-ranking Romani in the whole of Britannia, of course! For who else would protect them when Procurator Decianus, the second highest Romani in rank in Britannia, together with all his cronies, had just fled, leaving them leaderless like a flock without its herder. Rome would never let these traders down, not when their pioneering spirits had brought them to these furthest outposts of the Romani Empire, sacrificing

174

their own comfort in the name of Romani entrepreneurialism. And not when Rome will need the port if it's to bring in any more legions from the Empire to replace the ones we've already destroyed. And anyway, these good people paid their taxes towards the protection that is their right. Londinium is ideally placed. If any one knows the value of that, it will be its own inhabitants.'

'So what did the Governor do when he got there with his cavalry?'

'He ignored their pleas and returned to his foot soldiers.'

'Never! But…?'

'Imagine what a shock it was to the Romani in Londinium! Their expected protection had turned up to rescue them only to deem the town undefendable and turn tail and ride away leaving them to their lot.'

'What happened next?'

'As you'd expect, panic set in. Some of them, probably those with little to lose, took Suetonius' advice, vague though it was, and travelled south as quickly as they could to the Regni, there they'd be sure to find sanctuary with Cogidubnus who still keeps his client kingdom on the coast loyal to the Romani.'

'Still?'

'Yes, madam, still. Neither he nor the Brigantes have rushed to join us, you must've noticed that.'

'I have, but you'd have thought they would've done so once they saw what the Romani had done to the Iceni and how hollow Romani promises are. Cogidubnus is taking a dreadful gamble in keeping faith with our enemy; surely he must know what we'll do to him and his tribe when our victory over the legions is complete. It'll be a high price to pay for the luxurious villa I've heard he lounges around in. I think I'll enjoy calling to collect that particular gambling debt personally.'

'Well, anyway, the borders of the Regni lands are not far from the south bank of the Tamesis. It'll only take the refugees days to reach safety, especially if they travel light.'

'Didn't Suetonius offer to take any of the Londinium inhabitants with him?'

'Yes, but he knew your horde wasn't far away and he didn't have long to scamper back to the main bulk of his force before he'd be in very real danger of being cut off from them by skirmishes from your outlying scouts. He didn't dare leave his legionaries leaderless and in chaos, especially because not all the legions of Britannia have joined up with him yet, and he probably feared rivalry between Romani officers of equal rank should he not be there to lead them. He is, you see, the only one of his status, the only Governor. No one else in Britannia outranks him.'

'According to Romani reckoning.'

'Indeed, my slip. Anyway, he did invite any inhabitant of Londinium to join him and enjoy the protection his cavalry might offer, he just made the proviso that they had to keep up and were their own responsibility. He didn't have enough leeway to take on slackers or those without their own horses, nor really for non-combatants. Once they'd gone and the last precious places upon the few remaining ships had been sold for the highest price their captains could squeeze, then the real panic began.

'Looting, of course, which is why I've kept this as quiet as possible: it wouldn't do for your force to realise there might be little left as spoils in the next town offered for destruction. Any such settlement will have its share of poor and wanting. With the rich flinging decadence and waste at them, as that sort tend to do, envy will flourish and take any opportunity to satisfy its covetousness. Those people will have taken the things of their dreams and scurried away to hide wherever they feel they might be safe. Then there'll always be those who choose to face their death with borrowed courage and drink their way to oblivion. Get drunk enough and you can face any fear, take on any foe. And we mustn't forget those so bound to their possessions they won't leave them even if it means parting with their lives.

'This, madam, I suspect, is the sort of thing you'll find in Londinium. There'll be no resistance; it'll be yours for the taking.'

'Sounds as if we don't need to hurry after all. It might be cruellest to let the inhabitants of Londinium work themselves up into a frenzy of imagining what we might be and might do. It might even give some of that borrowed courage a chance to sober up so we can have the excitement of at least a small challenge. Also, I think I'd like Suetonius to make his own way back to his legions; perhaps we can even lure them all back to their precious Londinium. I want to wipe the Romani out in one go, not be forever mopping up their fragmented military units, which is what they're more likely to disperse into if he's gone. Do you see any reason not to keep to our agreed gathering at New Moon?'

'Only one and that is a mixed blessing. There's a major contingent of Romani soldiers, an entire legion in fact, based at Isca. It's situated to keep both the Durotiges and the Dumnonii at bay. This legion two hasn't joined with Suetonius' force yet, and there's no information regarding whether those troops have set out in keeping with the Governor's orders. It'd be reasonable to presume, in the circumstances, that the absence of the legion is connected with the non-appearance of the two tribes it was set to govern over and which we expected to rise in revolt with us. Reasonable, but I don't know why nor whether it's to our favour.'

'If they don't join up with Suetonius, we won't be able to destroy all the legionaries in Britannia in one final, total victory and we won't have kept to our plans.' Boudicca was dismayed. 'There'll still be Romani legionaries out there waiting for us. Oh, I know, even if everything progresses as we'd hoped, there'll still be the other two client kingdoms to liberate, and scattered fortlets and castles to capture, but not a whole legion sitting at our backs! We'll have won merely a battle, not the whole war, and I'd really begin to fear whether we could demand that the tribes stay at Host. They'd start to distrust us and our strategies, and then the desertions will begin.'

'Better that, madam, than for our horde to meet Suetonius in battle and be overwhelmed by his numbers.'

'Which you've already calculated is impossible, Lovernios mine. We outnumber them ten to one. Let him gather every Romani he can muster, it'll still not be enough; we're used to much better odds. Ha! Reverse the odds, each of my Iceni champions could take on ten Romani easily and still triumph!'

Lovernios didn't have a chance to answer before they noticed Fand of the Coritani striding towards them. She was wearing a stern expression and carrying a bloodied sack. Most of the warriors had gathered with their families tonight, huddled close for maximum warmth around many, many camp fires glowing like isolated stars in the dusk, so she had to pick her way through the crowds, dripping blood on them as she passed. The remains of the hamlet were packed, the camp much larger than usual. The loose plan of announcing when the baggage train would reach the next major Romani settlement seemed to be working. It gave the champions, who rode out to seek glory far from the bulk of the force, a clear idea of where and when they could rejoin their kin. Although, of course, no one could be absolutely certain of the information reaching all the outlying warriors because no one could be definite about how many the horde comprised in total. Doubtless there were many others, scattered around the east of Britannia, who'd chosen not to return to the main camp tonight.

So, it wasn't totally unexpected to see Fand and her Coritani amongst those gathered with the horde tonight. What was surprising was the Queen's expression. Boudicca could almost feel the ground quake with each step of Fand's massive bulk, and as the distance between them lessened, she felt her own confidence and resolve falter.

Boudicca felt for her torc, seeking solace from Andraste's presence and power from the Divine. There was no response and she felt the lack of support, when she had come to rely upon it so often, as acutely as the sore hurt of loneliness.

Fand faced her squarely and dropped the sack at their feet. Once the rough material had held Romani flour, but now it was covered in clotted blood. Boudicca couldn't help but be curious about its current contents.

'Ask her what she wants, please, Lovernios.'

He did not. Instead he translated Fand's formal greeting and offered one in return as if that had been what Boudicca had just said. His eyes flashed a warning to Boudicca.

'Invite her to say whatever she wishes to.'

The great Queen's words were unintelligible to Boudicca but her body language and tone were all too clear. Fand was clearly furious about something and since she kept pointing to the sack it was obvious that it had something to do with her mood.

Lovernios questioned her repeatedly about what she was saying, trying perhaps to get the meaning correct or to persuade her to some diplomacy before he translated for Boudicca. His perseverance was obviously not sitting well with the Queen who gradually raised her voice until it was a voluble tirade which drew quite a crowd. Lovernios gestured for her to calm down and for the crowd to disperse. Some did, respecting the authority of a Druid immediately, but others appeared to take their place, too curious to mind rank.

'Fand says she found this sack in the ruins of Caesaromagus, madam, barely hidden. The contents, she says, are disgusting and this sort of thing should not be allowed. Apparently, the sack is full...' Lovernios swallowed with awkwardness, 'of severed members. From men. Romani men mainly,' he elucidated. 'They are hardly identifiable as such and at first she thought she'd found some offal from some Romani butchery. On closer inspection she recognised them for what they were and knew them to have been taken by Celtoi from Romani corpses. She tells me many of the Romani bodies left for the birds at Camulodunum were mutilated in this way, and that now it's started again. It's honourable to take heads, but not other parts, and not from fallen Celtoi warriors as is now happening. She wants this practice stopped.'

'Tell her I, too, have seen the bodies she described, but in the interests of tribal relations and diplomacy I'd let the customs of other tribes continue unchecked. It's not for me to decree what's proper and what's not. We're many differing tribes here, we've differing practises, we should live and let live.'

'Madam, I don't think I should translate that for you. You see, Fand thinks it's the Iceni who've done this. She's not asking you to find out who is responsible for doing this, she's telling you to stop.'

'Don't be ridiculous!'

'Madam, please, this is a most sensitive issue.'

'Why is she so certain the Iceni are involved?'

'This isn't the first sack to have been found, madam, and they're all flour sacks that were traded by the Romani to the Iceni. That's the meaning of these marks here, see? Madam, it would seem that there

178

are some amongst us who aren't well, here in the head. Not well in the slightest.'

Boudicca thought quickly. She decided to obtain a delay if possible, whatever the price. 'Can you placate Fand as best as possible? Give her my most humble apologies and pass on my assurances I'll do all I can to stop this immediately. Thank her for bringing this to my attention and try to convince her this is not the usual Iceni way.'

Lovernios did so. Fand grudgingly accepted what was said and stomped off, her select champions trailing behind her, casting belittling looks upon Boudicca as they left.

'Do you have any idea what's going on?'

'No, madam, do you?'

'I've one suspicion, but it's so dreadful I don't want to speak it until I've checked it further.'

'Even to me?'

'Especially to you. Can you get Sucellus to me whilst there's still some light? Don't disturb him if he's eating, and don't nibble anything yourself while you're gone.'

'What on earth have you got in mind?'

'I'll tell you when you get back, but you'll need an empty stomach.'

'No, madam, not that?'

'Don't worry, I'll do most of it. All you'll have to do is look.'

And she did. As soon as Lovernios had gone to get the smith she dragged the sack into the best light she could find in the deepening gloom, shooed some people away, and tipped a few of the gruesome contents onto the ground. She had to hold her breath to stop her stomach heaving, but she managed to sort the limp cuttings enough to examine the way they'd been severed from their respective groins.

Long before Lovernios returned with Sucellus, she'd convinced herself of the weapon used for the butchery and, by implication, the person who'd done it. Now she just needed to check. She looked a bizarre sight, her hands and arms splattered in dry blood to the elbows, and blood smeared upon her face where she'd wiped her hair from her eyes.

Whatever the reason, neither of the two men could bring themselves to look voluntarily at the gobbets she'd spilled from the sack, but she forced them to see what she'd found, trying to convince them to look at the penises as if they were simple off-cuts from any animal. They couldn't.

'Just look at the cut here, and here, and here, see? If you pick any of them, they all have the same sharp cut. It's as if a fresh knife was used for each laceration, right? Sucellus, am I right?'

'Yes,' he swallowed. 'Yes, you're right.' Then he turned his head away and retched.

Boudicca put all the members back in the sack and wiped her hands. 'That's all I really needed you to see. Those samples were from the top of the sack. I dug a few out from the bottom and checked those and they're the same. I take it you'll be prepared to take my word on it?' Lovernios nodded, white as a corpse. 'Good. Let's presume, anyway, that the pieces I showed you were some of the last to be cut, some of the last to be put in the sack, some of the last to be collected? It's reasonable, anyone gathering anything will throw everything into a sack like this and the most recent additions will be at the top. Right? Right. Now you saw the cuts with your own eyes, all razor sharp, all as if cut with a fresh blade. Which is not reasonable, right? No one carries that many knifes around with them. So they must all have been cut with the same blade, or at most a few blades. Yet the edge remained sharp despite cutting through, what, a couple of hundred men?'

'This could be the doings of several people.'

'No. The whole act stinks of secrecy and obsession. This is one person's work.'

'There's no such blade.'

'There is. One at least that I can think of.'

'What would that be?' Sucellus was interested as much as a professional metal worker as for the solution to this mystery.

'Andraste's sickle.'

'But you've …'

'It's lost at the moment, remember? Or however Lovernios wants to express the fact that I am not its Keeper for now.'

'"Transferred" will do, madam.'

'Sucellus, Andraste's sickle has been "transferred" to another and was with them when this was done. This is the only find we've seen for ourselves. Perhaps the previous members were not cut so finely – I can't even say precisely when the sickle went missing. All I know is that Her knife will put up with constant use, even abuse, and yet will remain as sharp as the day it was forged. Nothing can blunt it.' She shuffled her feet nervously. 'Do you think you could take my word on that, too? As to who did this… well, that's why I wish to talk to you, Sucellus. But I think whoever it was may have been at this mutilation way before they decided to bend the sickle to their grisly task.'

'Go on, I'll answer as best I can.'

'I can barely bring myself to speak my suspicion. Just understand, please, that I do so as much to help her as to stop this, this filthy… perversion.' Lovernios reached out to offer support. Sucellus nodded, willing to at least hear what he had to say. Boudicca took a deep breath. 'Sucellus,' she asked. 'You've shared many days with Maeve – my daughter Maeve, that is …' Lovernios withdrew his arm. Sucellus' face was stony. 'Have you ever noticed Maeve to have blood on her hands, or have been washing them too frequently for normal? I mean, apart from her constant bathing, of course. I've been unable to give her as much attention as I'd have wished of late and fear I may have missed some of these signs through my neglect.'

'How could you think such a thing? Not about Maeve. She's such a gentle, sweet child.' Sucellus was extremely defensive about his adopted ward. 'She wouldn't do such a thing.'

'You both agree with me she's been behaving strangely recently? Since the Romani attack she's been so withdrawn, where Grania has been healing, moving on, Maeve has just been… nothing. Maeve is just there. I simply wanted to know whether you'd seen any evidence like blood under her fingernails or on her clothes. It can be hard to shift, especially when it dries or stains. You'd have been more likely to notice this than me, even if you've dismissed it in the past. Think, please! You know this new Maeve so much better than I, her own mother. It's been as if the Faery have brought a useless, vacuous Changeling to fill her place; she's more stranger to me than kin. I'm not accusing or blaming, I'm just concerned. She's my daughter; I must stop her from harming herself like this. She only needs one of these Romani to be not quite dead and she'll be injured. And she can't fight back, she was never the sort.'

'Madam, you must have other reasons for thinking these things about your own daughter.' Lovernios was ever the voice of objectivity. 'Perhaps you should share all of your suspicions with us.'

'Lovernios mine, it was the things you said yourself about the nature of the Divine which set me off on this way of thinking. You know, as well as I, that Maeve projects the Goddess in a most pure form. And you must remember what you said about Andraste Manifesting through the easiest conductor. It made sense for me to assume that Maeve, my own daughter, had stolen Andraste's Presence from me, and left me bereft without my Goddess. The sickle will go with Andraste – it's Hers, not mine, and will find the best Keeper it can.

'I've suspected, since we left Camulodunum, that Maeve has the sickle. She has a smugness about her which I'd previously presumed was Andraste's rapture, but now I'm convinced it's there because she's successfully stolen what should be mine. She's not got any better since the Romani came to our settlement at Imbolc. She's still withdrawn and lethargic; in her mind she must be all churned up and disturbed. I dread to think what dreadful mental curses her wounded psyche must procure daily. All she does when left alone is to wash constantly and change her clothing, on what, three or more occasions a day? And she does this with her hands …' Boudicca showed them. 'Constantly wringing them as if unable to get them totally clean.'

Lovernios and Sucellus exchanged glances. They were still unconvinced.

'Without any outlet for all her sorrow and anger it'll eventually turn in upon herself. I'd begun to realise she meant to kill herself, with Andraste's sickle, offering herself as the ultimate sacrifice to the Goddess and ending her mental turmoil together. But now, now this crime has been discovered, I realise she *has* found an outlet. And her constant washing and cleaning is not simple obsession, it's actually necessary to rid herself of all the blood she wallows in whenever she has the chance.'

Sucellus and Lovernios were silent; thinking very carefully, Boudicca realised, before they answered her. The two men exchanged glances again and shrugs too. Had she been too emotional in explaining her suspicions to them? Had she frightened them with the force of her accusation?

'I still say, not that one, she wouldn't do it.' Sucellus was adamant.

'She would if she didn't know herself what she did. Perhaps she's been sleepwalking or led by Andraste herself. After all, our Goddess is terrifying in this Aspect, such is Her nature.' Lovernios was being skilful, Boudicca noticed, weaving a half-truth to satisfy both her and the smith. 'Perhaps we can't hold Maeve herself responsible for this act, if indeed it was her.'

Both Sucellus and Boudicca breathed a sigh of relief. At last someone was taking both their points of view seriously, both were being believed.

'But, madam, you haven't proved it was her.'

'I have ...'

'No, madam. She's nearly always had someone with her. Mainly Sucellus, but there are Druids too, mainly Sisters, who sit with her to project Healing and to experience the Benediction of her presence. Too many people for her to silence, too many concerned friends keeping an eye out for her welfare.'

'Just so, well said,' Sucellus seemed to be taking the accusation personally; he welcomed Lovernios' refutation.

'Nevertheless,' Boudicca flashed back at them, 'It can't be anyone else. I'll have her guarded and watched over. Then at least it shouldn't happen again.'

'I'd advise you to do so surreptitiously, madam.'

'Of course. I can be subtle, you know.'

'Occasionally, madam.'

'You do what you want,' Sucellus interjected into the brewing lover's quarrel. 'I've my own suspicions and I'll set my own watch. If it's all right with you two, of course.'

Chapter 13

Londinium

They hadn't intended, nor needed, to stay still and quiet through the dark, but somehow the fresh new moon cast a whisper of secrecy over their preparations which awaited only first light to see fruition. There were no campfires, horses were silenced with feed, and a command for no raised conversations had filtered its way to everyone, although no one could trace its source.

Until the first caress of dawn revealed the density and size of the crowds gathered around her, Boudicca had been uncertain how many the force would finally number. This, she gradually realised, was much, much larger than the huge army which had massed at Caesaromagus, the most recent gathering of the horde a few days before. It was testament to their discipline that Boudicca had been unable to gauge any idea of the numbers until there was sufficient light by which to see.

The silence though, was almost completely unnecessary. The budding town of Londinium lay just ahead, out of the forests and only a short charge along the Romani roads. Hated they might be, but it was the Romani's own roads which had made the movement of such a large number of people even feasible. That was why they'd been laid in the first place, of course, but not for these particular people in this particular way.

No, the silence was not essential, not as it had been with Camulodunum. The town of Londinium knew its fate, although it doubtless still prayed for a miracle or a rescuer or a sudden change of plan by the brooding horde somewhere to the northeast. Everyone who could leave the town had done so, the rest had rendered themselves senseless or invisible. So much was obvious from the Celtoi scouts and from the lack of sound from the port, which would normally carry even this far out. Londinium was a town of ghosts, empty and noiseless, awaiting its engulfment as placidly as if it had surrendered.

Nevertheless, silence there was, and it added to the mood of excitement and anticipation evident in every combatant's face. This was an event, the next great stage in the rebellion. To act without a warrior's caution would be to treat the deed too casually and with improper disdain, and might invite disaster. So, the atmosphere was set, with clandestine plotting and surreptitious planning.

That the disparate units of the horde had gathered in this one place on the same night was a marvel in itself, and yet another example, to Boudicca, of how crucial Druid communication channels were to the success of the revolt. Lovernios, she knew for one, had certainly been busy and he wasn't even with her now, too concerned with the final snippets of news and situation reports still being brought to him.

They were hosting at full dawn, when the sun would be completely above the horizon and the summer birds in full song. For now, the sun was still edging its way up, as if the earth kept tugging at it to keep its precious light hidden for itself. The early light was grey and pink and threw distorting shadows all around. It promised a day which would appear blisteringly hot but which produced merely a fragile warmth. Unbidden Boudicca found herself grinning. It was her favourite weather, not yet so hot for her to wilt with heat and feel uninspired to do anything, but still the whole day radiant and cheery with yellow sunlight. All it would need now, she imagined, would be a gentle tempest to stir up the tree branches, heavy with blossom, and cover her people in a sheet of petals. A rousing wind for them to race against and to send the Celtoi wild. That's what was needed, then she'd really be in her element.

Grania was with her this morning, their chariots drawn close together. Boudicca had insisted Mouse and Cloud were returned to her and she took comfort in their familiar neutral colour and in the knowledge of their sturdiness and fearlessness. These two ponies would never bolt in the midst of battle, neither would they refuse an order or suddenly rear. It was good to be able to rely on something for a change.

Grania was eager to be off fighting and maiming. Boudicca had agreed that blood sacrifices would recommence from tonight; Grania was so keen to hunt the victims it was as if she imagined they would provide feed for herself. Her daughter's mood showed all over her body as her eyes flitted over everyone and everything, alert for any movement, and she checked and rechecked her spears and sword and her chariot's harnessing.

Grania's actions set others off on the same checks, and Boudicca watched the pre-battle rituals ripple through the entire force as individuals started to sense departure was imminent and hurried to ensure they wouldn't be the stragglers of the host. Quite leisurely, Boudicca wiped the blade of her sword once more, testing the sharpness against her finger, before slipping it away into her scabbard. She hadn't yet mounted her chariot but instead stood by it, letting her ponies chew her clothing. She fiddled with Mouse's tack a little, where it felt loose, and pulled both big horses' heads to her shoulders, giving their necks a good rub. From there she could see the last checks petering out and the smell of nervous readiness informed her there should be little more delay.

They were awaiting her. Any longer and the moment and momentum would be lost. Boudicca was still unused to this responsibility on such a scale and still partly incredulous that the hosting depended upon her command. She savoured the feeling of power a while longer, stepping imperiously up and onto the chariot to stand behind her driver. She closed her eyes for a moment to experience the passion of so many spirits, all intent on hording, all pushing, all eager, all waiting on one signal no matter how slight.

She let the pent-up energy of the collective mind carry her to a crest of emotion and then over, letting out her war cry at the same moment that she seemed to fall in her mind. Her driver urged the ponies into a gallop and she reached out for a hold upon the wicker sides, the instant lost with the need to retain her balance. Once away from the forest cover, the light chariot bounced over the uneven grass, throwing Boudicca around and jarring her body with every violent jolt. She hung on tighter, using her weight to prevent the chariot from toppling over. All around her the rest of the horde streamed out of the trees and across the short stretch of grass to the road. The vast numbers of chariots were surrounded by even more fighters running on foot alongside and keeping up with the pace of the swarming host. Everywhere war trumpets blared, dogs snarled, and champions screamed and shrieked of the destruction they brought

Once at the road, the chariots travelled faster with no snagging grasses or mole hills to catch on the wheels. Those on foot started to lag behind, although the majority of the chariots were caught up in the huddle of warriors. Some of those on foot caught the occasional lift on offer, although the chariots were usually limited in space and weight to two passengers and a driver who sat upon the shaft. Far, far behind, the camp followers and the Druids heard the hosting and assorted war cries and made their own, more plodding pace, towards the town that would no longer exist when they finally reached it.

It wasn't long before the foremost charioteers passed the Romani tombstones lining the road into Londinium, but they didn't stop their onslaught there because there was nothing to stop them. No walls, gates, fortresses; not even a defensive ditch. Londinium sat completely undefended, like a lamb led to slaughter. There was no noise emanating from the straggle of buildings, nor any activity save for the odd plume of smoke from a hastily dowsed hearth.

Boudicca had instructed her driver to keep them to the front and centre of the advancing host. This position gave her the advantage of

185

being one of the first to observe the unfolding situation, yet also not be in any immediate danger herself. It also meant she was jostled and shaken by the pressing masses around her and deafened by the clamouring and the inhuman shrieks of the war trumpets. Her vision, too, was dazzled by the myriad flashes of complex tartans and lurid colours which the Celtoi loved to wear. Her confusion rose. It took her moments to realise that all the sound, all the colour, came solely from the Celtoi. This was like the meeting of two worlds; one noisy, one silent; one colourful, one bland; one alive, one dead. Londinium was dead already, even more so than Lovernios had warned.

A detachment of chariots from the Parisi, to judge by the battle paint daubed across their bodies, peeled off to the west, and gradually the rest of the horde scattered amongst the houses and hovels of the port. Everywhere there was consternation as Celtoi smashed open doors only to find whole warehouses empty of anything of value and every place devoid of people.

'Search harder! Keep looking!' Boudicca ordered. 'Andraste must have sacrifices tonight! Put everything to the fire, this driftwood town will catch ablaze as soon as the first torch is put to it.'

And you, she thought, you my peoples must have something for your effort; some trinkets of war, some blood on your spears, some supplies. Yes, definitely some supplies, for the horde was already beginning to run short as people used whatever rations they'd brought with them and then looked to their leader to supply their needs.

Then Boudicca felt a second emotion rise to join the anger she felt at having been thus cheated: she felt worry too – a stomach-gnawing worry at not being able to give her people, her wards, what they needed. And if she could not, would they then turn against her? There was no Goddess certainty, now, to ease that trouble, and she doubted in her heart whether there ever would be again.

She pushed such thoughts from her mind. She couldn't afford such negativity; too much depended on her to allow herself to sink into that frame of mind. She'd find Andraste a sacrifice, she knew there had to be someone suitable in this forsaken town, and the rats would come scampering out just as soon as their holes were aflame.

'Head towards the river,' she directed her driver and those around her, and soon they were flying past all the wooden structures that Londinium was mainly comprised of. The driver kept to the road, heading south and passing just two other streets running east-west, before they reached the river Tamesis. This, then, was the extent of the Romani's trading centre in Britannia: a road, a bridge to the south bank, two streets and some wharfs, all scantily clad with lean-tos and workshops, warehouses and hovels. It seemed a poor sight to Boudicca, especially when compared with Camulodunum.

She paused a while at the bridge head, sniffing the air, still rank from the smell of dead fish and tar, and surveyed the Romani prize her tactics had just won. It hardly seemed worth the effort. There was no glory in taking this ramshackle settlement and no apparent gain either. It all seemed very disappointing. Could this really be the same place the Romani spoke of with such pride, and where there was rumoured to be such riches? It was hard to imagine the place as bustling, let alone affluent.

She scanned the town and decided to make for some of the larger buildings to the east, along the north bank and dotted amongst the warehouses. Catus might not be here himself, but certainly his palace was, and if she could only find that... But none of these structures looked like palaces. Why, they were barely the size of some of the country villas they'd passed around Caesaromagus.

Boudicca stepped down from her chariot and hefted her spear and shield. Her sword she kept scabbarded because it was not her favourite weapon. She dismissed the chariot driver who turned the horses and insisted on accompanying her on foot.

'Madam, I'll come with you, then you can be certain your chariot will be available for your return.'

The young man seemed so earnest, bare to the waist with tattoos swirled over his shoulders and the first shadow of a warrior's moustaches, that she agreed, proffering her hand in a champion's embrace. He was the same charioteer who'd accompanied Grania earlier, a young nobleman named Laeg, and she knew she could trust him. Apart from anything else he reminded her of Prasutagus, back when he'd been very young and before the Romani had insisted she take a consort.

Quickly she tidied the memories away. Those days were long gone and the present was too busy to spend energy reliving the past. This driver was not Prasutagus. Prasutagus was dead, even though she still saw his eyes and expressions staring out of other men's faces.

'I thought we'd check these larger buildings,' she explained. 'I want to find Catus' palace and these look like they might be quite rich.' Then she strode away with long, bouncy steps, leaving him to follow as he would.

The doors of most of the buildings had already been broken down and the ransacking begun. The single story building she chose to go inside first was bedecked with elegant wall paintings and hangings, mosaics and rugs. Boudicca was astounded by the luxury confronting her and the level of comfort and airiness afforded by the design of the rooms. Even the floors were warm – she could feel them through her boots – and when she stooped and ran her hand over the neat tessellae she couldn't help a little gasp escaping her lips. What had been said about the Romani nobles was true, then. Could she have come to expect such a lifestyle eventually, had she kept faith with the Romani? Would it have been worth it?

Despite all this decadence before her, she still felt the palace to be cheerless and devoid of some essence, and she would have reached such conclusions even had the building not been stripped of its valuables and ornaments that doubtless once filled the many plinths and niches. She was more suited, she decided, to the humble earth beneath her feet and nature's own beautiful surroundings for decoration. What was the point, anyway, in painting leaf and frond upon your walls when you could so easily step outside and see them in their native majesty? And how many Romani slaves, she wondered, or other citizens of Londinium, had their place upon a ship sacrificed so a precious object might be saved from the horde instead?

She strode through the rooms, one after another, in incredulous wonderment. She followed her nose into a food preparation area, where the scent of fresh bread still remained. There she heard a thin piping sound and she crossed to the alcove from where it appeared to come. She pulled back a curtain and could barely believe what she saw. There, encased in clay, were trapped mice, only their heads sticking out from the sealed pots and seemingly straining for sustenance or escape. She picked up one of the creatures and examined it. What strange traps were these? And how inhumane not just to kill the pests but to keep them alive and tormented. She puzzled over the little rodent, whose calls had heightened on her approach, and wondered whether its desperate cries were intended to warn off others of its species.

Boudicca stooped to check her idea, scrabbling quickly over the floor. The traps must work as quite an effective deterrent, in the same way as Celtoi hung up dead foxes or rats, for there were no mouse droppings to be seen anywhere around. Whatever the reason, she felt her heart tug in sympathy for the pathetic creatures.

'You're no longer under the dominion of these tyrannical masters,' she told the first dormouse, as she stood up again. 'Be free now. But remember it was Celtoi who released you, so stay away from Celtoi grain!'

Then she broke the clay as gently as she could and helped the tiny animal out. The poor thing was vastly overweight, its limbs shrunken and unused where it had been stuck in the pot for so long. Unable to run away, it tried to pull itself across the shelf, vainly searching for food and still piping demandingly.

Boudicca realised in total disgust that the Romani had been purposely catching and fattening these dormice. She felt sick. Not at the thought of eating rodents – even Celtoi nobility would stoop to that given a poor harvest and a bad winter – but at the cruelty in the method. These alien people seemed to be the antithesis of all of nature itself – was nothing sacred to them? Nothing unexploitable?

She did the kindest thing she could think of, breaking each of the clay moulds in turn to check whether any of the mice could run away. Then she took those who could not and tenderly placed them on the floor, bringing her boot heal down quickly and sharply upon each one. As she did so she spotted the reason for the pleading calls of the dormice. Slumped in a corner of the larder where she wouldn't have noticed it had she not been bent over and if the mice calls were not stopped, was an unconscious body, snoring gently over a spilt amphora of wine.

She went to the inert figure and kicked it in several places. There was no response. The middle-aged man carried on dreaming his drunken dreams, oblivious to the vomit over his once-white tunic. Boudicca didn't want to waste precious moments deciding what to do with this Romani so she called over her driver.

'I can't even be bothered to waste my strength or the sharpness of my weapons on this dirt,' she announced, 'Take him – he's yours. Practise dealing death upon him.'

Boudicca left the charioteer fumbling with his belt knife and had one last look around the stored jars and baskets for any useful supplies. So far, this house had been disappointing in its yield and by the sounds of dismay wafting through the corridors, she sensed that something would have to be found soon else the Celtoi in the horde would become bored with what Londinium had to offer and start to doubt whether it was worth their while to continue plundering the Romani.

Suddenly she heard the slightest whimper, so soft it could so easily have been her boot scrape on the sawdust on the floor. Then she smelled it: the subtle scent of a mother's milk. Quickly, she knocked over a pile of baskets and lifted the largest one up. There, curled up beneath, was a terrified woman, her eyes wide with abject fear and her arms encircling a swaddled babe whose mouth had been packed with rags to stop it from making noise. Someone had hidden them here; they could never have arranged such a nest by themselves.

Boudicca turned to look back to her driver. 'Have you finished with him yet? Hurry it up, he was braver than he first appeared.'

Laeg drove his knifepoint into the yielding flesh of the drunk's throat, sending a gush of blood flowing over the floor towards the young mother. She sobbed and held her baby tighter, trying desperately to crawl away or make herself smaller. She seemed to become even more disturbed at the man's demise and now appeared utterly distraught.

Boudicca grabbed the woman's hair and hauled her upright. She was short, as most women were in comparison to Boudicca, and she had to stand on tiptoe to prevent her hair from being pulled out by its roots. Still she held the baby close, as if it was a part of her.

'At least we've got something to show for raiding this spewing little port,' Boudicca snarled. Then she looked at the Romani infant and suddenly all the pain, anger and jealousy, which her conversations with Grania had stirred up, rushed to the surface. She felt an immense hatred of the woman and her baby. She didn't know whether the child was a boy or a girl, only that it was the woman's, not hers, and, by rights, it should never have been born. Boudicca glowered at her catch, burning inside with an abiding passion, only vaguely aware her internal heat had been considerably stoked since the inception of the revolt.

'You'll do for my Goddess,' Boudicca purred to the woman who dangled uncomprehendingly. 'Fertile Romani women for Andraste to feed upon. And fertile you certainly are, as you've proved so brazenly with your little tot. But you don't need it any more, it was just a qualification for entry.' And with that, Boudicca released one hand from her hold on the woman's hair and whipped the babe out of its mother's arms. The woman clung on desperately, incurring dreadful pain as she did so.

Boudicca pulled on the child, trying to tug it away from its protector who'd started to scream in protest. Boudicca tugged on her hair, more jerkily now, and the woman started to kick at her tormentor. Then the woman let loose one hand from its hold on the babe to claw at Boudicca's face, and the Queen saw her chance. Holding her own head back and out of reach of the woman's fingernails, she grabbed one of the baby's arms and yanked hard, dashing the child against the packed earth floor.

The woman's screams reached a crescendo as her child smashed against the floor. But she'd never let go, not completely. She still held one leg, the bone pulled out of its socket, and she cradled that now, close to her breast. Boudicca could do nothing to prise it out of her clenched fingers.

'Keep it, then,' Boudicca shouted into her face, making the woman shut her eyes from flying spittle, and she pulled her away from the room and out of the palace, the woman still screaming in panic and grief.

Once outside, Boudicca stepped atop her chariot again and instructed her driver back up the main road into Londinium. 'Not so fast,' she ordered. 'She's to remain alive.' They set off at a gentle trot so the Romani woman could still run behind, albeit with difficulty. Boudicca still held onto her by the hair, but now the woman reached up to Boudicca's hands trying to scratch at her to let go. A few slaps and an increase in chariot speed and the woman resigned herself to just holding on to the hands which restrained her, trying to keep Boudicca's hands in contact with her head and prevent her hair from being tugged too much and also keep a tight hold of the remains of her baby. The tactic worked, for Boudicca could see she wasn't in too much pain. She did, however, become tired more easily without her arms to assist her running, and before long she was puffing and panting and as red in the face as her erstwhile baby had been.

Boudicca chuckled at her captive's predicament. What power to be able to make your victim choose which torture they preferred! Boudicca revelled in the hold she had over the woman's well-being and the control she exerted. Surely Andraste would return to her just as soon as she'd made her psyche a suitable receptacle for her Goddess? Surely this was exactly the level of cruelty to encourage Andraste's return?

But there was no return of Goddess consciousness, she noticed sadly. No presence of the Divine in her spirit. Perhaps she'd have to try harder, descend to deeper depths of depravity? They stopped just beyond the outermost buildings, the obvious place to meet up with the wagons due to join them by nightfall. Already other Celtoi warriors had started to gather, taking a respite from the fun of plundering to bring their booty to one place, to share what could be shared and to display what they chose not to. Boudicca was relieved to see that a poor but fair amount of trinkets and delicacies had been found and piled together. She hoped it would be enough for the horde to feel Londinium had been worth the waiting. Pickings might be small but at least there would be few Celtoi casualties today.

Several other Romani women had been found amongst the hovels and houses of the town and Boudicca pushed her contribution towards the huddle of sorry looking female captives. The woman tripped with the force, stumbling into a haughty matron with a huge hooked nose and excessively painted face. This older Romani woman immediately started pulling disgusted expressions at the uninvited physical contact, brushing at her clothing where it had been fleetingly touched, as if she had been in contact with a plague victim.

Boudicca looked at the confused and worn Romani women without being able to muster any sympathy for their plight. Some of them sobbed or stood close together for comfort, most of them looked resolved to their fate. Only the one haughty woman stood really apart, obviously considering herself above such things, or were the other women secretly glad she chose to stay away? Boudicca was dismayed at the cowed and subservient behaviour being demonstrated. A Celtoi woman would never be taken like this, she'd prefer to die. Yes, and take a few of her foe with her into the Summerlands, too.

She doubted whether even these dainty and gracious captives would be so submissive if they knew the nature of the death awaiting them, the style of sacrifice desired by the Goddess. Boudicca smirked. Even if the plunder from Londinium was somewhat lacking, the amusement to be derived from the deaths of these women would make it all worthwhile for every single Celtoi in the horde who dared to watch the terror Grania had devised.

But she could not sit around all day thinking about the evening's entertainment, she had an obligation to her people to continue with the scouring of this settlement, so she called her driver over to one of the amphorae of wine and invited him to drink with her. The wine was not good quality but rather sharp and watery; fine enough to quench a thirst but not much else.

'Thank you for accompanying me,' she said to her driver. 'Would you stay with my chariot until my return?' The driver started to protest but she interjected. 'I'll be fine, Laeg. Occasionally I enjoy being Boudicca without being Queen. It's easier to do that if I'm on my own without a noble's chariot.'

Her driver remonstrated a little more. 'But you won't be safe alone, madam.'

'No, really, I will,' she insisted, unused to having to press her point. 'I'm quite capable of looking after myself. I do this often, there's no danger. Londinium holds no threats. You've seen this for yourself.'

But still he argued and still she was adamant she wanted to go off by herself and would be fine doing so. So used to having her demands met immediately, she found herself dwindling into childish pantomime in an effort to insist on her own way. Finally she stamped off without him, unconcerned whether he decided to tag along puppy-like behind her or sit in the sun and drink himself into relaxation.

The first group of Celtoi she joined were dismantling a lean-to hovel piece by piece even though it was barely standing upright by itself. They were convinced there was something within, alive and hidden. They lifted off plank after plank, pulling out rags and fishing nets cautiously, surrounding the structure with alert warriors in case whatever was inside would make a sudden break for freedom.

Then there was a rustling as some supports settled and a distinctive scrabble for air, and those nearest the noise tensed themselves in excitement. Suddenly a cat dashed from the heap of wood which had once been someone's home and hurtled away from the town hissing and with all its fur standing on end. 'Of course! Pussy would decide to do his own looting in a fishing hut,' someone joked, and all the Celtoi laughed at the moment's anticipation gone as quickly as it had arrived.

'There won't be anything of value in there.' Someone kicked at the remains.

'Only some fish hooks. Doubt if they'll be needed for a while,' volunteered someone else.

'Burn it, then,' they chorused and torches were brought and set to the dry tinder. Just as the smoke started to stream from the hovel and the Celtoi were relaxed enough to look around for their next target, a whole heap of wood shifted and a grey head pushed itself out of the pile. It blinked, rubbing dust from its eyes and spluttering with the smoke it had breathed in. It was an old person, sex quite indeterminate, and it tried, albeit vainly, to move out of the flames before they caught upon its ragged clothing. One foot was caught under a heavy timber support and it bent shakily down to try to free itself. As it did, a loose rag trailed near enough a flame to catch alight and soon its whole body was ablaze with a whoosh of heat. It staggered out of the pile, waving its arms desperately for help and moaning unintelligibly, shambling towards the river only to collapse after a few paces.

They let the flames die out before they turned the body over to look into the rheumy eyes which had already started to glaze over. There was a dreadful smell which no one wanted to stay near for very long. They checked it was dead and then sauntered off to a warehouse which looked more promising.

Boudicca left them to it, joining instead a crowd picking over the remains of a food shop. She stooped under the awning to pick her way through some cracked samian ware, each containing a different sample of luxury Romani treats. Some of them she knew through her own trading but she'd never seen such rare goods in these quantities before, and she felt indulgent enough to nibble at dates and nuts as she sorted through what was worth taking and what was not.

'We've got everything we want from here.' Someone shouted. 'Get out before we fire it!'

'Wait!' Boudicca ordered. 'I want to save some more of these delicious dates. Have you tried them?'

'No, get out quick!' they replied.

Boudicca was simply not used to being ordered about like that, not even when the Iceni royal enclosure had lived in the very presence of a Romani occupation. She was so surprised by the sheer audacity, she found herself stuck for a terse and authoritative reply. She was about to dispute the command when the heady smell of smoke wafted to her and she realised she didn't have that long to stay where she was. She jumped out of the terraced shop, still not the last to leave, and clutching a handful of dates.

The woman who had argued back was unrecognisable to Boudicca. Her body paint said Coritani but she could not be completely sure. Certainly, Boudicca expected to be recognised by someone who was so obviously a noble herself, but wasn't that the whole point? Should she ruin her apparent disguise, her ability to merge with the bulk of the rebellion and experience what was really going on amongst her people first hand by throwing her royal weight around in retaliation?

Boudicca decided not to create a scene. The noble had obviously not thought much about the whole issue; it was not personal. Other Celtoi had rushed to obey the command, too. It was just a sharp warning, a caution. Other warriors had more sense, did as they were told and moved on with their comrades. Other warriors had not brooded upon questions of rank, but were more concerned with questions of self-preservation. Dying in a shop fire was not exactly a hero's death, after all.

She watched this particular group of Celtoi move on. The noble woman had already forgotten the whole issue and was arranging teams to clear the next line of shops. Boudicca was relieved but nevertheless confused at the woman's lack of acknowledgement of royalty, not least the figurehead of the whole rebellion itself. Surreptitiously pretending to put a date to her mouth, she felt for her torc, checking it was well covered by her robe. For a moment she stood rooted to the ground; the torc hadn't been concealed at all, she'd forgotten to hide it in her urgency to be away from her driver. Quickly she regained her composure and pulled her cloak up so her neck was covered as she had become accustomed to do. There must have been some sort of oversight: perhaps the noble woman was shortsighted or simply unobservant, possibly even blatantly ignorant.

Boudicca turned away and tried to focus on the things going on all around her in order to distract herself from the nagging worry at the back of her mind that she simply did not want to listen to.

Londinium was a wealth of fires now, and here and there a refugee bolted from where they'd been smoked out, straight into the arms of a waiting Celtoi. It was easy to spot the Romani. Even those who strolled nonchalantly away from their hiding places were too distinctive. They stood as much chance of hiding their impractical clothing and terror of the horde as of covering their latent disgust that such savages should destroy their town so ignominiously.

The Celtoi who waited for them, like so many hunters at a fox's earth, were under instructions to keep only Romani women alive, most especially so if they were expecting a child. Boudicca smiled to see so many Romani women obviously relieved not to be killed immediately upon being found. She knew rumours would have informed the Romani that the revolt was taking no prisoners for ransom or slavery. They still weren't. Boudicca was looking forward to the moment when those stiff and formal Romani matrons made that discovery themselves.

Such thoughts made her mind turn instinctively to Grania. Her warrior daughter had been amongst the first of those chariots to hit Londinium, and she wondered now where Grania had got to. She scanned the scattered shops and houses to see if she could spot the unique pattern woven into Grania's tartan trousers. She could not. Then, uncertain why, she meandered west, against the flow of the river Tamesis, keeping a keen lookout for her daughter all the while.

The riverbank was dusty and gravelly, except where the Romani had built gigantic wharfs for their massive ships to embark. Such ships took the lifeblood of Britannia – food and essential supplies, even people – and what did they bring back? Trinkets and baubles and other useless commodities you could not use and did not really need. The Romani must have seen the Celtoi as so many magpies, thought Boudicca, wise and cautious but easily tricked by a pretty shiny thing to mesmerise the eye.

Could the tribes really justify being seen in any other way? Wasn't that the trap they'd so easily flown into? Was it so wrong to admire objects of beauty and craftsmanship? She remembered then a magpie she'd watched once, totally absorbed in brief flashes of sunlight reflecting off a waterfall. The water had been so beguiling that the magpie was joined by its mate, and then another two pairs, until six birds perched around the clearing. Each one had been equally mesmerised by the play of sunlight and oblivious to her presence. They followed every dancing droplet with jerky little movements, not missing a single facet of the tumbling liquid. After a while, she too had stopped looking at the magpies and allowed herself to be ensnared by the sparkling drops of water, like stars twinkling by day. She wondered now whether she'd been watched in turn by something else? And then the sun had gone in and they were all released from their spell back to their dull worlds. Life could be so cruel, so drab; why not rush at any chance to own something which promised to transcend life's limitations, even if only for a moment?

Just as Boudicca was thinking of the magpies, she saw a glint of something sparkle for the briefest instant. Instinctively she whirled around to see what had caught her acquisitive attention and realised that whatever it was had been golden. She squinted, unsure of her eyesight at this distance. Then there was some more movement and she recognised Grania's tartan before it was gone again, just as quick.

Running, she made her way to where she'd seen the signs of her daughter, and then spun around for her. She was nowhere to be seen. There were still quite a few houses and other wooden buildings in this part of the town, all bundled together in a stinking community. Judging by the number of bodies scattered around, this had been where people had been unable or unwilling to leave their homes for want of mobility or desire or even because they had so little anyway they deemed themselves unlikely to be the main concern of the horde.

Boudicca could not help but look in pleasure at the number of bodies here. More Romani dead, of any type, was a welcome thing. Less to fight, less to kill later when they would systematically sweep the whole of Britannia for Romani and their sympathisers, more rumours to be spread about how indefatigable the Celtoi were. She crept around the houses, calling softly: 'Grania, Grania mine?'

Then at one body she noticed the groin was bloody and she froze where she was. The mutilation had begun again, but now she was amongst the mutilator's prey, in the territory of the deranged. The blood looked fresh on this corpse, and on the next it hadn't even started to clot yet.

Grania! She was so brave. Boudicca's heart pounded in her breast; her daughter was in such danger. Grania would stop at nothing, she knew. She must have seen where the perpetrator skulked and gone straight after them, seeking a personal confrontation so the whole incident might die out without any further fuss or effect upon the cohesion of the horde.

Oh, my brave, clever daughter, thought Boudicca, creeping silently amongst the corpses and shadows, using the full benefit of the squalid light to stay unseen. She rounded a corner and gasped loudly. There was Grania, crouched over a corpse, obviously ahead of Boudicca in the trail to find the owner of the disgusting mind which was carrying out this act.

Boudicca coughed to make her presence known. 'Daughter mine, Grania, thank Mother it's you! Have you found who's doing these things? You're so clever to have tracked them here, I'm so proud of you.'

'No, mother mine,' Grania looked up from inspecting the corpse. The groin area was bloody on this one but still intact. 'I think I must've surprised him whilst he was working on this one, but he can't be far away.'

'Oh, my child, my child, quick we must get away; we might be in danger ourselves. We must've frightened him enough, so close behind his gory trail, that he daren't do the same for a long while yet. And there is one other Blessing to come from this, too.'

'What's that?'

'Why, Maeve, of course. She's under a heavy but unobtrusive guard, by my orders. Now I know for certain that she didn't do this, it's such a weight from my mind. Tell me,' she steered Grania away. 'I don't suppose you noticed whether he had my, I mean Andraste's, sickle, at all?'

Then they stopped talking, for they'd heard an eerie sliding noise, approaching from a side alley. An odd stride with an unusual pace, as if someone dragged their leg or walked with a disabling limp. The two women held onto each other, Boudicca certain she'd never emerge from the warren of hovels again.

Just when she thought her heart would be certain to explode with its heavy beating, the newcomer appeared and announced himself with a bow, limping towards the two terrified women.

'Sucellus!' Boudicca was astounded to see him, yet also deeply confused, all her worst fears rising at once. 'I thought you were making sure Maeve was all right?'

'Oh, I am, madam, I am. That's why I'm here. That's why I've been here for quite a while.' Then he bowed again, twice, acknowledging each of them separately.

Chapter 14

Dark Moon

No one spoke a word as they made their way back to the outskirts of Londinium, where it had vaguely been agreed the horde and the camp followers would meet up. Not that any tryst needed to be so specific these days; it was hardly possible for such large numbers of people to avoid knowing the location of each other. Nevertheless, Boudicca supposed, the policy did serve to reassure those left behind with the baggage where their loved ones might be and when they might see them again.

Boudicca and Grania walked with their arms around each other, in familial solidarity, Grania's head fitting snug against Boudicca's breast. It felt so good to have one daughter, at least, back in the fold where once their intimacy had been common place.

She sensed Grania's need of her and nervousness of Sucellus, and she held her daughter tight and protectively, keeping her own body between Grania and the blacksmith. Right now, Boudicca felt she would do anything to maintain this renewed level of closeness and trust with her daughter; that certainly included siding with Grania's mental rift with Sucellus by joining with her daughter in displaying a physical distance from him.

Lovernios had already arrived in Londinium, one of the first of the camp followers to get there. Immediately he had sent his Druids to mingle with the pillagers and scavengers of the horde and obtain whatever information they could about the progress of the sack of the town. He looked drained with nervous exhaustion, Boudicca noticed, and she felt reluctant to go to him, not wanting to add to his burdens and responsibilities. He was pointedly ignoring the ever-increasing huddle of Romani women taken from the ruins of the town, and was ensconced in debate with tribal leaders and returning Druids, busy building his own version of events from the conflicting reports being brought to him.

'Madam?' Sucellus was trying to gain her attention very formally. It was his first use of her title for quite a while, she noticed.

Feeling Grania stiffen, she acknowledged him with a nod, shielding her daughter and refusing to look him in the eye. What had happened between these two? Sucellus had been so trusted. She'd even let him stay with Maeve. What could he have done to Grania to make her this disturbed?

'Will Grania… Rather, will you both be here for a while?' he asked.

Boudicca nodded curtly, trying to make sure he was aware this was all the attention she was going to grant, leaving Sucellus to speak as politely as he could to her back.

'We're not going anywhere,' Boudicca replied, trying to keep her voice as neutral as possible, not wanting to give Sucellus the satisfaction of knowing how uneasy she felt.

Sucellus nodded and limped off to join the queue of people waiting to see Lovernios. Boudicca watched him go, hiding her face in Grania's hair, and saw Lovernios look up at his approach and call him over immediately. She saw the two men look briefly at her and Grania and then look quickly away, hoping she hadn't noticed, before they returned to their agitated whispering. The furrows on Lovernios' brow deepened the longer he spoke to Sucellus and he started to rub his beard absentmindedly.

'Mama mine?' Grania hadn't seen what was going on between the two men. She was facing the opposite direction and greedily looking at the Romani women. 'Do you think it might be an idea to build some sort of cage or pen to keep the sacrifices from escaping?'

'No, there's no need. They've no life or will in them to run away, and where would they go anyway? Besides, they don't know what we've in store for them; they probably think we'll set them free.'

'But mama, they're devious. Look, the old one with the paint, she looks clever and she sits apart, see? And she watches, keeps watching, for a warrior to catch her eye so she can call him over and prattle. She knows the ways of men, you can tell. She's used to getting what she wants from them.'

'Perhaps she is, Grania, when she's in her finest clothes and is clean and her hair isn't all tangled and half hanging out of its clips. Look, her paint's all smeared. She'll never attract a man looking like that.'

'Well, look at those young ones over there. The one with the piece of raw meat, is it? She keeps showing it to the others and wailing. She'll start an insurrection before long. We should ensure they're boxed in in some way.'

'It's not necessary, their will was broken before ever we got here. They won't run.'

'But think, mama, think! What if one did get away? Despite all our precautions, all the warriors we've set to guarding them, all the things we know about Romani women; what if one actually managed to escape? Imagine how annoyed Andraste would be.' Boudicca tensed. 'The Goddess is probably here now, watching, anticipating their blood. Think how cheated She'd feel if we didn't deliver to Her all we'd promised, all we're promising now simply by setting these woman apart for Her pleasure.'

'That wouldn't do. Not at all,' Boudicca agreed.

'No, mama, it wouldn't.' Grania continued her persuasion. 'For if we don't keep faith with Andraste and hold to our pledge with Her, She might abandon us. And what would we be without Her?'

Boudicca stared, unfocused, at the Romani women. Suddenly she saw their inactivity and placidity as a trick, a wily subterfuge, to lull the Celtoi into complacency. She daren't risk incurring Andraste's wrath: if she did, the Goddess might never return to her.

'Yes,' she hissed at last. 'We must cage them.' She called over some of the guards and ordered them to build something to keep the women from escaping. 'It doesn't need to be too sturdy or too elaborate,' she explained. 'Just enough to pen them in. Perhaps wooden pallets could be used and some of the rope the Romani left down by the wharfs? If you build cages over the backs of the wagons it'll be easier to transport the women to the Groves.'

'Madam,' the guards were nervous. 'Those Romani are too tired and frightened to be any trouble. What you're suggesting isn't really necessary. There are some Romani slave chains in one of the warehouses not far from here, perhaps we could chain the women up? Certainly it'd be quicker and easier.'

Boudicca opened her mouth to argue, surprised her command was questioned. Before she could speak, Grania butted in. 'We need this done immediately.'

The guards bowed and scurried off to do as they were told, and Boudicca watched them commandeer a couple of wagons and strip them of their contents before erecting wooden bars all along the sides. She breathed a sigh of relief that soon the Romani women would cease to be recalcitrant and unruly and she'd finally be able to rest, assured that Andraste would have all She'd been allotted. She was satisfied, too, with her continuing ability to control the horde and the individuals in it. Those guards had certainly set about fulfilling her demands almost as soon as her order was given. It was kind of them to make alternative suggestions, but ultimately, they must have known it was not their place. There had been moments, over the last few days, when she had felt as if the horde had been trickling away from her drop by drop, but now she felt relieved it had only been a passing fancy. It seemed there was nothing untoward with her authority after all.

She stood with Grania, the two women still embracing each other, until the cages were built and the Romani women herded into them. The women were terrified, so much was obvious, and the guards had to prick them with their spear tips to hurry them up and goad them forward. Boudicca was certain some of the women were seeking a chance to escape as they milled around, trying to respond to conflicting orders issued with a spear point. But most of the women clung to each other, now they were forced to be so close, and actually seemed more alarmed if a command appeared to try to separate them from those they held onto. Boudicca suspected it was all just a ruse, appearing more concerned with staying with one's fellows than effecting escape, whilst all the while she could see they'd really take any opportunity to run for their lives.

Most of the camp followers had made their way into Londinium now. The wagons were drawn round in a wide circle to provide shelter from the wind for the camp-fires which had been started for the comfort of those returning from ransacking the town. Lovernios and Sucellus finally made their way over to Boudicca and Grania, at Sucellus' pace and with their heads bowed close together in continued conference. Boudicca and Grania had not moved from where Sucellus had left them. Boudicca was conscious of that and had stayed there partly on purpose. She had been too wrapped up in ensuring every single one of the Romani women were securely caught, and in giving Grania the affection her daughter had rejected for so long, to bother with disobeying the smith. She had also not wanted to give Sucellus cause for complaint; she was aware he had some grievance and she did not wish to provide him with any excuse to suspect her further. If she did as he asked and stayed put, surely he would have to deduce she was innocent – was it not only the guilty who sought to avoid justice?

'Madam?' Lovernios addressed her formally. His face was stern; there was no welcome for her here. 'Sucellus has something very important to say to both of you. It might be best if the four of us move away.'

Grania clenched her mother tighter. Boudicca walked forward, as Lovernios suggested, virtually having to drag her daughter with her. 'Grania, Grania, daughter mine, it's all right,' she soothed. 'Mama's with you. Mama will make sure you're looked after.'

When they were out of earshot of the rest of the camp, amongst the tombstones of the Romani straddling the road into the town, she motioned for Sucellus to begin. Both he and Lovernios looked so grave-faced and serious Boudicca wanted to laugh at their expressions. What on earth could she have done which was so dreadful? She ruffled Grania's hair, still holding her daughter to her. Grania's warmth was reassuring, even though her daughter hid her face and refused to look at either of the two men.

'Go on, Sucellus,' Lovernios encouraged. 'Exactly as you told me. Unless this issue is aired, we won't be able to help her.'

Sucellus looked extremely uncomfortable as he began. 'It's about your allegation that Maeve is the one responsible for the mutilation of the bodies.' Boudicca nodded. 'I've reason to believe Maeve is not responsible.'

'So do I,' Boudicca flashed. 'She's been heavily guarded since Caesaromagus, as I dare say you've already verified. Why, her wagon has only just come into camp, I saw it myself just a moment ago. She can't have been responsible for the mutilations which the three of us, all too clearly, saw in Londinium, because she couldn't possibly have been there. I'm so glad we agree. It was a relief for me, I can tell you, now I know it's definitely not someone close to me. Now, if that's all …' Boudicca started to move away.

'Wait, madam.' Lovernios restrained her. 'A while longer, please. Sucellus has more to tell you.'

'It wasn't Maeve who was responsible. I was certain of that even before you made your accusation at Caesaromagus, Boudicca. But it still means somebody else was.'

'Yes, and Grania nearly caught them too. Didn't you, Grania?' Grania nodded her head fervently from within the shelter of Boudicca's embrace.

'Grania was ideally placed to catch them,' continued Sucellus. 'I watched her for quite a while. Unbeknown to her, of course. I saw what she did to the bodies and I saw what she used to mutilate them. You were right; Andraste's sickle is being used for this disgusting act. Grania could've caught them very easily, as easily as owning up that it was her.'

Boudicca was livid. 'What a ridiculous thing to say! This isn't true, is it, Grania?'

'No, mama, it wasn't me. I swear. I nearly had him, I was sneaking up on him to take him alive.' Grania's voice was muffled where she refused to turn her face away from Boudicca's breast.

'See. If Grania says it wasn't her, then it wasn't her. I won't hear another word of this stupid accusation.'

'Grania?' Lovernios' tone was gentle but firm; it would accept no nonsense. 'What did he look like?'

She sniffled. 'I don't know,' she pleaded. 'I only saw his back. He was big, broad shouldered, dark, hairy… Leave me alone, it wasn't me, it really wasn't me.'

Lovernios and Sucellus exchanged glances. 'I know what I saw,' Sucellus finally stated.

'And I know what I saw, and now I've heard what my daughter has to say about it, too. As far as I'm concerned, Sucellus, it's your word against Grania's and you should have no doubt, either of you, about who I'll believe. Somewhere among our peoples there's a monster of a man and you're both stood here frightening an innocent little girl, when if you displayed half the bravery she did in trying to bring him to justice, he might be executed by now and the whole disgusting depravity brought to an end.

'Now, if you two men have quite finished, my daughter and I have this evening's sacrifices to discuss. I'm trusting this matter will go no further than the four of us. Please excuse us.' And with that, Boudicca tilted up her head and escorted Grania away and back to the camp.

Grania started to sob, still hiding her face in her mother's robes. 'There, there, Grania mine. You can come out now, they're not here any more. Mama believes you and mama won't let anyone else believe otherwise. Let's work out exactly how these Romani women will die; that should take your mind off that nasty Sucellus.'

'Will they let us use the Groves?' Grania spoke through her tears, her voice still shaky.

'They will if I demand it.'

'Good. Then we must make sure everyone is there to watch and take part.'

'Everyone?'

'Yes. Then we'll all be Blessed by Andraste, then we'll all be sacrificing to Her and the whole horde will benefit.'

'But …' Boudicca thought quickly, she didn't want the whole tribe to benefit. Of course, she'd known she couldn't have done it all by herself and she was expecting others to be there with her. But she had anticipated a select group of Druids, Chiefs and Ladies, and her own family, perhaps. If she shared the bloodletting with too many people, she might not be able to wallow in the sacrifices the way she intended; the way that might provide a nest in her psyche for Andraste's return. 'I think there might be too many people to organise,' she countered weakly.

'You managed it for the Eostar rituals, mama. You could manage it again. Look at the plunder we've taken from Londinium. There's hardly anything – a pittance to be shared amongst so many. Unless we provide some other diversion, we'll lose the horde. They must have something more definite than ideals to fight for.'

Boudicca could think of no arguments against her daughter's suggestion. Grania was so determined now, so very assured in what she wanted, possessing the very qualities Boudicca had felt lacking in herself since the sickle had gone missing and with it, Andraste's presence.

Looking closely at her daughter's expectant face she couldn't help but notice the unmistakeable slant to Grania's eyes and the cruel twist in her mouth. Andraste was here within Grania, so much was clear. But then, Lovernios had already admitted as much, back in Sucellus' clearing after their first encounter with Artio, when she'd forced him to tell her. What was the word he'd used then? 'Hospitality.' That was it; both her daughters had offered Andraste suitable hospitality, he'd said, and both of them could be helped to channel the Divine. Maeve had never needed to be helped, or so it had transpired. Had Grania now learnt to channel the Divine herself? It would be a help if she had, thought Boudicca, for without Andraste's presence within herself for guidance, she had felt truly blind over the last few days. If she could only derive Andraste's inspiration through Grania, second-hand as it were, just until she had won the Goddess back for herself. Surely it would be better than this nothingness, this empty space where Andraste should be?

Having used logic thus far, Boudicca set her mind to implementing what Grania had suggested.

'I'll need you to help me, Grania. I'll need you to invite the horde to the Groves with us, to ensure they watch and join in the rites. We'll stand together, but you'll need to address the crowds yourself. They'll listen to you.'

'All right, mama. I think I know what to say to get them to come with us. Now, how shall the Romani die?'

What would Andraste like best? What would bring Her back? 'I think it should be the most horrific death we can think of. Something to make even us sicken at the very thought.'

'So, what's the worst thing you could imagine happening to you, mama?'

Boudicca was caught in mid-thought. So many dreadful things had already happened to her, she had already seen more horror than it was fair to live through.

'Think, mama, think about the punishments these women deserve. How they flaunt their babes and their fertile stomachs. How they take, take, take from Celtoi. How we can make even the whole of the Romani Empire squirm in disgust at the things we can devise, so they'll fear to ever return to Britannia.'

Boudicca mentally flicked through the many masks of death and suffering she'd witnessed. They came so readily to mind, as if waiting impatiently for the slightest invitation to be recalled. A husband dead from some wasting disease which had stalked him for years, a still-born babe still wrinkled from womb waters, friends and family with expressions contorted in agony from their final wounds. Two beautiful, lively twin girls, with everything to live for and a kingdom to inherit, left ruined in the dirt.

'No. We can't do that to them.'

'What, mama? What can't we do to them?'

'Every woman's nightmare, Grania. Every woman's secret dread. The unspeakable crime. No. We're Celtoi. We've never done such things, we won't start now.'

Grania's eyes twinkled greedily. 'We can adapt the idea. Use a different 'weapon', one which will kill as it penetrates.'

Boudicca wished she hadn't eaten the Romani's dates earlier. Her stomach was churning at the thought of the distress she could inflict. She imagined the feel of her own body being pierced and skewered, bit by bit. The sharp bite of metal tearing her internals apart as it rose through her body. Then she felt a rush of excitement and titillation as she discovered the idea appealed to her very, very much. It answered the Romani back very neatly for what they'd done to her daughters and to countless other women, including, she remembered, Lovernios' mother. And paid them back, for that matter, for the cheap sexuality they displayed gratuitously in their homes too, their obscene statues and lascivious wall-friezes. This would teach them to regard sex with a new respect, as a sacred, caring act emulating the Goddess and Her Consort, not as something to be bought, sold and discarded when it was done with.

If she alone were capable of inventing such torture in honour of her Goddess, surely she'd prove she was still a suitable receptacle for Her. Then she'd be certain of coaxing Andraste back, wouldn't she?

'Yes,' she agreed, catching Grania's enthusiasm. 'Do it, arrange it for mama, speak to them now.'

Grania grinned with a huge smugness at having got her own way and at having been granted exactly what she wanted. 'Come with me, then, mama,' and she pulled Boudicca after her and onto the back of the nearest stable pile of rubble and wood. Immediately, Boudicca watched heads swivel to see them. They must have looked imposing; two women, one tall, the other destined to be, both with muscular frames offset with waist length, reddish brown hair and adorned with gold and almost garish clothing. But Boudicca knew it wasn't their appearance which made people look, it was their presence.

'Tonight is New Moon,' called Grania, and as she spoke, more of the horde stopped what they were doing and turned to listen. 'And New Moon is the customary phase for new beginnings. We are moving from the dark back out into the light again.' Her voice rung out clear and resonant, commanding attention from the masses. Other tribes-folk ran from the last of the plundering, urged by their comrades to move into listening distance. Boudicca watched as Celtoi from all over Londinium converged upon the camp, moving together as if drawn, unresisting, back into a unified whole. This, then, was power, Boudicca knew; no wonder Grania's face shone with exhilaration. Boudicca could hardly wait until the sacrifices had been made and her own psyche was remoulded and suitable for Andraste to Emanate through her again.

'I know you are disappointed at the spoils the Romani have left you in this place,' Grania roused the massive crowd. 'I know there's not the wine, nor the food, nor the combat, nor even the treasure you had dreamt of in sacking Londinium, but there are fabulous riches yet to be taken from the Romani. And there is a different entertainment for you tonight than Romani wine and Romani delicacies. One which will answer today's unmet desire for bloodshed.

'I know you seek gold, not just for yourselves but for sacrifice, too. You know that, in providing for Andraste, She will continue to bring you victory and triumph. You are disappointed there is not enough gold for you to satisfy your Goddess and you fear She will desert you. Do not be! For She has provided another means for you to keep Her sated, the way of blood sacrifice. And in Her bounty She has provided even the sacrifices for you so you need not look to yourselves for volunteers.'

Grania pointed to the Romani women, caged upon the wagons. 'Andraste demands the blood of these Romani women to be poured out for Her tonight. She demands you all bathe in their blood and you all join in Her rituals that you might be Blessed by Her. Let the Druids lead the way that the Paths may be Found, then follow me, every one of you, into Her Groves.'

Entranced by her daughter's power over the horde, Boudicca could do little else except hurry to keep up as Grania sped to take the lead of the shunting crowd edging its way north, back towards the forests. The outermost trees were not far away – the outskirts of forests never were, woodland being far more expansive than cleared land everywhere in Britannia. The wagons with their cages were pulled and pushed along in the midst of the heaving, excited people and a chorus went up of 'Andraste! Andraste!' over and over as if the horde had become a mob. Power, thought Boudicca. Grania might have power, but not control.

She pushed her way between a few people who barred the gap separating herself and her daughter. She suffered elbows in her ribs in the process, and knew the jarring would soften to bruising by morning. When she was level with Grania, she tried to get her attention, but her daughter was too involved in ordering Druids to lead the way into the deeper pathways of Andraste's sacred Groves. Desperate not to lose her and become subsumed into the faceless masses, Boudicca grasped for Grania's cloak. She caught a corner and held onto it for dear life, determined not to become separated from her daughter again.

They were beneath the trees within moments, the chanting stopping abruptly as each individual ducked beneath low-hanging branches and fell under the spell of the Otherness of the place they had Found. Boudicca felt the almost imperceptible shift of consciousness so reminiscent of a group Find. There was a sacredness in the air, a smell of musky leaves and an overwhelming profoundness which settled upon every Celtoi present. This was no longer a mobbing, even if Grania had been encouraging one; now it had been transmuted to a mystery, an appeasement of the Divine.

They brought the Romani women forward, singly. They had been taken from the cages one by one, unable to bring the wagons into the Groves, and pushed through the crowd independent of each other. Boudicca was at the front now, with Grania. The Grove was massive, like some vast cavern, and the people crowded in so they appeared like a field of weeds with faces for flowers. The horde was hushed with awe, the only sound being the screams from the Romani women as they were pushed forward through the packed tribes-folk, forced to endure contact with leering strangers with malevolent mouths.

Grania ordered torches to be lit and they cast an ethereal light around the gloom of the giant oak trees, beneath which they shel-tered. The wind was still up, although here, deep within the hearts of the trees, it was enough only to send the torches guttering a little. Boudicca was trying to stay close to her daughter as Grania moved around giving orders and directing others to keep to the scheme she was so carefully orchestrating.

Some of the Druids had started to chant hymns to the Goddess, fa-miliar enough for the tribes-folk to join in the chorus where the Druidic words could be remembered. The lilting refrains seemed am-plified in the steadily increasing dark. A detachment of Celtoi was gathering dry wood to heap together for a bonfire and a huge mound of timber was soon created. Once torches were set to it, it caught quickly, roaring into life and sending flickering orange patterns across the thousands and thousands of upturned faces waiting to see what would happen next.

It was quite oppressive for Boudicca, waiting here, watching Grania organise the ritual. She was without Lovernios' support and totally unfamiliar with the whole issue of blood sacrifice – she wondered where her lover had got to. These rites had not been practised for an entire generation; how Grania knew what to do was quite confound-ing. Perhaps the Goddess was leading her or she'd sought out Druidic historians for guidance. Whatever, Boudicca was reliant upon her daughter to take her through the liturgy.

The crowd seemed charged as they surged and jostled against each other. Grania was arousing and provoking them to action, stirring the tribes up and inciting them to do as she did. As Boudicca's gaze swept the horde, she noticed how the peoples had roughly divided into tribes. Kinsfolk stood near kinsfolk, keeping themselves distinct from those with whom they had no blood ties. The division was clearly per-ceptible by the subtle change in fabric colouring as she changed her direction of view. Grania had ensured that roughly the same number of Romani women were in the custody of each tribe. Where necessary, she reallocated prisoners, obviously aiming to provide equally for each tribe.

Grania started the formal Invocation of Andraste, building up the tension in the Groves. The chanting drowned out even the shrill pleas of the Romani women. Without knowing why, Boudicca looked over her shoulder far into the woods. There was a bear in the depths, she was certain, with the saddest eyes, but as she watched, it turned its back upon her and lumbered away.

Boudicca spun back, unbidden tears in her eyes for some inexplicable reason. She joined in the chanting with renewed vigour, determined to forget what she had just seen. She must get Andraste back and her best chance would be now, tonight. Her voice must be the loudest of all to invoke the Goddess. Grania was screaming with ecstasy, spinning herself around and around to induce trance. Seeing her daughter steal the privilege of ritual euphoria, Boudicca shouted herself hoarse calling Andraste's name, desperately grasping for the state of bliss which would make her so receptive to the Divine.

All around the clearing, other people, especially those more sensitive to the Otherworld, were being transported to rapture, whilst women swooned and children's eyes grew wild in the fitful light. Boudicca collapsed, gasping for breath and mentally exhausted. Her mind spun with twinkling colours and she sent out a prayer, in her head, for the Goddess to come to her. She'd emptied herself as best she could of the clutter of her mind; there was ample space now for the Goddess to return. She begged, with enormous exertion, for Andraste to please, please reappear.

Grania was officiating over the first of the sacrifices. She made the horde watch her carefully; each tribe was to repeat her actions with the prisoners in their keeping. She ordered one of the Romani women who'd been given over to the tribes-folk of the Iceni into the centre of the Grove, and her limbs to be pulled apart so she was splayed horizontally upon the ground like a five-pointed star.

Silence descended upon the horde, even upon the Romani women. Only heavy breathing and terrified pleas, which the Celtoi couldn't understand, could be heard from the first woman chosen to be sacrificed.

'This is how Andraste wants Her blood!'

Grania screamed the words, thrusting her spear between the woman's legs, carefully finding her birth channel, and pushing up, up, through her womb, solar plexus, and to her chest, until the spear point burst through her throat. Boudicca watched the woman's body buck in different places as the spear passed through her torso, and heard sinews and organs squash and puncture as they ruptured. Those warriors holding the woman let loose her limbs and blood spewed and gurgled from all her orifices as she twitched convulsively.

The horde cheered tumultuously as Grania ordered the still warm body to be propped up to lean upon the spear pinioning it. Around the Grove, the horde bunched around each of the remaining Romani women to continue with the grisly skewering.

Boudicca forced herself to enjoy the woman's torment and savour the exquisite pain being meted out around the Groves. It had been a long while since the oaks had resounded to such terrible wails, but the noise was like sweet music to Boudicca. She revelled in the torture exuding from the clearing and from the heightened senses of every person present, all attuned to the manufacture of pain and suffering.

Still she didn't feel Andraste's presence return to her. Her psyche felt hollow and craved to be full, like a child's hunger when the crops had failed. Striving yet to attract the Goddess back to her, she joined in the sacrifice of the other women assigned for the use of the Iceni tribe. Here she helped position the first thrust of the spear, expertly placing the point at the woman's sex. There she held an arm as it desperately tried to break free in its frenzied flailing. At another place she tugged a spear loose where it had stuck on some bone, then helped drive it fully into the woman until it was completely embedded.

When she finally withdrew from the slaughter, she looked down at herself. She was completely covered in blood, as if she had just helped at the delivery of a thousand babes. In the firelight her whole body seemed to glisten with gore and bodily fluids. But still there was no sign of Andraste for her. Mad with jealousy for the precious thing she had lost, for the Gift she could no longer live without, she sought Grania.

She found her daughter preparing rope for each spiked body to be hoisted up high in the oak trees. There they would provide food for the Goddess' ubiquitous crows, as had been done in the days of her ancestors.

Boudicca grabbed Grania by the shoulder. 'It's not enough,' she demanded. 'There must be something more we can do. Some further depravity to which we can sink. This blood isn't enough to purify my spirit. Andraste hasn't returned, She wants more!'

Grania grinned back. A madwoman's grin, her eyes as vacuous as Maeve's. In an instant, Boudicca doubted her daughter's sanity and her own for being led by her. Then the dullness in Grania's gaze lifted. Boudicca saw a flicker of evil leap into life, and the visage of the Destroyer sweep over Grania's face.

'There's still this, mama mine.' And Boudicca watched incredulous as Grania lifted up the folds of her robes and pulled out Andraste's sickle. Still amazed at what she saw, Boudicca saw Grania cut off the dead woman's breasts with the golden sickle and sew them roughly to the corpse's mouth with ivy tendrils and mistletoe stems. Then the whole horrific effigy was winched into the tallest oak branches and left to swing in the winds that were still busy whipping around and above.

Grania grabbed Boudicca's hand and pulled her on to the next corpse. She did the same again, cutting off this old woman's sagging breasts with one swipe of the blade and stuffing them in the corpse's mouth before securing them with a few basic stitches. Boudicca recognised the body. It was the painted face of the haughty Romani, the one who'd sat apart from the others. Barely distinguishable now, she looked like she was eating her own breasts, her own providers of sustenance. With the spear still protruding from between her legs, the sexual overtones were too blatant to be ignored.

Boudicca didn't have long to look before this corpse too was hoisted high into the air and Grania tugged her mother on to the next sacrificial victim. Boudicca couldn't remember how many disfigured bodies she looked upon, or for how long she ran behind Grania only to see another pair of bare feet disappear above her head before her daughter pulled her away upon another errand. It was like being upon a Faery carousel; a twirling, nauseous ride of glittering lights and horrific faces, flying in and out of focus and rendering her as confused as if she'd stepped into the Otherworld where nothing could be known and nothing trusted.

Finally they stopped and collapsed upon the ground. All around, the horde cheered excitedly, singing new songs of joy to Andraste as they celebrated Her Blessing being bestowed upon them as Grania had promised it would. With all the sacrifices creaking above in the oaks of the Grove, and the firelight disguising most of the carnage, the scene could almost be the jubilation following Lugnasadh fair. The dancing could be celebrating the bounty of the harvest. The carousing could be a thanksgiving for victory in the annual games. But it was not. The horde was high on hype and racket and Boudicca berated herself for what she'd unleashed. And what for? Still, she realised, there was no Andraste to fill the void within her spirit. Grania's suggestions had evidently never been the way to retrieve what she'd lost.

She looked at Grania now, still able to find compassion for the animal her daughter had disintegrated to. For she was, after all, kin. Boudicca took the sickle from her daughter and tucked it back in her own belt where it felt like it belonged. It seemed to sing to itself, happy perhaps to have been blood soaked for a while.

'So, Sucellus was right,' Boudicca whispered, half to herself. 'It was you all along.'

Grania lifted her head to answer, all light gone from her eyes. Before she could, something streamed past, quicker than Boudicca could see. Suddenly the revellers filling the Grove started to scream and panic, and stampeded away from whatever the hurtling thing was.

Boudicca noticed a child with long streaks of blood down its face being picked up by its parent and carried away. Then more people panicked as the threat seemed to lunge at them again. Boudicca stood, hauling Grania to her feet too.

There was another child, in the midst of the chaos, with no one to see to it. It was crying to itself and calling out for mama mama, unable, Boudicca could tell, to see anything other than thousands of legs, all as tall as tree trunks to it, and none of them familiar. Boudicca left Grania for an instant and went to the child, desperate to soothe its fear. Before she could pick it up, she felt something charge across her path, something with long threads of black hair which cut her face and stung her eyes as she almost ran into it. When her path was clear again she looked for the child, but it had gone.

Vainly she looked all around, aware the Grove was clearing fast, leaving just herself and Grania the only people not in a hurry to leave. Then she noticed Lovernios had arrived at last. He stood with Maeve and Sucellus and pointed.

Boudicca assumed he was looking at her and started to walk towards him. She did so slowly, for she was aware she was in no state to be embraced. He didn't look pleased.

'Go!' He boomed, in a voice filled with borrowed authority. Boudicca could feel Maeve and Sucellus lending him mental support in his command. 'Back to the depths of Other to which you were Banished and to which you must stay,' he continued.

Not knowing quite why, Boudicca turned to look behind her. Lovernios' command hadn't been directed at her after all. There, backing quickly away into the depths of the forest was a scrawny woman, her face virtually covered with dark strands of hair hanging down to her hips. As she vanished from view, Boudicca noticed the inhuman expression and the kicking, mewling infant in her arms covered in scratches from the woman's taloned fingernails. Boudicca recognised the infant as the one she had almost saved and she started to dart after the apparition. But it was too late, the gloom and the oak leaves had covered over the woman's departure and she may as well have never been there.

'Lovernios!' Boudicca called, not caring any longer for her appearance. 'What have I done? What have I let loose?'

He held her with reticence. Boudicca could feel his disgust and shame seep through his touch along with his affection. His answer surprised her though: 'Madam, you might well be asking me the same question.'

Chapter 15

New Moon

Lovernios held Boudicca for as long as she needed. It was good to feel human warmth again and to see a familiar, kind face, especially when she had expected some sort of reprimand. When she felt able to address the world again, Boudicca pulled gently away from her lover and stood without leaning against him. She had left blood smeared all over the front of his robes, but he didn't seem to mind.

'We should all return to Londinium, madam.' It was the first words any of them had spoken since the horde had left and the strange woman had disappeared back into the forests.

Boudicca nodded; she didn't feel like replying. The woods felt oddly deserted, more so for having just been the scene of such ribald merry-making. She imagined that, if only she could listen closely enough, she might still detect the ghosts of echoes ricocheting off the sturdy oak trunks.

'Let's make sure the Grove is Sealed as we leave, Sucellus.'

'I think it might be best, all things considered,' the smith replied. He was careful, so Boudicca noticed, not to look her in the eye.

Boudicca stooped to help Grania to her feet. Her daughter lay slumped where she'd fallen in exhaustion, waking only to start licking off the blood caking her skin, as if she were a wounded hunting dog. Boudicca pulled Grania's head away from where she licked and encouraged her to stand and accompany them back to Londinium. Grania growled a low warning, enough to make Boudicca pause before touching her again. Them Maeve joined her and softly stroked Grania's arm, leading her sister back to the horde which waited on the outskirts of the town.

Boudicca followed close behind the two girls, leaving Lovernios to set the strongest Wards of Sealing upon the Grove. Evidently he did not want this particular forest clearing ever to be accessed again. Soon, Boudicca felt the shifting of consciousness, which she was becoming so accustomed to, alerting her of a passage out of Other and into the material realms. Only then, as the last oak branches swung back to hide where they'd emerged from the trees, did she see the extent of the destruction of Londinium.

They had entered the Groves in late afternoon; now it was fully dark. The moon was new and offered scant light, less anyway than that afforded from the burning town. Billowing smoke had been visible by day, but was less impressive than this. Now the ransacked shells of warehouses, hovels and palaces alike had caught afire and the flames towered high as if reaching up to join with the stars. Not that there was any less smoke than earlier in the day. They were fortunate the wind had been energetic; without it the plumes would never have dissipated and the horde would not have been able to camp where it had, so close to the Romani town.

Here and there, Boudicca could see silhouettes run quickly across the backdrop of turning flame as it fed upon the dry tinder Londinium had been reduced to. This was no Camulodunum, built of stone and less flammable materials, this was a settlement endured as temporary by those who stayed for profit and as adequate by those who stayed hoping financial luck was infectious. Romani Londinium had not been built to last; it had been built to be inhabitable, but only just. It was the best indicator Boudicca had yet seen to suggest the Romani intended to stay only as long as it took them to strip Britannia of her natural resources. Judging by the heat she could feel even this far back, Boudicca would predict there would be nothing left but ashes come morning. Better, she thought, such description should apply to an invader's town than to a whole island.

She caught up with her two girls, who walked just ahead of her, and pointed to where she wanted them to go rather than telling them, uncertain she would be heard over the fierce crackling of fire and tumble of falling timbers. The three women veered off in the new direction.

'Madam, where do you think you're going?' Lovernios' question paused Boudicca but didn't slow her down.

'To wash. I think I need it, don't you? And probably to wash Grania, too.'

'Can't it wait 'til morning?'

'No. I don't want to look down at myself in the cold light of day and see what I can only imagine I must look like. Besides, the fires will dry me off as I walk back through Londinium to camp.'

'We'll accompany you then, madam. It wouldn't do for us to become… separated again.'

She very nearly snapped back: 'Please yourself,' but somehow she stopped herself and kept silent. Lovernios was showing her a lot of tenderness in holding back whatever remonstration she felt certain had been due to her. She was not exactly sure why yet, but she could maintain an almost-passivity until she had heard what he had to say.

They reached the banks of the river Tamesis by a circuitous route that avoided the burning of Londinium. It flowed rapidly, as black as Artio's cave, and seemed to twitch as if it were the sleek tail of a wildcat with a life of its own. Boudicca had watched such tails before, as they involuntarily translated the agitation of the wildcat in question, as if the predatory owner was too preoccupied with hunting to bother controlling its remote appendage.

Boudicca swung down from the wharf and landed upon the gravel which fringed the river's shallows. The river level was reasonably low and she had just enough room to stand between the wharf walls and the lapping waters without her feet getting wet. She started to undress and realised she didn't need to, her clothes needed to be cleaned too. The rough wool her cloak and tunic were woven from might shrink as they dried in front of the campfires, but she felt as if she had little choice if she really wanted to be clean from the evening's work.

She beckoned to Grania to join her, and her daughter jumped down with considerably more reluctance. Boudicca could see she might have to contend with tantrums as bad as any toddler's first bathing experience.

Slipping her shoes off and throwing them up to Lovernios, Boudicca started by edging a toe into the chill waters. Hag Herself! It was like touching ice, as if the blackness was not water but nothingness to freeze away all sensation. She would be here forever if she waited until each part of her body accustomed itself to the temperature. Dangerous too, she decided, and did what she usually did when faced with daunting tasks. Taking a deep breath she waded out until the river was waist height and then she sank, plunging herself completely under water. Knowing she wouldn't be able to endure the cold for long once the shock registered with her mind, she quickly doused her face and hair, feeling the ichors of the Romani women washed away from her skin. She felt clean and fresh and somehow new, then the cold hit her and she stumbled out of the waters, her damp clothes impeding her with their heaviness, until she was back upon the gravel, shivering and sodden but with the stickiness thankfully lifted from her body.

'Now you, Grania,' she ordered, her teeth chattering as she spoke. 'You'll feel so much better for it. I promise.'

Grania growled in that peculiarly feral way of hers and hunched herself away from her mother. Then Boudicca saw Maeve jump down and lead her twin with a placating hand, gently edging Grania into the river with no more than an animal's whimper. If anything, Grania's and Maeve's dips were even quicker than Boudicca's, and they emerged from the river with Grania shaking like a dog to dry herself but hardly free of the blood and mess from the sacrifices.

Boudicca let it go, reaching up for Lovernios' hand to lift her back up from the river-bed. Her daughters followed and wordlessly they trudged back to the camp and the rest of the horde. On this occasion they passed nearer to the heat of the numerous fires, Boudicca letting the flames warm her through and dry off her clothing as best she could. Bathing in a fast river at night, when the seasons had not yet turned to summer, was foolhardy, she knew. But it felt so good to have fresh skin again which did not stick to her clothes with every movement, along with anything else it touched. The waters had been invigorating too, reminding her that despite the sorrows of her life and the chaos she currently swam in, she was still very much alive, still capable of feeling.

When they joined the Celtoi camp, Boudicca was relieved to find they could do so without commanding much attention. They built their own hearth and set their own fire burning for Boudicca and her daughters to sit and dry out thoroughly. Lovernios discreetly got the attention of some of his Druids and requested they procure some sort of food for them.

'There isn't much, so don't expect a feast,' he half-apologised. 'We're running low on supplies and Londinium has been disappointing in many ways.'

Boudicca didn't bother replying. She was still unable to interpret what his mood was. Besides, she was too busy contending with her chattering teeth and didn't trust herself to be able to talk with any sense.

The Druids returned with enough food to stave off hunger, wine which had been well watered down and, without being asked, some blankets to replace their sodden cloaks. Boudicca could see her thick cloak would dry better for being spread nearer the fire and she let it be taken from her, Grania and Maeve doing the same.

They ate in silence, not even speaking to pass the wine around. Boudicca was confused and impatient to know who'd break the spell first. It would not be her, she would make sure of that. It was obvious she was in trouble, with Sucellus at least, and she was not exactly proud of the things she had done or been encouraged to do with nothing to show for it. Nor was she pleased with the way she had let her family loyalty override Sucellus' attempts to warn her about Grania, even though she felt he was being insensitive about the way he had virtually hunted her daughter. In hindsight, though, she could plainly see the clues she had missed about Grania's condition. She knew that she had deliberately ignored them before, not wanting to face the consequences of what it might mean.

She felt like a naughty child now, waiting for its parents to sufficiently calm down from their anger to be able to form the words they were presently too annoyed to bring themselves to speak. The best way, she knew, would be to ride out the storm, let them choose when they were ready, and quietly occupy her mind in the meanwhile.

So she listened and watched all she could see going on in the camp of her horde. They had not all fled, she noticed with satisfaction; most of them seemed to have left the Grove only to return to camp and the safety of numbers. Their numbers hardly seemed reduced at all and she could not forget there were still many Celtoi darting through the remains of the town. Perhaps they could not flee, she pondered. Most of them would have nowhere to run to, no homes left. Anyway, they were already implicated in what had been done in the name of the rebellion, and would thus be bound to destroy the Romani or die in the attempt.

Boudicca observed how kin and tribal groups had gathered together again and were chatting idly as if the sacrifices had never happened, or so she could glean from what she heard of the eavesdropped conversations. There was a hushed atmosphere over the whole place, as if every individual had been affected by what had happened, though. Shocked and disturbed, wondered Boudicca, or profoundly moved?

'I see you've got Andraste's sickle back.' Sucellus could obviously stand the tension no longer. Boudicca looked down. The golden handle was sticking out of her belt, glinting mischievously in the flickering light.

Boudicca nodded with what she hoped was credible submissiveness; she wanted to avoid admitting how she had had it returned.

'Do you believe me now?' Sucellus continued with his verbal prodding.

'I don't believe my daughter is the ogre you portray her as, no.'

'But Boudicca, how can you doubt so many facts?'

Boudicca crept nearer to Grania, drawing her close in a protective embrace. This then, was the confrontation she had been so dreading. Grania's frightened eyes flashed back at her accusers. She looked like a caged animal, terrified yet capable of dreadful violence if pushed too far.

'My daughter's been through more than anyone, especially one of the royal line of Iceni, should ever go through. She's lived a life's experiences since spring's dawn at Imbolc. It's hardly surprising if her behaviour is a little …' She considered the right word. 'Erratic.'

Sucellus shook his head in disbelief as Boudicca continued. 'I have the sickle back now, the mutilations can be stopped.' She chattered on, determined to convince the smith. 'Look, the horde's still here, no Celtoi has been hurt through what's happened – just a bit shaken, perhaps. We can keep this quiet, just between the five of us. Put out some story that Grania did apprehend whoever was responsible, with Sucellus' aid, in those crooked back streets. Then the whole nasty episode can all be forgotten about.'

In the space between the sound of her words fading and before Lovernios spoke, it was so quiet Boudicca could hear them all breathing and her own heart banging away within her chest.

'I'm afraid, madam, it's not quite as simple as that.' Then Lovernios bowed to Grania and said, 'It's not, is it, Andraste?'

Boudicca pulled away from her daughter in shock. Too many things suddenly slotting into place. 'Is this true?' she hissed finally. 'Did you steal Her from me?'

Grania did nothing. Boudicca shook her. 'Did you?' she screamed at her daughter.

'Madam! Be still.' Boudicca knew the tone – Lovernios' command would brook no nonsense. She sat in a sulk, aware she was so near to the thing she so painfully wanted back. 'If you pay attention, you should hear things that'll bear promise for you.

'You don't like Her, do you?' He was talking to Grania again, gently now. 'She brings out too many bits you're used to keeping tucked away, doesn't She?' Grania nodded once, the slightest assent. Lovernios continued. 'You don't really know what to do with all that limitless power, do you, Grania? But you might have done, you know, if you'd allowed your mother to help you train your psyche. But it's not too late – we can still help you, if you let us.'

Grania shook her head desperately. Then she pushed at her forehead with the back of her hand, as if she were a cat trying to loosen a tic without scratching itself.

'I don't want help; I like it here.' The words growled out from Grania's throat. 'She has imagination, this one, yea, and spirit too. The Trinovantes want to take Verulamium next. I'm going to let them too, just as long as I get more blood like today's.'

Then Grania sprung up suddenly and bounded off, too quickly for them to stop her. Only Boudicca had caught the expression of utter anguish upon Grania's face as her daughter had seemed to resist the urge to do as Andraste demanded.

Helplessly, Boudicca heard Grania rush through the camp. She saw Sucellus' and Lovernios' expressions as they, too, realised what they had all just heard. Then they heard Grania's voice again, loud and commanding, inspiring loyalty with every syllable. They sensed her presence immediately register with the crowds, inspiring the people to grant her their full attention. They felt the horde, spellbound, as she implored them to horde upon Verulamium and the Catuvellauni, and then they sensed the Divine command spread like the fires of Londinium through the massed force. They heard Grania beseech the Celtoi to yet more sacrifices, similar to the ones just made. The horde cheered back, confirming their own experience of Andraste's Blessing, which still roused their spirits from the evening's ritual.

217

Lovernios and Sucellus looked dismally unempowered as Grania's words rang out, yet they appeared deep in thought, too. Suddenly, Maeve stood, tapped Boudicca gently upon the shoulder urging her to join her, and started to walk in the direction of Grania's voice.

'I'd bring her back myself,' Boudicca sobbed to Lovernios and Sucellus, trying to remedy the situation before she set off with Maeve. 'But I don't trust my authority with the horde any longer. I can't seem to command respect from anyone at the moment.' Boudicca clamped her hand over her mouth as it suddenly dawned on her what she had just said. Her rash words, spoken from her emotional turmoil without full consideration, had starkly reminded her that in the last few days there had been several occasions when she had doubted her natural authority. Had she really only been able to command when Grania was with her?

'No, madam, you're right, you wouldn't be able to,' Lovernios confirmed. 'Andraste's with Grania, now. Of course, you haven't lost Her completely, none of the tribes-folk have. Those sacrifices called Her to us as effectively as Grania promised you they would.'

'You know about that?' Boudicca stopped in her tracks; this conversation sounded more urgent than going with Maeve.

'Yes, madam, I know about it. I can only begin to imagine how Grania manipulated you into thinking you could get Andraste back this way, letting you think it was all your idea. I can even understand how desperate you must've felt to go to those lengths, but I can't condone it. A lot of it I deduced, but I'm also not as stupid as some people think – nor are some people as clever as they assume.'

Boudicca wasn't too sure whether he was digging at her or at Grania, or at someone else altogether. This wasn't the place to argue though, so she let the slight go unmentioned. 'What do you mean by not having lost Andraste completely?' she asked.

'Do you remember the thousands of hares you saw, while in trance, bouncing around upon the entire horde?'

'Yes, of course.'

'Well,' continued Lovernios. 'That's more or less what's happened. Andraste's Blessing has been poured down upon the horde and Her Divine presence is with every one of us right now.'

'The blood sacrifices of our ancestors were very effective,' Sucellus explained. 'They still are. Andraste isn't just the horde's figurehead now. Andraste is the horde and the horde is Andraste, and the horde can very much direct itself. But when you're doubly Blessed, like Grania, it's possible for you to direct the horde to do additional things. Things it wouldn't normally do.'

'So, I'm not needed any more, then?' Boudicca asked more timidly.

'No, madam. You're needed more than ever.'

'I don't see why. I seem to be totally superfluous. You've just told me the horde doesn't need anyone to lead it at all, what with Andraste acting with it rather than through it. I might as well just fade away into notoriety.'

Lovernios smiled despite himself. 'I can't see you being eager to carry out that threat, madam,' he chuckled. 'But anyway, it'd be better if Andraste would return to you.'

'Better for whom, Lovernios mine?'

'For absolutely everyone, Boudicca.'

'Do I get the honour of an explanation, or shall I just accept it the way I usually have to?'

Lovernios and Sucellus looked at each other, trying, Boudicca presumed, to decide who would tell her. Finally, as if at some signal from Sucellus, Lovernios started to elucidate.

'Andraste's Manifestation depends on Her raw materials, so to speak. She is, as you have pointed out, acting directly upon the world through the horde's mass consciousness. Had that been Her only Manifestation, we could allow the transfer of direction and let the host have its freedom; we would ride with it, equally Blessed, and allow the authority of the Druids to counter any major problems as required. But that isn't the only Manifestation of Andraste. We all know Grania is, as Sucellus puts it, "doubly Blessed". Any interaction Andraste has with the horde will affect both of them: Grania will be able to exert her own influence upon the masses and the masses will mould her to them.'

Lovernios looked Boudicca directly in the eye for his next words. 'If it'd still been you, madam, the situation would be fine. Fine, but not easy; it would still be a demanding role, as you know. But you're strong, able to stand up to the horde, and fluid enough not to be subsumed by Andraste. And, with the greatest respect to your daughter, madam, the "raw material" with yourself is of a, shall we say, higher quality? Grania never learned to train her psyche, and the things which were done to her when the Romani came have unsettled her mind beyond repair, I suspect. Your daughter has not been healing from her experiences, madam, she's just been making herself sicker by indulging in her revenge campaigns.'

Lovernios paused before continuing. 'Unfortunately, when Andraste Manifests through such a filter... well, you've seen the results for yourself. It's like sunlight pouring through a piece of the Romani's darkly coloured glass and, although I recognise it as another aspect of a Goddess ultimately unknowable, there are occasions when even I have found Her almost unlovable. Truly Grania has brought forth the Divine in Her most darkest aspect.'

'A Goddess unknowable, certainly,' Boudicca agreed. 'Unlovable, occasionally. I can see that, Lovernios, but She is also uncontrollable. Just because you don't like the particular piece of glass you're currently forced to watch the sun through, doesn't mean you can pick the previous one back out of its box and hold it up to the light instead.'

'Actually, madam, we might be able to.'

Silence, for a while, whilst Lovernios' words registered with Boudicca.

'Might be able to what?' Boudicca asked incredulously. 'Control whom Andraste Manifests through?' She was becoming angry at this information. 'How? Why didn't you tell me before?'

'It's extremely dangerous.' Sucellus was very stern.

'What is?'

'The ritual. It's not something you'd undertake lightly,' Sucellus explained.

Boudicca turned away from the smith, refusing to accept his admonition, and faced Lovernios squarely.

'Do you mean, Lovernios mine, that you've had the means to bring Andraste back to me all this while? And that you let me go through that mental agony, like spiritual starvation, when you could've ended it all in an instant?'

'Not quite, madam.'

'But it's only now, now you don't like how She Manifests through Grania, that you want to do anything about it? You didn't actually care about me at all, did you? You wanted to see how She appeared through Grania first, before you even considered getting Her back for me, didn't you? Or did you? Have you been as confused, I wonder, as me in trying to determine through whom Andraste was Manifesting? Have you had to watch and wait until you were absolutely certain where She was?'

Boudicca's voice had become shrill with rage. When she spoke again she had regained some control.

'Lovernios mine, if it weren't for the fact I am desperate to have the touch of Andraste back upon my spirit, I'd not have any further part of this. But I've no choice; I can no more refuse than stop breathing. Don't think this acquiescence means I'm happy with the way I've been treated though.'

'Perhaps you'll understand one day,' Sucellus suggested patronisingly.

'After I've been through this mysterious ritual of yours or after I've got to the bottom of all the separate motives flying around and only just becoming evident?' Boudicca finally snapped, unable to control her temper any longer. 'After all, you seem pretty quick to have skirted around Grania's obvious distress. You want Andraste to reside in a more suitable receptacle so this whole rebellion can proceed how you had planned, whilst I want the Goddess back for my own selfish reasons. We both seem to have forgotten Grania herself in all of this. Do you think she'll give up Andraste willingly? More to the point, do you think Andraste will leave her?'

Lovernios looked decidedly uncomfortable. 'I don't know, madam. Neither Sucellus nor I can answer your questions. You might have to look at Grania yourself and decide whether forcing her to relinquish the Goddess might be the kindest thing to do. Consider your own welfare, too; Andraste might make you suffer for pulling Her back to your psyche.'

Boudicca turned and gazed into the distance, choosing to listen out for her daughter again and ignoring the two men in disgust. Grania had stopped haranguing the force and the horde had returned to its previous idle gossip or to sleep. Boudicca could feel the sense of peace settle over the mass readying itself to host again at first light. But where had Grania gone?

'Will you still be here when I return?' Boudicca asked.

'I'll still be here when the horde's gone,' answered Lovernios.

Boudicca looked puzzled. 'Aren't you coming with us, then?'

'Go and find Grania, madam. I think you need to. We'll explain everything when you get back.'

Lovernios and Sucellus signalled that the conversation had ended by moving to finish the wine. Boudicca could see she had been virtually dismissed, so she left them and went in search of her daughter.

She walked without torchlight, relying instead upon the large number of camp-fires all around. Many had been left to smoulder or had been banked for the night, but with one for each family or war band and larger ones for the Chiefs of each tribe, there was still plenty of light to see by. She moved stealthily, covering Andraste's torc out of habit, seeking anonymity amongst the shadows. She stepped over still bodies, tucked up as if in their winding sheets, and trod carefully around those still awake. She looked, she hoped, like any other Celtoi warrior picking an unobtrusive path through the crowd to relieve themselves in the night. However, although most Celtoi had bedded down to sleep, she was not the only one to be up and about.

Grania was nowhere to be seen or heard. Hawk-like, Boudicca scanned the faces of those still awake. Her daughter was distinctive enough. Even though her preference for garish clothing wouldn't show up in firelight, her long mahogany coloured hair couldn't be missed too easily. Boudicca had no doubts she would find her eventually, even though it might take a long while and plenty of perseverance. For once she did not seem to mind that. The chance to be alone, really alone, had been a precious commodity all her life and, especially since Imbolc, she'd now found another such chance. Working her way systematically through the crowds, by herself, answered her need in its own way. Not ideally, of course, but here and now, muffled in her cloak, she felt truly apart from the horde, quite separate, despite standing in its midst.

She fancied it might be how a ghost might feel. Moving amongst the living, unable to speak yet still able to hear, unable to touch yet still able to feel. Only she wasn't a ghost of the newly departed, she was alive and she could speak and touch whenever she wanted, aware only that doing so would destroy the concealment of her status. She was moving rapidly through the area where the majority of Iceni had camped, and still no one had recognised her. Every so often she tripped over a prone body and perhaps stumbled a little, knocking an elbow here or spilling a drink there. But still no one identified her and the only acknowledgement she received was a curse at her clumsiness. She smiled in memory of how peeved she would normally be at such lack of response and how much she had changed in not rising immediately to remonstrate that the elbow or drink should never have been in her way. Now she mumbled the briefest of apologies and glided away, letting the matter be forgotten.

Grania was not amongst her kinfolk in the Iceni, so much Boudicca could be sure of. She had listened with every fraction of her hearing, honed over the years for hunting, for Grania's voice, but it was nowhere to be heard. Boudicca set out for the next largest fire, taking especial care now not to trip over those whom she tentatively stepped across. She was amongst a different tribe now, people with different standards of behaviour, who spoke an unfamiliar language. It was up to her to pass through them with the very greatest respect.

She was still listening as attentively as she could for her daughter's voice or watching for her familiar red hair. As she walked, she caught odd snippets of conversation. In the main it was family gossip about distant members of Gerbfine or perhaps some boasting about the prestigious role an individual had played in the rebellion. The smattering of Celtoi jokes had caused her journey to be lightened, and the eavesdropping had been unavoidable when she had been so carefully listening out for her daughter's voice. Unavoidable, certainly, but not unpleasantly so, for Boudicca found any gossip entertaining, no matter how trivial it might be.

Here, amongst this other tribe, the language and accent were very different from the Iceni. Boudicca cocked her head to make sure she could hear clearly. It sounded like Coritani, she could almost be certain, and if she listened very carefully she could distinguish, through the thick nasal inflections, most of the root words of the Celtoi. The two languages had quite a lot in common but were different enough that she would not have to listen so carefully if she were to pick out

Grania's voice. On the other hand, she would have to pay considerably more attention in order to stand a chance of understanding any of the conversations filtering through the air around her.

Boudicca moved forward, trying to peer surreptitiously at the faces of sleeping and chattering tribes-folk while still pretending to be re-turning to a reserved place at a family hearth. After clambering over one particularly large family group, she heard a sound she had not ex-pected to hear: a woman crying. There had been plenty of squalling infants in the horde, teething perhaps or just plain over-excited, but she'd heard no adults crying. Until now. This was a distinctive type of tear – Boudicca had heard it on too many occasions before not to rec-ognise it and she could tell its meaning from the universal language of emotion, unbound by tribal limitations. This woman was grieving. In-trigued, Boudicca followed the sound to its source. Surprisingly, she had heard no other signs of bereavement in the horde up until that point. But then, she reflected, there had been very few Celtoi deaths since the defeat of the legion nine.

Boudicca stood within listening distance of the woman and her kin, shuffling forward, pretending her path was continually blocked by more bodies to bypass than there really were. Purposely she took a long while to cross a short piece of ground in order to prolong her stay within audible range, and she delayed further by fiddling with her cloak as if it insisted on continuously becoming undone.

She could not be absolutely sure, but it sounded as if this was the mother of the child who had been taken by the black-haired woman in the Groves. She was wailing and lamenting the loss of her son with ritual keening and loud prayers and entreaties to the Goddess. Boudicca peered at her as she passed by at the closest point. The woman had cruel scratches on her arms which looked as if they had been gouged deep and were already starting to turn septic. The wom-an's whole family was trying to offer comfort and it was in these attempts that Boudicca was most interested.

Quickly, Boudicca looked around. She might as well not be there for all the notice she was generating in this part of the camp. All eyes and ears were on the grieving family, so Boudicca folded herself down, as silently and slowly as she could, trying to look as if she had casually found the place she'd been looking for, and rolled upon her side, as if she was fast asleep, in order to better hear what was being said.

It wasn't easy to discern what the conversation was about with any level of precision, but Boudicca found her hearing improved still fur-ther when she shut her eyes so her sight no longer distracted her. She was also fortunate that those who were talking were confused and up-set enough to keep repeating their stories and reassurances. They did so in an attempt to ensure they had been heard and that they might come to believe what they were saying themselves.

Boudicca did not know how long she listened to the mourners' stories, but it was still dark when she eventually stood and continued her search for Grania. She had to rub her eyes to convince herself she was still awake, so she was not entirely sure she had not drifted off to sleep whilst she had been lying still, so fanciful had the stories been. Boudicca was sure she'd stayed a lot longer than she'd intended, though. At first, she had not believed what she had heard and, distrusting her attempts at translating, had stayed to listen to similar accounts which kept retelling the same tales of horror. Finally, she realised she must be interpreting the stories correctly; they were all so similar she could not be wrong, no matter how amazing they might be.

With her head spinning and still trying to sort this new information out, she pretended to wake from a deep sleep, still remembering to keep her movements as casual as possible. Somehow, the search for her daughter seemed less urgent now and she was unable to give the task the same degree of concentration as she had before. She was too busy going over and over what she had heard and trying to decide how to confront Lovernios with it. No wonder he had not reprimanded her the way she'd expected when he'd come for her in the Groves. The whole while he'd had his own guilty secrets to worry about!

Boudicca's movements were aimless now as she continued to wonder around the encamped horde. She meandered vaguely in the direction of the remains of Londinium, but on the whole her searching was more to delay returning to Lovernios. She carried on picking her way forward, still listening for the sound of Grania's voice, but without much hope of hearing it. As she passed through the horde she heard several different tribal languages jabbering away around her. What she could understand made her relieved no one had identified her. Some criticised her effectiveness in leading the horde, or questioned tribal unity, while others expressed their awakened passion at receiving Andraste's Blessing and their renewed confidence in Celtoi ability to destroy the Romani. Voices from the Trinovantes were excited about their anticipated revenge upon the Catuvellauni and boasted of the atrocities they would enact upon their erstwhile rivals. There was gossip, too, about how many the Romani might number by now and where the legions might be. Most of the camp members were able to suggest their own tactics for dealing with suspected Romani strategies, which ranged from the heroic to the ridiculous.

Boudicca absorbed everything she heard. Like fragments of a broken pot, she collected it all, thinking it might make sense or come in useful when it had all been put back together again. Her memory was Druid trained, able to store and recall vast amounts of information with ease, and it was second nature for her to sort and arrange her eavesdropping in her cavernous mind.

So intent was she upon these tasks that she failed to notice that she had wondered to the edge of the encampment. She stepped over a sleeping couple, hunched close together for warmth and comfort, took a few more paces without needing to interrupt her stride, and looked up, uncertain why the seemingly continuous lines of sleeping Celtoi had suddenly petered out. She had returned to the outskirts of Londinium, where a few isolated hovels and huts still remained standing amongst the burnt leavings of the main streets.

Boudicca turned away, intending to follow the rough outline of the camp limits south and west back to Sucellus and Lovernios. As she did so, she heard a strange, almost inhuman cry coming from the town. She was puzzled by the sound – intrigued too – and very aware that it was most likely to be something to do with Grania. She set off in its general direction, reassuring herself it could just as likely be some sort of night-bird or some pet of the Romani, mistreated like the dormice had been. Perhaps it was one of the incredible monsters the Romani brought to Britannia just to be killed by their slave soldiers in their amphitheatres. Who knew how many cellars there might still be in Londinium or what might lurk, trapped by fallen debris, within?

She loosened her sword in her belt, and felt for her daggers. Still there. Good, she'd be safe then. After all, she wasn't going to provoke whatever it was, just make sure that, if it was something to do with Grania, her daughter was not in danger. Her mind continued to race through the possibilities as she scampered soundlessly through the rubble and broken timbers, creeping through the shells of buildings and around the remains of walls. It was hardly likely to be wolves, not this far south in this season and with the horde so close, nor bears for much the same reasons. It could be a fox, although it did not sound like one, or a wildcat calling for a mate. The latter seemed the most likely.

It was so dark she could barely see where she was, and her lack of visibility made silent progress virtually impossible. The moon had only just turned new, and although the sky was cloudless it offered only a scant sliver of light to see by. At last the inevitable happened and she trod on a rotten timber which snapped beneath her foot and gave her presence away.

Boudicca froze, refusing to move, hoping that by some miracle the broken timber had not been heard. Then the noise started up again and she realised she had almost been upon whatever was producing it. She glared into the dark, straining her eyes to see whatever she could.

225

Gradually her night vision deepened a little and she caught the slightest movement to her left, then she saw it was human and was eating.

Then, as she watched, she saw an eerie, but nevertheless vaguely familiar, light come bobbing towards her. As she waited for the light to approach, as she knew it would, it illuminated the air around and she could see that the noise was coming from Grania. Her daughter was crouched down in the remains of a doorway, her long hair hanging in sodden tendrils and her face and hands caked in blood and filth. Grania growled and hummed tunelessly to herself as she ate what she held, or rather, as she gnawed the remains of what she clasped to her.

The light, with Maeve cupping its warm glow in her hands, just as she had before in Artio's forest, came nearer. Boudicca stooped to see what Grania was feeding upon. Grania pulled away from the light with a strange whimper, covering her eyes and dropping her food. Boudicca turned it over with her hand. Her stomach lurched to her throat and she swallowed, desperately trying not to be sick. It was a baby's leg, torn out at the hip joint, most likely from a Romani child – and she thought she knew which one.

Boudicca reached for her daughter, trying to pull her into an embrace. Grania clawed and bit at her mother, but Boudicca held on. Through the struggle Boudicca could feel something else, too – a tenderness, as if Grania sought to be held as well as to reject her mother. There were drops of moisture too, which Boudicca suspected were tears, although they might just as well be blood, saliva or sweat.

'Oh, my Grania, my daughter mine. Is this what has become of you? Is this what you've been reduced to? Little more than an animal scrabbling in the dirt with no sense nor reason?' Boudicca tried to soothe her daughter, gently trying to reassure her she was in no danger. But she already knew the answers to the questions she asked, even if Grania could not answer them. The things Grania was showing her, she put together with the gossip from the Coritani. Boudicca knew now that this was what could happen if Andraste Manifested in a certain type of... What would Lovernios call it? Raw material?

She looked upon her daughter with a new kind of pity. All thoughts of getting Andraste back for herself gone, Boudicca reached her resolution for a different set of reasons: no matter the cost, she'd try to free Grania of her spiritual burden. It did not matter how dangerous Lovernios' ritual was, she would not let Sucellus fob her off with warnings and scaremongering. Grania was suffering too much to continue living in this way; anything had to be an improvement.

When Maeve was near enough to them both, Boudicca saw her reach down and gently stroke her twin's head. Then Maeve led the way back to the camp, the Otherworldly light still glowing in the palms of her hands, with Grania following. Grania skulked in Maeve's shadow, hunkering along as if she were crippled, keeping her eyes averted from the witch-light. As she watched, Boudicca could see Grania's curious gait was due, not to an injury or wound, but to her body seeming to fight against itself in choosing where it would go. Clearly half of Grania yearned to keep close to her sister, entranced and enticed by the light, whilst her other half strained to be far away where the light did not reach.

Boudicca made up her mind quite impulsively and darted off to Lovernios and Sucellus to herald her twin daughters. She suspected the Druid would want to make some sort of provision for Grania's safety until the ritual could be arranged and enacted.

She ran as fast as she could around the outskirts of the entire horde, back to where she had left Lovernios and Sucellus. The two men had fallen asleep. Dashing up to Lovernios, she woke him by shaking him vigorously. 'Lovernios! Lovernios! We've got to perform your ritual and we've got to do it as soon as possible.'

Lovernios looked confused, probably because he was still half-asleep.

'Grania's coming. Maeve's bringing her. She's really suffering with Andraste's presence. It's not fair to let her live like this.'

Lovernios blinked. 'Madam, did I ever say that Grania would still be alive after the ritual?'

Chapter 16

Vernemetum

It was daybreak before Boudicca could persuade Lovernios to talk any more. The Druid had recovered himself quickly from his sleepy outburst, insisting Boudicca got some rest whilst she could. He'd obviously realised instantly that he had blurted out far more than he had intended to and strove to recover some sort of advantage by insisting they all rest.

Boudicca fumed in frustration at his refusal to discuss these vital issues there and then. But he was as stubborn and intractable as she thought only she could be, and he paid no attention to her demands or prodding attempts to awaken him. So, finally, Boudicca gave way to the needs of her body and slept.

When she awoke, it was well past dawn and she was surprised to see most of the horde already up and packed to move. The first meal of the day was, it seemed, to be eaten on the road. She roused herself, shaking her stiff joints where she had slept in clothes still damp from the previous evening's wash, and immediately started to worry about being left behind.

'Don't, madam.' Lovernios was trying to calm her down. Boudicca relented for a moment and then, just as suddenly, disregarded his reassurance as she remembered she could no longer trust him. She twisted around. It was all right, Grania and Maeve were still with them, although Grania fretted to be free of whatever Binding Maeve had placed over her.

'I'm glad to see you didn't kill her secretly in the night.'

Lovernios turned his head away in exasperation. 'There's no need for that, madam.'

'Isn't there?'

'We should talk.'

'Most definitely!'

Lovernios breathed a deep sigh of resignation. 'Let them all go on ahead. Sucellus will keep the girls safe and Maeve will keep Grania out of trouble and harm. The horde doesn't need a leader at the moment, although it might not know that. Everyone in it knows exactly where they're going and what they're doing, but it won't hurt for them to see two of their figureheads still with them. If they see your twins they'll know you won't be far away.'

'What about us? Where will the horde's superfluous figurehead be?' Boudicca asked.

'Right here, madam, with me. Sorting this out once and for all.'

'Being honest and truthful for once, you mean?'

'Well, madam, I will be. How about you?'

Boudicca smarted from the rebuke and her face reddened in anger. She felt tears pricking her eyes but she refused to give Lovernios the satisfaction of seeing them flow over, and she blinked to rid herself of their incrimination.

'Do you want some food whilst we watch them go?' Lovernios asked her, more tenderly now, and she smiled that yes, she did. Why couldn't she stay angry with him for long? Perhaps his concern was an indication of his willingness to erase the rift between them?

Lovernios brought forth some bread and a few eggs from within his robes. 'I went foraging very early,' he explained. Then he poked the fire, coaxing it into life with gentle breaths, and boiled up some water in the little pot he carried with him for stewing herbs. When the eggs were ready, they ate them straight out of the shells, together with mouthfuls of bread, which was already starting to turn dry.

As they finished their meal, the last stragglers of the horde started to move north towards Watling Street and the midlands of Britannia. Sucellus and the twins were already long gone, their departure brief as they hurried to catch up with the vanguard. The departing force left only camp debris, a ruined town and a cloud of dust.

'How will we catch up?' Boudicca asked what she thought was a reasonable question.

'If you still want to, after our talk, we can use your chariot. I ordered it left, by the waterside, complete with Cloud and Mouse.'

'Thank Mother you said "want to" rather than "can". At least I know for certain now that my own life isn't in any danger from you.'

'Boudicca, don't be like this, please. Think of all the things we've shared – the love, the intimacy. Don't throw it all away before you've heard me out. My explanations might bring some of our affection back. I hope they will. Why not give me a chance?'

'Because we've lost so much trust between us. I'm not sure we can get it back now that it's gone. Not for me anyway.'

'What if it wasn't trust? What if it was just misunderstandings?'

'Go on, then,' Boudicca conceded.

Lovernios paused, thinking carefully.

'What's the problem, Lovernios mine?'

'I've rehearsed this over and over and now my words seem too harsh, too blaming.'

'Try them anyway, else we end up staying here forever awaiting your Bard-talk, and lose any chance of ever catching up with the horde.'

Lovernios nodded. 'Madam, you made grave errors with Grania. Misjudging what was going on, I mean.'

'She's my daughter and she was very beguiling. Blood is thicker than water.'

'I'm not saying I wouldn't have done the same had it been me, but there were mistakes made and we have to deal with the consequences of those mistakes.'

Boudicca nodded in cautious agreement. 'And you made errors, too.' She accused him openly now. 'I think you knew what was going on more than I did, but you chose not to tell me. And don't forget the appearance of your mother.'

Lovernios blanched. 'Can we come back to that point? Later?'

'All right. But we will come back to it; I know too much to leave it unsaid.'

'Madam, I don't wish to press the point, but you were very naive about Grania's condition. I understand why now. I understand a lot of things now that I didn't before, about Andraste and Her effect upon those She Manifests through. But you must've noticed something was seriously wrong with Grania's behaviour?'

'Both my girls… they've been through so much. I didn't know how to interpret what either of them were doing, how either of them were reacting. I've never known any woman who's had that done to them. You know this, Lovernios, it just doesn't happen amongst Celtoi. Add their rank to the situation and the whole atrocity becomes inconceivable. You can hear yourself how difficult it is for me even to name the crime. Rape. There, I've said it, the unthinkable act. You must realise how alien the very idea is to our peoples.'

'Sucellus is still aggrieved about your blaming Maeve.'

'What was I to do or think, Lovernios mine? What is 'normal' behaviour for a victim of rape? Don't forget what I was going through, too. Don't underestimate how much losing the Goddess meant to me.'

'Do you still want Her back?'

'More than ever. Not just because of what She represents to me or because I want this rebellion to mean the last of the Romani in Britannia, but also because of what She's doing to Grania. No. That's not true. Andraste's not doing anything to Grania. You know what I mean.' Boudicca chose her words carefully. 'I mean, how Andraste is showing Herself when She Manifests through Grania. I don't suppose either of them can help it really. Those qualities are there in our Goddess; none of us who know Her would ever deny that. Grania just happens to exaggerate Her most extreme characteristics because those are the ones which are emphasised by their merging, or whatever.' Boudicca paused to think.

'I don't want Her back at the price you've set, though,' she continued. 'It's far too high. Are you prepared to haggle?'

Boudicca smiled. So did Lovernios. It was the first indication to Boudicca that something might be salvageable between them. Suddenly the air felt lighter and the atmosphere warmer.

Then Lovernios dropped his ghost of a smile and apologetically admitted: 'I'm sorry, it's the only price I'm aware of.'

Boudicca averted her gaze. 'I don't think I can agree to paying it, no matter how merciful or right it might be. Isn't there any other way? What caused Andraste to change from me to Grania?'

'I don't know. I'm still trying to consider all the factors which could've prompted it. I'm fairly certain it's something to do with the phases of the moon, but beyond that ...' Lovernios shrugged. Then he quickly changed the subject. 'If the price is too high for you, madam, let's return to what's bothering you. I take it you've managed to work out that the apparition in the Grove was my mother?'

'I didn't exactly work it out! I overheard some conversations amongst the Coritani whilst I was searching for Grania last night and made an intuitive guess. I wasn't quite convinced I'd translated correctly until you just admitted it. Up until then you could've still bluffed your way out of it.'

'I didn't want to. If all else fails, we have each other, Boudicca. It's worth keeping when you find it. What did you hear?'

'It was the mother of the child who'd been taken. I heard her grieving. She had her kin around her for company and commiseration, and as I listened I was shocked to hear that hers wasn't the first babe to be taken, that although it was not exactly common, it was still hardly rare in the lands where they came from. They named her Black Annis and I remembered your mother's name then. Now that set me to thinking about the lands of the Coritani – they're in the midlands, sort of north west to Iceni borders.' Lovernios nodded. 'And Vernemetum falls within their territory, does it not?'

'It does.'

'And Vernemetum is where your father lost your mother?'

'It is.'

'So there is my connection. Loose, but you've just confirmed it for me. The only thing I couldn't understand was what she could be doing so far south. How did she get here?'

'The same way all the other Celtoi got here.'

Boudicca looked at him, astonished and completely confused. 'What? How?' She asked. Then sudden realisation dawned and her mouth framed a large oval of disbelief. 'The Paths,' she shrieked. 'The

Old Paths. You opened them all. She'd have been free to follow the horde, free to follow all the little children. Didn't you think?'

'Oh yes, madam, I did think. I thought, or rather I assumed, she wouldn't come south, not this far, not whilst my father was at Vernemetum. But he isn't any more.'

'How do you know?'

'Because of the news that the Romani are still without their legion two and the evidence that we're still missing any warriors from the Durotiges or the Dumnonii, or even a sizable contingent from the Silures. Legion two keeps those tribes under control, or at least, tries to. If they're roused to insurrection, legion two won't follow orders to meet Suetonius in the midlands for fear the whole of the west of Britannia will rise in the same way as the east has. There's only one other Druid who could unite those tribes like that; only my father's personal appearance could influence so many people, only he has the status.

'Why he is doing it, madam, I don't know. What I do know is that he is meddling in things he doesn't understand and which I haven't asked him to contribute to. When your force meet the Romani in the final, last, ultimate battle, whether it is triumphant or not, it won't actually *be* the last, final, ultimate battle because there'll still be legion two left to destroy.'

'Did he know the Paths had been opened?'

'I doubt if he checked; he doesn't seem to have bothered checking anything else. It's probably beneath him to have to ask his son for a progress report and he's quite capable of Finding his own Paths for his own purposes. He'd be unlikely to use, or even look for, ours.'

'So, Lovernios, all our carefully laid plans are being disrupted by other people not keeping to them?'

He laughed. 'Yes. It seems the Romani are the only ones to have done as they were told!'

Boudicca shook her head. 'The Romani are the only predictable ones in this whole game,' she countered. Suddenly the whole rebellion seemed another world away and she felt quite detached. 'But would you want to be remembered as predictable?'

'I don't have to answer you, do I? Well, not your last question, anyway. What I do have to answer is your curiosity about my mother.'

'If it's not too painful for you, Lovernios mine.'

'It's irrelevant how painful it might be for me; you need to know. You see, the thing about my mother is that she was once Manifesting Andraste herself.' Lovernios paused, letting his words sink in. 'And she was raped, as I told you, by the Romani. One of the other reasons why she appeared in the Grove was because she was attracted by the presence of the Divine. She wants Andraste back as acutely as you do. And this is what Andraste's possession of her spirit did to her ...' He let his words trail away into silence. Boudicca was concentrating very hard on what he was saying.

'Has anyone ever tried to help her?' She whispered.

'My father says she is beyond help. But she is still his wife and still my mother.'

'Does he know a lot about such things?'

'He is revered as being very wise, yes.'

'Is that what Grania will turn into?'

Pause.

'What do you think, madam? My mother, Black Annis, steals and eats a lamb or a kid, occasionally a child, every so often. That's all she does. And remember, it's her desire to get Andraste back which drives her to these extremes; she was never so depraved when Andraste was directly with her. What does Grania do, even now, even whilst Andraste resides within her? And knowing this, what depths would your daughter descend to in order to regain her heart's desire?'

Pause.

'Why are you doing this, Lovernios?'

'Because I believe the price is fair, madam. Grania can't live with Andraste, nor can she live without Her. It'd be an act of love on your part.'

'You're right, Lovernios mine. Of course you are. But right never takes account of feeling, does it? Annis is still your mother. Grania is still my daughter. There are ties here which are inexpressible. Let me think on it.'

'Then we should catch up with the bulk of your force whilst you do.'

'I'd like to follow them, but perhaps at a discreet distance, if you'll stay behind with me. It'll give me some breathing space and us the chance to spend a while together, just the two of us.'

'I'm forgiven then, madam?'

'If I've got to trust someone, it might as well be you.'

Boudicca's emotional reserve caused Lovernios to chuckle and he clasped her to him before they moved away to the waiting chariot. There was a different level of closeness between them now, one which committed them to each other simply on the basis of having to see out what they'd both started.

Cloud and Mouse stood so patiently and obediently by the banks of the Tamesis that Boudicca ran to them to scratch their ears as soon as she saw them. They were harnessed to the chariot in readiness for Boudicca's and Lovernios' use, tethered loosely to prevent them wandering, and had been left a small pile of Romani grain to keep them from boredom. Boudicca let them nuzzle her clothing in an attempt to locate any food she might have hidden about her person. She laughed at their tickling persistence and pulled Lovernios over to rub their necks.

'Aren't they wonderful?' She exclaimed. 'This one was my husband's favourite. Prasutagus even chose him as the model for the depiction on Iceni coins. He's sired a whole herd of foals!'

Lovernios stroked Mouse reticently, getting his fingers caught up in the pony's snaggly mane, and rubbing Cloud along his distinctive white-blazed forehead. 'I have to admit, I don't really know what I'm looking for, but yes, they both seem rather magnificent.'

'I shan't give you a lesson on horsemanship, Lovernios, I could bore you for an age. Basically, though, it's their build I admire. Their frame is so stocky and sturdy. Strong too; ideal for pulling our chariots. Then there's the intelligence in their eyes, so obvious, and the condition of their coats, and this gorgeous mottled grey they've both inherited.'

Lovernios looked at the features she referred to as if he was her most attentive pupil. Then he stroked Mouse with increased confidence until the little stallion adjusted his stance, pulling forward in the certainty that Boudicca had a tasty root vegetable upon her person, and trod on Lovernios' foot in doing so. 'Mother of all!' He swore, tugging at his leg and pushing at the pony to move.

Boudicca found his efforts most amusing. 'I see you've finally found something more stubborn than you,' she jeered, and pulled Mouse's harness until Lovernios' foot was freed.

'No, madam, I found her quite a while ago. Now, just what is the appeal?' The Druid spluttered, flexing his foot to check his injuries were not permanent.

'Let me show you,' Boudicca replied. 'Come on, they're both keen to have a run,' and she pulled him up onto the chariot, freeing the tethering as she passed. 'Now, hold on tight because it's the closest thing to flying!'

Boudicca flicked the reins and Cloud and Mouse responded instantly to her command. She felt them both fall into their even strides, matching each other perfectly, and then she steered them onto the road which ran north from Londinium. 'I presume this is the way to Verulamium, the way the horde went?' Boudicca called behind without looking; she didn't want Lovernios' to distract her if he was pulling nervous expressions. There was some vague reply and Boudicca took it as a 'yes'. She touched the reins again, causing the chariot to speed up, and she let the exhilaration of the ride course through her.

The wind was still up today, although there was less sun. She had even wondered whether it might rain later, although she dismissed such mundane thoughts for the while and concentrated upon handling the horses and the swinging chariot. She loved fast winds when she was hurtling through the air like this. They made the chariot feel like it was travelling at twice the speed it really was, and it seemed as if spirits of the air played with her clothes and caressed her hair. This was so exciting and dangerous, demanding full concentration as she swerved to avoid potholes and fallen branches. It was as if she played an enormous game of dare with herself. One false move, one lapse of attention, and the chariot would twist and buckle and crash to the ground to be pulled behind the ponies until they realised they could run no more.

She smiled her crazy grin, her maniacal smile, that betrayed her love of adventure and risk, and she soared through the air, seemingly flying as the ground and scenery rushed by too fast for her mind to register its details. She was lost totally, for precious eternity, in the sheer joy of being utterly alive yet so near to death. It was the proximity of death, seemingly less than a knife blade away, a mere mistake away, like simply stepping off the caravan of life, which made her feel yet more alive and fully awake.

Then she remembered Lovernios hanging on behind and that right now she was responsible for another life and not just her own. She started to slow the horses, gently enough for them to respond in a controlled way without bolting. The surrounding fields and trees clarified from a blurred myriad of greens and yellows into distinct shapes and the wind stopped singing in her ears, leaving them burning with cold. Mouse and Cloud trotted along at a pace which needed little supervision, and she turned her head expecting to see a shaken Lovernios.

The Druid's knuckles were white where they had been gripping the sides of the chariot. So was his face, although she had expected as much. What she had not expected was his grin, as broad and as mad as her own, as if he was trying to split his face with his mouth.

'Wonderful,' he announced with a glazed look in his eyes. 'Now I know why the birds sing so sweetly.'

'But you've been in a chariot before.'

'Oh yes, madam, but not so well, not half so well,' and he stared into the far distance as if he was regaining consciousness from a trance. 'That was like Shape-shifting, exactly so, but just then I could feel the very blast from the wind and smell the air as we were buffeted around. Much more sensation than just seeing, as I'm used to. And being able to sense the freedom too, without being distracted by thoughts of mice in the undergrowth from the bird whose mind I'd requested to share.' He paused, still awed by the experience. 'The next occasion I ride with you, though, perhaps you could give me a bit of warning so I can get a good grip first.'

'Considering the next ride already, Lovernios? If you're so keen we can go immediately,' and she picked up the reins as if to spur her horses into action.

'So soon?' Lovernios gasped.

'Did I forget to praise the stamina of Iceni horses earlier? How lapse of me. Iceni horses are quite simply the very best in the whole of Britannia and the bravest too. They can run for days, live off the barest fodder, never cower in battle, pull loads as heavy as hundreds of their own weight, birth healthy foals without fail year after year, readily trained …'

'Stop! Stop!'

'I could go on. Iceni horses are the envy of all the other Celtoi tribes and the Romani; they have always raised a high price.'

'I'm sure you could continue for as long as your horses could run and I believe every word you're telling me, madam. I'm beginning to understand why the Iceni chose the horse as their totem; your wilful spirits are a good match.'

'They could run again, with ease, but the very last stragglers of the horde are just ahead. I can see their dust upon the horizon, and I want to keep back. No doubt their scouts know of our presence, although possibly not our identity, and that's fine, but I don't want to join them yet. Maybe in a couple of days.'

'After they've destroyed Verulamium?'

'Are we so near?'

'Your force is making good progress, moving much faster than before.'

'And Verulamium is so near to Londinium?'

'At this rate we'll be at Sulloniacis by nightfall, roughly half way there.'

'This is Catuvellauni territory, isn't it? Are those who inhabit Sulloniacis Catuvellauni?'

'Some are Romani traders, but mainly they're Catuvellauni tribesfolk living a Romani lifestyle, madam.'

'We won't be able to stop the horde then?'

'Would you want to?'

'No. The Catuvellauni deserve everything coming to them.'

'Aren't you forgetting Caractacus, madam?'

'I don't think so. That was a long way away, in the mountains to the west, I believe. I was only a child.'

'He was Catuvellauni and he fought the Romani.'

'He needed to. If the mewling, half-whelped princes of his tribe hadn't gone abegging to Rome, the Romani would never have come.'

'So you know about Adminius and Verica, then?'

'Are those their names? I don't know, I've told you, I was just a child.'

'Well, madam, let me teach you some history, or at least one interpretation of it, for there is always more than one version of the truth: it wasn't just the disposed Catuvellauni princes who went running to Rome, but other Celtoi tribes, too, who appealed to Rome against the territorial expansions of the sons of Cunobeline, namely Togodumnus and Caractacus.'

'You're going to tell me one of those tribes was the Iceni?'

'I am. There were others of course, but the Iceni were definitely one of them. And one of the first to not only benefit from but also to encourage Romani trade.'

'I don't know what you're getting at, Lovernios, but everyone can make mistakes – perhaps I'm just putting one of the Iceni's right. The Catuvellauni have always been our tribal enemies. We used to war against them every year as a matter of pride and they against us. We still sing with pride of our battle prowess. But our elders tell how they grew too strong and started to take too much, they subsumed whole tribes: our neighbours vanished and we worried they'd come for us. The Iceni suffered many threats from every quarter, our land is rich and our peoples resplendent in Druidic gold, what else should we expect? In a way, their envy is like a bitter compliment. We had to deal with the most urgent threat first, so we turned, with our neighbours, to Rome.'

'What I'm getting at, madam, is that your horde is now set to destroy every settlement in Catuvellauni territory. Your peoples give two reasons for this: firstly, because the Catuvellauni are pro-Romani and secondly, because they are hated utterly by the Trinovantes and it's their main motivation for staying with the horde after Camulodunum. The horde and Andraste are entwined now and She will continue to thirst for blood, until there is none left in Britannia, unless She is checked. There are other tribes who have sympathised with the Romani. To start with there are the other client Kingdoms of the Regni and Brigantes. Doubtless they're earmarked next for destruction after the Catuvellauni. And after them? Who next? All those tribes who didn't rise to join you?'

'Are you sick of the sight of all this blood already, Lovernios mine? Are you ashamed of what you started? Who knows what the future will bring? Don't you remember, even when Goddess possessed, my glimpses of what will be were vague and misted with symbolism? May I remind you, too, that our priority is to cleanse the land of Romani? So far we've done well, destroying their model Colonia and their trading centre. Now we go to destroy their legions. For want of better guidance from Andraste, we follow where the horde leads, directly to the midlands where the legions await us. It just so happens that the lands of the Catuvellauni lie on our way and part of our number have their own particular desire for revenge.'

'I'm not having a change of heart, madam, I just want you to know the likely outcome of what's happening.'

'The horde's like this chariot, Lovernios. At its maximum speed I can't stop the ponies dead in their tracks. All I can do is coax them into gradually galloping slower and slower. We must destroy the Romani and the horde's momentum is indispensable to that end, but I don't think we'll ever be able to stop competition between the tribes. There'll always be raiding; to be peaceable wouldn't be the Celtoi way.' She thought for a moment. 'Are you trying to pressurise me into sacrificing Grania for this ritual of yours?'

'No, madam, I despise human sacrifice almost as much as the Romani do, but I do keep forgetting we're only reacting and responding now and no longer leading and directing.'

'Then we should keep up.' She urged the horses to a trot. 'Then we can at least keep stock of what's going on.'

Boudicca could tell that the horde would stop overnight at Sulloniacis, so she drew her chariot up well before they reached the settlement and pulled the horses into the forest edges lining the road. She noticed Lovernios' cynical and playful delight in directing her not to bother Finding since the Paths had all been sealed, but nevertheless she set her own Wards around where they would sleep, to ensure against vagabonds and forest creatures, and against her ponies wandering off.

They woke with the day and greeted Artio, who appeared to have been watching over them through the dark. Then they readied the chariot and prepared to follow close behind the horde again. Their route lay through Sulloniacis, and although the horde had moved on already, it was fairly obvious what had happened. The settlement was in ruins and ashes, with here and there a few fires still burned themselves out. Anything edible had been taken and the pens emptied of livestock. Pots had been overturned in the search for food and valuables torn in the struggle for plunder. There were few bodies and Boudicca could only presume most of the inhabitants had run ahead of the horde, perhaps into the military zone where the Romani still pushed back their frontiers into the unconquered mountains of Britannia. A few women had not run, though, and they had suffered the same fate as the Romani matrons at Londinium, their skewered bodies planted along the road as grim testament to the rebellion's hatred of anything Romani.

Boudicca gave the place no more than a cursory glance before nudging her horses forward. So much will Verulamium be by evening, she thought, but she chose to keep her musings to herself. Instead she set her mind to thinking through the issues surrounding Grania's sacrifice. After all, she reminded herself, the reason why she had escaped from her responsibilities to the horde was to find some peace. So, to set the mood, she asked Lovernios to expand on his announcement the day before about human sacrifice.

'The Romani loathe us for it,' he started to explain. 'By us, I mean the Druids. It's their main reason for wanting to eradicate us – at least, their ostensible reason. Really, though, we know they're after Druid gold and, I personally suspect, they know that the Druids are the only uniting force of the Celtoi in Britannia and beyond. I don't understand them though; they have their games and their executions and their warfare. They're not scared of death as a people. I think what it comes down to is their insistence upon the importance of the individual in their culture. Whereas Celtoi put the tribe before the person and can easily accept it might be better for a few to die, or suffer, or lose, for the good of the whole.'

'And why do you hate it, Lovernios mine?'

'Because,' and now he stood behind her as she steered her ponies and held her tight. 'I'm no coward but I've been dodging it all my life.'

Boudicca said nothing for a long while. There was no need. She could feel Lovernios' hot tears trickle down her neck and she felt a great release of tension as if there was nothing now to come between them, no more secrets lying unsaid.

'Is this why you avoid your father?'

'Yes,' he whispered. 'I shared a womb with a dead brother. Such a birthing marks me out; it's my destiny, if you like. There aren't many who know. Some Healers, who are old or dead by now, my father of course, and my mother, although I dare say she still might not know it, but only be aware of it on a deep intuitive level. You can understand why I didn't tell you, can't you? I thought it might be too much for you after what you'd been through. I thought you'd never bother even trying to love me because of the risk involved. And then, as we grew closer, somehow it never seemed right ...'

'Oh, Lovernios mine.' She turned in his arms to kiss away his tears, letting the reins fall across the platform of the chariot and allowing the horses to plod aimlessly forward. 'There's risk in every love we offer, and you're not going to die. I'll do everything I can to keep you here, safe with me.'

'But everyone has to die at some point, Boudicca.'

'Then we should make the most of the days we have left, so that when we die we've no regrets about how we spent what was allocated to us.' And with those soft words she tethered the ponies and led him into the enfolding bracken. They made love as if it was their last opportunity to do so, both crying soundlessly throughout.

Afterwards, when they had finished and their bodies felt good all over, Boudicca lay naked on her back, exposing her body to the mull-

239

ing glow of the sun. The first summer flies buzzed nearby and the air smelt lazy. Lovernios twirled grasses along her stomach and she tried very hard not to imagine this must be what the Summerlands were like. It seemed such a sad thought but she could not dislodge it from her mind.

'This is so perfect,' she said at last. 'Wouldn't it be wonderful if we could escape together and never again have to worry about who we were and what we were born to be?'

'It wouldn't be perfect, Boudicca, not for long.'

'And why not?'

'Because of you and I, madam. We'd both be bored within days, you know we would.'

'That's so true, and I so wish it weren't. It's lovely once in a while, though, isn't it? I'm in no hurry to leave.'

'Nor me, my love. Actually, this reminds me of Vernemetum.'

'How so?'

'Well, how do you imagine the most sacred place in Britannia, madam?'

'Like Insula Mona, perhaps? Colleges and schools and Druid cells for contemplation.'

'Which is how come I know for certain you've never been there. No, Vernemetum is totally unlike Insula Mona. Try again, madam, and as you do, feel the sound of the place name, see what it evokes.'

Boudicca tried, testing each syllable over again. 'When I was very young,' she told him, speaking the first memory to come to mind. 'There was a massive storm one autumn night. I remember cowering, part out of fear and part out of excitement, as the bangs and crashes erupted outside. In the morning I got up and the land was all washed clean and new with the deluge. All the grass and leaves tingled with raindrops like polished silver.

'And then I saw what one of the loudest noises must've been. One of the most venerable oaks had been struck by lightning and lay prone, fallen upon its side. I couldn't resist,' she smiled mischievously. 'The temptation was too great, I had to go and look. Plus there were five magpies chattering at me to hurry up,' she explained, somehow seeking to justify herself even after all these years.

'So, despite the fact I knew I was going to return sopping wet, I crept amongst the upturned branches, silent as a huntress, although I still don't know why. Then, once within its secret folds I felt as if I was encased in leaves. As the sun brightened it seemed as if I were in a temple-tent of salad sunlight and all the drops of crystal rain shimmered upon me and around me until I was dazzled with wonderment.'

She stopped. 'Is that more like Vernemetum?'

Lovernios nodded, not needing to say anything for a while, not wanting to shatter the image she had recalled. 'It's as natural as Groves and Shrines should really be,' he agreed at last. 'Every waterfall and gurgling well is a venerated site. Every rolling hilltop a sacred place. There are no buildings, no temples, no altars, just the beautiful land in all its fertile bounty. As natural as our loving Mother intended it to be. The whole area is one huge site for Druid ritual.'

'Is that why only the Druids can go there?'

'Yes. I suppose we fear that Insensitives might not respect the place for what it is or misinterpret its holiness. And history reinforces our doubts, too. Remember I told you how one Romani officer and his men desecrated the Groves? He's but one of the fortunates whom we've dared risk allowing into Vernemetum in the past; few of them have repaid us with gratitude.'

'Is there anywhere else like it in Britannia?'

Lovernios' eyes shone with pride as he answered her questions. 'There are sacred places set aside all along Britannia. Sanctuaries for those who transport the Goddess' gold trade from Insula Sacra to Gaul.' He warmed to his subject, just as Boudicca had warmed to telling him about Iceni horses. He lavishly described the places he'd been to and loved in all their fruitful glory. 'They sweep in a wide arch from Insula Mona across Britannia and down slightly, into the lands of the Iceni. They're hidden well, so it's unlikely they'll be stumbled into casually, much more so that they'll be bypassed without realisation.'

'What about the Romani?'

'Oh, they look. They search long and hard but usually they don't look in the right ways and the best places. They hunt with gold greed in their hearts and to the forefront of their minds and then they wonder why they discover nothing. But the Romani have settled here for almost a whole generation now. They've raised children and tended fields and some have even grown old and breathed their last on these shores. Some of them have grown to know the land, to love it even and cherish it for its unique beauty.

'Occasionally,' Lovernios continued, 'There are such men in the ranks of the legionaries, although they are rare. When they're set to search, they do so with an appreciation of Britannia their colleagues lack, and often they Find what they've been set to look for. Then their comrades burst in with them and destroy the uncovered secrets. There's no gold to be taken. Instead there's something far more precious, but it can't be bottled or boxed or chained up for transportation and profit, and so it's destroyed. When you're so narrow-minded it's the only thing you can conceive of doing.

'Slowly, very slowly, Britannia is revealing Her secret beauty to the Romani. She does so unwillingly, as if Her clothes are being stripped from Her body, garment by garment. But, although She resists, their persistence wears Her down and She is powerless to stop the encroachment. So, too, are Her Druids, and gradually we are losing the sacredness from our lands.'

'But I thought your father was placing Wards around the sites?' Boudicca asked.

'He is, but I doubt their effectiveness. There are more incursions with every season; soon there'll be no Groves left. There's only one way for the Druids to survive: to totally destroy the Romani.'

Chapter 17

First Quarter

The horde kept up its furious pace throughout the whole of the next day, barely pausing for hobbling ponies or loosening wheels. There was a festival atmosphere amongst the Celtoi people, buoyed up by the prospect of pickings from the Catuvellauni who had grown rich from collaborating with the Romani. Pickings which were hoped to be sufficient to compensate for those missed at Londinium.

Boudicca and Lovernios hurried to keep up, following the deep ruts at the sides of the roads where, for want of room on the road itself, vast numbers of carts and chariots had passed. They listened for details of the joyous din which wafted back to them. Boudicca was keen now to rejoin the force and to take an active part in the sack of the third of the Romani showpieces. Verulamium, she knew, was notorious in its own way. Previously the Civitas Capital, or tribal centre, of the Catuvellauni, she could remember when the Romani had singled their most beloved allies out for special treatment amongst all the other capitals of Britannia. Verulamium had been granted the status of Municipium and its inhabitants were deemed to be Latins, a higher rank than the other Celtoi – who were merely Provincials – although still a long way off full Romani citizenship. Presumably, the Romani had conferred such privileges in order to encourage other tribes to emulate these model citizens and be awarded similar honours, but it had not worked. The jealously and rivalry festered away for years such that, when the boil finally burst, the rebellion had one more reason to demand settlement from Britannia's most hated tribe.

Boudicca and Lovernios caught up with the tail of the horde just before the warriors in the fore put on a further burst of speed and charged towards the town. Boudicca looked down upon the settlement from the advantage of one of the southern hills that cupped the valley of the river Ver; she was probably the last person to appraise its appearance before it was destroyed. There were a few isolated plumes of smoke, but otherwise few signs of life. The Catuvellauni, it seemed, had been even more reticent than their Londinium counterparts to wait out the rebellion's arrival, and in doing so, she felt, the townsfolk had revealed where their true sympathies lay. She watched as the horde approached from the south, flooding into the valley and battering through the flimsy gate as if it were so much matchwood, undeterred by the scant defences, and scaling the banks as if they were nothing more than a few slender tree trunks to clamber over.

Vast numbers of warriors and champions, together with nobles in their chariots, streamed into the town and fanned out along the streets. Boudicca observed them casually, as if she were still not wholly part of what was going on. Their progress revealed the town's layout as shops were set alight and open spaces swarmed with battle-lusting Celtoi. Verulamium, she saw, was bordered on the east side by the river Ver and by a defensive bank and ditch on the others. The town was rectilinear, rather than square, although the streets were still laid out as strict and regular grids which the Romani seemed to love and which mirrored their regimental ideals. The line of Watling Street, however, changed to a slightly more westerly direction near the theatre, disturbing the carefully planned rigidity. Somehow, that sight soothed Boudicca, lending insight that the Romani could not bend all chaos to their will and even nature resisted their attempts to impose order on everything.

Boudicca and Lovernios rode down to the town amidst the wagons. Her daughters would be with Sucellus amongst these camp followers, she supposed, but she hadn't seen any of them yet. The horde needed no orders or instructions on how to proceed. Already the first fires licked over the tiles of the nearest buildings, and storehouses had been plundered, with supplies being dragged out into the streets. As the flames took hold and started to rage, a few bewildered and confused Catuvellauni started to emerge from the buildings – how predictable that some would always stay! They came out from their hiding places like newborn mice blinking in sunlight, and the Trinovantes rounded them up for slaughter with loud whoops of glee.

The Catuvellauni were easy to distinguish from the other Celtoi, for they had already lived too long with the Romani and had become tainted by their ways. Their leggings, tunics and cloaks had been changed for flowing, loose dresses and voluminous togas; their long hair and warrior's moustaches cropped short; and their manners refined to sobriety. Boudicca saw a by now familiar expression on their faces as they were dragged off for slaughter. Quite plainly it appeared, just as it had on each and every Romani face she'd seen die. There, amidst the fear and distress, she saw disgust, too. Disgust at how the supposedly uncivilised Celtoi looked and behaved, disgust at being handled so roughly, and more disgust, not so much at dying itself, but at dying in this way and by the hands of these people. Somehow, it seemed, these townsfolk believed themselves to be above such an ignoble end.

The men were despatched immediately, almost as soon as they

were discovered. The women were dragged by their hair, screaming, down the narrow streets, until their tormentors had reached enough open space to sacrifice them as Andraste demanded. There weren't many who had stayed, but enough women were found to leave skewered bodies, pinioned upon Celtoi spears, all around the colonnaded forum to stain the stonework scarlet with blood.

Verulamium might be lacking in inhabitants, but they had fled without their belongings. The newly rich Catuvellauni could still remember being poor barbarians, and had obviously delayed leaving for as long as possible, trusting the horde would pass them by or never come. When they had finally left, it had plainly been a panicked and reluctant retreat, grabbing whatever could be quickly carried and hurrying away from the material things they adored. So there were plenty of precious things to steal and luxurious commodities to be won, wine to guzzle and sweetmeats to be enjoyed. By the state of some of the foodstuffs, Boudicca estimated that the majority of the townsfolk had only left in the last day or so; tonight there would be the pleasure of butter which hadn't yet turned rancid and bread which had not yet dried up. Such simple, basic fare would be welcome after some of the fancy Romani leavings which had turned her stomach.

Boudicca and Lovernios decided, first, to meet up with Sucellus and the twins, although where to find them amongst this heaving throng of people was another problem altogether.

'It's best if we stay together and head for a distinctive place, like the theatre, where they'll be able to find us.' Lovernios suggested. 'We can keep our eyes out for them on the way and I'll direct my Druids to look for them and send them to us, too. Have you…?' Then he changed his mind about asking whatever the question was, although she could tell by his expression it took an effort for him to hold back his curiosity.

She imagined she could guess what he wanted to ask, but she still didn't have an answer to his question, so she pretended she hadn't heard him nor recognised his restraint.

'The theatre sounds fine,' she agreed, noticing his disappointment when he realised it was all she was going to say. Then she turned away, reluctant to encourage eye contact for the moment, and urged the ponies to speed up. 'Am I going in the right direction?'

'Just around this corner, I think, madam. It seemed to be near the forum when we were looking down from the rise, and we've just passed that.'

Boudicca steered the chariot forward to where Lovernios indicated. The crowds had thinned at last and the little ponies were able to move at their usual steady walk, whereas when they had first entered the Municipium they had had to push to take each hoof-step. Celtoi were used to running alongside chariots in battle and Celtoi ponies were used to being brushed and pushed by warriors milling around them, but the confinement of these narrow Romani streets made the prolonged contact almost insufferable and Boudicca could see that several shunts had not been entirely accidental.

So they were able to ride into the theatre, into the semi-circular area before the tiers of seating, with a fair amount of dignity. Lovernios jumped from the chariot as agile as if he had been born to ride.

'I'll leave you to tether them,' he announced. 'I'll be back as soon as I've told my Druids where we are.'

Then he was off, leaving Boudicca to see to the horses and wander around the structure. The Romani's theatre was horrendous to Boudicca's eyes, as all their buildings were. She had heard a tale that Romani theatres elsewhere were of stone, that the Catuvellauni hoped one day to be able to afford to emulate such magnificence for themselves. In Boudicca's eyes, this theatre was already too grand and too false, and there was no roof either. What was the good of such a huge seating area when it rained? Or did the Romani think they could control the weather as well as everything else?

She hoped they hadn't learned to do that and shivered at the thought of Romani weaving Spells aroundto control nature. It was one of the first Druidic lessons she had ever learned about Workings: to keep them to the absolute minimum. Druids knew such lore, of course, but they rarely meddled, no matter how drought and deluge tempted. It was virtually impossible to garner the full repercussions of powerful Workings like those that altered weather. One could never be certain where one's Magic would end, or what other forces might be triggered as a result, so one usually left it to Mother's Wisdom.

She didn't think she would like to live a Romani life, she decided. She couldn't see any trees from inside these buildings and she had heard stories of how thoroughly the Romani cleared land before they started to build. Now that she listened, she could hear very little birdcall, and she missed it. The Romani were all browns and greys, she figured, whilst her people were an entire rainbow. It was obvious the Romani missed being able to see nature's bounty, for most of the houses she'd been into had had friezes and murals of plants and animals painted upon the wall plaster. Even this theatre had an artificial backdrop of sorts left in place, albeit torn and hanging at one end. But these painted tendrils had been specially designed, without a leaf out of place, and every frond twisting in perfect symmetry, just like the Romani's tidy, compact gardens. This was not the raw delicacy of life she was used to appreciating, this was a cruel training of something which should not be trained.

As she looked around, she noticed a packing trunk behind the painted backdrop, and she scrambled upon the stage to have a look within. It would, she excused herself, prevent her from getting too bored whilst she waited for Lovernios to return. The lid was held with two clasps which needed prising before they could be lifted. She worked at them with her knife and then Andraste's sickle as she realised they needed to be treated quite roughly.

What would Grania be like now, she wondered? Somehow she found it so difficult to imagine her daughter as being anything but whole and healthy. She could see her now, walking quite normally and laughing with her cheeky, occasionally painful, humour. Strong, brave Grania, decisive and independent and protective of those weaker than her. There would be pride in her face and fire in her eyes, just as there used to be, and she'd be reasonable and approachable and sane, too.

On every occasion Boudicca had left Grania recently, she'd expected her to be miraculously returned to her old self when they next met. Boudicca continuously allowed herself to get her hopes up and her expectations had repeatedly been dashed by reality. She had the same hopes and fears for Maeve, too, but less acutely; Grania's deterioration had been so much worse.

Finally the chest clasps freed and she slung open the lid to peer within. There did not seem to be anything of value as she rummaged inside, pulling out long cloths and holding them up to her body before hurling them around her as if she built herself a brightly coloured nest. Halfway into the trunk, her hand brushed something which was not cloth, and she grasped it and brought it out. It was a mask, with pinholes for eyes and a great drooping mouth with down-turned corners. Playfully, she put it to her face and looked around, imagining it was the only protection between herself and a vast Romani audience.

Grania's condition seemed bleak. Was there any way of saving her at all, or was it all too late and her spirit already long gone? Lovernios had stopped mentioning sending her to the Sisters for Healing. Had even he given up on her? Perhaps, it was fair to let her die; after all, you wouldn't let a dog suffer that way. Boudicca remembered a rabid dog she had to kill once. It had been a clever hunting dog, but it had received a bite, just a nip, from a vixen it had brought to bay and which had been defending her cubs. Boudicca had not wanted to kill the dog at first, reluctant to destroy such a fine animal which had taken so long to train. She believed it would heal eventually, but it hadn't. They'd tied it up for its own protection, but its fits had become dangerous and it had frothed and whimpered until she had to admit it was all she could do to put it kindly out of its misery. She could still remember its eyes blinking sensitively at her as if it knew what was being done and was accepting it as being for the best.

Would Grania's eyes look upon her just as kindly?

She put the mask back in its box, safe amongst the cloth and costumes, but upright so she could still see its miserable expression. There was another, too, but this had a broad manic grin, the like of which she had only ever seen staring back out at her from the depths of a mirror. Almost unable to resist, she put that one to her face too, to see if the world looked any different that way.

Grania was her daughter. Boudicca couldn't sacrifice her any more than she could cut one of her own limbs off. While she was alive there was still a chance she might improve, and the Mother's love could heal even where a mother's love might not. Aside from anything else there were no guarantees that Lovernios' mysterious ritual would have the outcome he desired. Although her heart still yearned for the return of the personal Manifestation of Andraste, she'd begun to doubt whether it was intrinsic to the continuing success of the rebellion. The horde swept everything before it now, as if whole towns were nothing more than tinder and the Romani little more than ants. Andraste was directly with the horde and leading them on to where She wanted them to be; there could be no chance of failure. Grania was under control, unable to affect the horde any further. The Romani were running away and the legions were nowhere to be seen or heard. Did she really need Andraste back at such a terrible price?

Two masks, side by side, in opposition to each other. One happy, one sad. Two ways of seeing the world out of thousands of possibilities; and there remained the crux of her unmade decision.

She heard an inhuman shuffling and scraping and she looked up. Maeve was walking towards her in her silent, unobtrusive way, with Grania close behind. Boudicca was appalled at the further changes in her two daughters. Where Maeve had become more serene and more Otherworldly, Grania had stooped deeper into the realms of the primitive. Grania's skin had taken on a deathly pallor and her eyes and lips were red-lined and raw. As Grania came nearer, Boudicca heard a dreadful gnashing sound too and, looking more closely, she could see how her daughter chewed at her jaw continuously. A thin line of blood-speckled spittle crept from Grania's mouth where she gnawed at the insides of her cheeks to make them bleed. This apparition shattered Boudicca's expectations of the hale and robust young woman she had allowed to build up in her mind. Once again, reality failed to live up to her hopes.

But still Boudicca felt overwhelming compassion for this poor creature being brought to her as if Grania's fate lay in her hands. Boudicca was used to judging tribal conflicts and arguments between kin, but this was different. This was her own daughter and Grania was not herself. It was not right that a mother should have to stand in judgement over her own daughter; it was too much to ask and she couldn't do it. She couldn't condemn her own daughter to death, let alone carry out the judgement herself, as she suspected she might have to.

No, Lovernios would have to manage with the three of them as they were. The horde would no doubt do fine without them, but if figure-heads were still required then they'd just have to be slightly tarnished ones.

Almost as if her thoughts had brought him to her, Lovernios came flying across the theatre towards her at a run which she would never have thought him capable of. With his black robe flapping around him, he appeared like a massive raven, but a fledging one at that, for he nearly tripped upon the folds in his hurry to get to her. As he approached, she saw his face was not carrying his usual delight at seeing her again, but was instead contorted in anguish as if he was holding back his grief until he could reach her arms.

She dropped off the stage to reach him more easily, and held out her hands to him. He collapsed onto her, burying his face in her shoulder and sobbing uncontrollably. She stroked his back, remembering Prasutagus' tears in suffering dreadful pain, and waited for the Druid to speak. He was like a boy-child, she decided, coming home to mama to let her put it right, and she reached up to stroke his hair.

Finally he spoke through the tears which it obviously stung him to show, slow words which she had to listen carefully to before she could decipher them.

'They've fired Vernemetum,' he sobbed. 'There's nothing now but black, burnt fields, for as far as an eagle can see.'

She didn't need to ask who 'they' were. 'Wasn't your father there to stop them?'

'No. No. The old fool's gone south, as I suspected he had. He's at Isca, stirring up trouble which is none of his business, instead of protecting the oldest, most precious place in all of Britannia.' A fresh wave of tears broke free. 'They did it to bring us north, to meet them in battle. We are, evidently, taking too long in coming for them and destroying too much on our way.

'Suetonius is no doubt short of food,' he continued. 'He can choose where he will wait for the horde and make his last stand – we've known that would always be his ultimate advantage – but now he's trying to force when.'

'We're ready to meet him, Lovernios mine. The horde has never been more ready. We're at the peak of our strength and numbers and Andraste is with us still! We'll make him pay for this desecration and we'll sprinkle these ruined fields of yours with Romani blood to make them grow back strong.'

Lovernios looked her straight in the eye with a determined and meaningful gaze that demanded her attention. 'You must do it, Boudicca.'

'No. It's not necessary, Lovernios.'

'It is. We must be assured of victory. The horde must have Andraste Manifest within someone who is capable of being a strong leader. We can't take any risks with this battle. Andraste won't allow Her enemies to live after this desecration; we must Serve Her as best we can and allow no room for error.'

'But I thought you and Sucellus were still uncertain whether this ritual would succeed?'

'We must try, Boudicca. We must try'

'But Grania might die needlessly.'

'Better that than she lives as she does.'

Lovernios was pleading with her, begging almost, his voice taking on an almost whining quality as he cajoled her into doing as he asked.

'Why aren't you certain it'll work, Lovernios?'

'Because we can't use the Groves for our Workings. They're Sealed now to keep my mother in the north, so we'll have to make our own Sacred Space for our ritual. And there's one other thing too. I still haven't determined what conditions occur to prompt Andraste to move to one who's more suitable, as She has done in the past, if indeed there are any.'

He was dismissing his doubts as he spoke, pretending to be reassuring her when he was really reassuring himself. But his tears had stopped and she responded to him on a mother's level, striving to keep his tears from flowing.

'There's no other way?' She flicked a glance over at Grania. Her daughter was scratching at herself and rolling in dust to cover where she'd just soiled the ground.

'No. There's no other way.'

'Then let some good come of this whole dreadful episode.'

Lovernios grasped her by the shoulders and kissed her hard in thankfulness. 'I can only appreciate what a hard choice it's been for you, madam. I'll do all I can to make sure it's the right one.'

'You realise, Lovernios, that I have chosen, now, between you and my daughter, between my lover and my own flesh and blood. This is a turning point for me and a bestowal of a privilege I would not have you treat lightly.'

'I understand, madam. I will honour your decision.'

'We'd better start, then,' she said in a whisper without looking around to her daughters. 'The horde will want to be moving again as soon as they hear about what the Romani have done. They'll see it as a challenge, and I should be at their head for their next hosting.'

Lovernios nodded, all seriousness now. His tears had dried, leaving stains upon his cheeks, but he looked no less for it in Boudicca's eyes. The Druid was a Bard with a poet's spirit; how could a heart sing if it was not subject to emotion?

'I've already arranged for Druids to surround us. Even now they delineate a Sacred Space for us, as they stand hand-in-hand forming a circle around this theatre. I ordered it to be done outside of these theatre banks so as not to alarm you, although these material barriers will not show within the Otherness we create.'

'You already knew I'd say yes?'

'I wouldn't have let up until you had, madam. Shall I start?'

'What about Maeve?'

'She'll have to stay. She's the only one who can soothe Grania.' He held up a hand to stop her objection. 'There are already too many variables, madam, too many ways in which we don't keep to the rules. But we're desperate people, pushed to desperate means, and we must try.'

Then he turned from her and started to pace out the area he had set aside for his Workings, walking with slow, measured steps and gesturing with a hazel twig. He muttered words and spoke strange invocations which Boudicca couldn't understand. Grania licked herself disinterestedly, looking up every so often to see how far the Druid had progressed. Lovernios' movements were stiff and careful; there was none of his natural serenity about him, none of his usual fluidity in casting Workings. He was worried, she could tell, and it was showing in a tenseness reflected throughout his whole body.

Grania became more agitated as Lovernios neared the completion of the circle he was marking out. She paid more attention to his movements and followed him with sudden, twitching movements of her head, as if he were a pretty, flitting thing she wanted to catch. Then, as Lovernios joined the beginning and end of the circle, Grania gave out the slightest moan and hunkered down to curl at Maeve's feet.

All this while, Boudicca had been motionless, keeping a distant and impassive watch on the proceedings. Then she felt the distinctive shimmer in the air as Lovernios finished the first stage in his ritual, dedicating a place in this Romani town to be as sacred, albeit temporarily, as the deepest Groves. The atmosphere within changed perceptibly, somehow rendering the outside world quieter, and the inner seemingly heavier, like the tension before a summer thunderstorm. Truly, Boudicca felt between worlds like never before, the set-asideness quite tangible.

Lovernios gestured for the four of them to come together. Boudicca could see how the energy he'd expanded so far already affected his countenance. He looked haggard and spent. She hoped he hadn't overexerted himself too soon, hoped he might have strength enough to carry them through his ritual; she wouldn't want to be kept here for eternity.

'We should be safe enough,' he wheezed. Boudicca worried for him and for his ability to see this task through to its end, wondering what unconsidered consequences might arise from the day's work and whether any of them might be the same tomorrow. 'There's a ring of Druids surrounding us, and a triple inner ring of my own Wardings. There couldn't be anywhere more holy.'

Boudicca had to trust to his training which she knew would have exercised facilities in his psyche, making him capable of storing quantities of inner strength she could only dream of. Whatever, it was becoming apparent to her that this was the last opportunity there might be for such rituals. Not only were their chances of finding the physical space and requisite number of Druids becoming more difficult, but also she could see quite clearly that Lovernios would be unable to expend so much energy, in one go, very often during his life.

This realisation firmed her resolve to continue, even though doing so meant placing more trust than she cared to place in anyone, upon Lovernios. Overwhelmingly she had to agree that there could be no turning back. The days of living in peace and plenty had passed long before even Prasutagus had died. She, personally, had been unable to return to her own shallow reflection of the domestic dream when she had first raised a voice in protest at her daughters' violation. For each person in the horde, that instance of no turning back would have come at a different moment. Probably it hadn't even been noticed until long after it had happened. Perhaps, by chance, they had looked back one day only to discover they were irrevocably committed to whatever they had helped set in motion. Since then, Boudicca, like the horde, had had no choice but to move on, even into uncharted territory where the future seemed increasingly uncertain and unsafe.

Once again she jumped, taking a leap of faith and complying with Lovernios' instructions, forgetting on how many other occasions she had done so since Imbolc. She grasped Grania's hand, as instructed. It was clammy to the touch, almost slimy. Lovernios took Boudicca's other hand, Maeve took Grania's. Then, forming a linked line of tightly held hands, they followed Lovernios' steps as he led Boudicca, then Grania, then Maeve, through the steps of the world's oldest dance.

Into the centre of the labyrinth he strode, twisting before reaching the centre and turning back upon himself. They trod precisely, careful not to miss their footing and step out of the pathway being woven, even Grania did as the others did, her poor mind overwhelmed by the power buzzing around them. The maze was unmarked, but Lovernios remembered the way and led them unfaltering to its end. There were many mazes Lovernios could have chosen. Each consisted of one single strand which led, eventually, by swirls and loops, in and out and back upon itself until the Walker reached the sanctity of the centre. As

Druid, Lovernios would have had to commit them all to memory, would have had to be able to remember the subtle meanderings of each and every one so he could recreate them, and their associated Workings, whenever they were needed.

As they reached the stillness of the centre, Boudicca realised a profoundness had settled upon her again, another alteration of consciousness so slight as to be almost imperceptible. She felt at peace within, almost beyond everyday cares and somehow beyond awareness of where or when she was. She looked back at the marks in the dust which their passing feet had made. There, all around her, were the lines of the labyrinth, regular and mysterious, representing the spiritual journey they had just made, every step symbolising a lesson and a transformation of their spirits.

She turned to look at Lovernios. His face was furrowed with strain, but his eyes shone with what he had accomplished. Grania was still, for once, and seemingly resigned to what must be. Maeve held her sister's hand tightly, supporting her and lending her strength.

They stood close together, crammed in the limited area that was the sacred centre. They were almost touching and Boudicca could smell her lover's hot breath and hear her daughters' heartbeats.

'We are all agreed on what we do? How necessity has brought us here?'

Lovernios asked the formal questions and Boudicca was surprised to see both Grania and Maeve answer separately and with sense. There were still things happening here which she did not understand, things which she felt she had a right to understand since she played such a key part.

'Then the waiting is over,' he intoned. 'And we should do what we have come for.'

Grania lifted her neck, revealing her throat as fully as she could. Maeve gripped her sister in comfort.

'Take Andraste's sickle and cut here, madam.' Lovernios ran his finger over Grania's jugular. 'Do it quickly and cleanly. Don't hesitate and don't stop to think.'

'It's just a lamb or a pigeon,' Boudicca recited in her mind. 'Just a piglet for butchery or a deer for sport,' she repeated over and over, pulling the golden sickle from her belt. 'Just a hare you have brought to rest. Kill it quickly; you know how to cause the minimum of pain. Quick, it's cruel to leave the creature waiting when it knows what's coming.' Then, as she looked at the throbbing pulse in Grania's throat, she saw the hare again. Bouncing, bouncing away from her. It must come back to her; it must not go without her. The whole horde depended upon the hare being made to stay. But it was bounding away, it was escaping.

In her mind's eye she saw herself draw a dagger and hurl it after the leggy animal. The dagger caught the sunlight and span in the air, rolling over and over until it shook in its quarry. Pierced with a hunter's precision, the hare ran no more.

A red mist cleared from Boudicca's mind and she blinked. Grania's blood had spurted out from where the golden sickle had cut her throat. Boudicca's daughter gurgled and quivered a little in shock. Maeve and Lovernios held her with clenched, concentrated expressions, seeking to untangle Andraste from Grania's spirit and guide Grania to the threshold of the Summerlands.

Boudicca stood rigid, alarmed at what she had done, forcing herself to watch the last moments of her daughter's life, the last she'd see of her beloved Grania this side of the Summerlands. Open mouthed and aghast, she saw Grania die and felt her spirit pass from this world to the next. She reached out for her daughter, surprised to see Grania's face turn less pale with death, and heard her whisper 'Thank you'. Then she saw Grania squeeze, with the slightest touch, the hands which supported her, before her body crumpled.

Then the sky darkened and the winds rose, whipping around their cloaks to almost pull them off balance. They let Grania fall to the ground, freeing their arms to hold onto each other so they might not be blown from the circle. The temperature dropped, setting them shivering, and the winds increased in speed as if they spun around and around, leaving the three of them seemingly in the centre of a whirling vortex. Boudicca strengthened her grip upon Lovernios and Maeve, scared she would lose them and be swept off into the terrifying nothingness which threatened all around her. She was frightened by the sudden change, shutting her eyes to the dust which the winds had now sent flying into their faces to sting against their skin. She ducked her head down so she might breath a stiller air.

Then she heard the spirits which came next, and she resolved to keep her eyes firmly shut so she might not have to look upon them. She heard Prasutagus call to her, begging her to step over into the Summerlands and share eternal bliss with him. His deep and gentle voice tempted her beyond reason, but Lovernios wouldn't let her pull away. She strained to hear the half-forgotten lullabies of her mother's voice and the melodic harp playing of the tribes' Bard just as it had sounded when she was a child. She heard a baby's crying and recognised the distinctive sounds with a sharp pain that caused her to take a sudden, deep breath. Her baby, her baby boy! He needed her so much; he was in pain, lost without mama. If only she could reach him, hold him in her arms, see his sea-blue eyes alive instead of dead, then they'd all be family again. So many of those she loved had already gone, surely it would be best if she went to them that they might be family once more?

She looked up for an instant and immediately regretted doing so. Grania was beckoning to her, Grania wearing a wonderful, benevolent smile. Her beloved daughter wasn't dead at all, but alive and well and it had all been her own imagination casting her into a living nightmare. Disorientated, she started to waver and swoon, not knowing which voices to believe, which bodies to hold to. What was real, what was not?

Lovernios caught her as she started to collapse and Maeve, surprisingly, started to talk to her: 'Mama mine, ignore the voices, they are phantoms come to test you, for we walk where we should not walk and Cast Workings unpractised for many generations. Come with me, both of you, I shall guide you back to safety. Stay close, I am the only way out.'

Eyes tightly shut and her mind shuttered against the things she heard, Boudicca let Maeve lead her away. She felt the air freeze in places, and when it did she would peer out of her blinkered lids to see herself pass through the trailing wisps of ghosts. She felt Lovernios step over Grania's poor body, left to lie where it had fallen, more normal in death than she had been lately in life. Then they were retracing their steps as Maeve pulled them from the labyrinth and the hauntings gradually lessened and the sky lightened as if it were dawning.

Feeling, at last, hopeful that she might return to the material realm alive and with her mind intact, Boudicca's thoughts lightened with relief and turned to the welfare of the horde. She wondered whether any of her people would still be there through these extreme weather changes. She couldn't blame them for scattering, if they had. Even with her own knowledge that such portents meant Workings of vast importance, she might have panicked and been tempted to run from the repercussions if she'd been watching from without.

And what of Andraste? Where had the Goddess been sent? She was not back with Boudicca, that much was evident to her. She wondered whether the Goddess had been released from Grania or whether She had finally refused to release her daughter. Perhaps She had moved into the Void which was all around – that would explain why they suffered now from such traumatic experiences. But she didn't panic. Lovernios would be able to answer her questions – he had to be able to, these things were beyond her comprehending. And who knew, perhaps the Spell did not complete until they had retreated their steps from the labyrinth? Even now, were they walking around inside a Spell?

Such thoughts gave her a smattering of confidence – enough for her to continue her journey. She bowed her head down, gripped Maeve and Lovernios tighter than ever and strode forward with increased purpose. She had done her part in what had been asked; she could not be faulted on that. Now it was up to Lovernios to show her it had been a success.

The first she knew about stepping out of the labyrinth was when

Lovernios and Maeve dropped their hands from hers. Her fingers had tightened into claws where they had gripped so firmly; they felt set in their rigidity and she flexed them to loosen her joints. The maze was nothing now but a kicking of dust in the middle of the Romani theatre. Grania's body had completely disappeared from its centre and the day had returned to its early summer warmth.

Maeve reached out to embrace Boudicca and the two women hugged each other in solace for the sister and daughter they had both lost. Lovernios darted over to undo the protective circle he had Cast, Working widdershins around the delineated area. Then he ran out of the theatre, the urgency of his task helping him to find yet more physical strength when it should, by rights, be depleted.

He returned in moments, his flagging pace revealing the real extent of his exhaustion. 'We've lost five,' he panted. Then explained in response to Boudicca's puzzlement, 'Five Druids died holding the circle. That's good, considering.' He looked relieved, despite being shocked at the loss of his colleagues. 'The rest are regaining their strength.'

'What about the horde?'

'What about the horde, madam?'

'Is it still here? Are they frightened out of their wits? How were they affected?'

Lovernios paused, incredulous, before replying. 'That, madam, is why so many Druids died. They held the circle – nothing escaped, nothing got in. The circle stayed intact throughout; the horde would've known nothing about what happened. Didn't you realise?'

Boudicca shook her head. His next question was almost an accusation.

'Madam?' Lovernios looked more worried than she'd ever seen him look before. 'Andraste has returned to you, hasn't She?'

His question pleaded with her to reply positively. His insistence frightened her, but she couldn't give him the reassurance he seemed to demand.

'No,' she admitted. 'I thought it was still to come.'

Lovernios cradled his head in his hands and dropped to the floor.

'I'm sorry,' Boudicca added. 'Did I do something wrong?'

'No, Boudicca. But I obviously didn't do something right.'

'Then, where is She? She won't just have disappeared, will She?'

They looked at each other, both confused, then looked up. Maeve was standing over them, offering them a hand each to get up from the dirt.

Then Boudicca's quietest child advised: 'The Romani are to the north. We should host against the gathered bulk of the legions soon, for that is what I most desire.'

Chapter 18

Gibbous Moon

Yet again, Boudicca felt strangely detached from the scene unfolding before her. She stood in her chariot, together with Lovernios and Maeve, and watched as Maeve did something that Boudicca never thought she'd see her usually timid and retiring daughter do.

'Think not of us as Queen and Heir,' screamed Maeve, letting the wind catch her speech and carry it to the furthest reaches of the horde. 'But as Celtoi: ill used and maltreated by the Romani just as every one of you has been.

'Look at their tiny numbers and compare it to our massive strength. Half of the Romani have fled, the other half lie cowering in their forts. This excuse for an army is all that remains between servitude and the eternal liberation of Britannia. They will never face the roar of our thousands: we outnumber them by twenty of us to every one of them. They will falter at our charge and fall before our hand-to-hand combat.'

Maeve paused for dramatic effect, taking a deep breath before she continued.

'Consider Romani judgements and compare them to the vengeance of our Gods who are still behind us in our quest for Celtoi justice. We have destroyed countless settlements and a quarter of their legions already – and that was in the days of our youth, when we were still growing in numbers! We could not have come this far without Andraste, and She is with us yet. We can all feel Her lust, still growing at the thought of the bloodshed to come!

'Even now the Romani quake as they realise the strength of our numbers and the justice behind our cause. Even now they will be deliberating whether to stay or to flee. Even now their resolve is crumbling away; no doubt they will be gone even before we attack.'

Then Maeve screamed at the horde: 'Victory is already ours and Andraste's! This battle is merely a formality; its outcome is certain. Follow me, then, or submit to the Romani's yoke forever!'

The horde's response was so loud that Boudicca put her hands to her ears. No translations had been necessary for any of the various tribes-folk. The breeze carried and turned the Goddess-inspired words as easily as if they were autumn leaves. Maeve hurled her spear as far as she could – the traditional signal for the battle to commence, clearly given – and the crowd surged forwards after it. Then Boudicca turned the chariot neatly, as arranged, and drove Cloud and Mouse back through the horde. The crowds of tribes-folk parted as the horses pushed and the chariot passed through the host. A chant of 'Andraste! Andraste!' rose through the ranks which roused Boudicca's heart, piercing even her sombre mood.

All around, battle frenzy took over the horde as individuals looked to their own glory and grew oblivious to what those around them did. Once they'd worked themselves up to their battle mentality, there wouldn't be one champion in the whole of the gathered tribes who would not try to take on the might of the entire Romani army arrayed before them. In such a state, death held no fear for a Celtoi warrior, and maiming was something which always happened to someone else.

Boudicca felt the rush swell within the crowd as her ponies shoved laboriously back towards the wagons. Although they moved away from the Romani, the horde was oblivious to them already. The ritual of war had well and truly begun and brightly painted warriors paraded upon their chariots for the pleasure and excitement of all those watching from the carts and wagons. The atmosphere was like that of a fair or a Beltane-gather and anyone who couldn't fight had climbed as high as they could onto the tops of the wagons so they could see the slaughter of these hated Romani without missing any of the action. To facilitate this, the Celtoi had done what they usually did during war and drawn all the vehicles up in a loose semi-circle behind the massed horde. In this way, everyone could be assured of the best possible view in compensation for not actually being able to participate in the fighting.

This was proper; it was the Celtoi way for one's kin to watch one's prowess in battle and it made good sense. After all, was it not the babes, those who would remember what they saw, who would tell of the battle to their children's children long after those who'd fought had died of old age? And was it not the old, those who were near to death, who'd be sure to be singing tales of heroes in the Summerlands to herald those self-same heroes when their turn came to pass over?

Thus, the tops of the wagons were packed, but even so, many of those who had been brought in on them had found some last reservoir of strength and joined the horde, just this once, not wanting to miss out on being a part of Andraste's glory. Consequently the horde was thronging with a fair proportion of unblooded children and hobbling wounded, perhaps seeking to slip a dagger in a fallen throat here and there, that they too might be included in the ballads of the brave. The Druids were amongst the ranks, too, swelling the numbers even further. Their black or pure white robes flashed distinctively amongst the vivid checked cloaks or blue-woaded bare flesh of the rest of the Undedicated. The Druids mingled amongst the Celtoi, keeping their spirits high and calling down Andraste's Blessing. The Bards, too, wanted to be part of the battle that they might invoke its atmosphere more accurately when they finally came to compose their songs of remembrance.

The horde had never been bigger. Boudicca felt it like a great hovering cloud upon the land. Such vast numbers of people; it seemed like the whole of Britannia had risen in revolt, not just half a dozen tribes. No wonder there had been so much trouble with feeding these numbers, no wonder the line of the host had stretched out to reach one town as the stragglers were still leaving the last. It was a pure miracle they'd come so far. To mobilise such a force, to keep it together, was a feat incomprehensible without Andraste's Guidance and Will.

Boudicca could still feel the Goddess' Presence albeit in a rather subdued way compared with what she had once been used to. However, she suspected it was in a way which was similar to the experience of every individual in the horde. Being able to also remember both life before Andraste and life with Her, Boudicca could compare and contrast the three stages of Divine Presence that she'd been familiar with. This more universal awareness was certainly more profound and heightened than before she had come to know the Goddess personally. She could understand now why the horde was so entranced by the experience, which would be new for most of them, and why it had affected them so deeply.

However, compared with the personal experience of Andraste's Manifestation, it was like seeing in black and white when she had previously been able to see the most vibrant colours. And, looking back at her life before she had ever felt Andraste's presence, well, in contrast to that, it was as if she had been blind then.

Boudicca still missed Andraste's presence as acutely as ever she missed Prasutagus, her late husband and consort. Lovernios' love had gone part-way to healing the first wound, but nothing, it seemed, could ease the emptiness of losing the Goddess. Being able to feel the universal Blessing bestowed upon the horde was a scant substitute for the prize she had once known, and nothing else mattered to her. But Boudicca was tired now, tired of being pulled around this country and being made to do things she would never have considered a season ago.

And the Queen had aged, too. Catching her reflection in the clear waters of a Romani well, what, three nights since? Yes, it must have been for the moon had been over a quarter full and waxing and now it was full. Certainly there'd been enough light to see her wavering face peer back at her from a mass of greying hair. There were new lines, too, around her eyes and mouth, which had never been there when she used to look in her own bronze-backed mirror at the royal enclosure back in Iceni territory. And her bleeding was late again, contributing to her overall sense of feeling like she looked.

Where had that dark, portentous well been? Had it been Bannaventa or Tripontium? They had passed through so many settlements and killed or scattered so many Romani or Catuvellauni. The horde had maimed and burned its way up Watling Street, searching as it swept the land for the legions that waited for it somewhere to the north-west. She could remember the names quite easily; after all she did have a Druid-trained memory. There had been Durocobrivis and Lactodurum, they had left them soon after Verulamium, she was sure, and Magiovinium, too. But they were all a blur and she could no more recall their order than retrieve Andraste.

Some of the settlements had been little more than one or two huts, rudely built around a Romani staging post. Others had been substantial and emerging towns, or villas at foundation stage. They destroyed them all, leaving just corpses and ash. Something had kept the horde moving at its tremendous pace all quarter; Boudicca knew it hadn't been her. The horde had been seemingly self-driven, rushing on and travelling unbelievable distances, being hindered less than was reasonable to expect with so many people and so much baggage to transport.

The pace had slowed at Venonis, where Watling Street crossed the Fosse Way and where everyone had seemed to expect the Romani legions to be waiting. If the legion two had come up from Isca, lying to the south-west, then that was where it would have met up with Suetonius. But they were not there. The Romani had not been passed on the way north, so they could either be further along Watling Street to the west, or further along Fosse Way heading northeast. The Romani had already travelled partially up along Fosse Way, so much was known. They would have had to have done so in order to reach Vernemetum. But whether they had then returned and backtracked or continued to their legion nine's fortress at Lindum was anyone's guess.

The horde had now passed into Coritani territory, so they immediately gained access to intelligence concerning the lie of the land and possible Romani positions from Fand and her tribes-folk. Fand insisted upon pointing out interesting landmarks and describing the delights of her tribal land, and Boudicca had had to put up with the chattering monologue for the last couple of days. Maeve, too, had been unusually vocal, but Boudicca had kept her distance, even though the return of Maeve's voice had previously been so eagerly desired. Fortunately, Maeve's diplomacy had also returned and Boudicca was able to hand the task of inventing polite questions, to fuel the Coritani Queen's narration, straight over to her daughter.

Maeve's handling of the situation disturbed Boudicca even further. Her priestess daughter had never been adept in social situations; even before the Romani had hurt her, she was far more comfortable in the world of shadows and secrets than the world of politics and war. She used to keep herself hidden away in the Iceni temple for days on end, even whole moon phases, only to emerge with some enigmatic phrase or guidance which was meaningful solely to the Druidic hermits who wandered from tribe to tribe. This new willingness to mingle in the ways of the world was clearly not Maeve, because Maeve had never behaved like that. This was plainly yet another aspect of the Goddess' Manifestation.

But Sucellus had shielded Maeve well since the Iceni first came to his forge clearing. His protection of her had kept her from too many prying eyes or strangers' curiosity, and Maeve's condition had been successfully concealed from those who might be affected by knowing the state of one of their figurehead's minds. In particular, very few in the horde knew of Maeve's scrub, scrub, scrubbing which left her skin red-raw and stinging, although Boudicca was relieved to see her daughter had finally stopped trying to wash herself clean of whatever she imagined still contaminated her.

More than anything, Boudicca wanted to be free of the whole lot of them. Lovernios sought to offer some comfort, but she could tell he felt too ashamed for persuading her to take part in the ritual that had sacrificed Grania. For her part, she felt too tired and too exhausted to lay blame upon anyone. Wherever Grania was now, it was almost certainly better than the living hell her daughter had become ensnared in before her death. Boudicca wished she had the energy to convince Lovernios not to put up needless barriers between the two of them. After all, she knew she could live more comfortably with the knowledge of what she'd done if only she had his support.

Just as soon as all of this was over, she promised herself, she would take herself and Lovernios off to the forests. She would not have to wait much longer; today's battle would be the beginning of the end of the Romani's rule. The forthcoming defeat would represent the pivoting of power. And it would be Beltane soon, the true start of summer, when the days would be long and lazy and they could rejoice in a newly liberated Britannia and be together forever. For Boudicca, the future and Lovernios were inextricably entwined. Every dream and hope involved her Druid lover and she'd ensure there would be nothing to separate them, nothing to come between them, ever again.

She would worry about the boredom if and when it happened.

Lovernios, it seemed, had picked up the signs of her fatigue and, probably as part-recompense for Grania's death, had devised a strategy to take the pressure off Boudicca and let Maeve do most of the diplomatic duties. It was he who had pointed out how much of a resemblance Maeve bore to her mother and he who had, very lovingly, explained how much the rebellion had sapped Boudicca and aged her since Imbolc. She was, he insisted, still exceedingly beautiful and a good rest and a few nights of decent sleep would soon smooth the crow's feet and soothe her furrowed brow. But, he had continued, the horde would probably not be able to tell the physical difference between her and Maeve, and they might be better off making the best of the situation and allowing Andraste to lead through Maeve, if that was what the Goddess wanted to do.

Boudicca had found it surprisingly easy to acquiesce, especially since she'd half-feared Lovernios might suggest sacrificing Maeve, too, in a repeat of his ritual. The Goddess could not be controlled; She had proved so much by now. Boudicca felt she might as well relax and let the Divine tide take her where it would. Perhaps, when they were at last alone and comfortable together in the wilderness, she might ask Lovernios to cast Workings upon her to ease the grief of losing so much, especially for losing Andraste's Presence. She had felt led and manipulated for so long now, a while more would not make much difference.

Sucellus hadn't been pleased with their plan, of course, and he and Lovernios had had prolonged and agitated discussions as soon as the smith discovered what had happened to his ward. He had glared at Boudicca with a look which exactly expressed her own decreasing sense of self-worth. But even the stubborn Sucellus was persuaded to the merits of Lovernios' rapidly redefined plan and had to admit that Maeve's condition was at least better than losing the Goddess altogether.

Andraste was still with them and they still had the advantage. Without Her, it was painfully obvious that luck would not have been on their side. Too many settlements yielded just the right amounts and types of supplies, too many wheels buckled only for an exact replacement fit to be found discarded at the next hamlet. The Goddess' Hand seemed to be upon everything, creating too many coincidences and making a gruelling journey seem leisurely. And Maeve, too, seemed a good vessel for Andraste to reside in. Her character coloured Andraste's Emanation to one which was more caring and nurturing of Her people. This Manifestation was encouraging and creative, too, but without losing the terrifying aspect of the Goddess in this form.

Venonis, then, had been quite a surprise. Up until then, things had progressed so neatly that when neither the Romani themselves, nor an indication of where they might be, were evident, a breeze of consternation and disappointment swept through the horde like the wind rippling ripening corn. Even Lovernios, who always seemed to Boudicca to know everything, was momentarily taken aback by their missing foe. He had apologised profusely, explaining how those Druids loyal to him were now all numbered amongst the horde instead of being convenient messengers and scouts. Also, he admitted, his powers of reconnaissance had been severely curtailed as soon as he'd Sealed the Pathways to the Groves.

But Maeve had taken control almost immediately. Whereas before, since they'd left Verulamium, she had restricted herself to individual inspiration and to insisting, as soon as they entered the Romani military zone, that the forts were avoided in favour of the easier targets, now she addressed the crowd as if it were something she had been accustomed to do for the whole of her short life. Even Boudicca and Lovernios found themselves almost forced to let her command their whole attention and they listened, quite beguiled, to her words.

'There are fortlets and Romani soldiers everywhere,' Maeve spoke as if she were holding a normal conversation with every single individual person in the horde. She projected her voice as naturally as if she were Bard-trained. 'I can smell them and so, no doubt, can you.' She sniffed the air, as if she could detect a scent. 'But it's not those whose trail we seek. No, we want the legions that await their deaths, those who have conveniently gathered together to make their slaughter easier for us. They have destroyed My Groves and now they must die, so scout for Me and discover where they wait for us. Scout out along all four routes of this crossroads, for a day's ride out at most, and then return immediately. Do not rest except to save your horses. Yes, scour every quarter of this realm! Even back the way we have come, for they may be seeking to attack the rear of our horde. Then report back as soon as you know where their lair is; I am impatient for blood and so are you.'

Almost before she had finished speaking, the horde had organised scouts to ride out to hunt for the legions. Charioteers and warriors acted at once, as if the horde were one now, a single organism with one mind rather than many, many thousands of separate individuals. Boudicca was amazed at Maeve's control, and knew instinctively that her level of power over such a large crowd could derive only from the War Goddess' direct influence. Boudicca gripped Lovernios' hand for security and prepared herself for a wait. All around, the more practical element in the horde busied themselves with gulping down a quick meal and ensuring their families did likewise.

It did not take long for the first scouts to return with news of where the Romani legions were. Those who found them had only had to ride a mere half-day's journeying further northwest along Watling Street. The Romani had been busy desecrating all the temples and Groves in a large area all around the Coritani's territory and even further west into the lands of the Cornovii, seeking to incense the horde into rash and unconsidered action. It had not been difficult to work out where the legions would be.

The Romani were, apparently, short of food and desperate to meet in pitched battle. So much so that their commander, Suetonius, had sent out members of his cavalry with the express purpose of making sure they were seen by any of the rebellion's scouts who might be looking for them. Maeve's scouts told tales of how they'd been virtually led to the place by a tantalising flash of a red cloak amongst the trees or the sun glinting off a polished helmet from a fair distance away. The scouts told of how they had crept as close as they could to where the Romani were pitched, and how they had spied for as long as they were able, in order to learn everything they could about the legions' position.

There was a flood plain ahead, belonging to the sweeping river which the road loosely followed, the scouts reported. Off it were several narrow defiles that opened out onto the river plain through which the Romani's road ran, created from where a ridge of rock had produced a long, steep escarpment. The Romani had holed themselves in the approach of the defile nearest one of their fortlets. Some of the scouts had ridden tantalisingly close to the Romani den, but none of the soldiers had taken up the challenge of a fight. It seemed the Romani legions had decided nothing would move them from the site chosen as their last stand. It was up to the horde to go in and flush them out.

Further questioning revealed how the terrain changed suddenly from open plain with little cover to a thickly wooded rise behind the valley of the defile. Such protection to the Romani's rear, if the reports were accurate, would prevent any sizable infiltration – especially now the Paths were closed – and effectively prevent any Celtoi outflanking strategies. The defile itself, they were assured, opened into the river plain, and narrowed sharply as it backed onto the slope of the escarpment. The horde would, therefore, be forced to advance into a valley of diminishing width. Suetonius had chosen a good defensive position, the Celtoi could acknowledge as much, but he had to do so: he had pitifully few men under his command, too few not to use every edge he could wring from the situation. In fact, the odds were so in favour of the Celtoi, it was probable there would be a rush for heads during the battle and it was unlikely there would be enough to go round.

Maeve ordered the horde to keep moving along Watling Street as soon as she heard in which direction the Romani were waiting. She listened to the finer details whilst on the move. A handful of chariot-eers were left at the crossing of the Romani roads to ensure those scouts still to return from their reconnaissance would know where to meet up with the rest of the horde. They could travel faster than the heavier baggage wagons and it made better sense for them to catch up later than for the horde to be kept waiting. For now, the Celtoi were eager to be at the Romani and she let them have their head, urging them onwards and making use of their enthusiasm rather than wasting it. The same tactic, Boudicca noted, that she had once utilized herself when she had been in command of the horde.

The Celtoi camped for the night just out of sight of the Romani position. Such precautions were traditional rather than necessary; the Romani had scouts out combing the countryside, just as the Celtoi did, and it would be virtually impossible for either army to hide their presence when such vast numbers were involved. Come dawn, the Celtoi had moved down into the river plain, like so many grains of sand trickling into a recently dug pit, and the wagons had been drawn around to provide viewing platforms. The sun was high above the massed armies before the entire horde had shifted into position, but still the warriors jostled each other for the prime places. The Romani must have shivered to see such a massive force, but they did not show it; they just stood in their orderly ranks, unable to move without orders, and listened to their commander's speech.

As soon as Boudicca had led Maeve to address her people and backed away again, the battle had begun. The Celtoi carried every advantage except position, and the Romani were painfully afraid to relinquish that, so the horde dictated the course of the battle, insisting they war as the tribes had always fought. Warfare for the Celtoi was virtually an art form. Trained from an early age, this was the purpose for which many of the nobles in the horde had been raised. There was not just the Romani to defeat, there was the glory of the tribe to be won and the accolade of heroes to be gained.

Boudicca desperately, desperately wanted to watch, so she manoeuvred her chariot, unwieldy with three people in it, around the line of the wagons and back to the flanks of the horde. In this position, she hoped to gain an uninterrupted view yet still be able to send orders to her commanders in the ranks where necessary. The wagon was difficult to handle, not least because it felt like it carried more than just three people. Boudicca had not yet felt able to grieve for the loss of Grania, and she could not help wandering whether her daughter was still with them, especially on the day of this eagerly anticipated battle. Certainly, Grania's absence had not caused any noticeable consternation within the horde itself, so perhaps her people could also sense

Grania's spirit. But Boudicca was aware of her own current inability to think straight and she was tempted to dismiss her mind's illusion as just another symptom of the madness she seemed to be being sucked into. She tried to focus her mind on the forthcoming conflict and to ignore the more extreme promptings of her imagination; it was the only way she could think of to cope.

Starved of their birthright to raid and war upon each other by the enforced peace of the Pax Romana, this battle was the culmination of all that these tribes-folk had been born for. Considering their rivals carefully, the Celtoi deduced that the Romani were not about to go anywhere; they might have an easily protected position, but it was also one which trapped them. For now, the day was plenty long enough to display and boast battle prowess as if the floodplain were a circus and all the horde travelling acrobats. The armies would not come together in pitched battle until the Celtoi had demonstrated all their refound skills and the trapped legionaries were reduced to quivering wrecks.

The Romani may well have been carved of stone for all they moved. Stern and stiff, they stared out at the horde as impassively as if they were merely upon a practice parade. Only at the back of the orderly ranks was there some urgent action as plans and formations seemed to be being minutely adjusted. Even the horses in the two blocks of cavalry to either side of the legionaries stood patiently with unnatural obedience.

The inactivity angered the horde, who roused themselves to new heights of fearlessness; pushing their chariots so very, very close to the Romani ranks as to almost run over a hobnailed toe before darting back. But still they could elicit no response. They taunted and jeered, gestured and exposed themselves, flourishing the numerous heads they had taken from Romani settlers. Amongst their trophies was the golden head of the Romani's Claudius god, taken from the Temple at Camulodunum, which had been stuck upon a long pole so all the Romani might see it. Champions were nominated from the tribes to show off their sword skills, blurring their blades in lightning twists as they strove to intimidate the Romani. Then warriors practised throwing spears back and forth between them, turning them as soon as they were caught and casting them back. Such a skill was vital where weapons were in short supply. To be able to use an enemy's own weapons against them was the ultimate in thrifty battle practice and explained why so many warriors asked Druids to Bless their swords against such an event. The most prized weapons were those which had had such Workings Cast upon them as a guarantee that they could not be used against their owner nor turned against them.

Boudicca clapped her hands at the wonderful displays of skills arrayed before her. For an instant, she was entertained enough to forget

266

about the gaping vacuum in her spirit left by Andraste. No worry that vast numbers of the horde were armed only with farm tools and makeshift weapons, today's outcome could be nothing other than pure, unadulterated victory with these highly professional experts amongst them and Andraste's Blessing upon them.

The chariots returned to the head of the massed army and the warriors disembarked, instructing their drivers where to wait for them should they need to be taken from the battlefield. Then the trumpets blared and the war dogs howled and the horde drove forward as one, the nobles and champions to the fore where they could be first to clash arms and the first to win glory. They were a hotch-potch of colours, Boudicca noticed proudly, almost as varied as the brightest finch wing or the shiniest fish scale. Sucellus' shields showed up well so the individual tribes, with their own distinctive colours and designs and emblems, could be picked out and identified even amidst the chaos of so many pressed people. In contrast, the Romani were like silver and red statues, proud and awe-inspiring but monotonous and sapped of individuality.

The open plain required a long charge, and soon the fittest were separated from those who found the necessary sprint harder to maintain. The horde spread out further as it neared the legions, with the elite troops at its front. Boudicca watched for interminable moments as the Celtoi approached nearer and nearer to the Romani troops. Still the champions and nobles did not slow their pace, despite hollering and bellowing their battle crics at the motionless enemy. Footfalls behind, other warriors kept up with their Chiefs and Ladies. For a while, Boudicca thought the Romani would never move and she started to wonder if the Goddess had spirited their beings away, leaving only the ineffectual shells of legionary uniform as a token foe to test the Celtoi faith. This was all so strange, with only one army moving; would her horde just keep charging until it crashed into the unresisting legions?

No, it wouldn't happen that way, it was too much to hope for. And anyway, a fair fight brought more honour. What would happen would be what always happened: at the crucial moment, just as the foremost warriors came into range, the Romani would step back, as one, and each would unleash a single javelin into the horde. Boudicca watched it unfold even as she thought it through, the Romani moving in exact discipline as if they were mirror reflections of one single soldier.

The Celtoi lifted Sucellus' shields, deflecting the Romani spears where they could. Some were not fast enough and fell to be trampled by those closing fast behind. Those who had succeeded in catching the spears on their shields tried to pull them out to hurl them back at the Romani, but the javelins were made of soft iron at their necks which bent on impact making them useless after one volley and too twisted to remove. Even as the Celtoi realised this and dropped their shields, now cumbersome and unwieldy, the Romani unleashed a second wave of javelins which shot into the horde, causing dreadful damage. Fand fell in this first onslaught. Struck in the chest as she swung a massive axe around her head, then sinking under the weight of the mob, as if beneath an insensate surge of sea surf. The din of battle rose to cover the peaking shrieks of the dying and wounded, concealing any noise Fand might have made in her passing. Yet still the Celtoi rushed onwards; they had only lost a tiny proportion of their numbers. Now it was the Romani's turn to die.

The two armies clashed and there was a tremendous roar as iron hit iron. Both sides pushed and shoved for all they were worth, while slender spears sneaked in to pierce Romani armour and jabbing swords snaked out to wound unprotected Celtoi skin. For every fallen warrior, another appeared to take their place and continue with the push to destroy the enemy. The line pounded and heaved as it gave here and held there, as if it were a giant earthworm tortured by some dreadful injury. With both sides equal in skill, Boudicca relaxed, realising their superior numbers would easily win the day. She breathed deeply, wanting to savour the sweet smell of revenge and understanding at last that it had all been worthwhile, in a way, to right the wrongs that had been done to herself and her daughters, and the peoples of Britannia.

She let her spirit soar free above the battlefield as her training had once taught her to do. The crows and ravens were already coming in, gathering for their feast, and she felt vindicated in her forthcoming victory. Andraste was with the horde so strongly now. Even Boudicca could feel Her Presence increase quite tangibly as the blood flowed heavier and the smell of sweat mingled with it to sicken the air. Boudicca drank of the scent as if the very atmosphere was vital sustenance.

Then something disturbed her, the slightest movement, and the Queen returned to her body to find Lovernios pulling at her robe.

'What is it, my lover mine?' she asked, more relaxed than she had felt all year. The forthcoming revenge seemed to lift a massive burden and weight from her mind as if the pain of the past was being flushed out along with the Romani lives.

'Maeve's gone. She left for a moment to relieve herself, but she's been away for rather a long while. I'm fearful she might have left to join the battle, madam, what with Andraste being upon her, but I thought it best if you go to investigate rather than me.'

'How very delicate of you, Lovernios.'

'She might appreciate it, even if you don't. Please go and check for me. She isn't trained as a warrior, is she?' Boudicca shook her head.

'No, I thought not. Well, if we lose her in the fray who knows what might happen to Andraste. If the Goddess withdraws now, it could turn the whole tide.'

'All right, I'll go look, just for you, but promise me you won't disturb me when this is all over. Let me have one long peaceful contemplation without you butting in.'

'I promise.' He sealed his word with a kiss.

Boudicca took a final all-encompassing scan of the battle and, reassured that her horde needed no further intervention on her part, jumped lightly down from her chariot. She trotted quickly round the wagons, listening out as well as she could for any sound of her daughter over the noise from the plain. She glanced around cartwheels and behind cattle, over discarded waste and peered between huddles of Celtoi too engrossed watching the fighting to notice the frantic searching of their Queen.

At last, when she had run nearly halfway across the flood plain behind a good majority of the wagons, she spotted a flash of blue, by chance, crouching down in the shade of a wheel-shaft. She squinted to see better, not wanting to disturb someone else or to appear foolish by creeping up on a stray piece of cloth. No, it was definitely Maeve, and she looked as if she was still relieving herself.

Boudicca approached, unembarrassed by seeing her daughter in such a position and anticipating that Maeve would feel the same. The closeness of tribal life, and particularly travelling as a horde, left little scope for privacy even for personal functions, and especially among immediate family. It was quite usual in such situations for conversations, if not household tasks, to be continued without a break.

'We wondered where you were, daughter mine. Lovernios was concerned you might have joined the battle.' Maeve looked up from her squatting with tears in her eyes. 'Why, whatever's wrong, Maeve?'

Maeve looked distraught, the blue crescent moon painted upon her forehead standing out stark against her wan skin. Suddenly, she started to sob quite loudly as if she were a child whose toy had been taken from her. Boudicca hurried over, as protective as if Maeve were a toddler to be toilet trained all over again. She flapped her arms, all ready to clear up whatever mess her daughter might have gotten herself into, her maternal protectiveness needing only the slightest provocation before it stirred into action.

Maeve shifted guiltily above the pool of urine which she was still bent over. Boudicca put an arm around her daughter whilst instinctively craning her neck to examine what might be the problem. The acrid urine was draining quickly into the dry, sand-like earth, but the soil was flecked with heavy splotches of thick blood. Boudicca looked closer. Maeve didn't appear to be wounded anywhere. Then a thick clot fell to the ground from between Maeve's legs and Boudicca understood that it was simply her daughter's menses.

She ruffled Maeve's hair, reminding herself that both her twins had been born far more recently than she wanted to admit. No doubt Maeve's body changes would still seem new and alarming to her; she was probably only just becoming used to womanhood.

'Does it hurt?' Boudicca asked.

Maeve nodded her head vigorously. 'Yes, mama. It cramps and I feel sick. I don't think I can move. I never knew it was going to be this bad.' She panted out the words as if she was in great pain and every breath brought her more discomfort.

Boudicca was inclined to dismiss it as something Maeve might just have to grow used to, but then she remembered how long she herself had taken to adjust to her own body when she'd first budded and she softened her reply. 'It does get better, daughter mine, usually after the first babe. Has it been this bad before?'

Maeve answered her with a puzzled look which confused Boudicca further until she thought about the things which Grania had told her about her twin. 'Maeve?' She broached her question as carefully as she could. 'Is this your first bleeding?' Maeve nodded affirmation, with huge eyes full of self-sympathy. 'No wonder you're like this! It's all a bit strange when it first happens, isn't it? Never mind. Look, grab some of this moss and put it here, see? Now come back to Lovernios with me, you don't want to miss seeing our wonderful victory, do you? There, lean on mama if it makes things easier.'

Boudicca steadied her daughter, helping Maeve to her feet and taking most of her weight. She was weak, so much was obvious, but she could not have lost that much blood. Maeve sagged against her mother and Boudicca decided to carry her back to her chariot. Lovernios could call a Healer to check there weren't any rare complications if Maeve didn't improve soon.

The battle sounded louder now as Boudicca made her hampered way back to her lover, and the combat could be heard fractionally closer than before. Those upon the wagons had started to shriek in excitement too; perhaps the fighting was nearing its conclusion already. She could have guessed that so few Romani would not have been able to resist their superior force for very long, but she was surprised it was all over quite so quickly. Perhaps, when she had finished depositing Maeve with Lovernios, she might wade into the masses and take a few heads for herself. Grania would have approved of that.

As the volume increased still further and her chariot came into sight, just around the curve of wagons, Maeve started to cry more and more. Her tears were those of grief, now, rather than of physical pain. Boudicca paused to ask what was wrong, cradling her daughter against her breast in the same way she had done years before when attempting to distil comfort to two demanding toddlers.

Maeve sobbed some more, a distraught sound which screamed of a deep and rending loss. Then, taking a deep breath, she yelled, venting her grief as forcefully as she could manage: 'Andraste's gone!'.

Boudicca hesitated for the briefest instant before tightening her hold on her daughter's frail weight and darting to her chariot and the waiting Lovernios as best she could. Her breath lumbered in her lungs. The sound of her pounding feet gained Lovernios' attention and he turned to her. She drew in a deep breath to tell him what had happened to Maeve, but then she noticed his face. Lovernios was utterly frantic, his expression delirious and his eyes totally crazy. Boudicca steeled herself to hear what his mouth was ranting about.

'My mother. My mother.' He raved unintelligibly.

As calmly as she could manage, Boudicca set Maeve upon the ground. Then she climbed upon the chariot to see for herself whatever it was that had turned Lovernios into this shaken and agitated creature.

Chapter 19

Full Moon

The slight vantage point of the chariot, and her own additional height, only just enabled Boudicca to see what had caused Lovernios so much anguish. The battle still raged ferociously upon the field, although astonishingly enough, the Celtoi horde appeared to have given ground to the Romani. This confused Boudicca, until she saw for herself how bewildered and somehow dispirited her host seemed.

She observed the fluctuating rhythm of the combat line heave back and forth upon the field, and tried to discern where the Celtoi weak points were so she might direct reinforcements to those places. She could see none specifically; rather it was the whole Celtoi line that was in danger of buckling. Her eyes darted further back, towards the Romani commanders, trying to spot how they were winning ground. All across the flood plain the Romani blocks of troops held firm and the lines fought unwavering. It was an unimaginative method of warfare, where every legionary fought solidly and identically to his colleagues with no opportunity for individuality. The Celtoi fought randomly and with passion, some burly warriors taking a handful of Romani with them on their journey to the Summerlands, whilst an opportunistic farmer might serve only as sword fodder before falling to relinquish his place to the next would-be Champion crowding from behind.

The clamour was hideous now, as if the spirits of the freshly dead had not yet departed their bodies but had chosen instead to stay upon the field to scream their outrage and terror at their slayers. The noise was so great and terrible that it could almost be felt, as it tumbled sheet-like upon those forced to listen. The corpses were starting to pile up under the Romani's feet already, hampering their steady advance and forcing them to trample and kick unyielding flesh before they could step forward.

Boudicca was shocked by what she saw and watched incredulous as the Romani edged marginally closer with every breath she took. But still the horde outnumbered the legions by a vast majority and the outcome, although slightly less certain, was a long way off. She monitored the tactics carefully, able to concede that Suetonius was at least putting up a good fight, yet still not believing that he had ever been able to defend his position, let alone improve on it.

And then she noticed what had caused Lovernios to blanch in shock. Far away and back amongst the thickly forested foothills of the defile mouth, so far that she could only just make out what was happening, she watched as some Romani soldiers struggled to bring something they had apprehended back to their commander's tent. These soldiers were quite distinctive and must have been of considerable rank, for their helmets were plumed like horses. Nevertheless, they were experiencing difficulty controlling whatever it was they had captured.

Boudicca wished she had been blessed with better eyesight for she had considerable trouble seeing whatever it was that had been caught. She detected a streak of black every so often and deduced it must be some sort of wild animal because the Romani seemed to be taking especial care not to be injured by it. Some of the legion's horses were being kept behind the tents to the back of the narrow valley, presumably so the commander could flee when the Celtoi broke through the ranks, and Boudicca guessed that a wolf or something similar had been caught trying to win an easy feed. They were a fair way north from Iceni territory now, it was not too unreasonable for an isolated wolf to appear up here, even this early in the summer. What she could not understand was why the wolf, or perhaps it was a bear, hadn't just been killed immediately.

When the Romani dragged the wild thing nearer to the tents, Boudicca could make out just enough information to glean why the killing had been delayed. The struggling, manic creature was forced to the ground in front of the commander's tent, inspected by another Romani, and a sharp order given with a cursory wave of a hand. Warily, the Romani restrained their captive as best they could, whilst keeping themselves back from the sword which was about to be brought down in summary execution. As it did, there was a feeble twitching and plenty of blood from the corpse, then some perfunctory kicks from the Romani around it, before they stood up, straightened their uniform and returned to whatever duties the creature had distracted them from.

As they left, Boudicca could at last see what type of animal had been brought in. One of the final random kicks it had received had been from a Romani who rubbed his forearm now as if he were newly injured from his grappling with the beast. It had been a violent enough kick to turn the body over, downhill towards the battle, and Boudicca felt sick as she recognised what, or rather who, it had once been. She gripped the wicker rail of the chariot to steady herself before jumping down to Lovernios.

The Druid was still shockingly white, although he had managed to control himself enough to tend to Maeve. He had placed a trembling hand upon her stomach, trying to Charm ease into Maeve's discomfort. Already, Maeve's face was showing less sign of pain, although her expression was still wearing the agony of abandonment.

Boudicca pulled Lovernios gently away. 'What was she doing there?' she demanded of him, her anger tempered by the grief she knew he must be feeling.

'She was attracted to the Goddess.'

Boudicca was relieved to hear that Lovernios knew instinctively to whom she was referring. At least he was not in the mood to play any of his mysterious and infuriating games. She drew in a deep breath, using it as an opportunity to calm her thoughts. She had so many questions and no idea where to start.

'Lovernios mine, just tell me everything. You know what I want, what I need to know.'

There was a flash of mischievousness in his eyes before his face changed to its more commonplace seriousness. 'I won't tease you,' he relented. 'I can tell it wouldn't go down too well at the moment.

'My mother came as near as she could to Maeve,' he explained, 'Or rather to Andraste. She must have travelled through the forests – at least I presume she did, using those few Paths which were still open to her or which she opened for herself – lured on by the thought of regaining the Divine Presence. The closest trees were those directly behind the Romani lines, a tremendous risk to her, but she would have been desperate and prepared to do anything to get Andraste back.

'And it paid off for her, too. You look surprised, madam. She got Andraste back, you know, at least for a little while anyway. It's so clear now; so obvious.' Lovernios shook his head in disbelief at himself. 'As soon as Maeve here started to bleed, the Goddess wouldn't stay, for that is the missing link. Trust me to overlook that! Trust a man, and one who has only recently come to know a woman at that, not to take such womanly things into consideration.'

Lovernios held his hands up in exasperation. 'Can you believe it? It threw me, I can assure you, but it all fits beautifully, Boudicca.'

'So why didn't Andraste come back to me? Why did She return to Black Annis?'

'Are you bleeding?'

Boudicca shook her head.

'I didn't think so, madam. I knew you weren't last night, but I expect my mother was. You're not due for quite a while yet, are you?'

'No. My menses should arrive with the full moon; so I'm expecting them, well, now.'

'Are you sure? Usually you're a little more, shall we say, 'restless', so soon to your bleeding.'

'Well, let's hope I'm not with child, shall we?' She paused, reminding herself that he was grieving. 'I'm sorry, Lovernios, I shouldn't have snapped. I could very well be later than usual. My body doesn't seem to know what it's doing and recently my cycles seem to be stretched and pulled between the full and the new moons each turn.'

'Well, that's definitely a display of the sort of 'restlessness' I meant. Perhaps you will bleed at full moon after all. Anyway, and before you answer me back, Andraste went back to my mother. It was a sudden, overwhelming change. Quite all surpassing. One moment she was creeping, step-step down the slope, darting between the roots and slipping underneath the branches of the forest edge, more enticed by the thought of working her way stealthily past the Romani to get to Maeve than by anything else. The next, a complete transformation. She had her prize as a gift, her most sought after treasure reclaimed, and she turned instantly feral. At first I thought nothing would restrain her and she'd attempt to take on the whole massed legions by herself and the Celtoi horde would only have to worry when she'd worked her way through to them. But then the Romani restrained her, and when she was killed ...' He shrugged.

'You know about that?'

'I didn't have to see it for myself to feel it, but you've just confirmed it anyway.'

'And Andraste?'

'Gone. Can't you feel it, madam? Hag knows, I can. The Divine is no longer with us.'

He was right. Now that she started to feel for it, there was a certain difference in the air all around. It was as if the sparkle had been taken from life and everything had been rendered grey. And the horde had been split into isolated units of tribes and Gerbfine, family and separate persons. They were no longer whole, nor were they unified, just splinters of a once greater completeness.

'But She must've had somewhere else to go. Surely there must've been another woman in the entire horde who was suitable?'

'There are too many requisites needed to have a psyche hospitable to Andraste, madam. You and your daughters had them, so did my mother. The bleeding is just one tiny factor in the many needed to draw the Goddess to an individual in such a personal way.'

'So,' Boudicca asked, 'It's not just the personal Manifestation which has been lost, but also Her Blessing upon the whole horde?' Lovernios nodded. 'Well, it shouldn't matter too much, this battle is nearly won. Once it's over we can disperse back to our traditional tribal disputes. We need the Goddess, all of us do, but not in such a direct way. Even I felt Her to be too strong on occasions. In many ways it'll be a relief to return to our state of separateness.'

Lovernios pulled her to him, holding her in a reassuring hug.

'Madam,' he whispered. 'I'm sorry. We can't win. Not without Andraste.'

'Don't be ridiculous,' she shouted in rage, pulling away fiercely. 'We outnumber them too well; we've nearly won. We can't give up now!'

'The line's already begun to break, the horde's already started to disperse.'

Boudicca pulled away from him in denial.

Lovernios continued calmly – too calmly. 'Madam, you don't need to look, you can feel it. You may not have the Goddess but you still have your training. Now use it.'

He ordered and Boudicca obeyed. Her spirit soared around the field, swooping upon the energies she could feel so easily as soon as she applied her mind. The horde was slipping away from each other and from the battlefield. A disorganised retreat had started, with individual warriors seeking to disengage from combat and slip away to save themselves. As champion after champion drifted away, the retreat became a rout and the tide turned to allow the Romani slaughter to begin. Boudicca felt it like a day of butchery as the legionaries waded through blood and hacked off limbs, swaying into their next sword strokes and carving a path of gore back to the wagons.

'Lovernios is right, Boudicca.'

Boudicca cleared her mind of what she'd Seen. Sucellus was speaking to her.

'It's only just started, but it'll get worse. Not all of the horde knows how desperate the situation is yet and there are still patches of resistance. Suetonius will send the cavalry in soon; you should go now.'

'But I …'

'Yes you can. You must, in fact. There's nothing you and Lovernios can do any more. Hag knows you've both done enough already.'

'What about…?'

'Maeve'll stay with me.' Maeve nodded, already keen to do as Sucellus was instructing her to do and smiling benevolently upon her mother. Boudicca felt as if she was being dismissed. Sucellus continued to speak. 'You two must go, as we agreed, Lovernios. You know what you must do, and I know what I must do. I'll buy you long enough to get to the forests. You can use the Pathways again, now they're safe. Find Artio, or let Her find you; She'll see you safe to the Black Lake.'

Lovernios nodded tersely and grabbed Boudicca's upper arm. She struggled but his grip hurt where his long Bard's fingernails, grown for harp plucking, dug into her skin. She glared at him in surprise, too shocked to pull away, and let him drag her off to the nearest clump of trees. A few steps further and she looked back over her shoulder to see that Suetonius had indeed unleashed his cavalry and even now the Romani horsemen were bearing down upon the horde, pressing the

Celtoi against the wagons to prevent any further escape from the carnage awaiting them. Maeve had stood, with Sucellus' help, and now held out her arms to Boudicca, her hands glowing with their peculiar witch-light as they formed the sign for ritual Blessing. Then she turned demurely and climbed upon the wagons, letting the Romani and the remains of the horde see her quite clearly.

'Lovernios, stop! Now!' Boudicca stuck her heels into the earth, muddy here, and pulled against him, halting his momentum for an instant. 'He's trying to pass off Maeve as me. She'll be killed.'

Lovernios stopped tugging her and gave her his most serious and condescending look. 'That's the whole point, madam. Quick, come with me or she'll die for nothing.'

There was no arguing with such a stern expression. Something hard in his eyes caught the little girl in Boudicca, rendering her defiance seemingly futile. Boudicca glanced back at Maeve, unable to accept the enormity of what her daughter was doing. Maeve stood proud atop the highest wagon, arms outstretched in a Blessing Salute for the dying. The cavalry had thundered into the sides of the horde now, massacring the draught animals and horses to keep the carts stationery, and methodically slaughtering those thousands of trapped non-combatants as if they were harvesting a field of corn. The sheer volume of sound from terrified animals and doomed camp followers swamped Boudicca's ears as if it had formed a tangible veil that wrapped itself around her. Such a sickening noise would be with her, she knew, for the rest of her life.

Numb at the sight of this torment, Boudicca stumbled after Lovernios, just as the first of the Romani cavalry galloped around the wagons, their horses' hooves hammering over the plain in their search for fugitives. The charge of the cavalry was enough to set the ground trembling, and the vibrations were powerful enough to kick Boudicca out of her inactivity. Refugees from the horde seemed to crawl across the flood plain compared to the speed at which the Romani horses stormed after them. Painfully the Celtoi sought to escape the cursory death that flew at their backs by hiding within tussocks of grass or diving into shallow ditches. Those who had regained the haven of their chariots fared better, able to put precious space between themselves and their pursuers.

Boudicca and Lovernios virtually jumped into the nearest trees, letting the branches swing back to hide them. There was a quick shifting sensation as Lovernios Found and the small clump of trees expanded to connect with all the other forests of Britannia. Finally, Lovernios relinquished his hold upon Boudicca, letting her push back the shielding leaves to watch the bloodletting on the plain.

From within the trees and the sanctuary of Other, the material world seemed less real and much quieter than it had moments before, as if it was being experienced through filters which blunted the senses. The sounds of the dying and injured were muffled and the action seemed slower, adding to Boudicca's detachment from the scene. What felt more real was Lovernios' body-heat at her back and his comforting hands upon her shoulders and dry kisses upon the nape of her neck. But he was easier to ignore, the Otherly events before her were not.

The Romani had scaled to the wagon heights now and were swiping at the old and babes as if Andraste's wrath had gone into the legionaries for want of better instruments of Manifestation. The soldiers moved cruelly through the ineffectual resistance which remained, ignoring pleas for mercy or clemency. Maeve's voluminous robes flapped bluely in the breeze, the only thing that seemed to move about her. It was as if the Moon Priestess stood at the centre of a tremendous maelstrom, trying to evoke peace and calm and eject it into the area immediately around her.

A thin band of warriors, led by Addedomarus and infuriated by the Romani's wasteful butchering of their precious ponies, had gained confidence from her presence, sending up a renewed, but ragged, cry for the Goddess. They held the main onslaught of Romani legionaries, allowing the Druids, whom they protected, just long enough to turn upon those who were left and start the mercy killings. The Romani death was too haphazard and ignoble; the Druidic method was quick and precise. It was always reverted to when a war could no longer be won, for the Summerlands were a better prospect than slavery, and as such this death was honourable to the Goddess, wherever She might be.

The Druids dealt with those who came to them for release, running sharp sickles across vulnerable throats before they finally used them on themselves. The Romani might hate the Druids and have a dreadful fate for them, but they were taking no prisoners, nor were they pausing in their violence to collect trinkets or spoils. Boudicca wondered at their training and discipline, so strict as to not even be distracted by a pretty face or a valuable piece of gold-work. Still they came on, whittling away at the horde and paring off its layers as if it were gradually being trimmed to nothing. Boudicca tried not to calculate how much longer the remnants might last, fearing she might wish the end into actuality.

At last, when there was little more but mopping up to be done by the Romani, and no further opposition from the Celtoi, a few legionaries dared to approach the statue-like figure atop the wagons. Sucellus saw them first, picking their way over cartons of supplies and jugs of wine, and nudged Maeve to alert her to the impending danger.

Boudicca tensed, wondering how her daughter and the smith would save themselves now, and gripped Lovernios' hand. Maeve nodded once and then both she and Sucellus took swigs from a tiny flask which the smith procured from about his person. The bizarre action, seemingly taking refreshments in the midst of a battle, paused even the Romani, who balanced themselves incredulous upon the supply wagon and watched as the strangely unphased woman and the crippled man with her, seemed simultaneously to collapse and topple into the surging murder below.

The Romani stepped to the edge of the wagons and leant curiously over to see what had become of those they had been tracking. Something dismissive about the way they casually sheathed their swords answered all of Boudicca's questions, and she broke from Lovernios' caress to go after her daughter. She started to run, heading back across the flood plain towards the wagons, not knowing quite what she would do when she got there, but the forest would not clear and the branches would not open for her.

'There's nothing you can do,' came a voice from directly behind her. 'The Pathways are no longer universally opened and I won't Find for you if you can't do it for yourself.'

Boudicca turned, angry and frustrated at what she had seen and at her powerlessness. Lovernios was only a few steps away; all her exertion had hardly moved her at all.

'Why not?' she asked, as petulant as a child.

'That's why not,' Lovernios answered, gesturing back to the flood plane.

A Romani cavalryman was heading directly towards them, his horse snorting heavily as it careered down upon them. Boudicca threw herself to the ground, rolling amongst the bracken to cover herself as best she could within the dense foliage, and concealing her head with her arms. Just as the horse crashed into the trees, knocking the branches aside, and Boudicca tensed in anticipation of trampling hooves, the forest went silent again and Boudicca nervously lifted her head to see what had happened.

Lovernios had not moved. The Romani cavalryman was nowhere to be seen.

'They can't get in here,' Lovernios explained.

'And I can't get out!' Boudicca snapped back.

'What good would you do?'

'I don't know, but at least I could do something rather than waiting uselessly in here watching everyone I love, and everything I have dreamt of and worked for, die.'

'If that's how you feel then you really should come with us, madam.'

'Us?' And she peered closer. Artio had appeared and stood close by

Lovernios. Half-hidden by forest gloom, she waited patiently at his feet, her eyes, like black jet beads, watched Boudicca intelligently. 'Do I have any choice, Lovernios mine?'

'Madam, you should know by now how unanswerable that question is. There's always a choice, there are always alternatives available. Only you can decide how viable they are and whether it's worth struggling against what fate has led you to.'

'Is that a yes or a no?'

Lovernios laughed. 'Come with us, Boudicca. It's a good while yet to new moon at Beltane and I would enjoy your company whilst we travel.'

'Let me have one last look before we leave, then.' And she turned back to see the Romani readying themselves to leave the field and return to their fort. The skies had blackened with the onset of evening and above her was a vast rustling and cawing as the rooks and crows and night-birds of the Goddess took to the wing and swarmed down upon the carcasses which should, by all rights, have been Romani.

She joined Lovernios, moving sadly with him through the undergrowth. The Pathways were narrow now and uncleared, allowing roots and brambles to catch upon her cloak. It was almost as if even Lovernios' Workings had been tarnished and limited. There was a silence and a resignation, too, about their movements, and at first she took little joy even in the beauty and splendour of the late spring woods. She grew cross at the thorns which tore at her skin and the dew which dripped upon her head, but did not allow her real anger to be expressed. She tramped through the scrunchy leaves and sucking mud, not caring for the noise she made or the tendrils she bruised or the snarling creepers which her passing snapped.

Then as the days passed and still they journeyed onwards, she began to grow less immune to the fragile treasures which nature displayed to her. The fresh oak and beech leaves were newly unfurled and seemed almost edible in their verdancy. Bluebells had sprung up in hollows to create an almost violet mist effect which trailed across the forest floor. Streams gurgled invitingly just as she needed to pause for a cupped hand of water, and wild mushrooms and herbs appeared when she needed to eat.

With her rediscovered appreciation of Britannia's bounty came unwanted tears. It had almost been as if the Goddess was tempting Boudicca back from whatever inner depths she'd hidden her feelings away in. This new provision of food and drink and wondrous sights seemed to have been provided almost to jar Boudicca out of her despondency and back into her sense of having her own especial place within the universe's own particular order.

Lovernios said little as they walked steadily, who knew where? Artio nuzzled her hand whenever she started to flag and the three of them snuggled close for warmth at night. There was not much that needed to be or could be said; they were together and the companionship held more meaning than a thousand words. And there was no need to discuss routes, as there was only one path, clear to follow and with no offshoots. Anyway, Lovernios seemed absorbed in his own world and his own thoughts, as if he were readying himself for whatever the next phase of his life would bring.

After several more nights – Boudicca couldn't remember how many exactly but it was at least a quarter judging by the moon – they were disturbed in the late afternoon by a rustling in the forest close by. Artio put up her muzzle and sniffed the air before sinking back to her supine position and Boudicca tensed at the prospect of a threat.

Lovernios continued to turn the spits of the fat pigeons he had caught, and was slowly roasting, calling out without being distracted from his task, 'Make yourself known. You're among friends. If you're hungry, it'd be best to come out before we eat.'

There was a bit more shuffling of undergrowth and then a very dishevelled figure emerged from behind a tree. It was ragged and dirty, with bits of fern and twigs sticking from its matted hair, and could look at nothing except the makeshift hearth, or rather what was roasting above it.

'You'd better sit with us, although supper isn't ready yet. If you eat it now you'll be ill.' Lovernios spoke as if he were talking to himself out loud, indicating to Boudicca to stay silent. Even so, Boudicca couldn't stop herself from watching the newcomer, and her curiosity drove him to shy away from the Queen and draw himself up by Lovernios.

The Druid continued to tend to the meal, asking Boudicca to look for some more mushrooms in order to make the meat go further. Boudicca did so, knowing instinctively now just where to look for the spores. She peeled back leaf-mould to reveal the pure white flesh, pristine for being shielded from light, and pulled the globes from the soil, gathering her harvest in her arms. All the while she thought about where she'd seen the inexperienced eyes of their guest before. When she was ready to return, she'd worked out who he was.

'Teirnon,' she asked gently. 'What brings you here?'

No sooner had she started to speak than Sucellus' erstwhile apprentice darted up and bounded for the cover of the trees, leaving Lovernios to glare at her in remonstration.

'I'm sorry,' she said to Lovernios, then louder once again to the patch of trees that Teirnon had disappeared into. Nothing. Then: 'It's a shame some of these fresh mushrooms and plump pigeon will go to waste now, there's far too much for the two of us. I suppose we could leave some of it for whoever or whatever comes along in the morning, but I daresay it'll be cold by then and past its best.'

More rustling, but further off now. 'You're amongst friends, and friends would like to be able to help you.' Lovernios took the pigeon off the spit as he spoke. 'There, that's ready. Mmm! Smell that pigeon, madam, done to a turn. Can't beat it this fresh. How are those mushrooms? Don't those herbs enhance them perfectly?' He divided out the food. 'There's a little too much, isn't there? I'm ravenous but I don't think I can manage it all. How about we put what's left over on that hillock, perhaps the Faery folk might like a treat, too?'

Boudicca and Lovernios ate a pigeon between them and fingered dripping mushrooms into their mouths. The flavours were sweet and succulent and their noises of delight and appreciation, feigned at first to lure Teirnon to his portion, soon became genuine and led them to forget, momentarily, about the fugitive lurking in the shadows.

There was a movement behind, by the low tussock, but neither Boudicca not Lovernios responded to it. Boudicca burned to look up and check that it was indeed Teirnon who was eating the food, but she knew better now than to risk frightening him away again. They came to the end of their meal, licking their fingers clean of juices and wiping their hands on the grass. Sounds of voracious chewing came from the hillock still, noises which didn't sound fully human in their gluttony. When the sounds of gorging died down, there was more furtive rustling and only then did Lovernios sneak a look behind.

'He's gone,' Lovernios announced, part disappointed and part resigned.

Boudicca felt deflated at the news and wondered whether they might've been better restraining Teirnon forcefully rather than attempting to entice him to them. She felt rising frustration too that Teirnon no doubt carried information with him which they would probably never hear now. Lovernios seemed unshaken and unrepentant of the way in which he had dealt with the situation. Placidly, he stirred the hearth fire again, setting more tinder upon the dusty ashes in preparation for the heavier branches which would burn through the night.

Then she became aware of renewed skulking behind them and, unable to stop herself, glanced up instinctively. Teirnon tried to shrink from her gaze, but she smiled and he crept nearer.

'I, I thought you'd like a drink after your meal,' he stuttered, holding out a large golden cup to them. 'I've already had some and the water here is good.'

Lovernios turned and took the cup gently from him, as naturally as if the gift had been expected and there was nothing unusual or tense about the scene. Teirnon relaxed visibly at the lack of formality and attention he was receiving, so much so that Lovernios was able to ask: 'Would you like to share our fire?'

There was something so basic and primeval in the invitation that Boudicca was instantly reminded of how much they had lost and how little they now had between them. Fire was an instinctive need; the offer was both primitive and yet astoundingly generous. There was a long pause whilst the enormity of the question sank into the host and the prospective guest. When Teirnon finally accepted, Boudicca discovered she'd been holding her breath awaiting his reply.

She drank deeply from the cup when it was offered to her; the water was indeed pure and quenching. Before passing it back to Teirnon, she poured a little onto the earth by her side as a libation to the spirits of the place, allowing them to share in the Blessing of their meal. As she did, she noticed the golden cup was most unusual and she lifted it to her face to examine it closer. She had presumed at first that it was some spoil from a Romani home, a tiny part of a fine dining service, but on inspection she saw that it was the head of the statue of the Claudius-god which the horde had destroyed at Camulodunum.

Boudicca caught Lovernios' eyes, wondering whether he had noticed its origins too. He winked at her surreptitiously, obviously imploring her not to ruin the moment with an accusation, no matter how vague. Teirnon was still skittish; it would not do to alarm him again. It was not until the evening progressed and the fire became more welcome that Teirnon started to join in, gradually, with Boudicca's and Lovernios' conversation.

'I wish I knew what had become of the Druids after the battle,' sighed Lovernios.

'And I wonder whether any of the tribes still fight on,' added Boudicca, seeking to hook Teirnon.

'How many got away, do you think?'

'Not many. Teirnon here is the only other warrior we've met so far. I don't suppose he's seen anyone else.'

'What do you think the Romani are doing now?'

'Perhaps they've given up chasing the fugitives and are busy escorting their civilians back to their settlements,' Boudicca guessed out loud.

'There were a few others who left when I did.' At last, Teirnon bit, making his own contribution to the conversation.

Pause.

'Thank Mother some of the Iceni survived!'

'But we split up almost immediately. We could see the battle was lost. We weren't cowards or deserters, we just thought we'd be better off leaving to reform, perhaps with some of the tribes who hadn't yet joined us.'

Pause.

'They thought I was too obvious, with this.' He held up the gold

283

head, the edges bent over to serve as a drinking vessel. 'They thought that I'd bring Romani wrath down upon them. Luckily, there were the forests. I didn't realise they were so close. I was just thinking so hard of Sucellus' forge and how much I enjoyed my training and suddenly I was lost, here, in the midst of all these trees.'

'It's a latent talent,' Lovernios noted. 'Have you seen anyone else?'

Teirnon shook his head. 'There was talk of resistance. But it'll be from individual tribes, not from Celtoi. The tribes blame each other now as much as the Romani. The legions were ferocious when they came after us. I don't think they'll leave us be until they've punished all who took part in the revolt and harrowed our lands. I've nowhere to go now. I haven't even seen any Druids and I thought the woods were full of them.'

Lovernios nodded to himself, mulling over Teirnon's words carefully.

'You can't come with us,' the Druid announced. Boudicca's head whipped up to glare at his apparent callousness. 'It's not the path for you,' Lovernios tried to explain. 'Perhaps you should start by getting rid of your 'cup'. I think your comrades were right and you would be safer without it. How do you feel about dedicating it to the Goddess at dawn?'

'You mean giving it up to the river? What if it washes into Romani hands? That sort of thing could incriminate whole tribes – that's why I've been taking such care of it.'

'If you give it to the Goddess, She won't relinquish it unless it's appropriate to do so. Let the waters have it, then I'll lead you to Iceni territory. Do you know the lie of the land in the north? Good. For that's the best place to set you, as you'll be sure to meet up with other pockets of resistance or else you can go to ground until the Romani terror has ended.'

'Is this what you want, Teirnon?' Boudicca asked him gently, more aware than Lovernios of just how young Sucellus' apprentice was. 'You don't seem terribly pleased at what the Druid has suggested.'

'I'm not frightened, great Queen, honest I'm not. And don't think I'm reticent or ungrateful for your suggestions. It's just that I'm not too sure if I'll be able to recognise any part of Iceni territory if I return.'

'Why's that?'

'You didn't see the Romani's wrath, Madam. They want to destroy all traces of the rebel tribes from Britannia. Nothing less will suffice for them, and I believe they can do it, too. First they will hunt down those who fought at the Place of the Chariots, as if we're nothing more than slinking wolves. Then they'll send whole families, whole communities, into slavery, perhaps in the hope that their sweated labour will repay the lives of the lost Romani. It won't be long before Britannia will be unrecognisable, that's how dreadful their revenge will be. Suetonius doesn't check his men; he allows them free rein as a reward for their discipline during the battle. There's even talk they'll attack the vast hillforts to the south and west.'

'No. Those places are totally impervious.' Boudicca dismissed his words as absurd.

'Not to the Romani, Madam. Nothing can stand against them. The legions will wear even those vast bastions down eventually.'

'So, are Iceni lands to be handed out as sweeteners to those good and loyal tribes who didn't rise against their Romani masters?' Boudicca asked imperiously.

Pause. Boudicca's question seemed more rhetorical than answerable. She started to laugh. A mad, high cackle; half tearful.

'I can see Cogidubnus even now waddling around our royal enclosure, aghast at the blackness of our soil and our lack of rolling hills. So far from civilisation! Perhaps the taming of the rough Iceni lands will be the death of the old sycophant. I can't help but hope so.'

'In the morning I'll do as you've suggested.' Teirnon spoke calmly, hoping perhaps to bring the Queen back to some edge of sanity. 'And I shall take my chances once more against the fierce Romani. But Madam, what will you do when you return from where you're going?'

'Return?' Boudicca questioned him instantly, without thinking. Then she realised that returning had never really been an option, and she started to chuckle eerily, the vibrations emerging like breaths from deep within her stomach. Disbelief at the impossibility of her situation drove her laughter to build, until the great gasps of air mingled with the loud clattering of a single magpie winging through the heavy branches around them. Lovernios just turned away.

Chapter 20

Beltane

'I understand you make good griddle bread, Boudicca. Would you cook some for me?'

'But I… I don't have a griddle,' she replied. Such a strange question, totally unexpected, made her jump and respond involuntarily. Trapped, as she currently was, inside her own manic world where nothing seemed permanent or trustworthy, the question itself did not seem quite so odd. Gradually, the last few lunar cycles had taught her not to be surprised any more at anything which happened in her dreamlike life. Thus it was that only after the words had left her mouth did she look around for the questioner.

About twenty paces away, where the clearing edged into trees and where the magpie had just disappeared into the forest cover, stood an ancient man, dressed in Druidic robes. Boudicca had never seen a Druid garbed in such a way before because, rather than being clothed totally in one colour, his under-robe was of the purest white, save for the hem which was brown where it had dragged along the forest floor, and his cloak was of the deepest black. He waited passively for them all to acknowledge his presence, observing them with a benign and patient smile which betrayed some sense of having caught them at a disadvantage. An orator, then, Boudicca deduced, if he were able to project his voice so clearly, and she started to look for other clues to his identity, too. Something tapped irritatingly at Boudicca's mind, telling her she should know who this person was, but she just could not make the connection.

But she knew his infuriating smile, all too well. Perhaps it was a Druidic characteristic: an unquenchable smugness born from bearing a vaster wisdom. Certainly there were numerous occasions since she met Lovernios when she had wanted to take a damp cloth and wipe his superior smirk right off his face. Seeing this man watching her, and wearing an identical expression, almost had her reaching for the edge of her cloak to wet it in water and rub at his mouth.

She glanced at Lovernios. He had sunk to the ground and hung his head in his arms, refusing to look at the newcomer. She reached out an arm to comfort him, running her fingers through his hair in gentleness, then looked up again.

The Druid was talking to her once more. 'I have a griddle you can use and some special flour which mustn't go to waste. It's been finely ground from the highest quality grain, taken from the final sheaf gathered in last year's harvest. I want you to cook me the best cake you can, just as if you were cooking for your daughters.'

Beneath her fingertips, Boudicca felt Lovernios shake with the convulsions of his tears, and she clasped him to her, seeking to fortify him with her love. He reached out and grasped her hand, clinging to it as if to his own life, and his hold turned her knuckles white where he gripped so tight. She knelt, cradling him closely, and tried to loosen his hold where he was beginning to hurt. But he would not let go, pulling now at her whole arm to bind her to him, as if he sought to combine himself totally with her.

'Hush now, Lovernios mine. Whatever's wrong? It's all right, I'm here with you.'

'I can tell you what's wrong, Boudicca.' The Druid had approached and was now interrupting their conversation. 'Lovernios,' he continued, 'Does not appear well pleased at meeting his father.'

Boudicca swayed a little, returning Lovernios' desperate grip in order to steady herself. So this was Cathbad, then. As the old Druid neared, Boudicca fought against an almost compulsive urge to kneel before him. Using all her inner strength and willpower she resisted as best she could.

'Why did you come between my army and the legion two?' she hissed, her pride determined to have an answer before she gave way to her buckling knees.

'You got away, didn't you?'

'What do you mean?' Now she had to force herself to look him in the eyes, as Queen to Druid, when all her body yearned to bow in homage.

'Do you honestly believe, for one moment, that the two of you would have stood the slightest chance of getting away from the battle if the Romani force had been twice as large again?' Cathbad asked. He shook his head. 'I rather think you should be thanking me for using my influence over the Dumnonii and the Durotriges. They were rising to join you, you know. Eager to tread the Paths my son had so magnanimously opened. But I persuaded them they could do more harm to the Romani by staying in their own lands and threatening havoc upon the very headquarters of the legion two at Isca itself. They didn't have to actually come to blows, I told them, just act unruly as if an insurrection was imminent.

'It just so happened their legatus had already left for Glevum where he could contribute to keeping the Silures under control – another of my personal touches – so the whole of legion two was under the temporary command of their praefectus castrorum, which was altogether very convenient. You see,' Cathbad explained, 'As well as being second in command to the legatus, the praefectus castrorum is the liaison officer for the legion as a whole. His rank is the highest any legionary can achieve, unless they are Romani aristocracy, of course. So, he's the most influential commoner of them all, a real 'man of the people' and as such is ideally experienced for resolving disputes between the legion and those multitudes of non-combatants whom they have to deal with on a daily basis.

'Let me illustrate.' Cathbad put his hands in a teaching position. 'The legion needs grain? It's his responsibility. Drunken soldiers causing trouble? It's his job to sort them out. Relations need soothing between the indigenous people and the pervading shadow of the fortress? Then he must stay until the troubles have been calmed down again.

'And stay our Poenius Postumus, praefectus castrorum of the legion two, did. Bringing shame upon himself and his legion for being torn between his duties and for choosing unwisely. But nevertheless, the whispering voices I set to gnaw at his ear and persuade him to the easier option bought you both precious space in which to escape Suetonius' massacre and meet me here.'

'We'd never have needed to run if we'd not had Andraste stolen from us.' Boudicca was still determined to argue.

'Annis was one of the factors over which I had no control, nor wished to for that matter. After all, how many Celtoi do you know who can control their wives?' He chuckled. 'Seriously, though. Andraste is not an asset to be manipulated. She is too volatile. She could have left at any point, you know. You're lucky to have kept Her so long. Others before you have tried and lost. Yes, they have, but I'll tell you of that later.'

He seemed such a reasonable old man now, all fatherly and wise. Boudicca was quite taken in. And then her legs finally gave way and she found herself kneeling in supplication to him.

He chuckled again, half to himself. 'Ah, yes. I forgot about that. I can't help it, something which comes with the rank, I'm afraid. There. Does it ease it if I step back a little? Good. Well then, daughter mine, we shall have to remember not to get too close, eh? And now I must see to the others.

'Artio,' he directed. 'Take Sucellus' apprentice here and see him safe to Iceni territory. Oh, and get rid of that hideous little godling head, would you? I think Lovernios was correct about consigning it to a stream. It'll be all right, Teirnon. Follow Artio to the Edge, then spend tonight in the safety of the forests. At dawn dedicate the cup to the Goddess and follow the first Path you see when you look up from the water; it'll lead you to the best place for you to be. Act as a messenger for your people. Tell them the Devoted One will bring a new Guardian of the Land and they won't have to suffer for long. Bring them a promise of hope.

'And now my son.' Cathbad knelt by Lovernios, taking over from Boudicca's comforting. 'So many tears. It must feel like you're weeping blood.'

'Where did He go?' Lovernios asked in anguish.

'Perhaps to the same place Andraste went to in the years between leaving Annis and finding Boudicca. A mystery, but these two aspects of the Divine are the eternal lovers and will continue to seek each other out; our histories record they have always done so. What was unusual in this Manifestation was that there were so many women who met Andraste's exacting requirements. It must've unsettled the Young God with every transference.'

'And now He is gone completely,' Lovernios whined. 'How did you ever cope?'

'Well, there was no guidance. Most of those who've known the God or Goddess so personally never even try to adapt to life without them. Once the Divine is lost, they treat their lives as if of little importance or else go mad with the attempt to regain what they've lost. So, coping was hard, I can tell you. But I worked through the pain to a deeper, more constant love, until I connected with the entire universe rather than the specific presence of one aspect of the Divine.

'But none of these options are your path,' Cathbad explained. 'You were born in different circumstances to mine. You are marked out, you know this even though you always try to deny it. Plus there is the agreement you made with Sucellus and the thousands of lives which depend on you.'

Lovernios looked up, scowling at his father. 'Is there really no other way?' he asked in a hoarse whisper.

Cathbad shook his head gently. 'Could you live with yourself knowing what you hadn't done?'

'No, father mine, I could not.'

'Then there's no other way, Lovernios mine.'

'How far is it?'

'Not very, we'll be there by sundown tomorrow, but for you it'll seem like forever.'

'It already does.'

'I know. Artio will be back soon; would it feel better to walk?'

'I think it might.'

'Then follow me. Artio can catch up later,' and Cathbad started off down a worn path which Boudicca hadn't noticed before. Lovernios trudged after, leaving Boudicca to assume she was to keep up too. Expecting Artio to rejoin them at a lumbering pace eventually, she ran to catch Lovernios' hand as he strode through the long grass, cutting away from the forest clearing.

This path had not been trodden recently. Pungent mosses crept over the flattened earth and fern fronds enticed their way around legs, causing a slight hindrance. Lovernios did not want to hold her hand to begin with, refusing too to meet her gaze. Then he relented suddenly and returned to the firm but desperate grip of earlier. But still he would not maintain eye contact.

After the sun had passed below the trees tops and the air had cooled, Cathbad stopped suddenly. There was something he wanted to show Boudicca. She came up close, responding to his gesture to keep a fair distance and to look at what he wanted her to see.

'There, can you see? The oak, third from the left?'

'What's wrong with it?'

'Tell me what you can see.'

'The bark is flaky and tinged with grey.'

'And the leaves?'

'I hadn't noticed those. My eyesight isn't as good as it was. Why, they've curled at the ends and turned brown. It isn't autumn, though, what can have caused it?'

'The Romani. You should consider Artio's coat, too.' Boudicca turned; soundlessly the bear had appeared at her side. 'Underneath, where it's all matted. Can you see where her pelt just hangs down in tatters?'

Boudicca nodded. 'But how can the Romani have done this, I didn't think they'd got into the forests so deeply.'

'No, they haven't, not yet. But their smoke has.'

'Smoke?'

'Yes, smoke. From their tile kilns and their vast furnaces. Slowly and insidiously it is poisoning Britannia, for the land isn't used to industry on such a massive scale.'

'What can be done about it?'

Cathbad glanced back at his son and then at Boudicca's up-turned, expectant face. 'Did you know Caractacus came very close to uniting Britannia against the Romani?' he asked, ignoring her question.

'No. I didn't. What's that got to do with it?'

Cathbad looked around. The sun was peeking between the uppermost branches now, growing larger and rosier as it neared the horizon, and sending out shafts of light to pierce through the leaves. 'The day is drawing to a close. I'll tell you as we walk, although Lovernios knows most of this already.

'Druidic histories,' Cathbad began, 'Tell us how the Romani first came to Britannia years and years ago, way before any of us were born

– excepting Artio, of course. A Caesar god led them then, and brought a very muddled and hardly successful expedition, for the Romani only stayed a short while. They came back the following year and took a few more token hostages and accepted homage from some of the tribal kings in the south. Kings, you notice! Even back then they didn't entertain the possibility of women leading, which just goes to show how they've always looked at Britannia with only one eye open.

'Well, our shores never heard anything more after that, leastways not until four or five generations had been birthed and cremated, and then the Claudius god came with his four legions and his elephants. But the seeds of our downfall had already been sown. In the long interval between the occupations, our links with the Romani were strengthened. They traded with us and they wooed us to their ways, some of us even fled to them when the Catuvellauni became too threatening. And when the Claudius god came we were forced to look upon the face of our eager bedfellows with truthfulness.

'The only person strong enough to repel the Romani was Caractacus. But being Catuvellauni, he wasn't popular with the other tribes, so the Druids gave him their full backing in the hope that our authority, at least, would be respected and the tribes would be united. I was so much younger then, just coming into a realisation of my Powers, and I had the most beautiful, the most graceful, wife. A daughter of Hibernia, a princess of royal blood, my Annis.

'Annis was so many things, but most importantly she had a certain affinity with the Goddess. You, of anyone Boudicca, should understand what I'm trying to tell you without me needing to explain.'

Boudicca nodded that, yes, she understood.

'Well,' Cathbad continued. 'I gave Caractacus my fullest support and we rallied what we could of the Celtoi to fight the Romani. I was as spirited as young Lovernios back then and really believed I could oust the Romani from our shores. And Caractacus ...' he shook his head wistfully in reminiscence. 'No matter what you might have heard from your Iceni elders, he was a magnificent warrior. Broad and tall like a gnarled oak tree, with great long moustaches that drooped in whatever he drank, and muscles etched in sinuous scars from a life spent in combat. He was a man to give your heart to and to lay down your life for.' He sighed. 'But too many tribes were ensorcelled by the pretty baubles the Romani enticed them with and didn't answer to our cause. So Caractacus lost his stand at the first battles in the lands of the Cantiaci and eleven kings surrendered to the Romani. Kings again, you note, no Queens! Caractacus had no choice but to flee west to the mountain lands of the Silures and Ordovices.

'Now, those small, dark mountain folk are renowned for their warlike temperaments, even amongst the Celtoi. And with Caractacus persuading them that Claudius could be sent back to Rome in the same way Caesar was, the focus of resistance centred upon their continued guerrilla warfare. This state of repeated attack and counter-attack went on for several years until after one battle at Cafn Camedd in the mountains, Caractacus was forced to flee northwards into the territory of the Brigantes.'

Boudicca was listening very intently to Cathbad's story. He was providing far more detail than she had ever known; things were becoming clear to her that had previously been only misted legend. Her concentration showed in her expression and Cathbad continued.

'Brigantia, as you know, is a vast area of land far to the north and back then it was a tribal confederacy ostensibly ruled over by their Queen, Cartimandua, but riven by deep divisions. The Romani hadn't yet conquered the tribe, which had client status, but that didn't mean the Brigantes were immune to Romani diplomats who were busy further exploiting those self-same tribal divisions. Cartimandua was loyal to Rome. To give her her due, I can understand she might have had good reason.' He paused as if in thought. 'Another story for another day, I think. Anyway, she handed Caractacus straight over to the Romani. In thanks for past favours, I suppose.

'Not that the loss of their commander was going to deter the Silures enough to stop them fighting. For one thing, they were protecting the Druids now that we'd seen how determined the Romani were to eradicate us, and for another, they had Annis beseeching them to continue with the bloodshed. The Goddess' darkest aspect was upon her and her battle-lust fuelled their obstinacy in perfect counterpoint.

'It took me a while to work out exactly why the Romani were coming down so heavily upon the Druids. I could understand we were the one unifying factor of a scattered bunch of tribes, and thus the main threat to the legions' tactic of divide and conquer, but that was never the reason given by them. No, they always claimed they hunted us down because of our practice of making human sacrifices.

'Personally, I've always had a lot of difficulty accepting such an argument from these people. They make no effort to conceal the atrocities they commit in their arenas of death. It's not just professional gladiators who lose their lives within the stone walls, but all manner of wondrous creatures and undesirables too. As a race, I consider them to be more familiar with inflicting torments than we are.

'Like us they keep slaves and like us they execute their criminals. But unlike us, their slaves constitute a third of their population, and some of them are kept in the most appalling, inhumane conditions. And they're taken unfairly: through poverty and debt, through petty crimes and misunderstandings, or just through being in the wrong place at the wrong moment. Our slaves are more rare, taken in battle

292

or during raids, and their kin always have the option to steal them back.'

Boudicca nodded vehemently in agreement. Their system of slavery was far fairer!

'Their criminals suffer dreadful deaths with no heed to the tempering of their suffering. Their families are treated as equal with the offender and they lose their lives and possessions all together. Ha!' Cathbad uttered a single sarcastic attempt at a laugh. 'They consider it unlucky to send a virgin to her death, so out of deference to their superstition, they commit the unthinkable crime upon the most innocent maids before despatching them to their premature ends. It is a waste of life. Those we execute always take the dreams and wishes of the tribes with them to the Gods. And they always pass into the Summerlands with the minimum of pain.

'I tried, once, to halt them,' Cathbad admitted sadly. 'I met a small number of their most influential legionaries, and bound myself to a promise that the Druids would stop their human sacrifices. Soldier-diplomats they were, but my assurances were not enough for them.' The old man's eyes misted over as he looked back at Boudicca. 'The memories of that day are still painful, I'm going to trust my son has already filled you in on the details. Some sorrow, it seems, never goes away, it just becomes muted until you awake the hurt with a fresh pain. Then all the grief one has ever felt seems to amalgamate into one vast emotional wound where all the feelings clamour to be heard the loudest.' He paused, momentarily distracted by his thoughts.

'Anyway, our bloody sacrifices stopped on my orders, replaced by the giving of gold, and the Gods seemed content with the new gifts. Then I found out what the Romani really wanted: Celtoi gold. But I couldn't let them take it, for how else could the tribes repay the Goddess for her never failing bounty?

'The ferocity and direction of Andraste had left us, too, with Annis' "departure", for want of a better word, and I could see no way in which we could continue to reject the Romani. So, I directed the Goddess' trade route into hiding, that the gold might continue to pour into Gaul rather than Romani purses, and I sought to persuade those Druids who'd still listen to me to head west. There's a certain liberty in creating only a minimum of ripples as you pass through the world, and my philosophy found a welcome in many a receptive heart.'

'But didn't you fear they'd come after you? Even unto the Insula Sacra?' Boudicca burst in with her first real objection since Cathbad had begun to speak about the Romani invasion. 'And what about the people you left behind? What about the ordinary folk? Where would their spirits find peace now? How could they exist without Enchantment in their lives?'

'The Romani way is to expand and to conquer. To acquire and to use. That they will eventually come to the Insula Sacra is perhaps inevitable. But we'll be gone by then, long gone, west perhaps, over the far seas. This isn't as defeatist as it sounds, for our individual lives are almost translucent in the wider scheme of things. Our ways and stories will have already been implanted in the folk memory and we'll never be forgotten. Conquerors will come and in turn be conquered, but an abiding sense of affinity with the greenness of Britannia will survive. Such is our legacy to these future peoples.'

'Is it enough?'

'It'll have to be. I think the tribes-folk are spent now and the Druids are ready to leave. There's just one last act before we drift away into the foliage of the Old Paths.'

'What's that?' She whispered, half of herself, not wanting to know the answer.

'Suetonius' wrath must be curbed. Already he's rampaging untamed through those tribes who answered your call to rebellion. He hunts for those who fought and he punishes those he considers are implicated. Teirnon didn't really comprehend the true enormity of his wrath. And there were no crops sown this year, so there'll be no harvest and the Celtoi will starve in their thousands. Nothing seems to halt him and I fear he won't be spent until the dead lie piled all around him and the land lies barren and infertile. It's as if Andraste has passed, now, into him, although I know this can't be possible.'

Cathbad changed his tone. 'The Devoted One must bear our wrongdoings and beseech the Gods for mercy.'

'You want to bring back human sacrifice?'

'No, Boudicca. You brought back human sacrifice. You and your Goddess-saturated daughter, who together soaked the oak groves in blood. It was you who broke the pact.'

'What if it doesn't work?'

'There are never any guarantees offered, but this is the triple death – the outcome is likely to be successful. And this is a night of power, a Beltane Eve, Blessed with a New Moon.'

'And there's no other way?'

'No.'

'Will I feel any pain?' She gasped, begging for some leniency.

Cathbad looked intently into her eyes. 'Yes. I think you'll feel the most pain of us all.' She returned his gaze with a look of abject alarm. He smiled. 'That is even though you're not the Devoted One.'

'Then who?'

Cathbad looked past her to his son.

'No!'

Cathbad smiled his benign patient smile. 'We're here now,' he explained. 'In the assigned place and moment. There's no other way. For one death, many thousands can be saved. Such a small price comparatively, although it isn't easy for me either.'

'I'm not too sure if I can go through with this. I don't know if I'm strong enough.' She was panicking at his suggestion; the enormity of his words and their implication only just making sense to her.

'I think that's the same dilemma my son faces. But you must find the strength. You both must. Let me show you.' Cathbad led them forward to where the trees thinned. 'We're in a pocket of land, due north of the Place of the Chariots. Tucked between the mountains to the west, the Brigantes to the north and the Romani military outskirts to the south. Possibly the only safe place left in Britannia tonight, the last remaining Grove. But there are Romani all around and we must be secretive.'

It took a while for Boudicca's eyes, accustoming themselves to the tiring light of day meeting dusk, to see where the Paths had brought them. There was a low hillock, possibly one of the burial places of the Faery, a loose circle of oaks and the smallest of bonfires, embers smouldering cheerfully. And a hunched over figure tending the driest wood, kindling the need-fire, or tein-eigin, by increasing friction to a rotating wheel. A sacred fire to Taranis, the Thunderer, then, but this was such a poor fire – enough to cook by, but not enough to cleanse the flocks and herds of a tribe. And not enough to be seen by Romani spies. Despite the unusual frugality of the flames, Boudicca couldn't help the unbidden shiver of Beltane excitement course down her spine, before she stopped herself, remembering this year's circumstances.

The ground was springy with the heathers underfoot as Cathbad beckoned them over to his side. He had drawn close to a dew-pond that had naturally collected rainwater and rising moisture into shallow puddles of pitch-blackness. There was little light now, save from the thin firelight, and gazing into the pools was like peering into eternity, where there was nothing upon which to focus one's vision.

Her eyesight disorientated, Boudicca noted the customary sensation of the water surface misting over and the images forming. Then the fog cleared and she saw a Celtoi settlement, the grain pits scraped bare for want of food, and a few dogs, skinny and whimpering. There was a girl-child, only just out of toddling, being passed from Romani soldier to Romani soldier, oblivious to the unthinkable being perpetrated upon her tender body, screaming, screaming for a mama who no longer bore a face.

Boudicca tore herself away from the scenes unfolding before her. Tears welling sullen in her eyes, she tried to distance herself from the child, hardening her heart to the sympathies tugging at her conscience. A more ruthless person might argue that Cathbad was manufacturing images with which to deliberately manipulate Lovernios and Boudicca into doing his bidding from guilt, but Boudicca could not, in all honesty, dismiss these particular visions so easily.

They were upon the threshold of summer. The nights were already beginning to draw in later and the stars appeared more reluctantly with the passing of each day. What would this year's summer bring? The unpredictable seasons always carried the threat of crop failure and stock loss, thus this quarter feast was celebrated at a point in the annual cycle of great potential danger and uncertainty. Only this year the danger was less of a threat and more of a certainty.

'I can't let you do this.' She turned to Lovernios, forcing him to look at her squarely in the eyes. 'I can't lose you. Not you, too; I can't bear the thought. I won't suffer this pain twice in one life. I won't do it.'

'I'm sorry, Boudicca,' he mumbled. 'I'm so sorry I've let you down. I should never have let things progress so far between us, with all you've been through before, but I so hoped... I don't know, perhaps that things would be so very different.'

Lovernios averted his gaze from her but continued to speak. 'This is something I have to do, although not one part of me wants it. It's not the dying but the losing of you which hurts the more. My father is right: I was born for this moment, birthed alive into this world along with death, and all my life has brought me inexorably to this place where I am the perfect sacrifice. Somehow this end has been unavoidable, although Goddess knows I have tried. There are no scars upon my flesh, no wounds, I'm free from disease, and it's been exactly a year and a day since my graduation. No one is more fitted for this honour. I should be proud to be chosen to die for my people, although the Summerlands will feel cold and empty whilst you're not there with me.

'Remember this, too, Boudicca my love. Death is only an extension of life. When we see clearly, we realise there are no barriers between all things. Everything co-exists and mingles in an eternal realm. Think not that we are losing each other, but only a part of ourselves.' Then the Druid lent gently down to touch his lips to hers, with a soft kiss which seemingly lingered forever.

'Wait for me, then?'

'If I can, I will,' he promised.

'This is like a dream. No, like a nightmare.'

'Think of it that way if it makes it easier for you to cope. Pretend it's not real, so you might survive the experience. And then we'll meet on the other side of the dream when we both awaken.'

'Will you return Andraste's sickle please, Boudicca?' Cathbad startled her with his request, and she turned reluctantly away from her lover, aware that on some deeper level her whole being screamed at her not to do so.

Trance-like, she reached within the folds of her robes, using her fingers to search for the sickle she still carried. At the first touch, it nicked her skin, as if it had bitten her, anxious perhaps to be passed on to its new owner. Then, as if she were performing some part in a well-practised Druidic play, she held out the golden sickle, trusting that someone would be there to take it from her.

A child took it, a hooded beatific child, sex-less in its prettiness. The same child, Boudicca noted on some detached level, that had escaped from Insula Mona and who had passed her the sickle originally. So, everything of Andraste was returning to its source. At last. Would it have been better if She had never emerged? Would the Romani have simply allowed the Iceni to rebuild their shattered, wealthless lives in the aftermath of that fateful Imbolc day?

'We need the sickle to gather all-heal. There are oaks here, rich in mistletoe. I promised my son he'd feel no pain, and I intend to keep my word to him. That is a greater promise than that made by other fathers to other Devoted Ones, although you won't know about that. The Workings are not diminished by mercy, and I have never understood why this way isn't adopted more often. It's the death, not the suffering, which opens doors.

'And now, Boudicca, cook me some griddle bread. And cook it as if you're cooking for your daughters: bind your love in with the batter.'

He led her to the fire, showing her the griddle which had been allowed to heat through, the sacred lambskin upon which to bake it and the finely ground corn from last year's harvest. She mixed the cake batter together, using the milk he had procured for her. It would have been taken, as was traditional, by stealth from a local dairy cow. Without requesting leave, such thievery would result in the farmer's morning ponder on why his cow had run dry and blaming the mischief upon the Faery. In this way, Druidic rituals had gradually become imbued with mystery and superstition, and the Druid way had become inextricably associated with the Otherworld in the minds of the common people.

To see her through the bread making process, she thought back to when the task had been second nature and she could flip the flat-scones with one hand and hold onto a wayward child with the other. She could see a tearful Maeve before her now, patiently expectant for the treat to cheer her childish sulk. And she imagined young hands edging forward to help in the cooking, only to burn one edge of the bannock bread and the spoilt meal having to be eaten immediately. She shut her eyes and for an instant was there, back with Prasutagus and all the love a woman could ever wish for.

The slightest hint of smoking roused her from her thoughts. Hag Herself! The griddle bread was burnt. Just a little. On the side, about a thumb-print size, and doubtless no good for Cathbad's purposes. She felt around in the bag of flour, wondering if there were enough ingredients to put together another cake. The light was so dim now, she could hardly be sure where anything was.

'What's wrong, Boudicca?'

It was Cathbad. 'I cooked the bread a little too close to how you told me to,' she tried to explain. 'When I used to cook for my girls, I always let a small piece of the batter catch in the heat and burn. They were allowed to eat any I ruined straight away, you see. And I'm afraid I've just gone and ruined this one, too preoccupied with memories of my daughters. There isn't enough flour left to make another.'

'It doesn't matter, Boudicca. You'll see. Let me have the bread.'

She passed the still warm cake to him, holding it in both her hands to stop it crumbling. It was very dark now; so black she couldn't see anything at arms distance. The night had rolled in swiftly, bringing with it rising mists which trailed damp across her eyelashes. Cathbad appeared as little more than a silhouette, orange embers highlighting his strongest features, as he tore the bannock loosely into five or six pieces and placed them in a crane skin bag he carried. There was a sound of movement from not far off and approaching steadily, a creaking and heavy breathing which carried on the still night air, causing Cathbad to pause and nod.

'Romani?' asked Boudicca, unsure what to make of the strange ritual unfolding around her which she neither understood in itself nor her own part in it.

Cathbad shook his head, sending a yellowy reflection from the tip of his straight nose where it caught the firelight. The breathing grew stronger, until Boudicca could just make out two huge plumes of steam. Had they awoken the dragon which slept beneath this hill to protect the Faery gold? Anything could happen on a Beltane night. This breath must be from its giant nostrils and the creaking from the rubbing of its spines as it thrashed its tail behind it.

'Don't you want to greet your beloved ponies, Boudicca?' Cathbad asked.

What? Before the dragon ate them?

Then she saw what Cathbad meant. Cloud and Mouse were producing the steamy breath, and they pulled her chariot towards her, rescued somehow from the battle with the Romani. She could just make out the lightning strike blaze upon Cloud's forehead; quite unmistakable. But how on earth did they get here?

And then she stopped herself, pulling herself up for being so ridiculous. It was all just a bizarre and strangely lucid dream, wasn't it?

So, in that case, of course her ponies would be with her. Obviously her psyche was gathering everyone she held dear to her to soothe and comfort her addled mind. Why, these two hooded figures leading her ponies must be her daughters, tall and majestic. And Lovernios was here, seated by the dim warmth of the fire upon a stool which had magically appeared and bearing a cauldron, a symbol for the love he offered her. And this authoritative old man with a regal bearing must be her first husband and consort, which was why he'd asked her to do something as basic as cook for him. That simple act must represent their domestic relationship, whilst the child bearing a sprig of mistletoe must be her stillborn son.

She felt herself relax as her imagination convinced her reasoning that this was all make-believe. A befuddled calm fell over her and she became limp, like a rag-doll, waiting for the next indication of what these dream-entities wanted her to do.

Cathbad was pounding the mistletoe with an ancient pestle and mortar, the stoneware scarred with the actions of years. He added the remains of the cow's milk and a few colourful pinches of powder, extracted with a flourish from somewhere within the copious folds of his robes. When he had finished, he produced a good cupful of a glistening liquid which he sniffed at with satisfaction. Next he gestured for them all to gather around him and Lovernios, offering the leather bag, and its contents, to his son first.

There was a long pause while Lovernios studied the pieces of bannock bread he was being shown. During the wait, Boudicca realised just how quiet they all were. There could be Romani everywhere, eagerly spying eyes casting about for the hint of Beltane fires in order to destroy yet more Druids or celebrants of the Druidic way. The slightest noise and they could all be betrayed. Boudicca noticed the sense of oppression all around, not uncommon in her recent dreams, and the almost natural way in which she had slipped into whispering. Even the ponies weren't whinnying and the very air seemed tense as if the whole of nature was poised to leap away at the slightest hint of trouble.

At last, Lovernios reached for a piece of barley bannock quite decisively, the first movement he had made for a long while. He showed it to his father briefly before popping it in his mouth and swallowing. The flash of bread, even in this light, had been enough to reveal that he had quite deliberately chosen the blackened piece. He swallowed it immediately, and that was all Boudicca needed to know that he had not wanted the chance to rethink his decision once it was made, and that his mouth had now turned quite dry.

Cathbad offered around the remaining pieces, ensuring that all of the bread was taken and eaten. Cathbad nodded his head gravely, touching his son reassuringly upon the shoulder. Then he motioned for the two hooded figures to take their places on either side of Lovernios.

'My son has chosen willingly,' he intoned. 'May he be pleasing to the Gods.'

Ritual words and ritual comfort in this strange situation where, yet again, Boudicca knew neither her place nor her role. Perhaps, she decided, that might be a Blessing, for would she truly want any part in this affair? Best to stay observer, quiet and out of the way, passive and yielding, to be used as and when required, just as she had been for most of her life already.

Cathbad gave his son the concoction of all-heal he had just mixed, precisely monitoring the amount Lovernios drank and wiping his bearded lips as gently as if his son were feeble minded. All of a sudden, Lovernios had the saddest eyes as he gazed full upon her. Then his eyelids became weighted and drooped, whilst his body sagged. The look made her want to go to him and wrap him up safe in her embrace. But her arms felt like lead and her legs as if they were stuck in cloying mud. This was a dream, she told herself, and in dreams it can take an eternity to cross even the shortest distances.

So she stood motionless as they stripped her lover naked, tearing his robes from his body and formally insulting him, seeking to transfer their curses upon Lovernios so they might be removed from themselves. It was all an essential part of the Working they wove, but nevertheless Boudicca couldn't bring herself to add her trespasses to those of the others. Every action, she decided, had beneficial and adverse repercussions. How could she ever know when she had done wrong and when she'd done right? What should she scapegoat to the Divine Victim and what should she retain?

She continued to remain still, pondering Cathbad's conundrum about moving through the world with the minimum of ripples, while one of Cathbad's assistants held Lovernios up and steady. Then the other drew up an axe from where it had been placed in readiness and delivered one, two, striking blows to the crown of Lovernios' skull. Lovernios slumped further into unconsciousness, caught firmly by the other assistant.

'For Taranis,' Cathbad announced, before a third stunning blow, with the flat of the blade now, hit Lovernios upon the base of his skull. Boudicca could see how each of the blows had been carefully aimed to stun and not to kill. It made sense, after all there was little in her dreams which would want Lovernios dead.

Quickly, Cathbad's assistants propped Lovernios up upon his stool, righting the cauldron which had been placed upon his knees. They removed his torc, the Celtoi representation of a lifelong willingness to be sacrificed to the Divine if ever required. Boudicca touched her own torc – it was quiet now, but unnaturally so. Then they replaced Lovernios' torc with a thrice-knotted length of corded animal sinew around his neck and inserted a stick – replacing the symbol with the actuality. Rotating the stick quickly, they tightened the cord, the executioner gaining purchase against the cord by shoving their knee forcefully against Lovernios' back and pulling against his spine.

Boudicca heard the slight crack of Lovernios' ribs. Her daughters knew the art of death. Quick and precise, at the expense of neatness – a merciful killing. These executioners were trained Vates, the sacrificers and entrail-readers of the Druidic orders, but why were her daughters appearing in this guise? What was the significance of ths part of her dream?

'For Esus,' intoned Cathbad, offering this aspect of Lovernios' death to the Lord and Master. At the same moment, while the garrotting continued, the other Vates stabbed into Lovernios' throat, releasing an inky jet of blood into the cauldron until all the blood had been drained and Lovernios' head flopped down into the hollow of his shoulder.

Cathbad took the cauldron, full of his son's precious blood, and placed it reverently within a dip in the ground where it could not spill over. The chariot was brought forward and Lovernios' body placed, slumped, within it. Boudicca, Cathbad indicated, should steer her ponies, as charioteer, and follow after him and the Vates.

There was little need, in the end, for her to offer much guidance to the two ponies, who both seemed sure-footed and certain of where they were going. Leaving the tumuli and the shelter of the oak Grove behind, Cloud and Mouse kept close to Cathbad's heels, allowing him to lead them onto a wooden causeway. There was a distinctive change in the sound made by their hooves and the chariot's wheels – a far hollower thud – which betrayed the change of terrain to Boudicca.

She could see nothing now. The uncertain moon had risen, thin and new, and afforded minimal light. Everything was hidden save for the occasional stark birch trunk, appearing like a slender ghost amidst the blackness which clung like a shroud upon the world she inhabited. Mindful too of the body by her side, her eyes placed tricks on her mind, imagining corpse-lights bobbing around in front of, and just beyond, her reach. To dispel these visions, she relied instead upon her other senses, breathing deeply and recognising a rich peaty scent. They'd come from heath-land and birch scrub then, and were travelling deeper into boggy ground. The timber causeways would provide safe passage through such treacherous tracts, allowing a secret route into territory where even the Romani wouldn't dare penetrate at night.

She had no idea where Cathbad was leading them, nor how far they had already come. She wondered whether he took them through the path of a labyrinth of his own design, seeking to reach some distant inner realm before enacting the finale of this rite. She wondered, too, how fast they moved, for the constant moon, always elusive, seemed continually to follow them, no matter how their path twisted and turned.

There was water all around. She could feel it. Not one great expanse, but several pools of it, here and there reflecting some pale moonlight. She could sense too the slight change in humidity when they passed another pond, tickling the fine, downy hairs on her cheeks. And there were the clouds of diaphanous insects to shut her eyes to, the sickly smell of bog myrtle, and the feather-stroking of reeds for further clues as to her whereabouts. No, there were definitely black lakes all around, and Cathbad wove a circuitous path through them all, whilst their jet stillness gazed upon her like so many baleful eyes.

There was a tremendous sense of isolation amidst these dark sheets of water, with only the clomp of the horses' hooves against the timber causeway and the rustling of the birches to be heard. This was a lonely place, full of sullen murmurs which roused new tensions within her spirit. The magical patches of water called to her, even as they straggled together: This is a good place to lie down forever, they enticed, as if beckoning her out of her dream and into a more restful sleep.

There was a numinous quality about the whole place, rendering her more tranquil and at peace than she had felt for a long, long while. As she drifted through the night, she felt a Blessing arise from her heart and shower upon all things. Suddenly, with the outburst of Divine Love, she recognised her role in all this. Hardly impassive bystander, now she sensed that once more she was the Goddess Manifest. The woman alone, amidst the company of men, paraded amongst her people with her consort to bring Blessing upon them. No statue of the Goddess this year to be carried around the field boundaries, but a living representation of Her to evoke a deeper magic. From this almost drunken, wider perspective, she could just see how this could all make a certain wonderful sense.

Before she could reply to the water's beguilement, Cathbad stopped, the horses pulling up directly behind him. The slightest torch was lit, allowing a sparse light. The Vates took Lovernios' body, helped Boudicca down from the chariot, and they all drew up around the water's edge. Black liquid lapped against their toes, seemingly eager to pull them into its depths.

'For Teutates,' intoned Cathbad, and they eased up Lovernios' body, already stiffening with the blood loss, and lowered him gently into the

302

embrace of this life-sucking water. Softly it washed over him, the God of the Tribes accepting now His tribute from the Druid's sacrifice, until the body had sunk from sight save for the purr of a string of bubbles.

'It is done,' recited Cathbad.

'Not yet,' whispered Boudicca. She reached up for the torch and took it from him.

Then she knelt beside the lake edge, leaning out to feel for Lovernios' passing. There was nothing beneath the surface to be felt; he must have sunk rapidly. So, he had gone now, without trace, as if he'd never existed. Slowly she lowered the torch, extinguishing it in the waters to show where her lover had last been upon this earth.

There was a touch upon her shoulder and she sat back, allowing something to be pressed into her hands.

'This is the last of the all-heal, left from my son's last meal.' The instructions sounded as if they came from Cathbad but she couldn't be sure. His voice sounded so distant and unreal, as if it reverberated around her mind. So befuddled and bewildered was she by all the conflicting emotions which crowded with the threat of overwhelming her, she could do nothing but listen. 'One mouthful will send you into a healing sleep to work through the worst of the grief. When you awake you can choose your sanctuary from the north and the wild Picts, or you can follow me to the west and Insula Sacra. There will always be a place for you amongst the Sisters. You are a wise woman and have skills which won't be wasted once they're recognised.

'Or, alternatively, you can drink all the remaining potion. There's enough to send you painlessly into the Summerlands. You must choose wisely whether there is adequate strength left in you to continue the fight to live, or whether this is adequate living for one life. Both paths will bring you visions of what Lovernios' life has bought, and I will be pleased to learn what you've Seen if you ever find me in Insula Sacra.'

With that the speaker touched her gently once more and withdrew as hazily as a summer breeze. Boudicca was left all alone in the dark, without even her ponies. It was cold despite the season but she felt unable to call for Cathbad to return.

She was frightened, she realised. Not just of being in a strange place where spirits resided and the earth felt hostile, but also at having lost everyone and everything she'd ever held dear. They had been taken from her gradually, one by one, and she had fought the departure of each and every one of them desperately and possibly forlornly. There was just her now, despite her efforts, all by herself, in a seemingly unsupportive universe. She couldn't even contact the strength of the Goddess-within; she could only remember how that had once been, how that had once felt. All this hurt in a single assault now; far, far too much, and she yearned to wake up soon so it might all be over.

She pulled the tiny vessel of all-heal closer to her and sniffed. She wrinkled her nose. The contents of the pot smelt sour. She took a sip, trying to swallow without tasting. It was not as unpleasant as she had thought it might be, although there was a tingling aftertaste.

She took another tiny swig, glad to welcome any restful oblivion, no matter how artificial or how temporary.

Then she took another.

An Ending…

There was a nauseating sensation, as if she was falling back and up, then suddenly it was gone and she was in a state of liberation. She was soaring very high above the ground, swooping and plummeting as it pleased her. She flew for the pure joy of being able to catch the air currents and atmospheric dips, and she revelled in the experience.

The land sped by beneath her as she tumbled with the breeze, a fertile land packed with potent earth. She was one with this place, a vast feminine force to nurture and suckle in a myriad of incomprehensible ways. She opened her white-streaked wings of bluey-darkness to Cast her own Blessing upon everything which passed under their fold.

But there was an intrusion: a maleness new to the scene, which resisted the unknowable love she provided. A force which revered things of little true worth and closed its heart to the gentle warmth she offered. A pervading and tenacious aggressor who seemingly lacked emotion. And to temper its encroachment she had had to give up that which she cherished most. She could still remember the loss, although the pain had dulled considerably since she'd entered this heightened state.

There was hunger in the land below, and fear, and hurt and only this intractable male oppression, incapable of soothing even if it wanted to. But her sacrifice had bought ease for the land's suffering and she had felt the brutal invader yield. Its wrath had burnt out against a compliant people holding out for a promise to be kept, and it had gradually accepted and combined its own truths with hers. So she had allowed everything under her keeping to pass to a father's protection, although she kept her own love constant, ready to return to her Guardianship should she ever be called upon again.

And now she could relax and go where she would. Alone yet complete, not needed but content. There was nothing more to do and nothing else to feel and she could move on, finally free. No regrets and no sadness, and nothing missing any more, just an awareness of the turning wheel and the repeating of all things.

There was a rush of wind from behind her and a call of 'chaka-chak-chak' heralding another magpie come to join her. This one was especially welcome, she knew the look in his shiny eyes too well not to recognise him from before. There was no misery for him any more either. He'd lost the Divine for a while, too, and it had nearly torn him apart in his moment of need, but now they and the One were indistinguishable and would never be separated again.

Her mate dived straight at her playfully and veered off to the west, enticing her to follow. She changed direction unhesitatingly. He knew the winds' secrets better than her, having been here longer. And he knew where the others were …

About the Author

Helen K Barker has interests in neo-Paganism, the "Celts", and world mythology. She has a BSc and a MSc in Archaeology and has specialised in studying southern Britain in the Iron Age and Roman periods. She draws on her interests, qualifications and experiences as inspiration for her creative writing.

She lives in Hampshire, England, with her husband and two cats.

Visit www.mushroom-ebooks.com for free sample chapters and information on additional titles from Mushroom eBooks.

Printed in Great Britain
by Amazon